Bull's Labyrinth

A novel by

Eric M. Witchey

IFD Publishing, 2016

Bull's Labyrinth

A novel by

Eric M. Witchey

IFD Publishing, P.O. Box 40776, Eugene, Oregon 97404 U.S.A. (541)461-3272 www.ifdpublishing.com

Ebook Design, Cyberscribe, Inc.

First Trade Paper ISBN: 978-0-9965536-8-1

Originally Printed by IFD Publishing in the United States of America

Acknowledgements

The endless list of names that should appear here will only give my editor a heart attack, and I don't want to feel responsible for her death. I like her too much. So, I will limit the list. Special thanks go to Elizabeth Engstrom, Alan M. Clark, and Leonore Witchey-Lakshmanan. Without them, I would have given up on Nikkis and Daedalus a long time ago. I also want to thank Molly Moore Emmons for willingly reading a version of this book that required a hazmat suit for direct contact. In spite of the rough form of the book, she managed to provide valuable advice, all of which would have made this book better (and some of which I actually used). Thanks also go to my siblings, living and dead, for sharing my insanity and believing in my visions. Most especially, thanks to Leonore and Nick, my living siblings, for never doubting that stories are alive and important. I must also thank my father, affectionately known as Papa Ron, for teaching me to value story and the written word. Thanks also to Devon Monk, Nina Kiriki Hoffman, Leslie What, Jerry and Kathy Oltion, Ray Vukcevich, Barb and J.C. Hendee, Steve Perry, Tim Powers, George R.R. Martin, Connie Willis, Carol Emschwiller, Damon Knight, Kate Wilhelm, Jim Hunter, all of the Wordos, and, most especially, James N. Frey. Good Lord, this list could go on and on, and I can already see my editor grasping her chest in pain, so I'll stop. All of these people, and many more, taught me my craft, such as it is. While none of them are responsible for the shortcomings of my work, all of them are responsible for the things I do right. No story comes to the page without the support of a huge community of believers.

Special Acknowledgments

My special thanks go out to the readers who registered for the Imagination Fully Dilated (IFD) Early Access ARC Program. I was stunned to discover that each and every one of you found at least one problem that nobody else found. I am embarrassed by how many errors you found at such a late stage of development. Thank you! Without you, this book would not be as clean as it is. I take full responsibility for any errors that remain. I had it last, and sometimes I ignored your excellent advice.

In the order in which they appear in the IFD spreadsheet, the ARC participants are:

First buyer (because he lives in tomorrow) writer and teacher, Ryland J. Kayin Lee.

Staunch, life-time supporter and Ph.D. Chemical Engineer, Leonore Witchey-Lakshmanan.

Inspiration, amazing teacher, mother, yoga instructor, and niece, Nichole Studd.

Equally amazing husband to said niece, inspiration to me, and truly wonderful early reader, Rudy Studd.

Fabulous yogini, mother, and model of imaginative living, Michelle Witchey.

Amazon best-selling thriller writer, David Spiselman (a.k.a., thriller writer D. S. Kane).

Writer, friend, father, and community organizer, Justin James Tindel.

Friend, writer, and dog trainer extraordinaire, Ellen Levy Finch.

Author, professor, organizer, and sister by another mother, Molly Moore Emmons.

New York Times best-selling author and long-time friend and supporter, Steve Perry.

Truly amazing author and endlessly patient and supportive friend, Mason Mccan Smith.

Writer and voice of kindness and enthusiasm for all writers, Mark Beardsley.

Healer, writer, book lover, and daughter of a very dear friend, Joan Jackson.

Writer, long-time tolerant friend, and always supportive, Tf Gray.

If I have made an error or moission in this list, it is because I didn't have you to help me. If I have missed anyone, please accept my apologies and let me know so that future volumes of this book will contain your name. I also want to extend my thanks to the many people who purchased the Early Access ARC, read it, and left such wonderful reviews.

Dedication

This book is for Norya Bird, an inspiring old soul who flies high and free no matter how much the world tries to weigh her down.

History Repeats

Only a hedge and a chain link fence stood between Nikkis and freedom—between her and love. Evening shadows had hours ago grown into warm, summer darkness. Her luck and the dark of the moon were synonyms.

Seventeen was too old to never have been kissed, and if she let her parents have their way, she'd be in her thousands before love was hers.

Night creatures filled the air with songs celebrating love. Crickets, frogs, and cats urged her on.

Her parents' home loomed behind her, a Colonial red brick and pillared monster stabbing twin chimney horns into a clear, Oregon night sky and trying to intimidate her suburban neighborhood's split-level ranches and salt boxes with its patriotic shadow.

Her parents claimed to be American, claimed they had left the old ways behind, claimed they had never spoken a word of Greek to her in her entire life, and they denied that her fluency in Greek had anything to do with them or with anyone from the old country. Even though they claimed all those things were true, they watched her night and day. They treated her as if some dusty, third-world herder from the stony hills of Crete might steal her virginity at a Safeway or the Liberty Mall.

Not tonight. Tonight, she chose. She chose a new life, her own future. Not even the old ways of family handed down through history could stop that. Nothing short of dark magic could keep her from love.

She dashed across the dewy, back lawn.

A silent meteor streak cut the star-speckled sky—a teaser for the light show Daed had promised, the Perseid meteor shower.

At the hedge, she knelt. Cold dew soaked into the knees of her jeans. She reached through the tangle of scratchy branches, groping for the chain link beyond. Over her shoulder, she watched the dark house for light or signs of life. For a cold moment, she wondered if she'd reached through the bushes at the right spot, at the fence post where missing clasps gave the fence the most give. Finally, she grasped cold, galvanized steel wire. She pushed hard against the bottom of her father's fence. It lifted, and she shouldered the bushes aside and peered through a low, leafy archway into the dark alley beyond.

Holding up the fencing with one hand, she slid under feet first. A little wriggling and some cold wetness on her back got her through the shrubs and under the fence.

She sat up and checked the alley.

Between back fences and garbage cans loomed the dark form of a station wagon—*his* station wagon. Daed's broad, solid male silhouette filled the space behind the steering wheel.

She stood and tried to brush herself off and shake the twigs and leaves from her long, dark hair before he saw her.

A part of her had believed he wouldn't be there. She was pretty, and she knew it. Boys, men, and even women lit up when she walked into a room. Their silly grins or shy smiles or wide-eyed stares made her dismiss them as fools.

Not Daed. He was never foolish—always clear-eyed, intelligent, and intense.

He'd always been respectful—so respectful that she'd been afraid he'd decided to not show. She was sure he loved her—as sure as she was that she loved him.

She trotted to the car he'd rebuilt himself, an ancient, golden Ford LTD wagon named Helios—a glorious chariot made of steel and restored by his clever hands. Like the legends from her homeland, he was a clever god among the boys of her school. Daed was a hero worthy of her love.

He leaned across the seat and opened her door.

Another streak of light slashed through the heavens. It illuminated his face—smooth cheeks, a decisive chin, eyes the color of dark olives—rich and flavorful and filled with promises of nourishment for her heart and soul.

He smiled. Dark, curly hair glistened.

She held her breath. For a moment, she forgot her fear of discovery. The melodies and harmonies of crickets, owls, and tiny frogs stopped. The night held its breath with her.

As quickly as the meteor flash had come, it faded and left only darkness.

She slipped into the car and settled against him on the vinyl bench seat.

"I didn't think you'd come," he said.

His voice soothed away any fear she had that they would be caught. It convinced her that she had truly escaped her parents' home—that she and Daed were together in the night—for the night. She wanted to answer, but her breath was still short. She was here, and it was enough.

He nodded and let off the brake. On the alley's slight slope, the car rolled forward.

To Nikkis, the quiet crunching of loose gravel under tires sounded like summer thunder.

Beyond the fence and hedge, a light came on. Her father's sharp voice cut the night air, "Nikkis!"

"Go," she whispered. "Go *now*."

Daed turned the key. The headlights flared. The Ford's engine growled to life.

"Go," she said out loud. She amazed herself—that she would do this, that this man could convince her so easily to sneak out, to violate the trust of parents who had always done their best for her.

Except, Daed hadn't convinced her. She'd convinced herself. She wanted to be alone with him more than she had ever wanted anything else in her life.

Her father stepped out into the alley. His white t-shirt, bald pate, and heart-pattern boxers glowed in the headlights. "Nikkis Ariadne Aristos!"

Daed let off the gas. His fingers twitched on the wheel, reaching for answers. She had seen it before. He reached for solutions with his hands, as if he could feel them and draw them from the air, but this was no time for searching.

"No," Nikkis said. "Go!"

She stomped her foot down on his, smashing the accelerator. As his mind and heart joined with hers to move the muscle and bone of his arms and legs, he smashed down with her and hit the horn at the same moment.

Fire burned under Helios's hood. Four hundred horses leapt forward toward the darkness, carrying Daed and Nikkis with them.

Her father leapt from the path of the car.

She pulled her foot back, turned in her seat, and looked out the back window. Her father stood up. He waved his hands in the air, his face red in the tail lights. He screamed at her.

It was the first time she'd ever heard him speak Greek. She knew the curses from dreams or from whomever had spoken the language to her when she was young, but she had never used those words.

She would pay—tomorrow. She turned back and settled into the seat.

"He's okay," Daed said.

"Really pissed," she said. "I'll be grounded forever."

"Worth it?"

She grinned. "We'll see."

His hand found hers, and for half an hour they drove in silence, knowing one another's thoughts through the movement of fingertips on the back of a wrist, through the slipping of one finger from between two, from the occasional squeeze or caress.

When they stopped on a dark track in the foothills east of Portland, nothing in the world existed for her except this boy, this man who so completely left her empty of thought and filled with fire and hope.

"He'll still be mad when we get home," Daed said. "Are you sure?"

"The meteors. I'll tell them I had to watch them for a school project."

"Yeah-huh. Sure. And if he sends the police to find us?"

"I'll protect you," she joked, "I'll tell them I kidnapped you."

A white ball of fire lit the heavens, turned the sky briefly blue-white before it faded back to daylight blue, then darkest blue-black, and finally to a black that slowly filled with stars.

"Wow," he said.

She looked at him. He wasn't looking at the sky. Her hand sweated in his. Her face burned. The time was right.

Now, she thought. *Do it now.*

Kiss her. Give her that, at least, if not more. And nobody else could do it, and no matter how angry her father would be or how long she would be grounded or how she might be punished or how much her mother cried, it would be worth it.

Like he heard her thinking, he leaned toward her.

Just like the heroine in a romance novel, her blood made the sound of surf in her ears, and her pounding heart threatened to break free from her chest.

She could smell the spice scent of his soap, the thin smell of machine oil, and the certain power of chemistry in his sweat. She also thrilled to the flinty, stone scent—a thrilling, powerful smell that seemed to surround him and nobody else.

She tilted her head to make it easier, stretching to bring him to her sooner.

He hesitated, asking her permission—as if her being there in the car against her parents' wishes weren't enough permission.

He turned his head slightly and pushed past her lips to her cheek. His lips grazed her face, slipped in under the long, looping curls over her ear.

So close. Her nose touched his warm nape. His hair smelled of stone dust and oil from sculpting and working on the car. Deeper down, closer to the skin, he smelled of love for her. She smiled and pressed her lips to his neck.

"I have always loved you, Nikkis," he whispered. "I always will."

She knew men said such things to get what they wanted, but she also knew he meant it. She could feel the promise in his hands, the power in his words. He meant it deeply and more completely than anyone had ever meant it through all of time.

He kissed her ear.

She shivered. She reached to wrap herself around him, to become a part of him.

He pulled back and touched his lips on hers.

Her heart fed on his soft touch. The night sky lit up as bright as day. The inside of the car glowed—and she knew the kiss lit her world, and only the kiss, because she closed her eyes. Not even the Perseid meteors could fill the world with so much light and fire.

And she wanted it to last forever.

But it didn't.

The kiss ended. He pulled back.

Abruptly, Daed opened his door and got out.

The chill of the night air rushed in and closed around her.

"Daed?" she asked.

He screamed at the sky.

At first, she smiled, taking the scream for a howl of joy and triumph. She understood his happiness and slid across the seat to join him. She would howl at the sky beside him.

He screamed again.

The scream carried fear and rage.

It went on and on, longer and louder than she had ever heard anyone or anything scream. Agony and terror tore from his throat and spread out into the night.

A new shooting star lit him, showed him tearing at his shirt with one hand and his hair with the other. Falling starlight flashed in the wide whites of his eyes. His eyes—the dark, rich olives, the food of the gods—had become small, black, hard, and crazy.

"You're scaring me," she said. "Get back in."

He screamed again.

The sound tore her soul.

"Daed!"

He turned toward her. Spit flecked the corners of lips that only moments before had brought her so much pleasure. He said something to her—something fast.

It sounded like a dialect of Greek, but it couldn't have been. As far as she knew, he didn't know that language. Spanish, yes. German, some. No Greek.

His shirt tore. He gasped for air like a drowning man. He screamed again.

She scrambled out. Through welling tears under the intermittent flashes in the sky, she tried to grab him, hug him, and heal whatever terror had filled him and pulled him so far away from her. "No," she whispered. "Ohi, Daedalus," *No*, she said in Greek.

"Ne, Nikkis," *Yes*, he said. He pushed her away. "Again," he said. "Oh, God, not again," and he ran away into the darkness.

~~~

The next day, when her father found her and the car, Nikkis had stopped crying. She never cried again.

Nor, in spite of the advice of the therapists forced upon her and her parents' desires and attempts to find her a match, did she ever share her heart with another man.

To have so much and lose it so quickly.... She would never allow that feeling into her life again.

She turned to books and old, dead languages. She found peace there. For twelve years, her only passion was the language of the past—the language of her family's past, of Crete.
~~~

Modern Ambitions

Detective Andros settled himself into the nylon fabric of a tripod camping stool next to one of the folding tables his men had brought in by helicopter. His little compound of tan, geodesic camp tents surrounded him. Brilliant, Mediterranean spring sunshine warmed his skin and the oil in his hair. A quiet, down-slope breeze pushed between the ridges and along the valley floor, carrying with it the dry, ancient smell of heated limestone dust.

Between his loyals from the police force and the mercenaries he'd brought in from out of the country, the dig in a hidden vale not far from Mt. Ida in the White Mountains of Crete and some miles to the west-southwest of Knossos was as secure a place as he could make it.

Away, to the down-slope side of the camp, the new man, Yorgos, a huge Sfakian whose usefulness he still questioned, pawed through a pile of rubble brought up from a caved-in Roman cistern.

In dust and dirt on one end of Andros's pale, plastic tabletop lay a scattering of ancient artifacts: potsherds, bits of marble, a broken piece of gold and semi-precious stone jewelry. On the other end of the table, he had set up the silver umbrella dish of his satellite uplink and opened the high-impact hard case holding his military grade laptop.

The juxtaposition of the dusty, ancient craftsmanship of Roman and Minoan Crete against the shining, reflective craftsmanship of the plastic, global culture of the modern world touched Andros. He was, after all, a man of honor who had a very personal passion for the history of this ancient land. Moments such as these, moments of poetry, were the making of a man's soul.

He pushed a long finger through the rubble on the table, his manicured nail scooting this bit and that aside. Nothing of value gained his notice in the dust.

He had hoped for more from this site.

Certainly, the locals had shown their desire to protect this hidden place in many ways. That should have meant something. And they had not called in authorities. That also meant something.

Even so, his return on investment on this project had not justified his expenses.

He'd lost two mercenaries so far. The remaining men believed the missing had deserted. Andros knew better. He paid them five times the going rate for mercs. Greeks might walk away from that kind of money out of pride, though the current economy had certainly made them easier to buy, but Germans and Americans tied their pride to money.

The men were dead.

He had no illusions. It was why he had brought in Yorgos.

The giant Sfakian had not joined his group for money. Sfakians were the heroes of Crete—never conquered, never beaten, never bought. Throughout history, the mountain people had defeated enemy after invading enemy. During World War II, Sfakian resistance fighters terrified the Germans.

Yorgos had not joined for money. He had joined for some other reason—perhaps, as he said, to discover and protect the history and honor of his people. Andros certainly understood that sentiment. It was, he told himself, his own passion.

Yorgos, a barrel-chested bull of a man, stood erect near the dump. He held something up in the sunlight then turned toward Andros and shook his hand in the air.

Andros wondered if Yorgos could be trusted if things got ugly. Certainly, Muscus, the oldest and most loyal of his little group of workers, had taken an instant dislike to Yorgos.

When a dog snarled at Muscus, Andros knew that dogs could be trusted to understand the character of people. When Muscus snarled at a man, Andros had wondered what that could possibly mean. Certainly, Muscus considered the bigger man a threat, but whether from projection of his own twisted morals into the Sfakian's head or from recognition that the larger man might betray them all, Andros hadn't known.

Luckily, the Spaniard, Elias, and the Norwegian, Lukas, had decided to "initiate" Yorgos. There was beauty in motion in that fight. No one had died. No one had even been permanently injured, but both Elias and Lukas had spent three days in their tents flat on their backs.

Yorgos drank a little water, ate a sandwich, and went back to work.

Andros smiled and nodded as Yorgos approached.

Men with Yorgos's build often earned the nickname Hercules in Crete, and they evoked caution in the locals. Add this Hercules's military experience, and Yorgos became a potentially useful local tool.

Mediterranean sunlight glistened on Yorgos's sweat-dampened chest. Andros's sense of personal poetry refused to let him call the man's glistening skin bronze. Brass was better, but only just.

Yorgos's bulging arms swung outward from his sides, too powerful and large to hang downward like a normal man's. In one hand, he grasped something Andros could not see well. In his other, he carried a magazine.

"Yorgos." Andros acknowledged his man.

"Look." The big man dropped the magazine on the table. It sent dust up into the breeze.

Annoyed, Andros quickly closed the cover of his computer.

He scanned the magazine cover, which was graced by the face of a truly beautiful woman.

For a moment, the woman's face made him forget to breathe.

When he once more exhaled, he tried to analyze her face—to see exactly what had stopped his breath and thoughts.

Many beautiful women had such a straight and sculpted nose or such a fine line in the cheek and jaw. Many beautiful women had skin the color of fresh, amber olive-oil. Many beautiful women had hair that glistened and begged a man's fingers to caress. Such cliché genetic triggers of beautiful women graced the covers of magazines and center stage in commercials.

But Andros had never before seen such eyes—ancient and knowing and filled with deep compassion, suffering, and longing all at once.

He could not help himself.

He stared.

After another lost breath and a skipped heartbeat, he chastised himself for gawking like a teenager at the face of a woman on the cover of a magazine, but he did not look away.

Yorgos dropped a stone in the center of the face—a pale, white stone containing black striations.

Startled, Andros looked up. "Trash? You want me to look at a girl from the trash?"

"The stone," the giant said. "The magazine arrived in the chopper this morning. Read her article."

Andros cautiously turned his gaze back to the stone and magazine. The stone was flat on one side. In the marble surface, he made out glyphs, tiny marks scored with great care. He lifted the stone and turned it in the light. Certainly, the glyphs were neither Greek nor Roman. "From the cistern rubble?"

"Yes," Yorgos said.

"Then," Andros said, "the writing has to be Roman."

"The article," Yorgos said.

Again, Andros looked at the magazine. The words above the woman's face said, "Linguae Antikuitas." Below her perfect chin, block letters said, "Dr. Nikkis Aristos. A Projection of Linear-A."

Andros flipped to the article. A sidebar presented a table of glyphs. A mark on the stone matched one of those glyphs.

Quickly, he scanned the table of characters this American Professor claimed *should* exist if she correctly interpreted the ancient script, Linear-A.

He found two more of the glyphs in her table before he closed the magazine. He rolled it up. He stood. "You're absolutely sure this stone came from the heap?"

"Yes."

"Have you shown anyone else?"

"No."

"Get your pack. We're going back."

"Now?"

"Now."

"Yes, Sir." Yorgos went to gather his things.

Andros called out, "Muscus!" He opened his computer case and placed the magazine carefully inside then closed it and locked it shut.

"Boss?" The little man had silently come up behind him. Andros hated and admired that about Muscus. He was silent when he wanted to be. More important, he was silent when Andros wanted him to be.

"Organize a work party. Take everyone off the potholes and the cavern. Put them to work on the discard heap and the cistern cave-in."

The wiry little man squinted up at him. "The sun did this to you. I'll get you some water."

"Do it," Andros whispered. "Look at this." He held out the fragment Yorgos had given him. "Find every piece of marble that has marks on it. Gather them, crate them, and send them to the warehouse in the next chopper load."

Muscus took the stone. He turned it over in his hands. "Bricks from the cistern?"

Yorgos returned, wearing his camo and ballistic vest. He wore a backpack almost as large as Muscus like it was a child's school pack. The Walther PPQ holstered and clipped to the hip belt of the pack and the light, shoulder-slung XP-70 automatic—magazine in, round chambered—marked him as ready to make the hike back to the car.

Muscus quickly looked the man over. Yorgos's changed clothes apparently made him rethink his objections. "Yes, Sir." he said.

Better, Andros thought. Nothing demonstrated that he meant business faster than a man like Yorgos dressed to kill.

~~~

Andros knew of three ways to get from the dig to the trailhead where civilized roads ended: fly by helicopter; hike down the valley, climb down a cliff, carefully work your way along a long, twisted goat path down the main drainage for the area, climb another sheer scarp, and waltz into the parking area halfway up a ridge; or walk along donkey trails to, through, and beyond an ancient, unnamed, dying mountain village.

Helicopter was fastest, but he wanted to avoid high-profile activities for now. The cliff-drainage route was shortest, but only a goat or a fool who deeply desired broken bones would try it.

From the dig, the village trail followed contours up a ridge to a head ridge that curved around the high ends of a number of valleys. That trail made for easier travel but added half a day by meandering farther away from civilized roads before dumping into the village. That was the trail they took.

By late afternoon, they entered the high side of the village. Entering the village, Andros and Yorgos flicked off their safeties and hustled past the white-stucco church with its traditional blue dome and cross-capped bell tower. Such churches always occupied high points in these old villages. Some said the hilltop temple tradition went
~~~

all the way back to the days when Zeus ruled the gods. Others said it brought Greek Orthodox congregations closer to God. Andros suspected it made the buildings more defensible.

Safely separated and never looking in the same direction, they hurried along the cobbled alleys, past shuttered homes, and finally down past the giant, stone Minoan soldiers guarding the path from the lowland roads into the village.

Not until they had left the village and descended several kilometers of dirt path to the trailhead and vehicle turnaround where a dirt road dead-ended did the two men pause and reset the safeties on their weapons.

There, on the circular dirt turnaround that marked the end of the dirt road from the lowlands and the beginning of the trail to the village, they found their car, a blue-and-white police Peugeot, upside down.

For a moment, Andros thought it might have been faster and, perhaps, worth it to take the neck-breaking goat path instead of the village route, but he knew better. The mountain peasants were invisible unless they wanted to be seen, and whatever they had done to flip the car probably happened at night and certainly couldn't have been stopped. Not even armed guards would have made a difference, except that he would be down a couple more men.

Beyond the car, against the cutout, uphill bank of the turnout, a shrine the shape of the village's church marked the place where some beloved relative had died.

While someone from the village respected that shrine enough to keep it carefully painted and the tiny candles within burning to illuminate the little, stained glass windows, the locals had once more shown their disrespect and distrust for outside authority.

Andros flipped off his safety and laid his trigger finger over his trigger and trigger guard.

Even this near the civilized world, Andros wasn't fool enough to relax. He scanned the surrounding hills and goat trails while Yorgos attempted to flip their car back up onto its wheels.

The village in the hills above enjoyed obscurity in a rugged part of the mountains where no tax was ever collected, where no invading soldier had ever survived for long, and where the people did not admit to any government other than the one they chose for themselves.

They did not like police, nor did they like police cars.

Yorgos squatted low and gripped the roof of the car and showed Andros why people called men like him Hercules. From the thighs, he pushed. The car rolled onto its side, slid in the dirt a little, then lifted and caught on its wheels.

Yorgos grunted, and like some Olympian, he jerked the car higher, shifting his grip while the mass had momentum. He squatted deep, caught the roof under his palms, then pushed upward. The thighs of his fatigue pants split from knee to hip, and the car fell back onto its wheels, bounced, then settled in the dust cloud the effort had created.

"Done," he said.

The man wasn't even winded.

Andros decided that Yorgos was an asset after all. Certain that someone in the hills watched them, what they had just done would get around. A legend could be a good tool.

"Check it over," he said.

The big man didn't answer. He just began going over the car. With methodical, professional calm, he checked it for problems, bombs, and breakage.

Andros crossed the gravel and dirt circle to the replica of the village church, a shrine to someone, a place full of food, water, raki, and maybe chocolate—a place dedicated to some spirit or another believed to come to this place from time to time. Waiting beside the shrine, he settled his computer on a flat rock. He pulled out the magazine and set up his tiny, folding dish antenna.

The internet provides almost magical power for a man who has access to Interpol and NSA records.

Before Yorgos had finished checking and starting the car, Andros knew everything he needed to know about Nikkis Aristos, Ph.D., and her work with antiquities and ancient languages.

He sent her the first of several emails.

~~~

The last email of Nikkis's morning reading session was a man's flattering note and a suggestion that they get together to discuss her new article about possible missing glyphs in the ancient Minoan script, Linear-A—an article she hadn't seen in print yet.
~~~

The message included an embedded photo of a swarthy, olive-complexioned man wearing a white, linen shirt unbuttoned down the front. A few curls of dark chest hair drew the eye down to the outlines of his muscled torso.

Nikkis almost laughed. His dark, haunted eyes and brooding lips combined with his thick, product-slicked, black hair convinced her that his email was some kind of come-on from an on-line dating service. She imagined it was someone's job to search American university web sites and glean info about single Ph.Ds.

It wasn't the first time somebody had targeted her. In fact, she'd deleted and blocked two other emails from the same foreign address from her phone earlier in the day.

She'd had her fill of come-ons from fake, fraudulent, and occasionally honest men. She doubted that this man even existed; if he did, he most certainly wasn't a detective from the Greek Isles. His features, too sharp and too dark for a native Kritiki, revealed ancestral bloodlines from farther south or east than Crete—maybe Turkey or Syria.

Nikkis didn't bother to read the rest of the message. In disgust, she sent the address to her blocked senders file and wondered how cyber-stalkers got her address and how they knew her real name.

She slipped her feet into the simple, black pumps under her desk; then, automatically, she pulled her blouse out from her straight, charcoal-gray professorial skirt. The old habit kept her shirt from conforming to her curves. At the door to her office, she pulled her wrinkled suit jacket from the rack and slipped it on. The weather didn't require the jacket. The walk wasn't far. She wanted to enjoy the sunny, mid-May day, but she might run into unwanted attention if she didn't wear her carefully chosen uniform of discouragement.

In her hall mirror, she checked her chignon and horn-rimmed glasses. She'd have to change her glasses soon. The geek-eyed, pointed look was back in fashion. She'd need something harder and thicker.

She shook her head and sighed. That she hadn't even seen the article that had been mentioned in the stalker emails had upset her.

She needed a walk.

She left her office in the Argosy Building and set out across campus toward her mailbox in the Admin Building, where she hoped the university's postal services had caught up with the rest of the world and finally delivered her contributor's copies of *Linguae Antikuitas*.

Even walking the tree-lined paths of the common lawns on the sunniest day, the university never quite looked like Nikkis felt it should. The granite edifices weren't white enough. Even in the brightest sunlight, a part of her craved more light—light that reached into the eye to touch the soul.

She caught herself in her ridiculous musings about light and chastised herself.

Light is not alive. It does not change its nature from time to time and place to place.

She shook her head at her own foolish thoughts. She'd let the emails affect her more than they should have.

Granite was granite. Buildings were buildings. Light was light.

Squirrels played in the oaks and willows lining the commons walkways. She tried to shake off the feeling that the green of the trees was too dark.

Nikkis squinted, attempting to force the color to lighten or to pull some needed blue from the surrounding grounds. People, mostly students, hustled about, bundled too tightly in clothing that seemed foolish and pretentious. Some glanced her way then ignored her. Most just ignored her.

On a day when she should have been excited, even elated by publication, she felt annoyed and distant from herself, like her body and mind occupied two different worlds.

Again, she shook off the familiar odd feeling of displacement that came to her from time to time. She didn't dress much differently than anyone else. She had some fashion sense. Of course, she also dressed to deflect interest in any asset other than her mind.

Even after brushing aside the haunting feeling by ticking off the logic of her own experiences, she couldn't shake the feeling that she lived in someone else's idea of what her life should be.

Well, it didn't matter, she told herself. Today, the article put her one step closer to tenure, and she planned to be happy about it.

She stepped onto the soft, groomed lawn beneath an oak, paused, and took in a full, cool breath to clear her head.

A fat, red squirrel skittered down the trunk, ran toward her, realized his mistake, and stopped.

"Signomi, kirie," *Excuse me, Sir*, she said. "Ah, but you are an American squirrel," she added. "Like most Americans, I imagine you only speak one language. Pity, that."

"Some Americans speak more," a woman behind her said.

The squirrel ducked as if something had been thrown at it. It spun. Tail high, it sprinted back up the tree it had only just left.

Nikkis turned toward the voice.

Karin Anderson, Chair of the Department of Antiquities, a stout tank of a woman whose only vanities were the sharp press of her dark suits and her loose, faux-natural mane of highlighted hair—the kind of wild, loose cascade that would have drawn men to her from three hundred meters away if she had been ninety pounds lighter or two feet taller.

Like she fancied herself a model, Anderson flipped the hair over her shoulder onto her back. "Some of us speak four languages."

Nikkis nodded. "Or more." The game was old—academics meeting by chance and immediately testing one another, trying to establish who had the longer CV, who had the greater prestige, who should bow and who should crow.

Nikkis would graciously lose to her department chair, and they both knew it, but she would play hard enough to hold some respect. "Dr. Anderson," she said.

"Nikkis."

"Admin?" Nikkis asked.

Anderson nodded. Together, they walked toward the administration building, which held Anderson's office and Nikkis's mailbox. The magazine's treatment of her article and the subsequent reviews could determine her future—whether she would eventually gain tenure, whether she would one day be free of the power games and foolishness of pride and ego she constantly guarded against in her chosen life and profession.

"For a twenty-nine-year-old associate professor, your performance reviews show promise, Nikkis," Anderson said. "When the time comes, the tenure committee will probably be impressed."

Nikkis bristled. Anderson had used her first name twice rather than addressing her as Dr. Aristos. "Are the reviews ready for me to see, Karin?" she asked.

Dr. Anderson stiffened slightly, adding a bit more formality to the starch of her suit. That little pause and tiny straightening of spine revealed that Anderson played some deeper power game than normal meet-and-greet politics. It was okay for Anderson to call Nikkis by her first name, but it was a one-way street, and Nikkis had gone the wrong way. The game's rules and victory conditions weren't clear yet, but Nikkis understood the warning that the game had begun and she might be either a player or a pawn.

To cover the awkward moment, she went on, "I'd particularly like to see the student reviews. I think some of the techniques I tried last quarter worked well, but I'd like to see if the student responses were positive before I try them again."

"Yes," Anderson said. "Playing children's games with graduate students on the lawn of the administration building was a bit, well, *unique.* If your students hadn't scored so well in their comprehensives on Linear-B and Classical Period Egyptian, I think Dr. Bonnet would have gone gunning for you."

Nikkis smiled, enjoying a small triumph. Bonnet would love to see her canned. She'd spurned his advances half a dozen times. "I can handle him," she said.

They walked out from under the cover of the trees, and the sudden bright sunlight made Nikkis squint.

Anderson sneezed and swiped at her nose with a starched sleeve. "He's not an ugly man," she said.

"No," Nikkis started up the steps of the Admin building, Anderson in step beside her.

"He'd make a good husband and father. He'd also be a good political ally."

"I'm sure," Nikkis said. "You're divorced. Have you approached him?"

Anderson laughed, stepped forward, and opened the heavy, brass-and-glass door for Nikkis.

Nikkis casually ignored the unusual deference. She stepped into the building and stopped in the shadows of the gray marble foyer. Gray. Exteriors were red brick and brown granite. Interiors were maple, cherry, brass and marble. All the marble on the campus was gray.

No. She corrected herself. The marble was white with gray striations—gray-at-a-glance or in peripheral vision. It annoyed her a little. It was the wrong color for marble. *Just wrong.*

She dismissed her silly, campus Feng Shui thoughts and turned to the mailboxes—rows and columns of old, brass boxes set into the wall. She tracked down the rows and columns, aware of Anderson watching her and wondering why the woman hadn't said goodbye and walked on. The game wasn't over, Nikkis knew, but these things often played out slowly over days, weeks, months, and even years. Rules of the game included pretending no game existed.

She bent and spun out the combination of her mailbox. The box front swung open, and even before she reached in, she smiled. The journal. *Finally*. She memorized the image of it rolled and wrapped in brown paper in her box before she slid it out.

Once in hand, she enjoyed the texture of the slick cover and the thin sharp line where the slick disappeared under the rough brown paper.

"The Linear-A article?" Even in the dim foyer, Anderson's onyx eyes glistened.

"I think so," Nikkis said.

Anderson grasped Nikkis's forearm.

Nikkis flinched, but Anderson held her firmly. "Open it," Anderson said.

"Later," Nikkis said. She didn't want to share the moment with Anderson.

"How can you wait, Dr. Aristos?"

Now, it's Dr. Aristos. Now, she understood that the game involved the article somehow. She nodded, slipped the brown paper off and unrolled the magazine.

Anderson moved so they stood hip-to-hip, both looking at the magazine in Nikkis's hands.

A head-shot photograph of Nikkis filled the cover. Low on the cover across the hollow of her throat, she read the title of her article. She had been excited about the publication, but she hadn't imagined this. After a moment to recover, she whispered, "The cover? They put me on the cover." She looked up from the magazine to Anderson.

The department chair grinned, released Nikkis's arm, and flipped her hair back.

"It wasn't that important," Nikkis said. "And the photo. I didn't give them a photo."

Still grinning, Anderson glanced from side-to-side then leaned in and whispered conspiratorially, "The editor, a dear old friend, and I both recognize a talented, promising young woman when we see one." Anderson's arm snaked around Nikkis's waist. She squeezed then stood on tiptoes and pecked Nikkis on the cheek.

Shocked, Nikkis pulled away and faced Anderson. The game wasn't the game she'd expected.

"You're brilliant in many ways, Dr. Aristos," Anderson said. "It wasn't lost on Bonnet, and it certainly isn't lost on others."

Anderson strode off into the dark, labyrinthine building.

Nikkis, her new success suddenly cold in her hand, stared at the back of the department chair, the woman who had so much influence that she could get Nikkis on the cover of the most prestigious magazine in her field on her first time out, the woman that could make or break Nikkis's bid for tenure. Darkness and ice grew in her gut and started to hurt. It was one thing when a man in authority played with your life for all the wrong reasons. Men with power often became predators. Through the ages, women had learned to expect it, to undermine it, to deflect it, to avoid it. It was something else entirely when another woman did it. It was worse. It was terrible and hurtful and, and, and…

Nikkis didn't know what it was, but she wanted to run, to get as far from the school as she could, as far from Anderson as she could.

Outside again, Nikkis sighed in the sunlight. She took some pleasure in the warmth on her face, but she took no pleasure in what should have been a triumph—the magazine in her hand. As she passed a waste bin, she paused. It was a cheat. Socially manipulated success didn't count in her way of thinking—only in Anderson's.

Nikkis's heart had broken only once, but it was enough. If she thought of matters of her heart at all, she believed that first loss had broken her heart so deeply that it had healed into a hard block of white marble—pure, clean, polished, and cold.

Bonnet's advances were nothing. He could be dismissed by force of intellect and superior achievement. His male reaction to her would be a handicap to him; but Anderson, she was different. She was a creature of politics, and she would have to be dealt with from a position of power Nikkis didn't have.

Cheat or not, the article moved Nikkis into higher circles. She came to the decision to accept whatever accolades came to her, and she gripped the magazine tighter to keep it from accidentally falling from her grasp and being lost in the garbage in the bin.

It would take some thought and maybe some time, but she wouldn't let Anderson, or anyone like her, man or woman, steal her hope.

Modern Daedalus Returns

Daed's tortured mind cleared only while he poured his heart through his hands into his hammer and steel chisel and onto the wall. In the safety of his cavern in the White Mountains of Crete, white stone walls lit by the flicker of an oil lamp, the hammer rose and fell true against the chisel. The ring of steel on marble echoed into the ancient depths of his labyrinth. Stone dust rose around the chisel point. Characters appeared in stone—a letter to his lost love.

Nikkis, if a dog can find his way home across a continent, perhaps a madman can find his way home across half a world. Thanks be to the many faces of the gods for giving me the gifts of my hands. While my mind spins through the agonies of our curse, my hands have seen me across the world to Crete.

In this life, as your Daed, I have known you and loved you once more. And as in all the lives that went before, we have been torn apart by my madness.

How many years I wandered, I can't say. I can only record my clear thoughts now, in this moment. Soon, the clarity will be gone again. Soon, I will be filled with all the memories of all the lives we have lived, a terrible storm of thousands of years of pain and suffering and loss.

I remember fixing things: lawnmowers, automobiles, tractors, generators, scissors, toys. I remember being in a ship and fixing computers and diesel engines. I remember so many things, and even now I'm not sure which memories come from this life and which come from others.

What I know is that I came home again. I found my way to this cave, and I took up chisel and mallet, perhaps from the sheer force of habit thirty-five hundred years creates. Perhaps mere instinct drives me to return here like a lost dog who finds his way home from afar. In my madness I come here because I have no coherent thoughts to interfere with my sense of direction, the pull toward safety.

Home again, where it all began. The people here remember us, Nikkis. They have not forgotten. They bring me food. I fix their generators, toys, grape presses, stills, and stanchions. This I do in my madness. They take care to never approach me. They understand what I have become.

Only in the cave…. Only when my hands hold mallet and chisel does clarity of mind return to me. By the gift of a long dead Queen, my hands remember all, and only in the writing on these walls will it be preserved for all of time—for you, Nikkis.

One day, I pray to Poseidon whom I have wronged, that you will read these words.

Your Daed in this life, and in our first life Daedalus, I write again in stone—once more reborn as man and blessed to love only you—doomed to lose you again—and doomed to find this cave and take up mallet and strike the stone until my hands fail and my eyes go dark and once more the gods see fit to let me slip from ancient flesh to newborn flesh and begin anew the cycle of our curse.

How many times I have been reborn, the walls tell. My writings go far and deep into the earth's darkness. My sane moments are too precious to waste reviewing our past. To put the mallet down, to free the chisel from my hand, will make me once more the madman who remembers all the moments of all his lives. Each memory is a single gem caught in a basket ever shaken by a child's hand so no moment seems to follow another. Without this mallet, I have no thread on which to hang so many moments and see them as this life or as that life.

Here, even now, my mallet in hand and stone dust in my nostrils—in my mind, in the part of me that is not my hands, I remember you in our first life, Nikkis—beautiful Nikkis—even at the last so full of life and hope.

I remember you also standing at the stone gates to your father's farm in some other life gone by. It was my first vision of you in that life—sun on your golden skin, and dark eyes lit like bright coals, flashing fire and calling me. I see you there, the dark, molten bronze rivers in your hair burning like poured metal from my smelting ovens, and I know we were together then, that day alone, in that life. We met there at the gate, and by day's end we lost ourselves to passion and kissed.

Your lips linger in many memories, touching, burning, filling me with the passion that unleashes the flood of memories of lives we have lived, of the curse we live.

So much has changed over the millennia. Only the kiss remains the same. Only the flood of ancient memory. Only the loss of love.

In this life, we drove to a mountain top in an automobile—my Helios.

In this life, I nearly killed your father, so eager were we to find a place to seal our fates.

Always, the kiss comes. After that, you struggle alone. For me, the wandering—always, the wandering. Years, perhaps, lost in a fog of memories that make no sense in this world of our new lives.

Computers and cell phones and cars and trucks and airplanes.

So long ago, I built my wings—so long ago, but yesterday in heart. Long lost Ikarus, have you forgiven me?

In grief, I think perhaps I'll drop the mallet and the chisel and let the past flood over me, let the child shake the basket so I do not have to hear the scream of Ikarus—the scream that only Poseidon's embrace silenced.

So many lives, and I have learned so much. I know that in infinite time lies the certainty that we will meet and end this curse. Though I cannot leave this place or make a plan that I can carry beyond this wall, I trust in love and time and numbers.

The making of steam engines was once my trade, and once there were golden trinkets born of my hands, and once there were toys with wind-up springs. Always, my hands have gifted men and women and children, and always the kiss has come and torn my mind, and always then my hands have recorded memories here in this cave on this wall.

Here, where once a bull raped a Queen.

Here, where once a fool built frail wings from leather, feather, wax, and honey and then launched himself and his trusting son into the sky.

Here, where all of the history of the death of Knossos lies buried.

Come to me, Nikkis. Let us come together and end our curse in this life.

Hunger drives me away from the wall, and I now place chisel and mallet on the floor, and in placing them, I return to my torn mind. I love you still, but by our curse your beauty will bring you to the bed of another. It will bring you to be desired, but you will know no joy of love. Who can say which is worse, to love and be made mad or to have loved and lost hope?

Hope demands that I eat, Nikkis. Hope takes me to water as well. The people of our village have kept their promise these many years. I protect them. They protect me. Mad, I may be, but my hands can still repair anything man has wrought, and to me they bring their needs. To me they bring food and water. Eventually, another hunger, a deeper hunger of the soul, returns me to chisel and mallet and wall.

Nikkis, you are my balm and hope. You need only wait for me in one life. We need but meet again in one life. We need but love again in one life, and the curse will end forever.

Please, Nikkis, come to me. Read these words. Save us both.

Ancient History

When Daedalus chose the site of his quarry, he had searched for three things: first, a place where limestone, marble, and mica all came together in abundance; second, a curved ridge that descended to a valley floor to allow for ease of cutting and an access road with a gentle slope; third, a hill at the higher end of the valley to allow him to construct his foreman's shelter so he could see all of the work of the quarry and so the sounds of the quarry would be amplified and focused on his hut.

Patience, knowledge, and hard-earned political savvy had allowed him to put off Minos, King of the island of Crete, long enough to create a quarry that allowed efficient masons to triple the rate at which they cut and delivered stone for the new palace at Knossos.

With the palace nearing completion, Daedalus often took pleasure in looking out over the valley and the giant stairs of cut-stone terraces that made up the ridge wall where his men worked hard cutting stone. Women, sent from villages as a tithe to the king, worked off their duty by carrying water, by cooking, or by sewing the tarps and covers that kept working men from the sun.

From his stone-and-tarp shelter atop the hillock, he scanned the ridge-top over the cut-stone wall. Facing late afternoon sun, he held up his stone-hardened hand to shade his eyes. In the bright light where an arid, scrub-covered slope met the brilliant blue heavens over the Minoan island of Crete, a dust demon lifted and swirled like a churning column of white fire descending the quarry road.

The shining vortex marked the advance of the king of Knossos and his retinue of soldiers.

Daedalus called to a passing woman to bring water, and he returned to the shade of his Master Mason's awning and the study of his stone, a slab of mica as thick as the span of a man's hand, as broad as his own powerful, mason's shoulders, and as tall as the shoulder of a horse. The stone leaned against a single block of limestone carved by Daedalus himself to represent a giant bull's horns. The horns would soon cap the walls of the palace of Knossos. Until then, they served as an easel for his study of the newly unearthed treasure of transparent stone.

Beside Daedalus, his apprentice and son, Ikarus, also examined the stone.

"It flakes off," Ikarus said. He pinched the corner of the slab. Leaf-like flakes of clear mica fell off and floated to the dust around his sandaled feet. "It won't cut. It won't take scoring and breaking."

The king's procession had distracted Daedalus. His mind searched for reasons the king might visit the quarry. Kings were best managed at a distance, and they were least dangerous when they were sated and ensconced in their palaces. When a king moved, trouble moved with him.

Daedalus's dry lips and tongue made him ignore his son and search for the water girl he had called. He scanned the pale, angled quarry terraces, lashed-ladder scaffolds, and tented resting and carving areas. "Ikarus," he said, "You call them. Those girls will fight to be the one who brings you water."

Ikarus laughed. "Your thirst must be strong," he said. "You've never asked me to call the girls for you before." The younger man slapped his father on the back.

Daedalus stiffened. While he loved his son, he had also noticed that lately work had suffered, and Ikarus carried the gleam of unearned pride in his eyes. The boy had begun to believe himself important because he was the Master Mason's son.

Impertinent humor twitched at the corners of the boy's lips while he spoke. "If you let them tarry with you while you drink, you might find one of them pleasant company, Father."

Daedalus frowned. "Look." He pointed to the moving column of dust on the quarry road.

"A dust demon," Ikarus said.

"The king and soldiers."

The mischievous glint in Ikarus's eyes faded.

"Call for water, *apprentice*," Daedalus said, "for the stone. I want water to drink and to clean the stone."

A woman wearing the black-hooded robe and veil of mourning swept into the shaded space beneath their awning. The hem of her robe was raised, pulled between her legs then tied into itself around her waist to make walking easier. Her pale legs showed the fine, useful muscle of a woman who walks the hills with goats or sheep. She thrust a full water skin between Daedalus and Ikarus. "I have your water."

Daedalus took the skin. "Thank you."

"It was not a favor to you, Mason. I perform my duty to family, village, and king." Her smooth, cool voice told him this woman was no mere child who would flutter about giggling and hoping for Ikarus's smile.

Relieved, Daedalus nodded acknowledgement then faced his stone. He bit down on the water skin's stopper, pulled it free, then squeezed the skin hard enough to send a stream of water out over the mica slab. Stone dust sloughed away, and the shine of the amber, transparent stone beneath reflected his form and the form of the woman standing next to him.

She took the skin from his hands and dropped her hood and veil to take a drink.

Daedalus stared at her reflection in the stone.

Even with the curves, seams, and warps of the stone reflecting her face, her beauty trapped his eyes. Captivated by her face in the stone, he reached for the soft, bronze-gold curve of her cheek to brush away a dark, shining curl that had escaped from the leather band binding her hair back.

His fingers met wet, cold mica.

"You have the same stare as a ram when the ewes are in heat," she said.

Embarrassed, Daedalus pulled his hand away from the stone. He turned to face her.

Her eyes were on Ikarus.

Ikarus stared, wide-eyed and mouth a little open.

Relief and a little regret washed away Daedalus's embarrassment. Her stinging words had been meant for his son.

Of course Ikarus held her gaze. Women's eyes always found Ikarus. His height, golden curls, cave-ice blue eyes, and muscled, lean figure brought all the water girls to him eventually. This one was no different after all.

"Boy?" Daedalus said.

Ikarus closed his mouth and blinked. Head cocked like a rooster, a slow, sly smile spread across his face.

Too late, Daedalus started to warn the boy to keep his tongue.

"For you," the boy said, "I would gladly provide a ram's service."

She didn't giggle the way most of the girls would have. Instead, she said, "I'm sure you would perform like a young animal if I smiled and fluttered my lashes."

Ikarus blanched. He sputtered. "I'm no animal."

"You are certainly no *man*."

Daedalus stifled a laugh. The woman gave better than she got. He imagined that her strength and beauty had given her much more practice at deflecting men than Ikarus had at embracing women.

The woman went on, "Should I desire a ram, I will choose a man who knows a woman's needs."

Ikarus turned red. His eyes went wide at the insult. He lunged for her.

Too late, Daedalus moved to stop his son from dishonoring himself and the woman.

Her dark robe rippled as if a breeze had come up, but the breeze was her hand moving too fast to be seen. A long, thin, curved blade appeared at Ikarus's neck. The point touched just below his ear and behind his jaw. "I was mistaken," she said. "You have the stare of a pig surprised by a knife in the hand of the woman who has fed him all his life."

Daedalus inhaled sharply, and he raised a hand to her pale, soft forearm.

Her head snapped to the side. Her long, gathered hair flipped forward over her shoulder. Dark eyes challenged him. Sunlight caught bronze in her dark hair and sent rivulets of Hyperion blessings down her head and into cascades over the front of her shoulder and along the high curve of her linen-swaddled breast.

"Please," he said. "He's young, and he has not looked upon much of life's beauty."

Her eyes softened. Small, controlled smile lines appeared at their corners. Her forearm relaxed.

"My apprentice is a simple man." Daedalus bowed slightly. "As am I. Mere masons."

Now, she smiled full and true. Dark cheeks glowed bronze-red. Eyes sparked with life and glistening, full lips belied the sadness of her grieving clothes. Her smile kindled a long dormant fire in Daedalus's heart, and he realized he had heard the advice of his son. He willed her to tarry a moment, wished it with his whole heart.

Then, her smile was gone, and he wanted it to appear again. In that moment, he believed he might do anything to see it once more.

She pulled her arm free of his grip, and she slipped her blade back into the folds of her clothes. "He gapes and stares like a boy caught behind bushes where women bathe."

"Yes," Daedalus said. "Thank you for teaching him better."

She nodded, took her water skin, and silently left them.

Stunned, Daedalus admired the strength and confidence of her walk as she departed.

"Did you see her?" Ikarus asked. "Have you ever seen anything so beautiful in your life?"

Daedalus turned back to the stone, but he continued watching her departing reflection there.

"Is your heart only moved by stone?" Ikarus asked. "By all of the gods, that woman can make men kill and women cry."

"The king," Daedalus said, "will want to know what we will do with this stone." Still, he followed her reflection in the stone, walking away, her water skin on her hip, her long, strong calves and thighs reflecting sunlight, and the bronze-fire and charcoal of her hair flashing even in the amber depths of the stone.

In the stone, Daedalus also saw that Ikarus still stared after the woman.

"Even a king," Ikarus said, "would bow before that woman."

"No doubt," Daedalus answered. "But I think that woman would kill or die before even a king could touch her without her desire."

Ikarus put a hand to the place on his neck where her blade had touched him, then he turned to face the stone.

Daedalus silently thanked the woman for bringing Ikarus's attention back to work and stone. "I will not cut the stone," he said, "though I think if I had enough time, I might find a way."

"Then what?"

"We will split it lengthwise along the layers. We will make four stones, and each will become a roof stone. We will build around them. Sun through these stones will capture heat, and the heat will move air in the corridors of the palace."

Ikarus nodded, and the two men returned to the work of trying to understand the grain of the layers so they could cleanly separate one from another.

~~~

The king and his entourage snaked down the long, narrow donkey track into the quarry. Daedalus, as foreman of the quarry and architect of the palace, went to meet him. At the foot of the quarry wall where the track spilled out through limestone rubble onto the valley's floor, King Minos and his retinue halted.

Minos, king of the island, keeper of the trust of Zeus and Poseidon—bull among the herd of men—sat astride his revered and aging bull, Karskus, a kohl-and-dun creature. One horn had been broken in battle, but the other double-curved horn still swept outward from his broad forehead. Then, it curved forward along and above the scarred lines of his long face. The bull's dust-tired, red eyes rolled. He shuddered, and pale trail dust rose from his smooth coat and settled to the quarry floor. The retinue's clattering, creaking, and clinking bronze, leather, and bone armor settled to stillness.

Daedalus knelt.

The king lifted a leg over Karskus's thick neck. A soldier dashed forward and went down on all fours. The king lighted on his back and stepped to the ground. As tall as Daedalus but not nearly as hardened from working with his hands, his shoulders, or his mind, King Minos still ruled over the people of the farms and villages of Crete.

Looking at the man, Daedalus easily understood how, when still young, the king had been given the name Bull Among Men. Though the man's face might be rounder than once it had been, the oiled, black ringlets of his mustache and beard gave his face a squared, solid frame that matched the undiminished stature and pride that had powered the king's campaign to unify the island kingdoms and take his place as chief leader of men and messenger of the gods.

"Stand, Mason," Minos said. "We have not come to inspect your work. We are much pleased with you and your son."

Daedalus nodded and stood. Relief moved through his blood like a cool breeze sweeping the dust from the face of parched, pale stone.

"Where is she?" Minos asked.

"Who, good king?" Daedalus said.

"Gask!" Minos called. "Where is she?"

A narrow-faced, rat-like man pushed forward between ranks of soldiers. He stood no taller than Daedalus's breast. The rat man scurried clear of the soldiers,
~~~

Daedalus, king, and bull. He paced and turned in little circles looking for something or someone.

"Perhaps I can help," Daedalus said. "If you give me the name of the person you seek."

"Her name, Gask?"

"Nikkis." The little man spoke while he scurried about. "Nikkis. A goat and sheep herder. A girl from my village."

Daedalus shook his head. "I don't know her name. She may be among the cooks or–"

Gask, the rat-faced man, interrupted. "Water girl. Village work tithe. Tithe to honor The Bull. Duty of her village. One week work, then gone."

"There are many water girls," Daedalus said, but even while he said it, his throat tightened. A cold layer of stone dust settled over the newly inspired warmth in his heart.

"Terrible beauty," Gask said. "Terrible. Quick in tongue and blade. If you meet her, you know her." The Rat peered at Daedalus through narrowed, challenging eyes. Gask's sharp, broken teeth flashed in the sun. A pale scar creased his cheek and eyebrow to make his face all the more narrow and ugly. "He *does* know her. I see in his eyes. He knows her."

King Minos strode up to Daedalus. He looked Daedalus level in the eye. "In truth, Mason? Do you know of this rare and beautiful creature Gask has promised?"

Daedalus and Ikarus had traveled the world. They had learned irrigation techniques in Babylon. They had learned to make paper in Aegypt. They had learned to build ships in the islands of the wind. They had come to Crete to rest on their way home to Athens. Daedalus had looked a dozen kings in the eye, and he steadied himself and met the gaze of this one with eyes that knew water, stone, wind, and fire. "The only beauty here is in the stone," he said. "This is no place for maidens, courtesans, and courtiers."

"Goat girl," Gask said. "Shepherd. Dark-eyed, fire-bronze and kohl-haired. Nasty."

"A creature to bring fire to my blood line." The king stroked his beard thoughtfully. "A heifer to bear me a son."

The cold dust covering Daedalus's heart crystallized into hard, icy quartz. The words of Gask and the king left no doubt. Nikkis was the woman he had just met. His patron, a man who could order him killed on a whim, stood before him, challenging him on the word of a rat-faced man.

The little man was too ugly and ill-kempt for court. More likely, he was trying to save his own skin.

"Good King," Daedalus said, "Protector of the herd of men, I cannot swear such a girl does not walk in your quarry somewhere, but I can say with certainty that I do not know where."

Minos seemed satisfied with the answer. "Look for her, Gask." The king took a seat on a white stone block. Two soldiers trotted up and stood beside him, one on each side. Four more set about erecting a silk pavilion above him.

Gask ran up to Daedalus. He looked up. "You love her," he said. "I see it! I know! I loved her too!"

"I have work here, little fool," Daedalus said. "Do whatever you've come to do. Leave me to my stone."

"I'll find her," Gask said. "I will give her to the king for what she did to me. Give her to the king and be a rich man. Rich, and then when he has had her and used her up, I will buy her and own her and make the rest of her days as painful as I can."

Daedalus considered giving the woman up. He had other concerns. Hiding her would break the king's law and trust.

But the raw sewage stench of the little man, the way he bounced around on his feet like a rodent ready to run from a cat or a child's thrown stone, the desperate rage and vindictive anger in the man's voice, filled Daedalus with an unexpected desire to protect the woman.

Daedalus didn't know what Nikkis had done, but in the span of a hundred heartbeats, he had become very sure the nasty little man had gotten his scar from Nikkis's knife and that he had deserved it.

Daedalus looked to the king and received a gesture of dismissal. He returned to the mica stone, relieved to be done with the king's audience and hopeful that the nervous little man could not find a woman so competent and clear-eyed as the one who had brought him water.

~~~

Several hours passed, and Daedalus had grown confident that the hunted water woman, Nikkis, had left the quarry. He had also grown more confident that his techniques for separating the layers of mica might work.

He and Ikarus stood over a much smaller slab of mica, one Daedalus had prepared for testing his idea for sheering off layers from the larger stone. After etching a groove around the edge of the mica slab, they had secured a length of fine, braided copper wire between two rods. With the wire set to one layered edge of the slab, they wrapped the wire around the slab so it seated in a groove around the stone. They slipped the two rods through a stone yolk and snugged the yolk to the stone; then, together, they turned the rods to twist and tighten the wire. The wire loop tightened and bit into the layered stone. Twist by twist, the wire pulled tighter and slipped between layers.

A man's shout interrupted the delicate cutting. Amplified by the curve of the quarry and focused on the master mason's hut, the ear-splitting shriek froze Daedalus's blood and hands. He made out the words perfectly. "Here! Here! I found her!"

"Gask." Daedalus dropped his end of the rods and moved out from beneath the sheltering awning so he could see the quarry floor and walls.

"She is here!" Gask called.

The rat man's voice came from one of the mortar pits near the lower edge of the quarry wall. If the woman was there, she was cornered.

Daedalus searched for the king's soldiers until he found them. Alerted, they moved slowly through the confusing maze of cut stone, rubble, and scaffolds covering the valley floor.

Daedalus knew the maze of his quarry better than any man. He ran down from his hill. He leapt over stones. He dodged in and out between great cut blocks. Following the shortest path to Gask, Daedalus flowed like water along the troughs, channels, and bends of his quarry.

The little man screamed and squealed.

Soldiers moved toward the commotion, but Daedalus arrived first.

Gask and three water women stood on one side of a mortar pit, a square, shallow hole filled with clay slurry and cut straw. Several laborers, men sent from distant
~~~

villages as a tithe to the king, leaned on tools or against stones. Bets were made. Coins changed hands.

Nikkis, hood thrown back and dangerous fire in her eyes, stood trapped. Her back to a white marble wall, she was blocked on one side by the pit and on the other by Gask and two women.

The other women cursed her and closed the distance.

"Not too close," Gask said. "Not too close. She will cut you. She cut me, and I loved her."

The laborers saw Daedalus first. They stood straight. Money disappeared. Hands took hold of tools.

He glared.

Reluctantly, they moved away from the spectacle and back toward their work.

Rat Face saw him too. "Liar," he said. "She is here; you are here. You love her. You love her." He danced and sang his taunts like a child. "Who's a fool now? Who? She'll cut you like she cut me."

Nikkis turned to see Gask's audience. Surprise softened her face for a moment—surprise and, Daedalus thought, perhaps the shadow of a cloud of sadness at the possible loss of his respect.

He dismissed the foolish thought as more worthy of Ikarus and his romantic fantasies. Who but a fool in love believed he could know any woman's mind? He certainly did not know this one's. He had only just met her, and in his whole life and all his travels he had met no man who could honestly claim to know the mind and heart of such a creature as this.

"What has this woman done to you?" Daedalus asked.

"Tell him," Nikkis said. "Tell him what I did. Tell him what and why, or I will. If I'm going to die in front of an honorable man, I at least want him to know that I was never dishonored by such as you!" She spat on Gask.

Daedalus pressed past Gask and his harpies to put himself between the women, the Rat, and the blade.

"Nikkis? May I use your name?" he asked.

She nodded, but her dark eyes searched for some place to run, some way to escape.

"You think death seeks you here?" He edged closer.

"I will die before I let the king make me into one of his breeding cows."

"A rare woman refuses a place in the palace." He moved closer still.

"Gask seeks favor from the king and revenge against me." She shifted her footing so she could see around Daedalus to watch Gask. Her blade held steady. "He is a rat from my village."

Daedalus turned his back to Nikkis. Now, between her and Gask, he back-stepped even nearer to her. "What did she do?"

"See! See!" Gask touched the scar on his face.

"And you?" he asked the watching women. "What's your business with her?"

One woman said, "I would kill to live in the palace."

"She thinks she's too good for a king," another said.

"Back to work!" Daedalus commanded.

The cowardly cook-and-water women melted away into the gathering crowd.

"All of you! The king comes. Do you want to serve him in these pits instead of cutting stone or carrying water and cooking for masons?" Daedalus took one more step backward. He heard Nikkis's breathing behind him, felt her movement through the stone under his feet. He knew her blade was at his back, but it was not so ready as it had been.

The gawking men and women shuffled away toward their work.

Daedalus's hand, as hard as stone and as controlled as the finest chisel, shot back and caught Nikkis's wrist.

She squeaked in surprise and pulled back.

He turned and twisted up and away from her shoulder. The knife came free in his hand. When her grip on the knife broke, he released her, and she lost the anchor that held her upright. As if tipping a balanced stone, he let her spin away from him and fall.

Nikkis tumbled into the straw, clay, manure, and water mortar. She turned and rolled in the muck, trying to get her feet under her.

Daedalus slipped her blade under his own garments and into the leather strap from which he hung his mason's tools.

Gask laughed.

While Nikkis struggled in the muck, soldiers arrived and surrounded Gask, Daedalus, and the pit.

By the time Nikkis regained her feet, now a stinking, muck-covered, dripping, gray golem in the vague shape of a woman, King Minos had arrived.

Soldiers knelt. Daedalus knelt. Nikkis knelt, the liquid muck swallowing her body up to the breast.

Gask recovered from his laughing fit. He danced and pointed, too excited to kneel. "Here," he cried. "Here!"

The king strode up behind the dancing man and glanced at Daedalus.

"One of my mortar workers, good king," Daedalus said. "A matron in mourning."

"This mud woman is the beauty you promised me?"

"No!" Gask said. "I mean yes! Her! It's her! The mud!"

The king took a bronze javelin from one of his soldiers.

Daedalus shifted slightly in case he needed to place himself between Nikkis and Minos. Even while he moved, he wondered at himself—wondered that he would even consider such a thing for a stranger. Even while part of him wondered, another part deep in his heart drove his actions from a pure certainty. While he marveled at the thought, he also knew he would die here and now for this woman if need arose.

Behind him, she whispered, "My blade. Let me die by my own hand."

The king faced them, hefting the javelin, his dangerous eyes first on Daedalus then on Nikkis.

Daedalus held as still as any stone he had ever cut.

The king drove the spear downward into the neck and through the chest and back of Gask. Minos said, "Join your queen of mud." He kicked the dying, sputtering man into the mortar pit.

Minos, island king, turned and strode away. Soldiers fell in behind him.

Moments later, Daedalus turned to the edge of the pit.

Nikkis stood up from the mud beside the dead man. Again, she spat—this time on the little man's corpse.

"Queen of the mortar pit," Daedalus said. He went down on one knee and extended a hand as if to help a queen step up from the foul mix.

She laughed, took his hand, and stepped up onto firm ground.

The sound of her laugh and the touch of her slimy fingers lifted him from his knees. He tried to brush the gray and brown muck from her cheek, but it only smeared. He smoothed it down from her head, but his hand only matted her hair.

Still, she laughed a laugh that could cause vines to flower in stone. She grasped his hands. "Stop," she said. "It's no use."

"I see strength and beauty under the mud, I think," Daedalus said. "So much that perhaps you have been cursed by it."

"He pressed me for marriage," she said.

"The king?"

"Of course not." She pointed to the corpse in the muck. "The rat. I refused. He found me in the hills herding goats—he and two others. They tried to take me."

"I suspected something of the kind."

"Two died." Sun flared in her eyes, and pride sounded in her voice. "That coward tried to run, but I needed a living warning to other men who would try to take me against my will."

Daedalus pulled her blade from his belt and handed it to her. The blade's simple, well-worn olivewood handle belied the intricate and careful work of the metal. Long and thin, someone had taken great care in the cold forging of the copper and tin and in the etching of designs in the blade itself. "His scar?" he asked.

She took the blade and returned it to her own hidden belt. "No. He did that himself. Running from me, he fell and hit his face on a rock."

Daedalus chuckled.

"I shortened his manhood by half."

Daedalus stopped laughing.

"Thus, I honor any man who would treat me so."

"Ah," he said. He remembered her black robe. "You mourn a husband? He must be honored by your love."

"You travel with a son but not with a wife. Is she honored by your absence?"

Daedalus looked at the mud flower before him and wondered what in life had made her as sharp in tongue and mind as the blade she carried beneath her robes. "My wife died at his birth less than a year after we married. I was sixteen. She was fifteen."

"I'm sorry," she said. "I mourn my brother, and I wear the robes and veil so men will leave me to the honesty of my herd."

"Beauty and loyalty *are* your curses," he said.

She looked up into his eyes. Sun had begun to dry her mortar mask. Her face, though shaped with perfect care by the gods, now appeared to be a statue's face made of darker and lighter clays. The reek of her made his eyes water, but the gratitude in her eyes and the smile on her gray, mud-caked lips made his heart pound and his blood burn to hear her speak and laugh again.

She stood on tiptoes and pressed a dry, raspy kiss to his cheek, then slipped past him. "I need to find water," she said.

"Don't come back to the quarry," he said. "You have enemies."

"My village sent me. It's my duty to serve the king's tithe."

"It's my duty to enter the roles, check the tithes, and clear the debt of each village. Don't come back."

"Thank you, Master Mason," she said. "I owe you my life."

He smiled. "Daedalus," he said. "I have no need of payment."

Her hand went to the mud and muck of her hair, and she smoothed it back. It only made her long neck look more like sculpted stone.

"Go," he said.

She turned and trotted away through the maze of stone, ladders, and scaffolds.

~~~

Daedalus returned to the mica. There, Ikarus laughed and flirted with a new water girl, one Daedalus hadn't seen before. A mere waif of a girl, her wide eyes showed that she held the mason's son in awe, and her place on his lap showed that he willingly let her worship him.

"Girl," Daedalus said.

The girl jumped up. She grasped her water skin, and water squirted from the open neck onto Ikarus.

Flailing at the water, he scrambled to his feet, too.

Daedalus bit his own lip to suppress his smile. "Go," he said. "We've had enough water here for one day."

The girl scurried away into the quarry.

"She liked me," Ikarus complained.

"We have work."

"The stone cuts just as you said it would." Ikarus slapped the last of the water from his apron.

"Yes."

"You're disappointed, Father?"

"No."
~~~

Ikarus shrugged. "I meant no harm with the girl."

Daedalus peered into the stone, searching for remedies to the sudden strange feelings of foreboding casting shadows in his heart. "We have been too long away from Athens."

His son mimicked his deep stare into the stone. "Seven years."

"Gather what tools you wish to carry." Daedalus broke his stare into the stone. He regarded his son and felt certainty in his decision. "We leave tonight."

Shock brought the boys eyes up to lock with his father's. "No."

"We must," Daedalus said.

"Father," Ikarus said. "The palace. A month, and we finish."

"A day, and we are dead."

"What are you saying? Your fame is greater than this king's. People will come from all the kingdoms of the world to see our work."

"Yes," Daedalus began to busy himself gathering the tools he could not replace on the mainland. "And how long will a king tolerate the fame of a mason?"

"As long as you build for him," Ikarus said.

"Once the king and queen have their palace, what will their next project be?"

"Whatever glory they seek, we will build."

"No." Daedalus stopped gathering his tools. His son needed to know the full import of this moment. He took the boy by the shoulders and held him until Ikarus's eyes focused on his own. "We will not," he whispered. He glanced around to be sure he would not be overheard. "They have unified the lands of this island. They have built their palace. They have ships of my design to control the seas for many leagues."

"Peace," Ikarus said. With less certainty, he said, "A time of joy and prosperity."

Daedalus shook his head. "Think, boy. The king and the queen each stands as a holy messenger for different gods that each claims to be supreme. Two powerful rulers as the heads of two powerful religions in one land."

"In Aegypt," Ikarus said, "there are many gods and many priests and priestesses. The pharaoh's wife–"

"I have been reminded of this king's justice and appetites today. The king and queen of this island will turn on one another, and because *we* have built machines of war for them, they will never let us go. *We* will become pieces in their game."

"But the riches? The fame?"

He gave his son's shoulders an affectionate squeeze and released him. Smiling, he said, "The women?"

Ikarus blushed.

"None has value in the kingdom of Hades. Gather your things, my son. We go tonight."

For a long moment Daedalus's son looked at him before finally nodding his assent.

Daedalus sighed in relief. He did understand the boy's desire to stay. He had once been young. Even now, he could not completely ignore the charms of women. Daedalus found himself hoping Nikkis had made it back to her home and family. He gave up a silent prayer to Poseidon, who had guarded him and his son in their travels so far. He prayed that the rest of the woman's life would be blessed with love and peace. Even while he made his prayer, he let himself selfishly wish to one day see her again. He prayed to once more face her, to have her look at him the way she had, to hear her speak to him as an equal in mind and heart the way she had. Most of all, he prayed to hear her laugh.

Certainly, he had cared for Ikarus's mother, his wife by arranged marriage—so long ago. The gods had given him Ikarus and taken her. This, though—this new fire in his heart—a different thing, a madness, a beauty, a greatness of soul that he had never known before. He wanted to embrace it for a thousand, thousand years.

His thoughts were selfish, and he knew it, but he had never met anyone like Nikkis before. If he would pray to the gods to grant her peace, perhaps it was not too arrogant to pray that they would also grant him the small boon of love.

Modern Sanctuary

Even the precise and austere Dr. Nikkis Aristos needed a place to go if all the problems in her life erupted at once, if all the foundations of her work cracked, and if the only things she had left were the blood in her veins and her memories.

With unexpected relief, Nikkis texted her acceptance to her mother's invitation to dinner. She accepted exposure to the silent judgment of her mother and father because it was normal and bearable. She accepted the possibility that they might once more try to convince her that she lived an empty life without a man and children. Worse, they might bring a man to dinner—a chance encounter, nothing manipulative, just a nice man—a man *they* thought had things in common with Nikkis, which meant he was Greek or had some relative who had once known a Greek.

After her explosion following their last attempt at matchmaking, she didn't think they would—but the best indicator of future behavior was past performance.

Thankful for the silence of her hybrid's battery drive, she turned her silver Prius onto her parents' lane, rolled to a stop, and pulled the smart key from the dash. For a long moment, she sat and simply looked at the house that had seemed so huge and out of place with the world around her when she was younger.

Now, that pillared colonial looked to her like a church of dysfunction that would always take her in and honor her call for sanctuary.

She got out of the car.

May in Oregon can be as warm as Florida summer or as cold as Montana winter, but the norm usually falls somewhere between—with rain. The evening's drizzle and chill made her pause and thank the ancient goddess for the invention of weaving and the gift of wool. She wrapped herself in a scarf of Greek sheep's wool, a present from a man who once hoped to be her lover and had at least had the sense to recognize her passion for the old country she had never visited.

Approaching the front door, she noted the three other cars in the drive: her father's white Ford Taurus wagon, her mother's aging, blue Olds Cutlass, and a monstrous Cadillac Escalade.

The shining, giant SUV had dealer plates. It was brand new and blacker than night. She told herself that the man who owned it was obviously compensating.

Good. She knew what to do with male insecurities.

She hadn't even gotten to the front door, and her blood burned and she wanted to scream. She turned back toward her Prius. She thought about getting in and driving as far away as she could.

A single shooting star sliced across the night sky.

Her hot anger chilled instantly into the cultivated quartzite clarity that had guided her life for the last twelve years.

No stranger would take her only and final refuge from her.

She turned back to the house, crossed the lawn, and marched through the front door.

"Mother," she called in Greek. "I'm here." She pulled her scarf off and hung it on the ornate, maple hat tree inside the door and next to her mother's antique phone stand. The scarf tassels draped down over the ancient, black rotary phone her mother insisted on keeping because it was the kind of phone that belonged on an old phone stand.

"Back here, dear," her mother called in English. "I'm just putting out dinner."

In Greek, which she knew both her parents understood perfectly though they refused to speak a word, she said, "There's a car in the drive—a man's car. If you set me up again, it will go very badly." She strode along the hallway toward the dining room and the kitchen beyond.

She stepped under the archway into the dining room at the same time she received an answer.

"The car is mine, Nikkis." English. A woman.

Nikkis froze.

The table had been set for four.

Her father, crushed into a suit and tie the way her mother crushed ripe olives into cheesecloth to extract oil, sat at the foot of the table.

Her mother hovered near him, a silver platter of roasted chicken in her hands and her American sixties TV-mom apron covering her blue housedress.

Sitting at the other end of the table, Dr. Karin Anderson leaned forward against crossed arms. She flipped her hair and winked at Nikkis.

Nikkis breathed ice into her words. "That explains the car." It also explained how the visitor had understood Nikkis's Greek.

Her mother made a little squeak and turned away to busy herself with the platter of chicken at the sideboard by the wall. Her father looked down to avoid Nikkis's gaze.

Nikkis's place had been set to Dr. Anderson's right.

Not good. Not at all good.

An ice water spring opened up in Nikkis's gut and filled her belly and chest with cold, liquid rage that threatened to rise into a wave that would wash upward and out to cover the room like a tsunami. She let a controlled stream of the chill form words in her throat. She launched them at Anderson. "Why are you here?"

"It's okay, Nikkis." Her mother said before she turned and settled the platter of now dismembered chicken at the center of the table. She handed Anderson the serving fork.

Her father coughed.

"Isn't it okay, Papá? Tell her." The edge in her mother's voice said that they had come to some decision, a decision that her father had agreed to under duress and with the implied threat of castration.

"Yes. All okay, Nikkis," he parroted.

"We're happy for you." Her mother spoke her rehearsed words, only choking on them a little. "We *understand*."

Nikkis spoke while crossing to her father's shoulder, never taking her eyes off Anderson. "Understand what?"

"Well," Her mother began to untie her apron. "Your—well—your situation."

Nikkis picked up her father's glass of wine and downed it in a fast series of swallows.

She placed the empty glass back in front of her father. The fire of the wine did nothing to melt the ice in her belly. She did her best to emit ice lasers from her eyes, to drill them into the condescending, smug gaze of Dr. Karin Anderson. She asked her mother, "What *situation* do I have?"

Her mother seemed about to say something, but Anderson interrupted. "It's okay, Cliantha."

Nikkis said, "You are on a first name basis with *my* mother?"

Anderson smiled. She sat up straight and laced her fingers together. "I've been telling them about your brilliant article positing a possible reading of Linear-A and the implied additional ideograms needed to provide sufficiency to interpret coherent text for all known sources of the language."

Her father lifted the wine bottle and poured a new glass for himself. Before Nikkis could reach it, he had the fresh glass to his lips.

"And other things." Her mother crossed to the foot of the table and picked up the wine bottle. The bottle shook in her grip.

Her father put his empty glass down. Some of the red wine dripped down the side of the glass, made its way quickly to the white, linen tablecloth, and then seeped like blood into the weave.

Nikkis's mother frowned at the spreading dark stain, but she didn't comment or fuss over it like she normally would have.

That, more than anything else, told Nikkis how very ugly her *situation* was.

"Show them your article," Anderson said. "Tonight, we celebrate, Nikkis. You've arrived."

"We understand now," her father said.

"No more sons of our friends," her mother said. "We won't embarrass you anymore."

"What the hell have you done?" Nikkis glared at Anderson. "I expect a straight answer. I came home to see my parents, a four-hour drive, and I find my department chair sitting in the dining room. This isn't about my article, and it sure as hell isn't about dinner, so somebody please tell me what's going on."

"A celebration," Anderson said.

"Of, well," her mother paused, "your lifestyle." Her mother's olive cheeks turned a maroon color her father called, ripe red—the color of the best California wines.

Like callused feet crushing cold grapes, the truth came down on Nikkis. She asked Anderson, "What did you do? What did you tell them?"

"Please, dear. We're *down* with *it*." Her mother's Greek accent made the aging American idiom sound worse than silly.

Her mother rounded the table and put a hand on Nikkis's arm. Eyes red and glistening, she said, "Karin seems quite nice, Dear."

Nikkis's sanctuary walls crumbled around her. Home had become as complicated and empty as her article.

"Anderson? Nice? This shark? No." Nikkis gave her voice the chilled, razor edge she had cultivated to castrate selfish, male suitors. Her thoughts moved at impossible speeds, and the room around her became narrow, and dark. "Nor are you."

"Here it comes," her father said. "The ice queen. I told you this was a mistake, Mamá."

Nikkis took a breath. The ice water rose, mixed with the fire of wine, and somewhere in her throat, somewhere near her heart, it turned to a flood of words. "It isn't enough to try to saddle me with every man you meet at the grocery, the butcher's, the baker's, or the park? It isn't enough to trick me into parties, and weddings, and christenings so I'll meet some *nice boy?* Now, you bring a woman from two hundred miles away into your home—my boss, my work, and you corner me with *her*?"

"We don't mind." Her mother patted the air with her hands in an attempt to calm Nikkis. "We understand. Really. It was hard, but Karin explained it."

Cold, slow, and with all the promise she could deliver by voice and eye, Nikkis spoke to Anderson like her parents were not in the room, "You're pathetic, tricking them—trying to trap me."

Anderson smiled. "They called me, Nikkis. They were worried about you. It's okay to be afraid."

The patronizing tone was too much. "I'm sure you arranged for them to invite you." She turned from the table and strode to the arch into the hallway.

"Nikkis," Anderson called after her. "You can't run from this."

Nikkis turned. "Sexual harassment."

"No," Anderson said.

"Do you think your lies will hold up when a professional questions my parents?" She took some joy in the pallor that took over Dr. Anderson's round, corpulent face. "No, I don't think so."

"Nikkis. Honey," her mother said.

"Listen to me—all three of you. This will never happen again. I will never give any of you the chance to treat me like this. If you can't honor the life I've built, then you will not be part of my life."

She spun away, strode down the hall, and grabbed her scarf.

"Nikkis?" her mother called.

"It's all right," Anderson said. "I'll talk to her."

On the hall table, the stupid, rotary phone rang. Nikkis grabbed the hard, Bakelite receiver more to keep from screaming than to answer. "Hello?"

"Is this Dr. Aristos?" A man's voice—thick and heavy with an accent—a central Crete accent.

"Speaking."

"You have not returned my emails."

"Put us on your do not call list."

"This 'not call list' is an American professor list?" The accented voice sounded truly baffled.

"Who is calling?" she asked.

The man said, "First Detective Andros of the Department of Antiquities and Forgeries in Iraklion, Crete."

Nikkis looked back down the hallway. The dining table was lit as brightly as the university stadium during a night game. Her mother stared at her. Her father's back was to her. Moving shadows marked the progress of Anderson toward the hallway.

"What do you want, Detective?"

"I read your article. I believe we have found some of the characters you have predicted. I want to fly you to Crete so you can verify them."

Anderson entered the arch and blocked half the light from the dining room.

"You're a detective," Nikkis said. "I'm a linguist."

"We found the characters on stolen artifacts."

Anderson was halfway down the hallway. Nikkis wished the woman would become Xeno's tortoise. "When?" she asked.

"At your earliest convenience."

She locked eyes with the approaching monster. "Now," she said into the phone. "I'll pick up the tickets at the airport."

The man on the other end gasped, recovered, and said, "Ne, theespehmis," *Yes, Miss.*

"*Doctor* Aristos," Nikkis said.

"Of course, Doctor. Please accept my apology. The tickets will be at British Airways."

Nikkis hung up.

Anderson reached for Nikkis's cheek.

Nikkis deflected the hand and slapped her boss as hard as she could. The crack of flesh on flesh echoed through the hallway like thunder rolling through a mountain valley and providing final punctuation to a storm.

Nikkis turned and left her parent's house.

~~~

Until she reached the counter to pick up her ticket, Nikkis had been certain it would be there—that she was destined to do this thing, to travel to Crete and walk the land of her ancestors. Only when she arrived at the counter did she begin to doubt. She felt foolish asking for a ticket to Crete, and she expected to be told no such ticket existed.

When the smiling British Airways agent handed over the ticket, irrational certainty began a war with reason in Nikkis's mind. She should have questioned a man offering her a plane ticket. She should have doubted his credentials—his sincerity and honesty. She should go home, she told herself. She should get her job back, if she could.

Still confused by her choices and surprised to have found the ticket at the British Airways counter as promised, Nikkis boarded the plane. She wound her way through the lounging seats of first class, seats with their own privacy screens, with full reclining capabilities, with free headsets, drinks, and movies. In the coach cabin, she considered turning back, going back to deal with *Dr. Karin Anderson* by begging for forgiveness or by slapping a sexual harassment suit on her. It might be better than playing egg-in-a-rocket with all these other travelers.

"Can I help you find your seat, Miss?"

The *Dr. Aristos* correction loaded itself onto her tongue. She spun in the aisle, but she swallowed her attack. The blue-uniformed woman who had approached her was Nikkis's age—British, blond, pretty, and seemed to want nothing from her except to help her find a seat.

Nikkis's life wasn't the flight attendant's fault. She forced herself to smile, to lie with her face instead of biting and clawing and showing her anger and her anxiety over flying.

"Is it a long flight?" Nikkis asked.

The attendant's helpful look flickered. For the briefest of moments, she seemed confused by the question. "To Heathrow?" Her professionally helpful face returned. "Ten hours, Portland to Heathrow, Miss."
~~~

Nikkis recovered from having asked such a stupid question by adding, "I'm going on to Iraklion on Crete."

"Ah, that's something, then. Sixteen with a refuel." The attendant seemed apologetic. Maybe it was just her British accent that made her seem that way.

Nikkis imagined ten hours stuffed into narrow seats set into rows and columns of uncomfortable, stoic people making the best they could of being living cargo in a metal tube hurtling over the frozen North Atlantic. It wasn't Nikkis's idea of a good time. It wasn't anybody's idea of a good time, but she had trapped herself into it. It was like some weird, fated moment. The detective had somehow known when to call—where to call.

He was a detective, she supposed. The where wasn't all that difficult to find, and she had blocked him on her cell.

The when made her wonder if Detective Andros knew Anderson.

Impossible. Just coincidence. He had called at exactly the moment when she needed to find a way out, a path to freedom from the expectations and ideas of family and false friends about who she should be and how she should live.

Perhaps the gods smiled. That's what her mother would have said. Her father would have just nodded and said, "Opportunity."

Nikkis told herself that her article was good. The writing and research were sound. Only Anderson's actions had made it an ugly thing. Facing sixteen hours in the crowded airline cabin, she wished she had more patience and could be more accepting of the things life threw at her. She might have simply used the article for leverage. She might have used it against Anderson somehow.

"Miss, are you ill?"

Nikkis forced herself to focus on the pert young woman in front of her. "I'm fine," she said. "A little nervous."

"First time, then?" The attendant lit up a bit, apparently happier at the thought of a first timer.

Nikkis shook her head. "It's work stuff."

"Are you sure that's all? You have that don't-like-to-fly look. We see it a lot."

The sincere concern radiating from the flight attendant's face made Nikkis say something she hadn't even admitted to herself. "Something about flying," she said. "It's like I knew somebody who died."

"Ah," the attendant soothed.

"But I don't," Nikkis said.

In a trained, caring professional voice, the woman said, "You'll be fine. We shall take excellent care of you."

So much for sincerity. "I'm sure," Nikkis said.

"Your seat number?" The name tag on the attendant's blue vest said "Jennie."

Nikkis checked her ticket then looked at the numbers over the seats around her. Her anger had driven her too far into the aircraft. Embarrassment had confused her. Now, she stood next to row 24. "Seven-A." Nikkis offered her ticket to the attendant.

"Oh." Jennie's almost genuine concern returned. "We'll get you sorted." Her English came out in smooth, educated British precision. For a moment, Nikkis envied her for having grown up in England, far from Greek parents who wanted instant grandkids and believed they had something to hide in the shadows of the past.

Jennie smiled and gestured back toward the front of the plane and the first class cabin. She hooked Nikkis's elbow and turned her back the way she'd come.

As they passed into first class, Nikkis worried that somehow Anderson had gotten her called off the plane. "I have a ticket," she said.

"Yes," Jennie said. "You have. Come along, then." Jennie continued toward the front of the plane.

"I just want to sit down," Nikkis said. "My bags are checked." She held her boarding pass forward over Jennie's shoulder.

Jennie didn't even glance at the pass. Her hand hooked up and snatched it. After a moment, the attendant stopped. Nikkis nearly ran into her. Jennie held the ticket stub low over a console for one of the first class reclining seats. The number on the ticket matched the number on the console.

"Here you are." Jennie winked at her. "You'll go much better here."

The seat had a window and room to walk around it.

Nikkis blinked.

Detective Andros had given her a fully reclining first class seat with a little table, a laptop holder, power outlets, a phone, a television screen, and a surrounding privacy screen.

Jennie looked at the boarding pass again. When she looked up, her smile had picked up some wattage. "I'm sorry, Dr. Aristos. I should have intercepted you before you got yourself to the rear of the plane." She handed the pass back to Nikkis.

"Please make yourself comfortable. Lawrence will be along to make sure you have everything you need. Can I pour a nip for you before we take off? Might be good for a bit of nerves."

Nikkis checked her ticket. She rechecked the number plate on the seat. They still matched.

For the first time in the eighteen hours since her morning conversation with the squirrel, Nikkis smiled. She had, after all, always wanted to go to Crete. She had been to Israel and Turkey chasing the Linear-A connection to Colchian and pre-Colchian language, but she believed that Crete held a wealth of undiscovered examples of Linear-A. In fact, she often had vivid, almost lucid dreams about Crete.

She decided to test the hospitality promised by Jennie of British Airways. "Macallan 12? Neat?" she asked.

"Will 18 do?" Jennie's eyes sparkled with pride.

Nikkis rewarded the attendant with her brightest smile.

"British Airways," Jennie said. "Only the best."

Maybe tolerance wasn't the virtue she'd thought it was a few moments before. If Anderson hadn't pulled strings, the detective in Crete might not have seen the article, Nikkis wouldn't have gotten angry, and she might not be heading out in first class to her first tour of her ancestral homeland.

One of her father's favorite sayings came to mind. "Who knows what's good? Who knows what's bad?"

Nikkis smiled to herself, shut down her cell, and settled into the accommodations for her flight to Crete.

Ancient Escape

Under cover of darkness, they had managed to sneak past the palace walls and the causeway guard, a man named Yorgos. The whole time, Daedalus had worried that Ikarus would intentionally make enough noise that they would be caught. Young men who believed in love rarely thought clearly. Pulling Ikarus away from his status as second to the master mason who built the shining palace of the king of Knossos was like tearing at the grip of a starfish holding fast to a stone. The boy had a thousand feet, each gripping tightly to some bit of grit or sand and each tugging back at the merest suggestion of pressure to leave.

Midway between the palace walls and the docks at the foot of the causeway, Ikarus spoke. "I have to say goodbye to Adara." He unslung his rolled blanket from his shoulders. His tools, carefully wrapped in an oiled lamb skin, then wrapped again in a clean, cow-leather bag, still clinked in the night with each hurried step he took.

"The ships put in to the Kairatos River before dawn," Daedalus said. His own roll tied over his shoulder and across his back, he hurried down the causeway. Moving quickly and silently, he hoped the nighttime silence of crickets and frogs following them like a shadow in daylight would not alert any of the soldiers watching the paths to the palace docks. The other guards, he was sure he could trick, but it was his bad luck that Yorgos guarded the path along the stream, the Vlychia, down to the piers on the deeper, more reliable waters of the Kairatos. He'd seen enough of Yorgos to know the quiet man was no fool.

"She's as sweet as honey raki," Ikarus said. "She has the scent of passion flowers, and her hair has fiery rivers of molten bronze set into onyx shine."

"Tides do not wait. Hurry." Daedalus's feet knew every stone of the causeway. His heart and mind had designed the way, and his hands had cut the stones or taught the men who cut the stones. Behind him, wrapped by the silence of the crickets, he took some solace in the hurried footfalls of his son. But Ikarus's youthful musings might get them both killed. "Be silent, or we will be undone."

"I'm already undone," Ikarus said. "I will sit here and die." His footfalls stopped.

Daedalus stopped and turned in the darkness.

His son, a man's dark shade sitting on a pale stone beside the causeway, said. "I can't leave her."

"She'll be here when we return," Daedalus said.

"Old and fat. The mother of the whelps of some dog who had not sense enough to care for her well."

"How will you care for her with your head on a spike in the palace courtyard?"

"You're a coward, Father. We ran from Aethiopea. We ran from Aegypt. We run and run."

Daedalus said, "We're going home."

"I have been gone for so long that I don't remember what home looks like. Mother died before I can remember. We have no home. We can make a home here."

The words cut deeper for their truth, but the truth of his son's words ended with the idea that they could make a home on Crete. "We can't stay if we want to live."

"You can't know that."

Daedalus moved close. He put a hand on the boy's shoulder and squeezed, trying to reassure. He understood the fires of youthful passion. Though he had thought them extinguished in himself, the sight of the shepherd woman, Nikkis, had stirred cold ashes and revealed a spark and some heat still living inside him. It saddened him that he would never see her again; but he would not. "She is, to be sure, a rare beauty," he said.

"You don't even know her."

In his urgency to mollify his son and get to the Kairatos and safely on a boat, Daedalus nearly lied and claimed he had met Ikarus's lover. He caught himself, and he nodded in the starlight. "No," he admitted. "I cannot say I know Adara from any of the other girls who have tarried near you at the quarry, but I know this one lives in your heart in a higher place than the others."

"Heart? You have no heart. You love only stone and things wrought by your hands. Stone heart. Stone hands. You couldn't love a woman if you wanted to. You know nothing."

He couldn't let Ikarus stay and become a casualty in the cruel games of kings and queens that would soon sweep across this island. He knelt before his son. "You were born, my son. Could that be if I could not love? I can love. I feel. I have seen women here that tempt me to stay."

Ikarus turned his face up. Starlight caught and danced in his eyes. "The water woman at the quarry."

"Yes."

"She was beautiful, and she liked you. Strong and smart and filled with will. A man died for her. A king searched for her, but she smiled for you, Father."

"She is a woman a man such as I might come to love. You think me untouched by her smile?"

"I think she put a knife to my throat, and we are running again. Your heart is made of the stone you cut."

Daedalus swallowed angry words. The night wouldn't cover them forever. Yorgos or one of his men would eventually walk this section of the causeway. A fight with his son would not go unnoticed. "She did not cut you," he said, "and she was hunted by Gask and the king. She plays a part in my reasons we must leave, and we must leave now. If they find us, we will never be able to leave."

"You risked your life to trick the king and save her. She will always remember you for that. We can finish the palace."

"No. If we stay, we will become no better than pampered slaves—if we live."

"Since you liked that woman so much, you could find her, disappear, hide, and live with her."

Daedalus savored the romantic idealism of his son's thought—an end of running, of adventuring. He could see himself in a village with Nikkis—using his hands to help people who didn't fight one another or steal land from one another. He wanted to be done with people who believed that all thoughts they had were inspired by gods and better than any thought in the mind of any other man or woman.

"You." Ikarus's voice rose and cracked. "You can herd goats for the rest of your life and live with the dirty, ignorant people in the hills. I will take your job as master mason to the king of Knossos. There will be other palaces."

Only one response could stem this swelling of angry hubris. Though he had no memory of ever striking his son before this moment, Daedalus laid his open palm across his son's cheek. The crack of flesh on flesh made no more noise than the boy's words, but it put an end to the tide.

"You come from such a village," Daedalus whispered.

Ikarus's widened, wet eyes reflected starlight.

"We will die here, if you like," Daedalus said.

Silence surrounded them for a long moment before Ikarus said, "The shepherd girl broke you. She put fear in your stone heart."

"Yes," Daedalus whispered. "She made me realize I needed to think of more than myself and my work."

"Our work," Ikarus said.

"If it were only my life, I might risk staying and becoming the prey of a king's ambitions, but I hope to save us both. I hope to save our lives and the knowledge we have gained."

"My life is mine to risk," Ikarus said. "Go, Father. Save yourself from your shadows. Be alone."

"We ran from Aegypt because Pharaoh believed himself a god and us mere mortals to be used in the making of engines of war against his enemies."

"There was wealth in that," Ikarus said. "Here, the wealth comes from peace instead of war. Each stone we place is like picking up a diamond from the tunnels you built in Solamemnon's mountains of fire. This palace will make us legends, Father. Because of this, your work will be known across the seas and across time."

"Wealth and fame become stone dust driven in the wind. They cannot be eaten nor held."

"Fear, then. We ran from the mines because you were afraid there, too."

Sadly, Daedalus shook his head. He tried to explain. "War was coming. Greed begets war. Always."

"These people are not at war."

"This king and this queen have jealous enemies."

Ikarus whispered, "This king and his mad priestess queen rule over all this island and many others. The ships you designed make them safe, so they build palaces for their comfort and temples to themselves."

"Please, my son," he pleaded. "See tomorrow, when the palaces and temples are finished. What then?"

Ikarus chuckled. "They will find new reasons to build new palaces and new temples."

"Ambition cannot know peace. They will seek out enemies."

"What enemies can a king and queen who live on an island have?"

Daedalus wrapped his son's hands in his own. "I love you, Ikarus. Think. Use the mind I have helped you train. What enemies will they have?"

"None." Ikarus jerked his hands free and stood. "None."

"The woman today—the king coveted her. He believes all the women of his kingdom are cows in his herd. The king is opposed by the queen, who believes that all women hold in them the magic of creation."

Ikarus stood silent for twenty heartbeats. He gazed inland, a defiant statue of youth occluding the night stars. Finally, his squared shoulders slipped. His outward gaze turned to his father. "Let them fight one another," Ikarus said. "The villages live as the villages have always lived. I'm not like you, Father. I don't pretend to know the minds of kings and queens. I only know I am fallen. My heart melts from the heat of love."

Daedalus took his son by the shoulders. "Who will they turn to when they begin to fight one another? Whom did the Aegyptians turn to? And when their wars fail, who will they blame? What will happen to your lover? What would happen to mine should I take one here?"

Ikarus turned seaward and began walking toward the docks again. "I will come back here, Father. Once I have seen you safely to the mainland, I will come back for her."

"Of course you will, Ikarus." For expedience, he conceded the point. "I have no doubt. Perhaps, if gods and time allow, I will come with you." He turned to follow his son. Under the starlight, just beyond a line of scrub, his gaze met the gaze of the guard, Yorgos. The man stood as still as stone in shadows. His eyes shone. The tip of his javelin pointed skyward. His huge hands rested, clasped on the javelin. For a long, terrible moment, Daedalus could not breathe. He could not think.

Then, Yorgos dipped his head ever so slightly in a nod and turned away.

Daedalus hurried after his son. He had no time to thank a man he barely knew, and he had no time to wonder at the reasons hidden in the heart of one of the guards of the king of Knossos.

~~~

Just before sunrise, Crete's mountainous countryside sent its night chill downward along gullies, streambeds, and river valleys. Whatever gods governed in the heights
~~~

seemed to push their influence downward toward the sea, battling the coming heat of the day, trying to drive it away from the earth and into the realm of Poseidon.

Daedalus prayed for the moment when their broad-hulled merchant ship bound for Athens would raise both triangular sails in the estuary. The captain of the ship would use that down-slope breeze, the river's flow, and the falling tide to carry them through the sea harbor of Knossos and into open seas.

Lines were cast off. Sails rose and snapped to. Wood creaked and moaned. The ship surged forward on breeze and current and tide.

For the first time since he and Ikarus had come to Knossos, he believed they might be safe.

Daedalus stood amidships on a plank walk along the hull. Ikarus lounged with the merchants in the belly of the boat with amphorae of olive oil beneath him. The captain and tiller man stood above all on a platform at the stern.

They sailed far enough into the bay that the fresh wind lifted the scent of shore, harbor village, and salt to his nostrils.

Ikarus, a traveler since he could walk, had adapted to the boat quickly.

A mere hour into the voyage, and the boy had found his place in the stern. There, he toasted sunrise with several traveling merchants, regaling them with tales of the wonders of the lands of Babylon, the joyous pleasures of Gomorrah, the dark and strange peoples of Afrikae, and the mystical Pharaoh of Aegypt.

Daedalus smiled.

The air stilled.

A gentle wave slapped at the bow.

Daedalus glanced eastward in the direction of the distant island mountain of Thera. Streaks of orange light from the rising of the great chariot of fire burned the sky there. Soon, Helios would gallop full into the heights and drive all darkness away.

Thunder rolled across the bay.

It caught him in his moment of silence and vibrated deep in his chest. He scanned the horizon, but he found only the promise of a glorious day for sea travel.

A second peel of thunder sounded.

This time, Daedalus looked to the stern and the tiller man. There, the captain of their ship looked out over the waters toward the mouth of the bay.

Daedalus followed the gaze of their captain out toward a point of land that marked the boundary between the realm of the king of Knossos and the realms where fools and brave seamen dared challenge the will of Poseidon.

Dim morning light revealed a long, low ship appearing from shadow as if issued from the womb of the earth. The warship's shadow separated from the shadows of rock to become a new, swift thing upon the bay. The thunder rolled across the bay again. And again.

A war drum.

A warship designed by Daedalus himself.

His first thought was that Yorgos had, after all, betrayed them, but the man could have easily stopped them on the causeway.

No, The Fates played some other game now.

The long, sleek ship moved quickly under oar and without sail. It cut swell and wave, and the long ramming beam at its bow dipped in and out of the sea.

"Lower sails!" the captain commanded.

"No!" Daedalus dashed aft, dodging sailors who untied, released, or hauled on lines. "No! Sail on!"

The captain called orders to turn into the wind.

"Tack west! They will tire! I built their ship for speed in harbor defense! We can make the open sea and stronger winds before they catch us!" He stopped beneath the captain's platform. "Captain," he called. "I beg you."

The captain, a man who had been carved by the work of lines, sails, and storms, looked down on Daedalus.

"Please," Daedalus said. "I can pay!"

"Can you buy my ship and crew, Mason?"

"Yes," Daedalus said.

Ikarus and the merchants looked up from their drink and tales.

"Father?" Ikarus asked.

"Why are we stopping?" asked one of the merchants.

"I'll pay double wages and buy your entire cargo," Daedalus said.

"You want to be gone from Knossos badly," the Captain said. "Perhaps King Minos gives a reward for you?"

Several sailors had worked their way along the walkways attached to the hull. They gathered on both sides of Daedalus. One grasped his upper arm.

Daedalus had the strength to lift one of them from his feet and toss him into the sea, but that would change nothing. He pleaded with the captain. "Take this boat to sea. I will pay you a fortune to deliver us to Athens. You will buy a fleet with what I pay you."

"And anger Minos?" The captain shook his head.

Desperate, Daedalus said, "You will be wealthy in Athens. Your new ships will be free upon the sea."

Ikarus stood below, looking from his father to the captain and back. He seemed to grasp that the winds of fate were turning against him. "Father has the wealth," Ikarus said.

To Ikarus, the captain spoke in sad, kind tones. "You are a good son. I, too, have a son."

The man's words drowned Daedalus's tiny spark of hope. "Here?" Daedalus said. "On Crete?"

The captain nodded. "A new wife? A new son? Your money will let me buy them, too?"

Daedalus understood the man's plight. To run would be ruin. To save Ikarus and himself, he asked this man to ruin his family, his business, and the families of all the men aboard.

He nodded. "I bear you no ill will," he said. "The war ship comes for me, but Minos gives no reward."

The captain nodded. "I'm sorry, Mason. I have only heard good things of you."

"Please, my friend. If you have heard people speak well of me, then trust those words and take my son to Athens. I will return to Knossos, but this boy has no reason to stay, and the king has no reason to keep him."

"Father!" Ikarus scrambled to his feet.

"We'll let the soldiers decide who stays and goes," the captain said.

The war drums rattled the amphorae of wine and oil in the belly of the ship. Merchants covered their ears. Ikarus climbed the hull and clambered up onto the walk-plank with Daedalus. Together, they watched the long, sleek ship pull alongside, throw up a line, set a plank, and disgorge armed soldiers.

Together, father and son walked down the plank and made their way into the low, dank interior of the warship.

~~~

After returning them to Knossos, soldiers separated Ikarus and Daedalus. Daedalus spent half a day and a sleepless night locked in a chamber with no windows. He found small hope in the fact that he had not ended up in one of the cages or pits in which the king placed those who had offended him.

At daybreak, Yorgos and a smaller guard came for him and silently marched him out of the palace and to a high meadow surrounded by sheer, limestone cliffs on three sides. There, they joined the king and several other soldiers. All stood beside a chest-high, fieldstone fence that separated them from the meadow and sealed off the grassy expanse between the surrounding cliffs.

Daedalus listened to the droning, bluster of the bull-king. Soldiers, one on each side of Daedalus, stood in stoic silence—stone-faced men with active eyes filled with fear and distrust. Other soldiers, men who appeared to Daedalus to be equally afraid of one another, spread themselves out along the fence and the path that had brought Daedalus to the king.

Kings had long used gold, women, and favor to make men loathe their fellows and fear their tongues. He had seen it in other kingdoms, other lands. His murder in front of these men might yet be a tool the king could use to create fear and control.

The memory of the king's treatment of Gask came to him. Perhaps that death had created enough rumors to control the soldiers for now.

Daedalus thanked Poseidon that he still lived, and he prayed that he might yet use the gifts the gods had given him to fashion an escape—if not for himself, then for his son.

In the hope of saving Ikarus, he inhaled deeply, focused his thoughts, and listened to the words of the king.

"This, my roaming mason, is the reason I know my palace shall be the greatest of all palaces, the center of all the world. Men will look to me from across the seas, and they will feel awe. They will shake before the splendor of what I do here."

The king lifted a long, blue silk. It undulated, serpentine in the light breeze.

On the other side of the green expanse of succulent grasses, a pair of young men pulled a polished, bronze grate away from the mouth of a cave.

A magnificent white bull charged out of the dark maw of the earth.

The men scrambled up rock faces to safe perches.
~~~

The bull entered the sunlight. Its red eyes flashed like embers in a forge. The skin of the creature reflected the fires of Helios like polished marble; the breadth of the bull's noble face rivaled Daedalus's shoulders. Its lustrous, pale horns stretched outward then forward like man's arms spread to embrace a friend. Their forward sweep over the creature's noble face ended in white points so fine that Daedalus had to squint to focus on the tips.

"Poseidon sent this gift to me," the King said.

Daedalus nodded. He had not met a king or queen yet who could not tell him which gods had chosen them to rule. A man needed but listen a bit, and kings and queens would tell amazing tales not only of which gods had chosen them, but also of the why—the thoughts and moods of the gods and how such powers had come to be attracted to that king or queen.

The king said, "Tell me what you think of this gift of the gods, Mason."

Daedalus bowed and told the truth. "I have never in all my travels seen any bull as beautiful and magnificent as this one."

The king's eyes shifted and darkened.

Daedalus knew the king had recognized the court-craft Daedalus used to cover his doubt of divine favor. "Such a creature makes," Daedalus added, "a fitting gift for the king of this fabulous island." He hoped flattery would overcome the king's annoyance. It often did.

"It was sent to me from the surf," the King said, "and I came upon it while walking on the shores of my island."

"Ah," Daedalus said. "From the realm of Poseidon."

"And I have had a vision."

Daedalus held his breath. In his experience, visions seldom showed rulers how to bring water to fields, how to bring light into a mine, how to move grain across the land quickly, or how to cool a home in summer and heat it in the winter by changing the way air flowed through the stones of the house.

A ruler's visions seldom meant good things for the likes of Daedalus. Men and women who ruled rarely helped those they ruled. Righteous visions often justified ambitious actions. Kings had visions of slaughtering neighbors, stealing land, and bedding women who belonged to other men. Queens had visions of conquest over neighboring kings or their sons, of marriage for favored daughters, or of raising sons to kill their fathers.

"Is it not folly that I sacrifice this magnificent creature," the King said, "to keep the favor of Poseidon?"

Surprise hit Daedalus like a bronze hammer slammed into his chest. He exhaled. "What?" The word slipped out before Daedalus could check his surprise. He had expected so much worse.

"The priests order me to build a pyre, lead the bull onto the pyre; then, with my own sword, to let the creature's blood flow from its neck, and I, myself, to show my humility, must light the pyre. After accomplishing all, on my knees like a slave or servant, I must bring sea water to wash the ash into the river so the bull may journey once more to the herds of the Lord of Waves."

"A vision showed you this?" Daedalus let his surprise and relief show. The king seemed genuine in his belief that he should give up the bull as a gift to Poseidon.

"Just as a vision showed me where to walk the day I found the bull."

"Then the gods have given you a gift as a test." It seemed a safe thing to say. There could be no harm in killing the bull and burning the carcass—at least no harm to Daedalus or Ikarus. A simple sacrifice could bring no harm to the people of the land or of lands across the sea. If the king had called him to help in this ritual, perhaps Daedalus could garner the king's goodwill and leave as soon as the king believed Poseidon appeased.

"Yes," the King said. "A test."

"You wish my help, good king?"

"I have watched you since you came to us," the King said. "You, more than any man I have ever known or heard tell of, have cleverness in your hands."

"If so, then gods who have not made their names known to me bestowed what small gift I have."

"I say it is so. I say it is no small gift." Dangerous jealousy carried in the King's voice. "Since the gods test me and my love of them, I shall extend their blessing and test your craft and your love for your son."

The threat was not lost on Daedalus. The king had not yet revealed his true desires.

Daedalus willed solicitous words from his lips. "I will gladly be tested beside you, good king."

The king smiled, and in the smile Daedalus saw more of the wolf than of a great bull. "Build a replacement for this bull. Make a simulacrum, a thing that will fool the gods. I will bleed it and burn it as the vision bade, but I will not butcher and burn this creature. I will keep him in a cavern away from the sight of gods and men just as Zeus was hidden in a cave, not far from this place, and protected when he cried by the cacophonous din of the Kouretes pounding on their shields. I will lead my cows to this bull and mate them. I, Minos, King of this island and all the seas surrounding, the first priest of the strength of the bull, shall have a herd of cattle born of the blood of this creature of the gods."

Daedalus could not speak.

The king turned away and carried his ambition to rival the gods away across the fields toward his palace. Guards gathered into a column behind him. Daedalus watched the young men leap from their safe perches on the rocks by the cave. They ran into the meadow to herd the bull back into its cave.

The bull was worthy of the god from whom it had been sent. It killed two men before it retreated once more into the darkness.

Two guards remained with Daedalus. One, the smaller and meaner-faced of the two, chuckled and derided the hapless herdsmen. When that distraction ended, he turned on Daedalus. "You are undone, Mason."

The other, the giant Yorgos, said, "I wager on the mason's behalf. Two bronze spear heads that he can fool the king."

"What of the gods?" Daedalus asked.

"I'm a soldier," Yorgos said. "What do I know of Gods? I think if I were you, I would work to convince the king the gods have been fooled. That might save your hide."

Daedalus nodded his agreement with Yorgos. No man could hope to win in games against the gods. Ambitious kings, however, were another matter.

"Done," the first guard said. To Daedalus, he spoke with contempt, "So, *clever-handed one*, how will you fool a king and build a bull that bleeds and burns like a real bull?"

"I will not say." Daedalus did not know, but he would behave like he did as long as he stood before men who might speak to the king. He decided to test his position, to see what freedom this order of the king had bestowed upon him. He turned and followed the departing king. His guards flanked him, following him toward his home in the temporary village of tents for the men and women who worked on the palace of Knossos. While they walked, Daedalus pondered the question of how, indeed, he would fool the king. Fooling the gods was certainly not his problem. That was the king's sin. The gods would find a way to punish the king for his arrogance. But to fool the king, Daedalus would need to think hard and long.

He would do it, or he would die. He would do it, or Ikarus would die.

He would build the bull. All he needed was a vision of his own, a vision that showed him the how of it.

~~~

Daedalus's guards woke him in the darkest hour of the night. They pulled him from his tent. To their credit, they were quiet and discreet.

Daedalus didn't believe he was being taken to his death. The king needed his skills to deceive the gods. Still, he might be tortured in order to ensure that he would have a better disposition.

By pale starlight during the march to the palace, Daedalus saw his escorts smile. While he had no love for them nor them for him, he thought it odd that *both* would take pleasure in his torment. The thinner man, a cruel guard who sought favor by applying himself passionately to violence in a soldier's guise, certainly; but Yorgos, the great, quiet bull of a man, was not so base. After the incident on the causeway, Daedalus fancied Yorgos might even be a friend under certain circumstances—inasmuch as a man who could be ordered to cut your throat could be counted a friend.

Still, both soldiers, believing darkness covered their faces, smiled.

By the time they reached the palace and snaked their way through the labyrinthine corridors to the queen's quarters, Daedalus knew he would not be tortured. Their destination convinced him that the ambitions of others worked in the night. Such manipulations and games of court would never end, he thought, until the ambitions of men to rule men had died.

They ushered him into the queen's inner chambers. The hallway reeked of sweet incense. A layer of silks covered the arch between hall and chambers, a glistening, shimmering wall of dancing shadows and firelight cast from within the sanctuary of the queen—Priestess of Serpents, the king's first wife, equal to him in power and in the command of the fear of the people of Crete.

The silks parted.

A young man staggered out. He gasped and coughed. He fought to breathe.
~~~

Barely more than a boy, he was pale and gaunt. Sweat plastered dripping golden ringlets of hair against his skull. For a moment, Daedalus thought the boy's full lips oddly colored—perhaps painted purple.

Those lips shuddered like the boy had spent a full night in the far northlands wandering in winter snows. The boy turned and leaned against the wall, hiding his face from Daedalus and the guards.

Long, red welts streaked the boy's naked skin.

Realizing the color of the boy's lips came from shock and pain, Daedalus suppressed a shudder, but he couldn't suppress the question of what the queen might want of him. If torturing this mere child was the queen's pleasure, Daedalus was glad for his thick bones, broad shoulders, and dark skin and hair. He was as far from the queen's appetites as a man could be, but he also knew that decadent, royal appetites often demanded variety.

The boy staggered off, and no one showed any interest in helping him.

"Will he be well?" Daedalus asked Yorgos.

"Mason," Yorgos said. "Queen Pasiphae waits for you."

"The boy?" Daedalus asked. "He's hurt."

The guard's dark eyes narrowed, and for a moment Daedalus believed he had angered the man, but Yorgos said, "No one has ever asked after one of her boys before. You are the first."

"His skin–"

"This is no place to speak of such things. He is Athenian. He will survive. As to being well? That is another question. Have you seen the children of Athens die in the bull dance? Do you know of the Athenian who stole the daughter of the queen?"

"Yes." It was Daedalus's shame that the king took tribute from Athens in the form of children. Most of those children died in the arena at the center of the palace he had built. They died trying to play a Minoan game, a game they never trained for, a game they had never practiced. They died trying to leap the horns and back of a goaded bull. He harbored a secret joy that only a few years past an Athenian had beaten the bull and stolen the daughter of the king and queen.

"That child's pain," Yorgos said, "proves he lives. She scarred his heart, but he will grow and find a place here. The queen's attentions have saved him from death. The king would not be so kind."

From within the fabric walls, a large bell sounded, low and resonant. The thick vibration moved in Daedalus's chest.

"She waits." Yorgos thrust his javelin through the curtains and parted them. "Go, Mason. Please the queen if you value your health and son."

Daedalus entered. The guards did not follow.

Daedalus had designed the large chambers occupied by the queen and her servants, but he had not designed the arrangement of the curving corridors and chambers made from silk draperies lighted by bronze braziers of coals and low flames.

He wandered through a maze of women and male servants lounging, rutting, or sleeping. When he paused, some man or woman would point. He followed their direction.

Deeper, always turning inward toward the center, the almost narcotic stench of the incense growing stronger with each step, he traveled until he came to a circle of sheer, nearly transparent white silks. Within, a flame burned on a pedestal of stone. The flickering fire moved air and made the silken walls flutter. A woman's silhouette danced on the silk wall.

Her form would have called any man away from even the happiest life, and her lithe movements reminded Daedalus of the slow and graceful undulations of the arms of an octopus or the sinuous movements of a serpent through grass and sands.

"Come, Mason," a siren's voice whispered through the silks.

"My Queen?"

In answer, unseen hands parted the draped silks.

Firelight poured outward, and the woman stopped dancing. She turned, and Daedalus caught his breath.

He managed a step forward. The silks hissed closed behind him, and he knew they were as impenetrable as any stone gate. He was trapped in a web of beauty and danger.

"Mason." The queen panted from her exertions. The firelight made her oiled skin golden. Long, black coils of hair, the kind of hair that many women wished they had, draped over her shoulders and along the sides of her bare breasts. Her nipples, dark and hard, glistened and heaved. Her hands came up to caress her own breasts.

"Come, my mason." Gray ice eyes chilled him. "My dance ends, and my hungers are sated. You have nothing to fear from me." She turned her back to him and flowed in long, graceful strides to a pile of silken pillows. She collapsed there. Behind her, the silk wall parted. A pale hand reached through and offered an urn. The queen took it, and the hand disappeared. "Drink with me, Mason."

Unbidden, two hands offered two cups through the silks.

Daedalus had walked the halls of power in many lands, but he had never seen such a display of trust in absolute power. The silks were mere symbols, and he knew servants surrounded them, watching, peering through the sheer curtains, invisible to him from within. Each had a job, a role in satisfying the desires of the queen, and the queen feared nothing and no one in this place.

"You pale and quiver as though facing a thief who would kill you for a coin, Mason. Come, now. Sit with me. I have a task for you."

He had to move. Here, his life might hang in the balance against these small requests. He crossed to the queen's bed of cushions and settled himself cross-legged, facing her.

She, in turn, lounged, naked, alluring, still breathing heavily. She poured wine for him, and the humble gesture told him that whatever the reason for his summoning, she needed his cooperation rather than his servitude.

He took the offered cup.

"Drink to the gods who have blessed my husband with a white bull." She raised her cup in toast, then drank.

He touched the wine to his lips but did not drink.

"May I ask a question, oh queen of this wondrous island nation?"

"You may."

"What service can I possibly provide that you do not already have?"

She smiled and sipped from her cup again. Her smile was the smile of a cat. Her drinking was the lapping of a tiger. Lips wetted by wine, she said, "I would like you to build something for me."

"If within my power," he said, "I will gladly repay the hospitality of you and your people by practicing my craft."

"A thing of beauty," she said, "that will rival the white bull."

"The gods gave me my craft, but I cannot match the gods in craft."

"I will dance with the gods. You need merely build my stage."

Her words mystified him. He touched his lips to the wine once more. The touch of the wine to his lips seemed to warm him, or perhaps it was his relief that she only wanted him to build something—or perhaps some servant had slipped in unnoticed and added fuel to the fire.

The queen sat up. Even though she moved quickly, she held her cup with such grace that no drop fell to the silk cushions. She crossed her legs, and for the elimination of at least one distraction, Daedalus was grateful.

"Mason," she said. "I have seen the things you have crafted—the black head of the bull, the golden horns, the walls, pillars, and stone horns of the palace you built for us. I have seen your hands press the smallest details into gold and carve the finest lines in a marble seal."

His lips burned, and he looked into the wine in his cup.

She continued. "You are, indeed, gifted by the gods."

"Thank you, My Queen."

"Here," she said, "you may speak my name. Pasiphae."

A queen who pours wine for a mason and who gives her name to a lesser was a woman to be wary of. He told himself to put down the wine. He could feel his thoughts beginning to spin. Queen Pasiphae's flesh glowed in the firelight. Her sweet breath called to him like the scent of a cook fire calls forth ignored hunger.

To his shame, desire rose in his belly. He turned slightly, hoping to hide the insult of his lack of control.

"Build a cow for me," she said.

"A cow?" He set down his cup.

She moved closer, kneeling now before him.

"My Queen," he began, "you must not–"

She lifted her cup to his lips. She put her fingertips to his cheek.

Her touch set fire to his body. He could not stop himself from sipping from her cup.

She moved close, and her cold-mist eyes, wide and black, held his thoughts still, held his heart quiet between beats. "A golden cow," she said. "A cow that the white bull will see and desire—a thing so perfect and beautiful that no bull can resist it."

He had to squint to see her better. Her hand snaked behind his neck. She held him. She put the cup to his lips again. "Sip my wine, Mason," she said. "There are thousands of men who would die to drink from this cup."

He knew he should not, and he knew he could not defy her. He sipped again.

"Good, my mason," she said. "Can you build a cow of gold?"

"Yes," he whispered—though far in the distance where his thoughts were still his own, he was not sure he could.

"And make it hollow so a woman can fit inside?"

"Yes," he said. And already the distant mind planned, solved, saw the path to such a thing—the pits and molds that would be made, the wax, the fires and forges, the pouring and hammering. His fingers twitched, feeling their way toward answers. "Yes," he said again. "I can build such a thing."

"So that a woman within might mate with the white bull given to my husband by the gods?" She put down her cup and pressed her lips to his. His shame and desire grew. "Do this for me," she breathed into his mouth, "and I will give you such gifts as no man can imagine."

The fire in his blood rose to his lips, and only her kiss could quench it by adding fuel to his fire until it burned itself away.

His distant mind, that part that was still his, knew he had been drugged, and his drugged flesh betrayed him. He fought himself. He battled to keep from setting fire to his soul by touching this woman, this witch.

"I can," he said. "I will not."

She pressed him back onto the cushions and put her fiery hand to his loins.

Her touch focused his mind. Behind closed eyes, he found in his mind the stone he cut, the stones of the island itself, the deep, pale stone on which he had spent his energy, mind, and heart. He closed his hands around her wrists and willed fingers and palms to be the cold stone, to be solid and strong and push her away. He would not be thus humiliated by her. He would rather die.

His grip tightened.

Her eyes widened, and surprise paled her face. She jerked her hands free.

"You refuse me? You, a foreigner? You will build a bull for the king, yet you refuse me?" She spat on him, stood, and strode away.

Darkness rose around him, and Daedalus succumbed to her potions.

~~~

When he woke, two new guards came to him, lifted him between them, and half-carried and half-marched him to another suite of rooms in the queen's wing of the palace. Nearly recovered from her potions and still filled with fear for himself and his son, Daedalus stood silently, waiting for her to acknowledge him.
~~~

Three men guarded the queen. Each wore the ceremonial but effective bone-plate chest armor and helmets the queen favored. Each carried a sword of bronze, weapons of curved blade and double edge designed by Daedalus himself for fighting in close quarters—blades that allowed cutting in two directions while thrusting from behind a shield, blades that could be used to cut downward or could be used to slice deeply while being pulled back. These were weapons only the queen's guard used. The king's pride was too great to accept such changes in blade and tactics.

She busied herself near a fire set in the center of a ring of stones.

Daedalus had neither designed nor built that ring of stone, but it was well-built nonetheless. Unnatural fire licked at the air but sent no smoke into the chambers—none at all.

Queen Pasiphae naked, glorious, a distraction to any man who was a man, danced around the fire. A film of fine, shining sweat glistened on her pale skin.

One guard stared openly. The two men flanking him seemed too afraid of her to stare. They refused to look at her dance at all. One kept his eyes tightly closed. The other kept his eyes on Daedalus.

Daedalus watched all.

Pasiphae froze and placed her hands on the stone circle. Her back to the guards, her legs spread as if inviting them to her, she said, "Now."

The two flanking guards faced the man in the middle. One looped a cord around his neck and pulled it tight. The other pinioned his arms. The man choked and gagged. His hands clawed at his assailants. Eyes that had moments before coveted the queen's flesh now bulged with fear and pressure from the garrote.

In moments, he stopped flailing, the blood cut off from his head.

The guards dragged him forward.

The manner of his death had forced his already engorged manhood to unnatural size and strength. Together, the guards guided the corpse to mount the Queen. Together, the guards moved the man.

She set herself against the movements of the dead man, and she screamed, and her scream shook the walls of the palace with revulsion, shook Daedalus, and clearly chilled the blood of the two living guards.

"Enough," Pasiphae said.

The men pulled the corpse away.

Pasiphae gestured to the fire.

The guards lifted the dead man and tossed him onto the smokeless pyre.

The fire crackled as do all fires fed wet wood. Thick, greasy black smoke rose and rolled across the ceiling.

Daedalus knew he witnessed some dark craft of the queen, but he had never seen such a thing before and could not guess the purpose.

Fire consumed the guard like he was a sacrificial effigy made of dry sticks slathered in goat fat.

Queen Pasiphae began her dance again.

The guards took stations at the walls.

In moments, what had been a man was nothing—not even a charred form in the fire.

Nothing.

The guards left. The one who had watched Daedalus glanced at him again. His dark eyes showed concern, perhaps fear for Daedalus.

When they were gone, the queen slowed her frantic pace, stilled, and rested a moment. Breathing heavily, she regarded Daedalus. Finally, she addressed him. "Come, Mason. I would share secrets with you." She walked away from the fire. Sweat and animal dampness glistened on her thighs, rump, and back. Her long, dark hair curled in wet ringlets along her spine. Hers was the most terrible beauty he had ever seen. Hers was the sharp, bronze beauty of a perfect blade. It tugged at a man's hands to reach, to touch and test the edge even though to do so might wound or kill.

He followed her across the chamber and into an anteroom. There, she stepped into a stone tub, a luxury that Daedalus had designed and built. "Join me in my bath," she said.

He stood still.

"Join me, or I will have your son the way I have had the guard who spoke of my secrets to the king." She gestured to the ring of stones and the fire.

Still clothed, Daedalus stepped down into the perfumed water. Immersed to his hips, he stopped.

She lifted a sponge and handed it to him. She turned, and, just as if she were bracing herself against the fire circle again, she braced herself against the edge of the basin and presented her back.

He pressed the sponge into the water, lifted it, squeezed water from it, and began to wash her back.

"You are not a man," she said.

He smoothed the sweat from her skin.

"If you were a man, you would take me here and now."

He squeezed and let water pour down onto the back of her head. The water sluiced through her long hair and sloughed sweat and the dead man's ichor from the skin of her back. The water slicked her skin, dripped away, and mixed red and brown with the purer waters of the tub.

"Your son would not hesitate," she said. "My women have told me of his lusts."

"He is young," Daedalus said.

She turned to face him. Her breasts glistened in the yellow light cast by ensconced oil lamps. "You create a horror for my husband," she said.

He held the sponge out to the queen. She took it from him and began to wash her own chest and belly. While she washed, she watched his eyes.

While she washed, he watched hers.

"Yes," Daedalus said, "I have no control over his whims."

Her clay-gray, deep eyes showed no passion for life or for him. The only passion in those eyes came from the perversion he had just witnessed.

She dropped the sponge and moved closer.

He backed away.

She backed him up to the wall of the tub. She reached for his soiled clothing.

His powerful hands caught hers, held them, kept them from his clothing.

"Strong hands," she said. A flicker of light appeared in her eyes.

He did not wish to give her any pleasure—least of all that kind. He released her hands.

Disappointment darkened the spark of pleasure.

"That guard." She pressed Daedalus against the stone rim of the tub and lifted the sponge as if to wash his dusty clothes. "He refused me."

"Then," Daedalus said, "he died honorably."

"Oh, no," she said. "I didn't allow him to die." She pushed the cold sponge between his legs.

Daedalus shook, but he held still, clinging to a meager hope that he might still walk away from this room, from this insane woman.

"The ritual made him mine. His flesh has gone, but his spirit lives, and whenever I choose, I can pull him up from the darkness and back into this world."

"These are the lies you tell to make people fear you," he said.

"You, who have walked the halls of pharaohs and Nubians, should know better." She dropped the sponge and turned her back to him. The priestess queen of Crete climbed from the tub and crossed the room to a curtain-covered wall.

She drew back the curtain. Behind it stood a row of statues—some marble, some clay, some made of wood and inlaid with precious and semi-precious stones. None had faces. No eyes. No mouths. Mere bumps showed where noses might have been had the figures been flesh. The bodies of some figures were covered in tight leather or silk.

Daedalus shuddered at the thought that these clay men had been stitched into unnatural skins.

His soul froze when he realized that each faceless figure had been fitted with some grotesque parody of male anatomy—no two of the same size or shape.

She caressed one—a tall, muscular figure fitted with a distended onyx phallus.

On a pedestal next to the statues lay a hand bell and a tall, tightly woven basket. "My power is no lie," she said. She plunged her hands into the basket and removed two living, writhing asps. She held them high for a moment before she plunged the fangs of one into her breast and the fangs of the other into the statue, into the very stone of the thing.

Daedalus gasped.

She put the asps back in their basket. "My power," she said, "is the power of a goddess over earth and life." She lifted the bell and rang it sharply four times.

As the resonance of the fourth ring died, the statue moved.

She laughed. "Behold, Mason, what my craft can do."

The statue lurched forward. Its hands rose and searched its own face like a blind man seeking to know a stranger. The fingers traced the place where there might have been eyes, a nose, a mouth. The fingers traced the neck and chest. The hands began to shake, the shoulders to quiver. The thing seemed to be crying.

The thing's shaking, searching hands found its own manhood. It touched itself.

A moment later, it clawed frantically at its own face.

"Be still, my love," the Queen said. "Your fear will pass." She caressed the thing's phallus.

The monster seemed to shrink back. A low moan came to Daedalus—not through the air like a man's cry, but through the tub's stone floor to his feet as if the palace stones themselves carried the thing's cry of pain and fear.

"What torture is this?" Daedalus asked.

"This man who refused me, who spoke of my plans to my husband, he will be my lover for the rest of time or until I free his spirit from the stone." She put her hand on his chest, pressed her fingernails to the stone, and scraped along the chiseled muscles there. Finally, she took his engorged manhood in her hand and pulled on it. The statue stepped forward. "Lift me," she ordered.

The shaking hands of the thing grasped her under the arms and lifted her. She spread her legs over the shaft of stone. "Down, now," she said. The thing lowered her onto its stone phallus.

Queen Pasiphae sighed. She locked her legs around the monster's back. "In this way, Daedalus, I redeem those who oppose the will of my goddess—my will."

"No," he said.

"You." She gasped at the golem's thrusts. "Or your son might end thus."

"What do you want?"

"Again," she said, and the thing lifted her up and lowered her down as if she were nothing, a mere paper effigy of a woman. "Again," she gasped.

Daedalus looked for an escape, a place to run.

Perhaps she knew his thoughts. She said, "Leave me, Mason. Go into the next room and await my pleasure."

Glad to be away from her even if for only a moment, he retreated to the room where the pyre had been. Behind him, her moans and cries of pleasure grew louder. From the stones all around him, he believed he felt the vibrations emanating from the thing, the shaking terror, rage, and fear of the trapped soul within the stone slave.

While building the palace, Daedalus had crafted hidden doors and chambers. He considered the room in which he waited, but he knew that none of his clever doors had been placed in the queen's chambers. He tried the entrance to the chamber and found the door guarded. He tried the balcony and found only a deadly plummet to stone.

For a moment, he considered that path. Perhaps if he were gone, his son would be safer, but he knew better and could not bring himself to cause grief to his child.

He reminded himself that the designs of gods were like the secrets of stone. Only time revealed them. While he had life, he had hope. He resigned himself to waiting.

Hours passed, and darkness took the sky. The queen's terrible lust continued on and on into the night, perhaps driven by the goddess who brings life to the land.

Daylight broke on the balcony, and the light of Helios rising in the curve of the heavens broke Daedalus's fits of sleep.

Two guards stood over him. One gestured him to follow into the chambers.

Inside, the circle of fire was cold. He found no sign of the queen herself, nor did the stones cry or the moans of her pleasure come from the room beyond. He followed the guards in silence out of the palace and back to his quarry.

Modern Wings

During the long flight to Crete, Nikkis passed the time reading and sleeping. At one point in the long night over the Atlantic, she woke suddenly. She sweated and shook. A bad dream. A terrible dream.

She had had dreams all her life, and she never remembered anything about them except that they left her feeling happy, and she always wished she could go back to them.

This dream was different. She remembered a little bit of it, enough to want very much to never go back to it. She remembered that she'd been helpless, tied to a pole facing a man, and both of them were on fire, burning. While they burned, the man turned into a bull. Horns grew from his head. His eyes became wide and red with rage. He screamed, and she had heard that scream before.

It was all she could remember, but it was enough to keep her awake for a few hours. She watched the moonlit ice pack slide by beneath the aircraft. The endless miles of white, barren, empty ice soothed her.

A middle-aged marketing specialist from Athens was awake in the seat next to her. They chatted for a while, until she told him she was traveling to Crete.

His eyes hardened, and he said, "Crete. I never go there. *Those people* know seventeen ways to kill you with a knife." After that, he focused on his work and ignored her polite attempt to distract herself by chatting.

She shrugged off the man's rudeness as the product of a long flight and insomnia. Eventually, she managed to sleep again.

When they landed in Crete, she gathered her things, stretched the cramps and kinks from her body, turned on her cell, wondered briefly how the flight attendant could look so cheerful and put together after such a long incarceration in a plane, then shuffled along toward the door. As an afterthought, she realized she should probably accept calls from her benefactor. She unblocked Detective Andros's number.

She emerged from the plane into the brilliant light of a glorious Mediterranean day. Shielding her eyes, she paused on the platform above the stairs to the white, concrete tarmac below.

The glorious light soaked into her, warmed her, and touched something in her soul. She inhaled the sea air, fresh from its own journey from mainland Greece and the Aegean.

The flight attendant touched Nikkis's arm. "You'll have to go down."

"It's beautiful," Nikkis said.

The flight attendant looked around. "Yes," she said. "I suppose so. Would you like me to help you down, then?"

"No." Nikkis started down the stairs. On the tarmac below, people filed away from the plane toward a customs bus. Off to one side, away from the line of new arrivals, stood a huge man holding a hand-lettered placard that said, "Dr. Aristos." The man's blue-and-white uniform marked him as a policeman—that and the fact that he was meeting her on the tarmac rather than in the terminal on the far side of customs.

But his uniform seemed odd. It took Nikkis a moment to realize why. The uniform didn't fit the man. The pants fit well enough in length, but his thighs threatened to burst free from the fabric at any moment. His shirt and jacket looked like they were made for a child and worn by a man. At first, she thought he wore a bullet-proof vest under his shirt, but the buttons over his chest strained when he moved, and bronzed flesh appeared in the gaps between the buttons.

Nikkis descended the airline stairs to the concrete and started toward him.

A dark, solid woman wearing a bright orange airport security vest stepped up and barred her way. "I'm sorry, madam," the woman said in Greek. She gestured toward the bus. "The bus will take you to the customs terminal."

Momentarily confused, Nikkis said in English, "Excuse me?"

The woman repeated herself in sharp, impatient English.

Nikkis pointed. "That man. His card is for me."

The attendant glanced at the policeman. She looked doubtfully back at Nikkis. "Just a moment, ma'am." The attendant marched over to the policeman. They exchanged words. She came back a different woman. She almost glowed. "I'm sorry, Dr. Aristos. I didn't know."

Nikkis smiled. More first-class treatment. This trip was turning into a very good experience.

The woman escorted Nikkis to the policeman. "If you'll come with me, Doctor Aristos," the policeman said.

He stood taller at the shoulder than Nikkis in heels, and his darker skin seemed weathered in the healthy way of farmers or outdoor extreme athletes she had met. His smile showed crooked front teeth with dark stains between them. Oddly, his Sfakian accent relaxed her—reminded her of a pleasant dream she couldn't quite bring to mind.

He added, "I'm to make sure you find your hotel acceptable."

And he did.

The policeman, Yorgos, dropped her off, saw to her check-in, and carried her bags. Finally, he left her alone in her room, telling her only to relax and rest. Lt. Andros would contact her.

Even in movies, she had never seen such an opulent hotel room. The police had put her up in a three-room suite in one of the few remaining Venetian buildings in Iraklion—across from the government center and not far from Lion's square, historically important places Nikkis had read about and seen in pictures.

She stripped off her jacket and kicked off her shoes. Barefoot and alone, she walked across the plush, Mediterranean-blue carpet, letting the soft fibers caress her toes. Lightly, she touched the urn on her coffee table.

Minoan, she thought. No. Reproduction.

She had touched a thousand potsherds in her research, and her fingers knew the texture of each type of clay and each type of firing. Texture often told her the era of production.

The smooth grit of this urn surprised her.

Ancient, Palatial Minoan.

It couldn't be. She knelt in the soft carpeting and examined it closely.

Her close, expert examination confirmed what her eyes and hands had already told her.

Her hotel room had an actual, intact Minoan urn in it. It had to be well over three thousand years old.

She couldn't believe it. For a wonderful moment, she believed that all her many years of sacrifice and hard work were starting to pay off.

She smelled it. She touched her fingers to the clay again, then to her tongue.

It had been fired with cypress wood. The clay tasted of lime and gypsum. It was real.

A nervous giggle escaped her lips. She had to be dreaming.

She crossed to the heavy drapes at one end of the sitting room and pulled them open to let in the light. Bright sunlight hit her full on the face. She gasped, and her heart raced with joy.

It was *right.*

This sunlight was *right.* The blue of the sky was *right.* The air she inhaled tasted of ancient magic and thousands of years of lives and families.

Perfect.

It poured into her like a glowing elixir of healing. Her blood warmed. Her racing mind calmed, and she felt a certainty that she belonged here, in this place, at this moment.

Outside her window, beyond lower buildings, port warehouses, and a wide, flat concrete dock, the wide Mediterranean sparkled blue and green like a molten mixing of jades and sapphires. The harbor of Iraklion, with its many masts, giant ferries, and tan stone fortress walls amazed her. Near the water's edge, a steam locomotive rusted slowly away into dust, a monument to the folly of foreign governments who had many times attempted to occupy and control the stony, mountainous island where Western Culture had been born.

Nikkis spun in the sunlight, closed her eyes, and imagined living here in this place, filled with the joy the light carried, walking in the mountains, singing an old song of love, and–

"A goddess," a smooth, low man's voice said.

Nikkis froze and opened her eyes. She hadn't heard anyone enter, but she instantly recognized the man standing in her sitting room. Detective Andros, the man whose emails she had dismissed as come-ons.

Here was her benefactor, a real human being. His sharp features, dress shirt, and dark hair weren't some affectation of an online dating service.

"You didn't knock," she accused.

The man bowed. When he straightened, his dark eyes narrowed and a thin smile turned the corners of his mouth upward. "Dr. Aristos, I find myself once more apologizing to you. I hope I do not have a new habit in my life."

She arched an eyebrow.

"I am Detective Andros. The maids know me and know I reserved the room for you. They let me in."

She walked up to him. In her bare feet, she was several inches shorter. While smaller than the other policeman, Detective Andros was still clearly a powerful man. Standing close to him, she could see that the reason his linen suit wasn't buttoned had nothing to do with his vanity. His shoulders were so broad and muscled that buttoning the neck would tear the shirt. "Next time, knock." She held his gaze, fully expecting to use her beauty and icy stare to back him down.

He held her gaze, his crooked little smile almost a smirk.

"I will," he said.

She stepped back.

He continued, "But I must say I am glad that at least this time I did not. Your beauty in that first moment I saw you I shall remember until the day I die."

Her low opinion of the detective had been rising. He had read her work and understood it. He had rescued her from her parents and Anderson. He had paid for first class airfare halfway around the globe, and he had put her up in this amazing room. Suddenly, all his plus-side efforts meant nothing. Her opinion of him had plunged all the way back to where it had been when she thought him a cyberstalker. The way he came into her room and the way he now looked at her made the hair on the back of her neck stand up.

She shook off the feeling. It wouldn't help her. She had no place to go except home, and she wasn't ready to face that yet. She had come to Crete, and she decided to see it through. She said, "I'm tired, Detective. Do you want to discuss your case?"

He stiffened, and his little smile disappeared. "Of course you are," he said.

"Since you are here–" She picked up the urn she had admired earlier. "Are you aware that this hotel has Minoan artifacts as decorations?"

The smile returned. "No," he said. "They don't."

"I beg your pardon?" She let her indignation show. "I do know something about this."

"No. Not the hotel. Only this room. These pieces are here for *your* pleasure."

She almost dropped the urn. Instead, she carefully placed it back on the coffee table. "For me?"

"My background checks tell me you have not been to our country before, but your parents come from Crete. I thought you might want to spend some time examining some of the pieces we have at the museum. I had these pieces brought here for you. The pieces in this room do not go on display."

She looked around the room. Museum-framed frescos hung on the walls. A clay oil lamp decorated her nightstand. On a small shelf over the sofa, a palatial-period matron serpent goddess stood bare-breasted and brandishing a serpent in each hand. She was the most perfect example of that goddess form Nikkis had ever seen.

Minoan. All of it. Ancient and priceless. She felt honored. She felt angered. It was too much. It confused her.

"I'm glad to see that you truly appreciate these pieces."

She crossed her arms and shook her head. "It's not right."

"But you *are* pleased." His dark eyes narrowed to cat-like slits.

"Irresponsible," she said.

His eyes softened, and he held out his hands as if offering her the gift of the room. "But appropriate," he said, "to your desires and our needs."

"What are your needs?" She fixed her eyes on the goddess.

He let his hands fall to his sides and said, "Authentication and translation."

Uncomfortable with the disappointment in her benefactor's posture and eyes, she moved over to the goddess figure. She almost picked up the figure. Habit and respect stopped her hand. He wasn't telling her everything. Too much money had been spent to bring her here. The artifacts should never have been allowed out of the museum. Something was missing, and she wasn't seeing it. "I'm tired." She faced him. "I'm sorry. Would you mind if I rest before we discuss this further?"

He bowed again. "When you are ready, call the front desk and ask for me."

She nodded.

"A' Diosas." He bowed slightly, turned, and left.

Nikkis bolted the door behind him. Enough surprises. More than enough. Even if the last seventeen hours had been filled with good ones, she wanted no more. She only wanted to sleep.

She found the bedroom, checked to reassure herself that the bed frame was made of modern steel and that the sheets and linens were machine woven percale rather than recovered from some as yet unpublished dig.

Satisfied that her imminent collapse wouldn't destroy antiquities, she let herself fall onto the mattress. As she closed her eyes, she realized the artifacts had been a test. They had to be a test. The detective was smarter than she had given him credit for. She would have to be more alert, more careful.

Still, she smiled. She had passed his little test. She was in Crete. She had just held a short conversation over an ancient urn and in the presence of a goddess. Whatever he had not yet told her would come out after she rested.

She slept, and she walked into a dream.

~~~

Walking with her herd across verdant spring slopes after the final seasonal melt of the scant, high country snows and the recent passing of a soft spring rain, Nikkis believed herself blessed by the oldest of the goddesses, the nameless one who had given her the speed and wisdom to guide her giant bull, Titan, in the high country, to lead or whistle the bull in and out and around the gullies and slopes from one grazing vale to another.

Where Titan went, the cows and goats followed; where Titan went, no slinking, hunting cat or swooping kite dared go.

She grasped her lower lip and pinched, making a tiny hole between teeth and lip. She inhaled sharply through the hole, whistling two short, shrill blasts. Two shorts, and the bull lifted his broad black head. His curved horns, black as obsidian, flashed in the sunlight. The pointed tips, terror and mortality to any creature who dared challenge him, sparkled with lives and minds of their own.

One more shrill tweet, and the bull turned left and headed down slope.

She and Titan knew each other. He had been born when she was thirteen, and after seven years together, their friendship had grown beyond trust to an almost spiritual unity. Sometimes, she thought she could simply wish for him to turn and he would. Sometimes, she thought that if he sensed danger, she suddenly sensed it as well.

Titan headed at an angle downward and across the slope to a descending trail along a cliff edge. The narrow trail led downward into a valley. It met the valley floor at the mouth of a box canyon. They would spend the rest of the day in that canyon. She would rest, sharpen her blades, play on her wooden flute. Titan and his cows and goats would graze and sleep.
~~~

Nikkis set her staff to stone and rubble and picked her way along the high track, taking pleasure in warm sun on her skin and the smell of new-growth sage, of the wafting scent of warming stone, and of the musk of her bull and her goats.

Her life was a perfect life while she walked with her herd.

The only flaw in her world, she thought, was that she would wake.

~~~

Andros believed that a few men had destinies. He also believed that a man of destiny had a duty to his ancestors to fulfill that destiny.

His parents had met in the lobby of this hotel, the Imperial Hotel. Both were outcasts hired by the Greek hotel owners to manage troublesome travelers with whom no self-respecting Kritiki would speak.

Gustav, his father, was the bastard child of a German soldier from early in the war, an advisor to the Italians before the Sfakians had chased them back to Italy and the SS paratroopers had come and died. His mother's family shunned her because Turkish blood showed on her face. After three generations, her skin, hair, high cheeks, and sharp nose marked her as a throwback to failed virtue in the time of Turkish occupation.

The same handsome features marked him.

Walking away from the American woman's room, Andros wondered if he had just met a part of his destiny. Her beauty had haunted him even before he'd met her. Her face on the cover of the magazine had drawn his eye back to it over and over. Now, having met her, he could see that, even exhausted, her mind was sharp.

He shook off his thoughts of Nikkis Aristos. He could not afford to let himself believe in that particular brand of desire. The face on the cover of the magazine was not what he needed. The article inside had given him new hope that he could restore his family name more quickly than he had planned.

Fine Persian carpets in Greek designs covered the floors. The staff thought nothing of walking on such craftsmanship. Ornate, gold leaf recently restored to its original Venetian splendor ornamented the wainscoting. Cherubs flew above him, painted into wet plaster nearly two hundred years ago. Mahogany, cedar, and oak made up the wooden panels of the walls. Intricate parquet patterns covered the floor where Persian carpet craftsmanship gave way to Greek artistry in hardwoods brought from Israel, Mexico's Yucatán, and England.
~~~

That was the history of Crete—an endless string of occupations. Few of the Kritikos' bloodlines remained untouched. Who were these mongrel peasants to look down on him?

His mother and father had cared for tourists from Italy, Germany, and Turkey.

Now, the tourists were of a broader mix. None of the tourists from Iceland, Norway, Germany, America, or Holland looked at Detective Andros as a Turk or a German. They saw him as Greek. In Athens, even Greeks saw him as Greek. When he spoke to Athenians, they marked him Kritiki by his accent. That held some respect on the mainland where people still suffered under the influence of folktales about the ferocity of the men of Crete.

But on Crete?

No.

The people of Crete held onto their family memories and grudges. They looked at him, and he knew they only saw oppression, invasion, rape, fire, and murder. In his face, they saw a Turk—a man whose ancestors burned their ancestors alive in the purges. They saw German stature and remembered the firing squads that killed ten Greeks for each German hurt by the resistance.

They knew he was born on Crete, but that made no difference. Shadows in their eyes betrayed their thoughts.

"She's dangerous," Yorgos said.

Engrossed in his own thoughts, Andros had missed the big man's approach. Yorgos matched strides with Andros.

"She's my problem," Andros said, continuing toward the lobby doors.

"*Our* problem. Smart. Educated. She'll figure it out."

"We need her."

"Why?"

The other man Andros pretended to trust stepped out of the shadows near the bellman's stand. Wiry, thin, quick-eyed, and more of a weasel than a man, Muscus nodded and moved to hold the doors. "I'd like to hear this," he said.

Andros stopped at the doors. He glanced around the lobby. Perhaps his mother and father had met right here, standing in the light through these doors. "She is the only person on earth who can validate the new artifacts. Everyone else believes them fakes."

"So?" Yorgos said. "Fake or real, sell them. She's a problem. Send her home."

Andros ignored Yorgos. "So, because I order it, you will watch her and keep her safe."

"Because she's pretty," Muscus said.

Andros turned a withering stare on the little man. "Because," he said, "she makes the difference between a few Euros per piece and millions each."

Muscus laughed. "I see it in your eyes." He pulled the door open and held it. "You want this American."

"I do not share *your* appetites," Andros said.

Yorgos said, "Dangerous."

"Your job," Andros locked eyes with Yorgos, "is to make sure…" He turned on Muscus and poked him hard in the sternum. "…this little pervert leaves her alone."

The little man hissed and released the door he had been holding.

Yorgos stepped in, caught the closing door, and towered over Muscus.

"Me?" Muscus held up his hands and stepped back. "I haven't even looked sideways at her," Muscus said.

"And you won't," Yorgos said.

The little man stiffened and brought himself up to his full height in front of Yorgos. "You think you could stop me, stone skull?"

Andros pulled open the door, slipped past them, and stepped out into the sun. Behind him, the door closed off the sound of the bickering he'd set in motion. They would come after him soon enough, but they wouldn't bring up Nikkis Aristos again—at least not for a while.

Muscus would work to find a way to be alone with her.

Yorgos would protect her with his life. He had honor—a twisted, dark Sfakian's honor, but honor that included protecting women from the likes of Muscus.

Yorgos's question had never been answered. Andros found it easier to set his men to bickering than to try to explain why he had brought Nikkis Aristos to Crete. He looked up at the crisp blue sheet of sky. They could not understand the value of her work because, if she was right, the value she brought to his destiny went beyond mere money.

He needed her work, but he didn't really need her once the work was done.

At least, that's what he told himself.

He hated to admit that Muscus was right. Andros did want her, this American Greek woman. Any man would.

He also had to admit that his ancestors would haunt his dreams until his plans were accomplished, until he replaced the prejudice in the eyes of these islanders with respect or fear. To do that, he needed land, wealth, and power. Nikkis Aristos might give him those.

~~~

Her trilling ringtone sounded to Nikkis like a tiny frog in a dream meadow, but it roused her. The dream memory of her meadow dissipated like mists burning away under hot sun, leaving her with the sense that something important had happened, something beautiful she wished she could remember.

Between sitting up in bed and snatching her phone from the nightstand, she promised herself for the hundredth time that she'd start one of those dream journals.

"Ne?" *Yes*, she answered. Her black and copper hair fell over her eyes, and she brushed it back.

"Dr. Aristos." Andros's voice carried his smile, and it annoyed her when she caught herself sitting a little straighter in the bed. Her mind was slow, confused by the dream she wished she could remember.

"Dr. Aristos?" he said again.

"I'm here, Detective," she managed. She focused on the antiquities in her room to help her dismiss the vague images of imagination. She settled her thoughts into the more concrete memories of the last fight with her parents, the improprieties of Anderson, the joy and disappointment of her article, and her whirlwind trip to Crete.

Across the room, mounted on the wall, a black marble bull's head with an alabaster inlay band around his nose and double-curved, golden horns swept forward over his face stared at her through red, dilated eyes.

Rage, she thought. The bull is enraged.

"I'm sending a man for you, Doctor, if it is convenient."

"What time is it?"

"Three o'clock in the afternoon, Iraklion time," his smooth voice answered. "I hope you rested well and can begin work."

There it was. The work. The reason she came here. Her article. The glyphs and verification. "Of course," she said.

"When my man arrives, he will ring you. I look forward to seeing you again. Good day, then."
~~~

"Yes," she said. "Good day."

She hung up, but she couldn't take her eyes off the bull's broad forehead and the anger and confusion in his eyes. She told herself she was projecting, that there was no way a three- or four-thousand-year-old bust of a bull's head could carry any sense of emotion across the ages. The anger and confusion came from her and her alone, and she would not let them rule her life.

If opportunity could be had in this trip to Crete, she meant to find it and make it work for her. If Detective Andros's plans didn't offer opportunity, she would create an opportunity for her career in some other way. In the end, her parents and Anderson would become irrelevant. In the end, she would be what she chose to be and not what someone else manipulated her into becoming.

~~~

A young waiter settled a napkin next to Nikkis's plate. He wore blue jeans and a button-down cotton shirt. His pen rested in his shirt pocket. He would have fit in perfectly in the engineering school back at the university—careful grooming, short dark hair, solid frame and muscles.

"Thathelateleehograsee." The waiter asked in rapid Greek if she'd like a little wine. Nikkis stared at the young man. He was maybe 25, her age more-or-less, but in other ways not her age—both older and younger. His wife and daughter played in a corner of the taverna. Ever practical in the way of most Kritikos, the daughter's mother had used a length of picket fence to create a play area so the toddler could be a part of the family while they all worked hard to keep the tourists happy in this little corner of the summer trade.

Detective Andros had said they would be working, but Yorgos had driven them here. She was glad to be eating, but she didn't like having a late afternoon meal with Detective Andros. She didn't trust the way he looked at her. She had seen that look too many times—most recently, from Dr. Karin Anderson.

"Perhaps a small glass," she said to Andros, who had settled himself across from her after she refused his offer to seat her.

"Red, Christophé," he said in Greek.

She noted that he didn't bother to ask her what kind of wine she might like.

Andros added, "Tell Papá we're here."
~~~

Andros's sharp voice for the waiter was very different than the voice he used speaking to her. "Thank you" and "please" disappeared from his Greek-to-Greek exchanges.

The young man stiffened, shot a dark look at Andros, nodded, and answered like a soldier. "Yes, Sir." Frost crystallized the air in the wake of his words.

She'd have been a fool not to see that these people had history with Andros.

American TV dramas ran through her mind. He was a policeman, after all. A lot of people probably had history with him.

Christophé went away to get the wine and inform his father, who, apparently, everybody called Papá.

"Is this place also filled with artifacts for my benefit?" she asked. She hadn't meant for it to sound so pointed, but dinner with Andros was making her increasingly uncomfortable. She wanted focus, work, something constructive through which to channel her frustration and uncertainty.

Andros put his elbows on the table, laced his fingers together, and leaned his chin against his fingers. "I have a duty as a man of my country to bring beautiful, visiting women to an authentic taverna for dinner, Dr. Aristos."

"For cultural context?" She allowed herself a smile.

"If you wish," he said.

"Beneath poorly painted grape vines and plastic leaves?" She gestured toward the arbor painted on the ceiling.

Papá, an older man, arrived. Thin and hard-looking, his gaunt face wore five days of white whiskers, and he wore a kitchen-stained Asterix cartoon character t-shirt. He took up Christophé's station by their table. Like a Parisian sommelier, he had a clean, white towel draped over one arm. His other hand cradled the base of a dusty bottle of wine. The body and neck of the bottle lay back along his forearm, supported gently like the head of a newborn child. Nikkis smiled to see such a rustic creature handling the wine like a grand sommelier.

Andros inspected the label and nodded.

In silence and with ritual precision, Papá corked the bottle, offered the cork for inspection, received permission, poured a finger for Andros, waited for tasting, approval, and permission, then poured a full glass for Nikkis before pouring for Andros.

She smiled for their waiter, and his aged, hard features melted a little. Finished serving, he stepped back and stood at the ready to pour again or to take their order.

"Not many Greeks here tonight," she said. The taverna was empty except for Andros, herself, and the family of Papá and Christophé. "Back home, they say if you want a good Japanese restaurant, you go where the clientele speaks Japanese."

"Everyone here speaks Greek." Andros lifted his glass. "To the success of our partnership."

Nikkis wrapped her fingers around the stem of her wine glass, but she didn't lift. "Exactly what endeavor is it in which you wish to believe we have become partners?" she asked.

"Then to your health. Yassas." Andros sipped his wine alone.

When he had put his glass back on the table, she asked again, "Changing the toast didn't answer my questions any more than making a joke."

Out of the corner of her eye, she saw the old man's mouth twitching, straining not to smile. Instinct told her not to look, not to draw attention to the old man.

"We should order." Andros held his finger up, back of his hand toward Papá.

Papá topped off Andros's glass then told them about the dishes that his wife had prepared. Nikkis followed it all, and in spite of her annoyance with Andros, her mouth began to water.

Andros ordered for them both, again ignoring any desire she might have expressed given the chance.

When Papá had gone away to the kitchen, Andros said, "I don't like to talk shop in front of locals."

"Aren't you local?"

Andros ignored her. He swirled his wine in his glass. Light from behind him caught the liquid and gave it a wonderful, transparent rose color.

Nikkis decided to try a less confrontational tone. Perhaps humor would get her more answers. "So," she began. "You brought me halfway around the world for secret agent stuff?" She sipped at her wine. The flavor caressed her tongue then evaporated and moved up into her nose. Warmth melted down her throat. It was so smooth and flavorful that she wasn't sure it was wine.

"In a way," he said.

"Very good wine," she said.

"We have to be very careful."

She gave him her attention, now. She set her wine down and remembered what she had asked him. "I'm not yet sure there is a *we*; so, once again, I ask you why I'm here."

"Because, Nikkis, I enjoy to dine with a beautiful, intelligent woman."

With exaggerated calm, she gathered her napkin from her lap and dropped it on the table. "I've had enough of this," she said. "You *will* address me as *Doctor* Aristos. I agreed to travel halfway around the world to authenticate artifacts for you, but every time I've met you so far, you've made a pass at me. I can have stalkers back in the States. I don't need to come to Crete to find them." Nikkis leaned forward. She consciously brought the cultivated, professional ice of her heart up to harden her face and eyes. "If it isn't too difficult for you, Detective, tell me why you brought me here."

He closed his eyes for a moment. When he looked up, all the slyness and smirk was gone from his face. He looked more like a shamed little boy. He even bowed ever so slightly, though it seemed to pain him. "My deepest apology, Dr. Aristos. You are correct. It is very inappropriate of me to speak as I have to you. I do not meet many intelligent women as beautiful as you. Often, beauty makes life so easy that those who possess it need not learn more than how to smile or pout."

She said, "Your experience is very limited."

He stiffened as if slapped, but he quickly composed himself and presented a tight smile.

Nikkis instantly regretted her tone. The man was apologizing, and he had flown her halfway around the world because of her expertise.

He went on, "I admire you, Dr. Aristos, on many levels; however, I will speak plainly now and refrain from the romantic games of a foolish boy raised in Crete."

She reminded herself to allow for cultural differences. "Please." She lifted her wine, took a full swallow, and allowed it to sooth her.

"You are here to help me bring honor to my family name."

She set the wine down. "Excuse me?"

"Pure Kritiki blood does not flow in my veins. I am the most unfortunate son of Turkish and German parents." He peered at her as if what he had said should mean something important to her.

After a moment, he continued. "History, Dr. Aristos. Perhaps they do not teach the history of this part of the world in America."

"I have studied some of the history of Crete," she said. "I don't see what your parentage has to do with me."

"Perhaps you noticed the anger of Christophé and his father?"

"They were a little chilly."

"Toward me," he said. "Only toward me. With your beauty, you could be born of the oldest bloodlines of this island. You have the look of Minoan aristocracy."

"Detective," she cautioned with her tone.

"Only a fact, Dr. Aristos. You, they are glad to see. Their goodwill does not extend to me because they believe my ancestors murdered their ancestors. Which, to be candid, is true. They hate me because I carry Turkish and German blood in my veins."

"If they hate you, why eat here?"

"Because I take every chance I get to gain the respect of the people in this area. I go to the places where the prejudice is strongest in order to prove that my blood does not make me a monster, that ancestry and history do not make me evil."

Nikkis searched his face for more, for something that told her why he was telling her these things. Finding nothing useful, she said, "You are telling me your personal problems, Detective Andros, but you didn't answer my question."

"Smuggling and forgery," he said. "Your article gave me new insights into the smuggling and forgery of ancient Minoan artifacts. My job, you see. I investigate such things."

Nikkis shook her head. "Family histories and forgery. None of this has anything to do with me."

"Please," he said. "I am a detective. You can trust me, and after dinner I will show you what it has to do with you. Your skills with Linear-A can help me solve a smuggling and forgery case that will win the respect of these people and give peace to my ancestors."

Papá brought a plate of dolmades. In English, he said, "Our finest for your slut, Andros."

Simultaneously, Andros and Nikkis leapt up. Chairs fell. Wine glasses tipped.

Nikkis was faster. Her hand left its red outline on Papá's cheek. In Greek, she said, "My name is *Doctor* Nikkis Aristos. I came from America to do research on the Minoan Palatial Period."

Papá looked shocked. He stared at Nikkis. In Greek, he said, "Apologies. Apologies." He staggered back a step. "You are so pretty that I…." Her red hand print disappeared into the growing red of his whole face. "You are so much like the women he–"

Andros interrupted. His words came slow and low. "I will remember this."

The old man bit his lip, bowed, and retreated to the kitchen.

"You see, Dr. Aristos, how they treat me."

She did see. It was terrible. She'd been teased in grade school because of her darker skin. White kids called her a wetback because they thought she was Mexican. Latino kids called her a towel head because they thought she was Persian. The Persians called her an infidel. It had been terrible until she hit puberty and it had all changed. Except for one young man, people couldn't see *her* at all after that. They saw her skin, her face, her hair. They saw a walking icon of things to be desired and acquired.

Except for Daed.

Only Daed had seen past all that, had shown her the deeper love she'd dreamed of….

Daed.

She hadn't thought about him in a long time. She wouldn't let herself think about him now. No matter how bad Andros's life was, she came here to do a job, and if it helped him, good. If it didn't? Well, that didn't matter.

"I'm sorry for your uncomfortable situation," she said. "I have no expertise in social dynamics or therapy. I'm here to look at artifacts. That, I can do for you. I'm afraid that's all I can do for you."

"Ah, thank you," he said. "I'm sure it will be enough."

"I hope so," she said. "Shall we go?"

He righted the chairs and wine glasses. He picked up his napkin, shook it out, then sat down and settled the napkin on his lap. "First," he said, "we must eat."

"Here? After that?"

"Papá must recover his honor now. We will have a wonderful meal."

"How can you be so sure?"

"Hospitality to travelers, good food, and good wine are Greek traditions. Correct me should I be wrong, but these traditions survive even in your country?"

She couldn't help the smile that slipped onto her lips. Her mother and father had filled their home with people and many, many times fed friends and strangers. They could pretend they had shaken off their roots, but their Greek hearts always betrayed them.

She gathered up her own napkin from the table, shook it out, and settled into her chair.

Ancient Love

A bull to trick the gods and a cow to trick the bull—to create the effigies the king and queen had asked for, Daedalus searched the hills above Knossos for a cave, a perfect cave, one that would act as a workshop, as a refuge, as a place where he could create the illusions that would be needed to balance two ambitious rulers against one another, and, most importantly, as a place where he could plan his escape from them both.

He found an opening into a cavern complex perfect for his forming plans. He had known he would. The gods had long ago, maybe before men had been given breath, created the rivulets, streams, and rivers that ate away at the stone beneath the island nation.

Who could say? Perhaps the gods had known at the beginning of time and decided to create the caves he would use because it pleased them that he should use them. A man who works with stone sees the workings of the minds of gods in small creatures and seashells embedded in marble, in insects deep in amber, in the pattern of a fern hidden beneath the earth between two layers of limestone.

Men believed the gods spent their time playing games with the lives of men. Daedalus the Mason believed that the games gods played revealed themselves only over many lifetimes, over perhaps thousands of lifetimes.

Regardless of the plans of gods and men, he brought men from the quarry and from the construction of the palace to build walls and archways inside his cavern's main chamber. Even though his men were loyal and grateful for continued work, he carefully guarded his plans.

Each man worked on a small part of Daedalus's workshop, and no one worked on all of it—not even Ikarus—especially not Ikarus, who had abandoned the love of his life, Adara, in favor of less willful and more willing girls.

With care, planning, and cunning, inside of a month Daedalus had created a sort of warehouse out of the main chamber. He had used his mason's skills to create rooms and halls. Deep in the bowels of the earth, a carefully shaped chimney through the cavern roof and into the open air above completed his forge. The pull of that chimney under a mere coastal breeze created more powerful airflow than any bellows he might have built of wood and levers and leather.

Daedalus needed that chimney for a forge that would need no other man to help him in the creation of wire, brackets, fasteners, and the special poured and pounded metals only he could craft.

In the first few days of outfitting the workshop in the cavern, Ikarus dutifully helped. He toiled and sweated alongside his father and the other men. Daedalus was proud that the boy showed at least some awareness of the clouds of political trouble boiling around them. He even considered telling his son of his plans; however, Ikarus's sense of duty lasted only three days.

On the fourth day, three women sent by the king arrived at the work site. Beauties, each, they hailed from different distant lands.

Daedalus instantly recognized the trained nature of the king's slaves.

Ikarus saw only what the king intended that they both see—beauty and desire reflected from his eyes to theirs and back again.

The women were trained to please the eye, the heart, the belly, and the loins. One lithe girl had pale skin and long, loose yellow hair. A more curvaceous woman had dark skin and wore her hair in long, ebony ringlets. The last, their leader, was purest Minoan and surpassed the other two in beauty, grace, and seductive movement.

Daedalus met them in the main hall of his workshop. "Go," he told them. "Tell the king that if he wants his work finished, we must be left to finish it."

The Minoan beauty pressed herself against Daedalus. The other two pressed their charms against the more easily excitable Ikarus.

"Master Mason," the Minoan said. "We wish only to soothe so that your work may progress."

Her breath smelled of honey and wine. Her eyes were the color of a late afternoon sky. Her bare breasts, pressed against the muscles of his bare arm, were so soft and firm that he could not deny his desire to hold her, to take her hard against the cavern wall.

The queen had drugged and nearly taken him. That shame he carried, but he would not let it happen again. The king was more direct. The king would not trick him. These women were only pleasure. He would find no love in them. If he hoped one day to be free to love, he had to escape the king *and* queen. If he hoped to ever see his son well-wed, he would have to find a way out of the court and away from Crete.

In spite of his desire, he pushed her away. "Your help will only slow the work. Look around you, girl."

The working men had slowed their pace to stare. Several stood flat-footed, mouths agape. Most had never seen a courtesan working in her full glory—or at all.

Her pride showed in her smile. "We are a gift." Her craft showed in her pout. "We dare not return to the king. We will help. We can work." She knew her effect on him. She knelt before him. She bowed her head, and her breath caressed his thigh. She lifted her hands above her head and crossed them at the wrists. She held her palms up for inspection. "Please don't send us away."

His knees nearly betrayed his resolve.

"Father," Ikarus said, "let them help." The boy already sat on a cushion that one of the women had pulled into the cave. "They can carry water," he said.

A nearby worker spoke up, "Aye, Master Daedalus. Water from such as these will make the work go well."

Daedalus grasped the woman's wrists and pulled her to her feet. Her pout was deep, touching, and practiced. He saw only trouble in these women. They were the king's eyes and ears. They were the possible failure of Daedalus's efforts to manage and keep separate the ambitions of the king and the queen. Worse, they might end his own ambitions for himself and his son.

She whimpered under the vise of his grip.

Men stiffened and glared.

In his men's dark eyes, Daedalus discovered a possible path to greater loyalty from his men and to his own ends. To set his plan in motion, he freed her.

The beauty before him smiled and caressed his cheek. "How can such as we create such worry in so strong a face?"

He put a hand around her waist and pulled her hard toward him.

She giggled.

Men cheered.

His stage was set and his audience ready.

He twisted her around so her back was to him and his arm wrapped her. He once more gathered her wrists together and held them tight, now between her breasts.

"You come to help," Daedalus whispered into her ear. "Look at the men here. Do you see them?"

She kissed his hands.

He put his mason's strength into his grip.

She whimpered.

"Tell me what you see," he hissed.

"Father," Ikarus said. "You're hurting her."

The two women with Ikarus stood.

"No," Daedalus said, "but she whimpers like a kicked puppy for the benefit of sympathy."

She stopped her whining and writhing and relaxed in his grip.

"Now, tell me what you see, girl."

"Men. Just men. Like all men—dirty and tired from work."

"Men," Daedalus said, "Standing still. Watching you."

"Yes," she said.

The two women with Ikarus smiled.

"We have hard work to do for your king." He released her. "Go back and tell him we are too busy for you."

She spun to face him. "The king will have us beaten," she said.

"Or killed," the Nubian said.

"Or worse," the pale woman said. She wrapped her arms around Ikarus and pressed herself against his back to make him both lover and shield against his father.

The boy's face flushed red. His loin cloth already showed signs of sweat, and he had shifted his tool belt to be more comfortable.

"Father!" Ikarus said. "How can you be so cruel to such beauty?"

Daedalus could not have asked for a better player on his stage. He knew the women spoke the truth, that if they went back without succeeding in what they had been sent to do, they would be beaten. One of them would likely be killed to impress the others. If he let them stay, the work would slow and his secrets would be at risk. He and Ikarus might have a few pleasant days, but in the end they would be killed.

In his mind, he married the three women with the deceptions he planned.

He pointed to the mouth of the cavern. He made his face a visage of stone.

"Please, Master Mason," the Minoan begged, a note of true desperation now in her voice.

"Father," Ikarus pleaded. "If you turn them away, the king will want to know why."

He fought to keep from smiling. The boy was his son, and while he did not yet see as far or as well as his father, he was quick enough of wit to make his father proud.

Daedalus lowered his pointing finger. He softened his face and nodded.

The girls relaxed.

Workmen began to move again.

"We will make a place for you," he said. "Here, in this corner of the main chamber, we will erect a wall. You may stay and help in any way you can. As long as the men work, as long as the work progresses on schedule, you may stay and serve. If the work slows, you must go."

Several workers cheered. The women sighed genuine relief. Ikarus smiled and pulled the pale woman closer to him.

Daedalus turned and spoke to be heard by all his staring men. "If the work falls behind for any reason, they will be sent away. For each day ahead of our schedule, you will each receive half a day to do as you please."

The men immediately began moving more quickly, and Daedalus thanked the gods for the gift of these women. They would report to the king what the men knew—what he allowed the men to know. They would distract the men from his purposes. And, if he kept them in a separate chamber, they would see nothing of his growing deception.

He turned back to Ikarus, but the boy's face pressed against the face of the pale woman, and his hands had found their way into the labyrinth of her silks. It was the end of work for Ikarus, and that was just as well. Of all the men in the caverns, Ikarus had the experience and mind to understand the use of the tunnels, the movement of the winds, the coming and going of materials. Ikarus would ask the most difficult questions, and his lips would be hardest to seal.

To keep his son alive, it was best the boy's hands and lips had other things to keep them busy.

~~~

Two weeks passed. The chambers were finished, the forges in place, and the tools and materials secured.
~~~

Daedalus released the workers. He sent word to the king that what he now did need be done away from the eyes of men and gods.

Yorgos and the little guard stood watch outside the caves; on penalty of death, no man entered unless both Daedalus and the king had first named him to the guards.

Daedalus worked in the caves alone. His workmen returned to their chores at quarry or palace or home. Ikarus spent his time occupied with the king's women, who in turn were grateful to have so easy a task for a time.

Deep in the caverns, hidden by twists and turns and darkness, Daedalus opened panels and doors to channel the winds of the hills into his forge. The coals roared and glowed, casting his inmost chamber in red-white light that paled the torches set in sconces in primal, stone walls.

Daedalus, stripped to waist, dripped sweat and wished for water, knowing he could not stop now, could not let his molten mixtures cool until he had poured them into molds—molds cut from stone to create the joints and shapes that could not fool gods but might fool kings and queens. More important, the new metals he mixed, melted, and poured had to be liquid enough to flow evenly into long, spidery molds he had fashioned for his own purposes.

He grasped long tongs and lifted a white-hot crucible from the coals. With care, he tipped the vessel and let a long rivulet of glowing liquid flow into a mold funnel.

While he poured, he prayed that this time the metal would be strong enough, would be rigid and flexible enough—that this time it would cool to be so strong that it would not break.

When the pouring ended, he hung his tongs on a hook and stepped back from the furnace.

"Water, Mason?" a woman asked.

He spun, startled by any voice so deep in his maze of caverns.

One of the king's women, veiled and draped in silks, stood in the archway of his forge room. From her carriage, he believed her the Minoan seductress, though the forge made the skin of her arms seem redder, and shadows made her height seem greater.

As always, her silks both hid her charms and invited exploration. Her dark hair, loose and long over shoulders and breasts, shone red in the forge light. Above her veil, her dark eyes glowed with deeper fire, greater strength, and more intelligence than he remembered.

He shook off the feeling she had changed. He could not afford his own foolish masculine desire triggered by exhaustion. "Leave," he said.

"I've brought you water." From beneath her silks, she lifted a goat skin.

He knew that voice—*her* voice.

He crossed quickly to her and pulled the veil from her face. "Nikkis!"

"You were not so angry with me when last we met."

"You shouldn't be here."

She lifted the goat skin again. "No? You are not thirsty?"

He took the skin. Keeping his parched eyes locked to her cool gaze, he gratefully drank.

"I had to come," she said. "I can't sleep."

With difficulty, he swallowed her welcome gift. To clear his throat, he swallowed again. Then, he realized he drank and swallowed and stalled because of fear. A mason knows his own heartbeat because he must strike with steady hand in rhythm with his heart. His pounded now, and his throat tightened.

"My dreams," she said. "They brought me here."

His fear wasn't for himself. It was for this woman he barely knew.

He set the skin aside and took her hand in his. "Quickly," he said. "Come with me." He led her through the corridors and chambers of his cavern world.

After they had traveled past several splits and made several turns, he pulled her into a deep shadow and through a narrow fissure in the rock to the chamber he used for his most private planning, the chamber most difficult to find and that could not be found by accident.

In the well-lit room, the walls covered in parchments with drawings of bulls and cows on them, he turned her to face him. Cool air brought a chill to his sweat-slicked skin. "Your clothing," he said.

"You don't like this?" Awkwardly, she mimicked the movements of one of the courtesans.

Her unpracticed attempt to smooth her unflattering silks over the perfect contours of her body brought more heat to Daedalus's blood than any trick of seduction he had been shown by the more practiced women in the camp.

"No." He shook his head. "This is not you. They caught you? The king has done this to you?"

"I have heard that you and your son prefer this." Her tone accused him, and shame grew like a cold, thorn vine in his belly.

She removed a silk from her waist and used it to wipe the sweat from his arms. "No," she said. "They have not found me. They don't even look. I stole this dress so I could pass through your caves to find you."

He caught up her hands. Her strong fingers wrapped around his. The dampened silk tangled around their hands, joining them. "Why?"

Dark eyes looked into his. A dizziness washed through him—the feeling that he stood at the edge of a cliff looking over, both afraid of falling from the height and pulled by the precipice to fall, to feel the freeness of a bird in flight even if only for the moment before death.

"I came to ask…." Her strong voice cracked.

Fear burned in her eyes. He had no breath to speak. He only nodded.

"My dreams," she said.

"Awake and asleep," he said.

"Yes."

"Yes," he said. He pulled her to him, wrapped his arms around her, pressed his lips to hers. Their hearts beat as one. Their thoughts joined with the mingling of their breath.

Daedalus stepped off the cliff. He fell and flew inside the expanse of Nikkis's embrace, and when at last their lips parted, he breathed her name as if it were a sacred word passing his lips for the first time. "Nikkis."

"Forever," she said.

A chill breeze swept through his chamber. Someone had changed one of the panels in his halls, slid one to the side and diverted the flow of air. The cold brought him back to his mind. "This is not safe," he said. "Already, the king uses my son to threaten me."

"The Fates," she said. "What choice do we have against this feeling?"

"We have choices," he said. "I cannot be the cause of your death. You must go. Please."

"Come with me."

"I have to finish what I've begun. When I'm free, I will come."

"Come to my village. My people will hide you. They will hide your son."

"When I'm done."

"I loathe this king and queen," she said. "They battle as pieces on a game board played by old gods and new. Both need you in order to win. They will never let you go."

"Me, they must try to keep. Not Ikarus. I must get my son away. I will make them believe we both escaped. Then, I will come back. I swear it."

She touched his lips, his cheek, his neck. "I don't think he wants to go."

"He is my child. A father protects his child."

She nodded her understanding. "A good father."

"Please, Nikkis. Keep safe. Within a year, I will come to you."

"I will wait," she said.

They kissed again—a long kiss to savor in memory while they were apart. Then, he helped her move through the hallways to the mouth of the caves. There, they found Yorgos on guard. Nikkis covered her face with her silks. As they passed the big man, he nodded and smiled.

Once out of eyesight, Daedalus set Nikkis on a path into the hills. Against moon and starlight, he watched her silhouette. She flowed like a cat over stone and ridge and trail, and, like the mountain cats that were so hard to see, she disappeared into the landscape without trace.

He wondered at his heart, and he wondered at her skills and her silence. She had become part of the landscape of his cave by wearing the silks, and she had slipped through his protections as if they were nothing. Now, she disappeared into the mountains like a creature of the night and hills.

The gods were truly creatures of ill humor to have brought his heart to fire here and now amid such danger.

He looked to the night sky and the moving starlight.

"Forever with her," he whispered to the gods, "would not be long enough."

~~~

King Minos had bidden him to build the bull.

Queen Pasiphae had bidden him to build a cow.

The two effigies were not so different, and he had managed to hide both by building them at the same time and in the same forges and pits and molds.

When the day came to present each abomination to each royal fool, Daedalus took care to arrange that each be taken to its intended destination under cover of
~~~

darkness. No worker in the caverns ever saw both bull and cow together. Only hand-picked servants of the king saw the bull, and they were sworn to silence or death. Daedalus suspected they would die soon after he delivered the bull. To send them to the underworld meant they could not speak to men or gods once the trick had been played on Poseidon.

To continue to be useful might keep him and his son alive, but Daedalus would not trust his life and the life of his son to the cunning self-interest of a king—especially not a king who believed he could trick the gods.

So, too, with the queen's cow. Only her most trusted and loyal knew of the effigy she had commissioned.

The queen, however, only wanted to trick a bull. Her servants would not die. Though in many ways more treacherous than the king, Pasiphae was by far the easier of the two to serve in that she knew of the king's plan, so her heifer went first to the ancient cavern lairs of her religion, caverns in the same hills in which Daedalus had created his workshop.

He arrived in the queen's sacred cavern before dawn, tired from the efforts of many of Pasiphae's women, four oxen, and himself to cart the heavy creature across two ridges and into the deep chambers of the ancient religion of wombs, birth, and rebirth.

Serpent carvings covered the walls, and no woman entered the below-ground chambers wearing clothing.

No sane man ever dared enter. Those few fools who did never left.

Daedalus entered under the watchful guard of two women who might have given any male soldier a glorious death in arms. He and his guards followed the queen's acolytes, who moved the golden effigy of a white cow into the caverns.

A male on sacred feminine ground, he waited in silent respect, listening to the breathing of the muscled women and the tiny click of their knives against the scabbards they wore on naked hips.

Queen Pasiphae arrived. She shed bodice and skirts and stood naked before Daedalus. "The heifer is well wrought, Mason?"

Daedalus answered in low tones. "I have done what I can."

"I will do the rest."

"Do not," he said.

"My goddess will be served."

More than her words, the metal of her voice told him she would do this thing.

"What must I know?" she asked.

He looked her in the eye and said, "That an abomination is an abomination," he said. "This serves ambition. It serves no goddess."

One of the warrior women slipped a long, thin, curved blade from the scabbard at her hip. The ring of the bronze told Daedalus that the blade was well-made.

The queen put a hand on the woman's. "He has earned the breath to speak here and to speak thus."

The blade returned to the scabbard.

"What must I know to survive my ordeal?" Pasiphae asked.

"If you must do this, then you must do exactly as I tell you."

"So it will be, Mason. Speak."

He told her of the straps and bars and stirrups. He told her of oils and salves and tallow. He told her of tiring, preparing, and managing the bull. He told her of preparing herself, and he warned her that having done all she must do, she still could not prepare herself for what she planned.

He told her all that he had thought of during the making of the heifer, and he prayed she lived long enough to know how hard he had tried to keep her alive.

When she satisfied herself that he had done all he could, she sent him back to his caves so he could return to Knossos to serve the king's plan to parade the false bull before the gods and pretend to sacrifice it.

~~~

"Good King of Knossos and all of Crete." Daedalus knew well the flattery of courts; in their hunger to hear flattery that could be believed, all royal courts were the same. "Let my hands serve for the greater glory of your–"

"Enough, Mason," the King said. "You have brought the gift to Poseidon?"

Daedalus bowed. While he bowed, he prayed to Poseidon, who had been kind enough to not drown him on his many voyages. *Do not, God of waters and men, think poorly of me for my place in this.*

Silent soldiers brought the false bull into the arena of Knossos. Only Daedalus, the king, and soldiers Daedalus believed would soon be dead watched the strange creature, a bull made of wood and metal and goat skins and the fur of ermine and filled with bags of gore.
~~~

"Good," the King said. He stood and raised his arms and spoke to the walls and heavens and seas. "Today, great king of the sea, Poseidon, we return to you that which you have given."

~~~

In dark chambers hewn in white rock and lit only by torches held aloft by nubiles, the queen stood enraptured by the passion for new power burning in her body, the passion of power and magic that she had called upon herself from gods older than those her husband knew, older than those known by men in any country—gods who were old when they gave birth to her goddess, Rhea, and who were the gods of life and death, and whom others had only known the shadows of, the merest wisps of memory, but whom she knew in her soul and womb as alive and living in earth and sea and air and fire.

She let her acolytes caress her body with olive oil to protect her skin within the effigy. She let their hands stretch her and bring her to greater arousal, and she stood still while they greased her and the effigy with warmed tallow wrought from cattle and pigs. Finally, she climbed within the pale effigy built by the clever foreigner. She climbed within and wrapped herself in the nets and straps as he had instructed. She wrapped herself, tightened the leather thongs at knee, waist, and shoulders. She placed one strap between her teeth, for he had said that without it she might bite and crush her own teeth when Poseidon's bull came to her.

Then, she waited, and her mind filled with fire and anticipation of the great powers that would flow through her when her goddess's power mingled with the seed of the upstart god, the gift of the sea.

~~~

The king's false bull lumbered forward, riding on metal wheels, false legs bending and pretending to walk. Men walked beside it, shields low, foolish in the belief that they could hide the lie from gods. They led the cold, empty-eyed white bull up a ramp onto the altar to Poseidon.

The altar of flawless, virgin marble had been well-crafted. Unstained by crack, fire, or blood, it stood ready to receive the blood and spirit of the bull that had no blood of its own and no spirit to deliver up within tendrils of smoke to gods whom Daedalus believed could not be fooled by the short-lived hopes and ambitions of men. Standing, head low, beside the face of the altar, a face carved with ornate dolphins rising and falling in dance above an urchin-encrusted seafloor, Daedalus prayed.

The king lied to the sky and sea.

The bull halted on the altar and waited for blade and flame with the patience of the already dead.

~~~

Poseidon's bull came to the queen, and her acolytes warned her that it had arrived. She placed her feet in the stirrups Daedalus had made. She braced her presented sex against the cold, padded leather in the rear of the heifer frame. She told herself that the mason's reward would be great. To her goddess, she prayed.

In this, I do your will.

In this, I am your body.

In gratitude for this power,

gifts to the mason, Daedalus.

His shall be fame and power.

His name shall live through the ages.

Whatever else she hoped to add to her prayer left her mind when the first tentative sniff of hot bull's breath touched her. Her blood boiled. She moaned in anticipation of their union.

Hooves scraped against the shell of the heifer. The frame shook, but her stirrups held. She bit hard on the leather and pushed against the bronze bar Daedalus had given her as a brace.

Hooves scrabbled. An acolyte screamed. Something thumped hard against the shell. Another acolyte screamed, and she began to open her mouth to ask what happened.

The bull found her. He found her, and with none of the patience of men she controlled, he took her, drove into her, tore her and slammed her inward and forward against the nets and harnesses. Her question exploded from her throat as a scream of terror and realization that her imagination had lied to her, had told her of ecstasy that would not be.

The bull thrust again.
~~~

All thought abandoned her. She screamed in pain and fear. The leather fell from her teeth. The straps, nets, and stirrups held her legs mercilessly. The bull slammed against the frame, and his passions made the cushions into stones attacking the queen.

She screamed, and her screams echoed in the heifer shell and again from the cold, stone walls of the deep, dark chambers in which her travesty of ambition played out.

~~~

Daedalus imagined that he heard a distant scream echo from the hills south of the palace. It was a scream of surprise and pain, and he suspected Pasiphae had come to the truths of which he had tried to warn her.

The king brought his long, curved blade down quickly into the neck of the effigy. He did exactly as Daedalus had told him, and his blade found the clever cords and bags within. The bull lowed deep and loud as if it lived and were now dying. The head slashed to the side, as a bull would, and the animal fell to its knees then to its side, as though the king's blade had struck heart-deep and true.

The king stepped back, and he held the bloody blade high in the morning sun.

A soldier lit the pyre, and flames consumed Daedalus's work and the king's lie.

The fire burned, and black smoke spiraled upward.

In the hills, in a cave, a woman screamed.

The king looked down on Daedalus and smiled.

Daedalus hoped that smile lasted long enough for him to get Ikarus away from this island of lies. He hoped the smile never turned on him again and that he would be able to fulfill his promise to Nikkis.
~~~

Modern Mystery

Yorgos pushed their Toyota Celica's engine into a scream in order to pass the motorized tricycles farmers drove, the ubiquitous tourist buses, workmen's vans, and cars on the twisting highway through the rolling hills of the lowlands below Knossos.

Nikkis said, "During the Palatial period before the landscape was changed by the eruption of Thera, now called Santorini, Knossos thrived as a shallow-draft port city." As soon as she said it, she felt silly. Of course Andros would know that. He lived here. Even if he was an amateur, he was a knowledgeable amateur.

Andros chuckled. "You glow, Dr. Aristos," he said. "Excited?"

Embarrassed to have shown it, she nodded and turned her face to the window.

Olive groves floated past outside the car, twisted and ancient trees marching in rows and joined in ranks here and there by newer, younger trees less than one or two generations old. Long, low rows of pole and wire-trained vineyards interrupted the legions of olive trees. Tall, knife-like rows of cypress trees sometimes separated fields. Sometimes, low, white stone walls marked field boundaries. Sometimes, grapes simply gave way to olive ranks or the ranks stopped and made room for grapes.

Beyond the sloping fields, Nikkis thought she glimpsed the broken arch of the remains of an aqueduct. "Roman?" she asked.

"Yes," Andros said. "I'm surprised you know the different types."

"Not so hard," she said. "Besides modern works of steel, plastic, and concrete, only two post-Minoan cultures left architecture on Crete. Romans used bricks. The Phoenicians used stone. The structures reflect the materials in both form and deterioration."

"Of course," he said.

"There will be Linear-A in-situ?" she asked. "This isn't just some tourist event we're going to see."

Yorgos pushed the car hard. The little engine screamed in protest. Even so, the car obeyed him and zipped forward then into a space between the front of a bus and the rear of a tiny Smart Car.

Nikkis gripped her seat.

"My dear," Andros began.

She shot him a warning look, but he was looking away out his own window.

"Can you see out my side?" he pointed at a passing row of tall, narrow cypress trees.

"Cyprus," she said.

"Beyond the trees."

She leaned forward to better see through his window. She focused her eyes to see through the gaps between trees. Flashing past like a color zoetrope of a nineteenth century construction project, machines and men moved about on a low hillside. Suddenly, the site resolved into something she recognized—a grid of dig pits—an excavation.

"Knossos?" she asked.

"Yes, but not the part of Knossos the tourists see. Much more here has been uncovered than has been published."

Heat from Andros's breath on the back of her neck cooled her excitement. He had taken the moment to lean in against her side. His head was too close at her shoulder. She sat back, forcing him to take the back of her head in the face or to sit back himself.

On the other side of the car, shops had appeared. Vending booths blocked the view of anything beyond the road—Italian ice, books, maps, water, linens, beads, and a thousand other tiny trinkets for the tourists.

Confused by the sudden proliferation of tourist traps, she said, "I thought we were nearly there."

"We are there," Andros said. "The tourist entrance will not do for you."

Yorgos pulled the car into a gap between two booths: a postcard vendor and a shaved ice vendor. They rolled slowly along a narrow dirt lane then stopped in front of a tubular steel gate. Yorgos got out, unlocked and opened the gate, returned, drove them through, and got out again. He locked the gate behind them, returned to the car, and drove on another hundred meters before parking in a dirt lot beside several other cars, including a sky-blue police car.

"Visiting Knossos is one of my dreams coming true," Nikkis said.

"It pleases me," Andros said, "to live for a moment in your dream."

Again, she thought his tone flirtatious and patronizing. She wondered if his rudeness came from a cultural attitude toward women. Perhaps, as an American, she had misinterpreted the tone entirely, or perhaps he carried some darkness toward women in his heart.

She stopped herself from thinking about the things he had said about his mother and father. In terms of her work and time in Crete, it didn't matter what he thought of other women as long as he respected and needed her work.

She glared at him, and this time she caught his eye.

He showed no sign of apology or shame. Apparently, she had not been clear enough at dinner the night before. She reminded herself that she had been in such situations many times, and the moment would come when she would make it undeniably clear to him that only the artifacts and confirmation of her work in Linear-A interested her.

When she did, she would make it a public humiliation. Even persistent men usually left her alone after that.

Then there were the obsessive men—the stalkers—they were a different story.

While she could admire his hope to bring honor to his family and to protect the history of Crete, her instincts made her cold toward Andros. Even so, she didn't believe he could have his position if he were the crazy type of obsessive. He would back off.

They crossed the dusty lot to a smooth, stone causeway. Even though it was only nine in the morning, sweat beaded and dripped on her neck and arms. She was grateful for her loose hiking pants, t-shirt, and light boots. Had she believed she would be alone, she'd have worn shorts and a tank top, but she knew she'd be with Andros and other men. She would sweat rather than have to deal with them.

Her boots slipped slightly on ancient stones worn slick by the tread of bare feet and sandals over thousands of years. As if the stones remembered the passing of every foot, the warmth and history of ten thousand lives moved like a wave upward through her legs. Her heart raced. She paused to catch her breath. "The west gate entrance," she said.

"You know Knossos," he said.

"From books. Only from books. This… Look here." She swept her hand across their path, taking in the causeway stones. "Foot traffic has worn these stones so completely smooth. The literature talks about the worn stones and how the change in wear from outside the palace to inside supports that palatial period Minoans wore sandals outside and went barefoot inside." She took a deep breath and rushed on, "Touching the stones themselves—the feel and smell of the history of the place. The people. The lives. That isn't in the books."

"Such a romantic, Dr. Aristos."

She ignored his jibe and let the ancient feel of the place wash into her like a cool summer shower trickling over parched skin, smoothing twisted hair, and soothing tattered nerves. She felt like she had come home, like on some deep level she belonged in this place and had always belonged in this place.

She passed into shade beneath an arbor covered in grape vines. Their path met the path from the main parking lots, which she imagined provided parking for the local workers critical to any large-scale dig.

Her sense of the ancient grew into a full, vertiginous chill of déjà vu. It swept through Nikkis. Goose flesh spread from her spine, across her shoulders, and down her arms.

She reviewed the many explanations she had read for the phenomenon of feeling like she'd been here before: it's an echoing feedback effect in neural nets; it's a random boost in brain voltage; it's a moment of prescience; it's a moment of memory from a past life; it's a reassertion of an image seen in a book or on TV or somewhere else….

None of the thoughts cleansed her of the sense that she had once before walked under grape vines up to the west entrance of the vast Minoan complex of stone now called the Palace of Knossos.

The déjà-vu moment continued, and she believed she could have turned left and walked along the wall of the cistern house, but there was no wall.

Instead, on that side of the grape arbor, foot-worn cobbles stretched in a semi-circle toward a terraced drop-off and metal pipe railing. The terracing helped her shake the idea that she'd been there before. Whatever the cause of her déjà vu, it came from some subconscious imagery that didn't match the completely ruined palace.

Noticing that the pipe railing formed a circle, she looked more closely. Beyond it, two more pipe railings surrounded pits, each twenty feet across.

The cisterns.

She froze and stared. In spite of the sun and heat of the morning, icy cold settled in the bottom of her belly, and her heart slowed as if its silence would let her remember—feel something that she should feel but couldn't quite find inside herself.

"Come, Nikkis," Andros said. "There is much to see here, and we don't have much time."

His voice startled her. She stumbled forward.

He caught her elbow and steadied her.

"Be careful. I would rather you not come to harm."

His unwelcome touch cleared her mind. She jerked herself free, straightened her back, and glanced at the sun. It had only climbed a quarter of the sky. "We have all day," she said.

"Tourists. They will begin to arrive soon."

The pipe railings around the cisterns—they kept fools from falling in. She had seen the shops outside the gates, but she hadn't put them together with the idea that tourists were allowed to traipse all over these ancient stones. "They let people walk here," she whispered.

"Oh, yes," he said. "Every day. Guided tours. Buses full of people."

Before Nikkis could protest, a dark-skinned man met them. He was darker than Andros, and deep life lines tallied the years on his broad face. He gave Nikkis the sense that he had spent time on the sea, though she had no reason to believe the impression. She decided it came from the wear-shined leather patina of cheeks and the paled brown of his blood-shot eyes.

He spoke quick, fluid Greek. She imagined that she recognized an Athenian accent. His words ran together even more completely than Papá's or Christophé's. "What useful thing do you think *you* can do here, Detective?" the man asked.

Andros stepped in front of Nikkis, separating her from the man as if she needed protection. "We came to examine some of the old writing," he answered.

"You have not enough hidden away from us?"

Andros seemed to grow. He pressed close to the old man. "Rumors," Andros said, "mean nothing."

"They mean much to–"

Andros interrupted him. "Official business."

The old man stepped back a pace. "I was not informed."

"I hereby inform you."

The old man blinked rapidly and opened his mouth as if to speak.

"Yes?" Andros said.

The old man's mouth closed. He took a short breath and said, "The artifacts are in my care—my responsibility." He glanced at Nikkis. Leather lids hooded his eyes. His frown and glare told her what he thought of her. She'd gotten that same look from Papá just before she slapped him.

"He seems upset," she said in English.

"American," the man spoke it as an insult. "As curator of the exhibit," he said, "I cannot let you in as some private entertainment for your," he paused and gave Nikkis another dismissive glance, "your *friends*."

Nikkis's blood heated. She knew the type, the men who never saw her, who looked at her parts: her skin, her legs, her breasts, her hair, her eyes. They decided she had been given everything in life, that she was as vacuous as a hedonistic, hair-flipping shampoo commercial.

In her perfect Greek, she said, "Not *friend*. Colleague. Nikkis Aristos, doctor of archeolinguistics. The detective assured me access to examples of Linear-A here. So far, I have only seen a continuation of a last century dig defiled by reconstruction to serve the tourist trade. I doubt there have been any significant finds since Minos Kalokairinos began his digs or since Sir Arthur Evans got down to the business of organized excavation."

The curator's dark skin took on a red-copper burn as his brown eyes widened. "Doctor?" The man's English was weak, but his contempt was not. "Ancient languages?" In ancient Greek, he spoke to her, "Whores and mules can both wear silk, but only the mule will carry water to the grapes."

Her blood burned. Her hand stiffened to slap the man.

Andros spit on the pale stones at the curator's feet.

The curator and Andros locked eyes for a long moment.

Nikkis used the moment to regain her composure. In ancient Greek she replied, "A man who cannot share his grapes will have no friends to help make wine."

The curator looked away from Andros and reassessed Nikkis.

Suddenly, he turned his back on them. In English, he said, "Come with me. To your *American* academic, I will extend the privilege of seeing our treasures."

Andros took Nikkis's arm, and she let him.

A few minutes later, inside a restored, palatial-period hallway, they stood before a display case. Inside, mounted in a half-circle bracket, rested the Phaistos Disk. Nikkis recognized it at once. As it always did, even in pictures, it set her mind to spinning, to trying to make sense of the odd glyphs, the undeciphered language that spirals around on both sides of the fire-hardened clay disk. From the flower at each center to the double-blocked glyphs at the edge, she tried to read it. Some instinct in her compelled her stare, told her that if she only looked long enough and hard enough, she *could* read it.

Of course, she couldn't. Nobody could. Not yet. Some speculated that the language of the disk was a precursor to Linear-A. Others believed it to be a phonetic hybrid between the Linear-A and the fully deciphered Linear-B. She believed it to be a ritual, a hymn, perhaps even a prayer. Such disks must have once been common among the elite as a way to carry messages or to record rituals. She hoped one day to prove it.

She looked up and realized that she'd been lost in her own experience long enough for the curator to launch into a long, boring explanation of the nature of writing, its origins, and of how the disk fit into that development.

At first, Nikkis blinked and looked at the man's white teeth flashing between dark lips. She understood the words he spoke. She understood the sentences. He was speaking English, he believed for her benefit, and he managed to continue to convey insults of tone in every word. Even so, the sentences he spoke made no sense.

She shook her head.

"Am I going too fast for you, then, my American *colleague*?" he asked.

"No," she said.

"Then I shall continue. As I said, the disk is written in undeciphered Linear-A."

"No," she said again.

"Excuse me?"

"Not Linear-A. In fact, it isn't even close to Linear-A. It may be early Thracian, but as far as I know, nobody has identified the root language or offered a definitive explanation for the creation of the disk."

The Curator's white teeth disappeared behind his dark lips.

"You have done nothing but insult us since we arrived," she said. "Your contempt drips from your lips like bad wine from the lips of a drunk, and I'm tired of it." She poked the man in the chest with a long finger. "I came halfway around the world to help this man stop the theft of *your* artifacts," she said.

"I doubt it," he said.

"That is why she is here," Andros said.

"And," she continued, "the Phaistos Disk wasn't found in Knossos. While it has, *perhaps*, combined components of Colchian, Linear-A, and Mycenaean Linear-B, it is not pure Linear-A. I came to look at Linear-A, and you show me this? Admittedly, I'm fascinated and thrilled to be in the presence of such a rare object, but the professional hospitality I have been shown, well...." She let the words trail off into a short, awkward silence before continuing. "Had you come to the United States, we would have offered you every resource possible to make your stay productive."

Eyes wide, the man gaped.

"My field is Linear-A," she said. "My name is *Doctor* Nikkis Aristos, and if you don't mind, I'd prefer you quit wasting my time with your vacuous, erroneous tour-guide patter."

She turned to Andros, "If you want me to see something here, show me. This man won't help us."

Andros beamed. "Come, Doctor." He took her arm again.

They left the little building. The curator hustled along behind them. "Dr. Aristos! Please! Not that way! My apologies. Please!"

She ignored him.

Behind them, he called out, "Tylissus!"

As if the name were a cattle prod, Andros jerked and picked up the pace. "Come, Nikkis." He hurried her forward along a wall toward a roped-off area.

She stumbled along beside him, trying to pull her arm free. "Slow down."

"The tourists will be here soon. We must hurry and finish before they arrive."

A man blocked their path. "Finish what?" he asked. A few inches taller than Andros, he wore blue jeans and a nearly sky blue cotton shirt. He might have been a tourist, but his Kritiki accent marked him as a local, though she thought his accent was from the west of Crete and not from the central coast or east. He might even be Sfakian, one of the people even the historically ferocious warriors of the rest of Crete called unconquerable.

Andros put a hand out to the man. "Tylissus," he said. "Docent duty for you?"

Tylissus looked down on Andros's hand and clasped his own hands behind his back. He took a military position of at-ease, but he conveyed more of a sense of stone wall. "When I can get the honor of accompanying artifacts from the museum in Iraklion to temporary displays for the benefit of the people," the man said, "I take it. And you have come here because?"

The curator caught up. Catching his breath, he spoke in his fast Athenian, "He abuses his power. He will give away knowledge of our finds to this American scholar."

Tylissus put a large, square-edged hand on the curator's shoulder. "I will speak to them," he said. "Nothing will be broken, stolen, or lost."

"But she's an American. She's a doctor. A linguist."

"Dr. Nikkis Aristos," Andros said in English, "I introduce to you the Chief of the Tourist Police unit for this section of Crete, Tylissus Baptiste."

More gently this time, Nikkis once more removed her arm from Andros's grip.

"Dohktaar?" Tylissus drawled.

"Dr. Aristos is an American expert in ancient written languages," Andros said.

"I see." Tylissus held out his hand to Nikkis. In practiced Ancient Greek, he said, "You honor my ancestors with your interest."

"More ancient than that," Andros said in Greek.

The curator went on, "You can't let her in the–"

"Please," Tylissus said. "I will deal with this. It is a police matter." He put a hand on the curator's shoulder and gently guided him into a turn that propelled him back toward the disk's temporary home. Clearly upset, the man looked over his shoulder several times.

Nikkis swallowed hard. She was moved by the sense of depth and sincerity the policeman projected when he spoke, but she didn't want to show it. She wanted to see whatever it was they had come to see, and Tylissus appeared to be a new obstacle.

"I'm sorry," Tylissus said in English. He extended his hand again.

She placed her hand in his, and he clasped his other hand around hers. His hands were huge and hard. It was like hiding her hand inside a bowling ball.

"I'm pleased to meet you." As he said it, he leaned forward, almost bowing. "Have you come to study our Minoans and their language?"

Tylissus still held her hand. Her palm sweated in the giant's firm, gentle grip. "Their writing," she said. "I specialized in Linear-A."

"And you travel with *this* man?"

"Tylissus," Andros said. Then, in Greek, he went on. "I will not tolerate interference with my investigations."

Tylissus nodded to acknowledge Andros. "A viper, this man," Tylissus said in English.

Nikkis worked her hand free.

"But perhaps you are a viper as well," he said in English. "I watch these ruins," he said. "My eyes see all, here. Do not give me a reason to detest such a beautiful and intelligent woman." He turned and made his way off into the maze of broken stones and restored walls.

"What was that about?" she asked.

"Jealousy. Professional rivalry," Andros said. "You must have these things in your country."

She thought of Anderson and Dr. Bonnet. "Yes," she said. "I'm afraid we do."

"He believes, as do you, that we stand on sacred ground that should not be touched by modern hands. What are the words in English? I think you would call him the zealot. Righteous zealot."

"Then you're both on the same side. He must hate forgeries and the theft of antiquities."

"He does. He also thinks I cannot do my job well enough because my parents were German and Turkish. Many old wounds scar this land." He held out his hand to her. "Come, Nikkis. I will show you something no tourist sees."

She started to take his hand, but his familiar use of her name registered. She stiffened and pulled back.

"Ah, still you do not trust. Perhaps Germans and Turks have history in your country as well." He turned and continued along the worn, stone path.

Ashamed to have treated him like the others and relieved that they were at last getting to work, she followed.

All around her, bits and pieces of the giant palace had either been restored or were in the process of restoration. Carefully restored, intentionally visible layers revealed construction techniques of the time, demonstrated the cleverness of the people who had built the complex, and showed the ancient grandeur while not destroying the site.

Beside her, a broken, layered wall rose from rubble to freshly finished, pristine glory. Its heart was made of raw-cut stone. Mortar covered the stone. Plaster covered the mortar. Bass-relief fresco covered plaster, and paint covered the fresco in intricate, geometric designs popular among the Palatial Minoans. The palace must have been a spectacle and wonder of the world at a time when many cultures had barely learned to build houses and some had not.

She followed Andros through the ruins toward the ropes, her own professional righteousness waxing and waning as her anger over site desecration fought with wonder and awe triggered by bits of restoration.

He led her along pavers to a half-restored wall, part ancient stone and part new mortar and paint. A rope channeled tourist feet away from a descending scaffold ramp that filled a gap between the walkway and the wall. At the gap, he ducked under the barrier rope, turned and descended the ramp into a shadowed hallway below.

She followed, asking, "What does Tylissus think of the restorations?"

"He believes they defile the memory of his people."

His people. She wondered for a moment how much Andros's choice of words meant.

Where Nikkis thought the hidden hallway dead-ended, Andros turned again and disappeared into a tunnel that could not be seen from the scaffold or the tourist perspective above.

She paused at the dark maw into the underworld.

From within, his silk-over-sandpaper voice came to her. "It's safe, Nikkis. The roof will not fall."

"It isn't the roof that worries me," she said.

"Haven't you wondered why I would trust you? Did you think your article so stunning and new that I just dropped my investigation and negotiated the funds to bring you here?"

She peered into the darkness. "I have wondered."

He reappeared in indirect light. His eyes sparkled, wide and black. "My dear Nikkis, I considered your article just so much American hubris. Americans like to believe that if they think of something it must be the first, best thought anybody ever had."

"Dr. Aristos," she corrected. "Americans do not monopolize that trait."

"Workers discovered this tunnel only a year ago. We completed excavation only a month ago."

"And?"

"It was discovered in the west pavilion, the active dig we saw from the road. We first found its other end beyond the highway. This tunnel runs under the highway, beneath the West Court, under the West Wing Magazines, and, we suspect that it once went all the way to a spiral stair beneath the Throne Room. It had been missed before because of very cleverly disguised doors at each end, a careful arrangement of stone weights and slides. Ingenious, really, and unknown in all the world for that period."

"Minoans had palace intrigue," she said. "So?"

"At first we believed it a late addition."

"Probably," she said.

"Except that when we washed away lime accretions, we discovered that the walls inside the tunnel held inscriptions in Linear-A. Several of your posited glyphs appear here."

"You have a light?"

"Ah," he said. "Follow me." He disappeared into the darkness again. A few moments later, lights came on in the tunnel. Twenty meters into the tunnel, an overhead wire supported light bulbs every two or three meters.

She followed him. After a few strides, she came to the light switch hanging from a wire on the wall. "They didn't have enough wire to light the whole tunnel?"

"They didn't want light coming out of the tourist end of the tunnel."

"Of course," she said.

He pointed. At the midpoint, as near as she could tell with the lighting and without pacing off the entire tunnel length, the wall was native bedrock—white marble with black striations. An area of the marble, she estimated about a quarter meter square at eye-level, was as smooth and flat as wood someone had planed, sanded, and polished.

Cut into the flat were rows and rows of glyphs.

Nikkis moved close enough to the stone to inhale the scent of it. She examined the glyphs, her heart beating faster and faster. She placed a hand on the wall and traced fingertips over the perfectly preserved symbols. An hour or a minute might have passed. For Dr. Nikkis Aristos, a lifetime of work became a moment of realization.

Andros interrupted her perfect moment. "Was it worth the trip?"

She took a deep breath and stood straight. She took another breath before she could speak. Finally, she said, "In this one wall, there's more original Linear-A than appears in the entire literature of the history of the language."

His low, rich laugh echoed in the tunnel. "We have only begun," he said.

She ran her fingers over one of the glyphs, an hourglass shape, and the déjà-vu feeling hit her again—the weird certainty that she had stood just there and placed her hand just so against the stone.

The touch of Andros's hand on her shoulder startled her. She jumped to the side to escape him.

"I'm sorry," he said, and he did seem sincere. "I saw goose flesh on your arm. I thought you had taken a chill."

She chastised herself for such ingratitude to a man who was helping her make her career. "You just startled me," she said.

He smiled and nodded, and she wondered if she could like him. She wanted to like him. She thought she should like him. But something about him made her chest tight, gave her the feeling that something hid in a shadow—that if she turned around quickly enough, she might catch him retracting claws or hiding fangs from her.

She shook off her little girl fears. She was in Crete. She had just put her hand on the material that would free her from real monsters like Anderson.

"Come, Doctor," he said. "We must go to the car. Yorgos will drive us to a place where there is much more to see."

~~~

Yorgos stopped the car in front of a warehouse on a long dock jutting out into Iraklion harbor. Nearby, a giant ship with Greek letters on the side, *Daedalus*, waited in silence, a metal titan soon to challenge the sea of Poseidon.

"Daedalus," she whispered. The name flowed from her tongue like a word she'd spoken a thousand times, a name that brought pleasure just in thinking it.

"Excuse?" the driver said.

"The ship," she said.

"Ah. The ferry."

"Ne." *Yes*. She searched the tall, white-and-blue hull of the ship for some sign of what it was that warmed her and made her feel at home here in this dirty industrial area.
~~~

While she watched, one end of the ship split open and lowered like a drawbridge to the dock. Automobiles began to drive off the ship onto the dock, all driven by madmen who would soon find their way onto the streets and highways.

Her door opened. The movement startled her out of her musing.

Andros's hand appeared, palm upturned as if asking her to rise and dance.

She slipped her legs out, but he stood too close and the car was too low to let her stand without grasping his hand to pull up. He steadied her during her climb from the seat into the bright, afternoon light.

"What do you think of the harbor, Dr. Aristos?" Andros asked, still holding her hand.

She locked eyes with him, delivered her best ice queen stare, and said, "The drivers here are insane."

He smiled. "The best drivers in the world."

The man was unbelievable. She'd made a terrible mistake allowing herself to get excited in front of him in the ruins. Now, her best withering glare only seemed to encourage him. She tugged at her hand.

He did not release it.

"I don't know how you can say that," she said. She pressed toward him, expecting him to step back.

He did not. Instead, he let her bump into him, her hand in his between them. She smelled the spiced oil in his hair and the wine and garlic of his breath. She pushed harder. He held his ground. She tried to sidestep, but he gave her no room.

"If they were not," he said, "you would see many more deaths on the roads, don't you think, Dr. Aristos?" Finally, he stepped back and freed her hand. "May I now have your permission to call you Nikkis?"

Angry heat pumped up from her chest into her face. "No," she said. "You may not."

His smile wavered just enough to let her know she had chilled his ardor. Only a moment passed before the smile rose again, twisted a little, and settled into a double curve that reminded her of the enigmatic horns on the bull in her room.

The chill she'd tried to create had taken up residence in his eyes, and she began to suspect he might be the kind of man who would let it live there for a long time.

"*Americans*," he said. "You look a man straight in the eye like you want his attention, and then you put a blade to his passion."

Suddenly, she thought she understood his odd behavior. She said, "In my country, when a woman looks a man in the eye, he gets out of her way."

Andros cocked his head to one side and narrowed his eyes as if considering her words. "Truly?" he asked. His voice had lost its edge.

"Often," she said. "Certainly, he will keep his manhood longer if he doesn't assume he has an invitation."

"So very sad," he said. "Americans must be very confused much of the time."

"Detective," she said, "you called me here to work."

"Always the ice and fire. Always the work." He turned and walked. Over his shoulder, he said, "Come, then, Dr. Aristos. To work." He crossed open concrete from the car to a nearby warehouse door. There, he waited for her.

She glanced around the empty industrial parking lot. Yorgos still sat in the car. Through the tinted glass and his sun glasses, she couldn't see his eyes, but she could make out his smirk. He stretched a long, muscled arm back across the seats and pulled her open door shut.

She joined Detective Andros at the warehouse door. "I thought we would be working at the police station or the museum," she said.

"Perhaps later." He held the door for her.

Behind her, tires crunched gravel as Yorgos and the car pulled away.

Nikkis passed Andros. She had to duck a little to keep from hitting her head on the top of the doorway. The change from such bright, Mediterranean light to the dim, cave-like interior of the warehouse made her eyes hurt.

The door behind her closed. She paused in near darkness, and she had the sudden feeling that it was hot, that something was burning, and that she should run, but she couldn't find a direction and couldn't move her feet.

She tried to tell herself to breathe. She forced herself to take a long, slow breath. The warehouse reeked of rancid olive oil, hot metal, and ancient stone. Her eyes began to adjust, and she brought the moment of panic under control, replacing it with practiced, rational thought. She was here on a job. She had seen enough to know Andros was a real detective. Yorgos, and presumably Tylissus, knew where she was. They certainly knew who she was with.

She searched the interior walls that made up the hallway—metal ridges and ruts. Rust stains and peeling paint covered the corrugated metal. The walls resolved into giant boxes—metal cargo containers.

The containers further resolved into blues and browns. Each had the name Daedalus stenciled on the sides.

"Daedalus, again?" she asked.

"A mythic hero." He tried to take her elbow.

She shook him off.

"It's dark," he said.

"I know who Daedalus was," she said.

"Sometimes the floor is slippery."

"The father of crafts and tools. He built the bull that let the queen of the Minoans be mounted by the white bull, the gift of Poseidon, and hence give birth to the Minotaur."

"How would it look if our visiting expert fell and broke her neck in a warehouse on the docks?"

She knew the flat tone in his voice. She used the same tone to warn off men. It carried an undefined threat of unpleasantness. She needed to force him to a decision here and now while the door was still close behind her. She could match his warning, and she could bury him with details. She would work, or she would leave. "Daedalus built the wings that let him and his son escape from Crete to the mainland, but his prideful son, Ikarus, flew too near the sun. The wax that held his feathers in place melted."

"And he fell," Andros said.

"To his death in the sea," she said. "Daedalus also built the labyrinth in which the Minotaur was hidden from the light of day and the sight of the gods."

"A maze," he said, "where foreigners became lost and were sacrificed."

"Until Theseus ended the practice by killing the Minotaur."

"You are a rare pleasure, Dr. Aristos—a woman with such a mind connected to such a tongue." He chuckled, a rattling growl of a sound low in his throat.

His laugh sent a chill across Nikkis's skin. Grateful the dim light hid her rising goose flesh, she ignored his casual chauvinism and her physical response. She said, "So, why is 'Daedalus' stenciled on all these containers?"

"Do you know what happened to princess Ariadne, who helped Theseus?"

"Daedalus's name was on the ferry outside. I thought it was the name of the ship."

"Theseus," he went on, "took her on his ship and sailed for Athens."

"Yes," she said. "And his crew disliked her, thought she brought them bad luck, so he left her on an island—stranded her there alone, helpless, without food, water, or friends." Nikkis stopped talking. The walls of dark, steel containers suddenly seemed too narrow to move between. They closed in around her—heavy, ancient, and dangerous. Where her long pants and loose shirt were much too hot in Knossos, here the wisps of fabric provided neither warmth nor protection against the sudden chill.

In the shadowy light of the warehouse, Andros's eyes once more reminded her of the bull in her hotel room.

He said, "It will not be my fault if you fall or lose your way in this maze," and he moved deeper into the building.

She exhaled her relief. His decision was made. It was her turn. The door or the shadows within?

Over his shoulder, he said, "Daedalus is a shipping company. That's all. They own this warehouse."

She chose, and she followed, lifting her feet and placing them carefully.

He turned several corners then slipped into a gap between two shipping containers. A heavy, metallic sliding sound came from inside the gap. From between the containers, white light slashed outward onto the grease-stained concrete in front of Nikkis.

She glanced behind her. By the light now spilling into the corridor between containers, she saw several side-tunnels—a warren of dark corridors she had not seen while she had been focused on following Andros.

Until that moment, she'd believed she could turn around and go back to the door and the daylight. Suddenly, she knew that somewhere in the maze of steel, she had become lost and not known it.

She followed him through the gap between containers and into a gymnasium-sized, open area surrounded by walls of cargo containers. Her parents' house could have fit in the brightly-lighted area. The concrete floor supported rows of sawhorse-and-plywood tables, folding steel chairs, and electric floodlights mounted on tripods or strapped to step ladders.

Among the tables, a small army of young women wearing latex gloves, white filter-fiber masks, and white-room Tyvek coats sat or walked. They wielded dental picks, toothbrushes, cotton swabs, and various magnifying lenses.

She recognized the tools and the intent concentration of the women.

Cleaning and restoration—on a huge scale, a scale she'd never seen before—never even heard of before.

She gasped. Her mouth and nostrils filled with welcome smells of dust, ancient clay, solvents, water, and the chemical smell of the prophylactic clothing.

Antiquities covered the tables: potsherds the size of her head; intact, decorated pots from Minoan, Doric, Roman, and Phoenician cultures; pottery sculptures; brass masks and helmets; alabaster busts; and marble—more ancient, marble statuary than she had ever seen in one place at one time.

She moved quickly to the nearest table.

A petite young woman, her dark hair pulled back and bound in leather so it hung between her shoulder blades like a brown club on the white fabric of her coat, leaned over a bench-mounted multi-hand tool. The tool, a medusa of articulated arms and clamps arranged beneath a large magnifying lens, held a gold earring—a crafted spiral surrounding an eight-petal flower. The girl deftly moved a fine, dental pick along the crease between spiral curves in the surface of the earring.

"Beautiful," Nikkis whispered.

The girl started. Her dental pick slipped across the soft surface of the gold, scoring it slightly.

Andros shouldered past Nikkis. Firmly, he grasped the young woman's shoulder and moved her up out of her chair.

She came up, sputtering excuses and apologies in Greek, her eyes wild and afraid.

"It was my fault," Nikkis said. "I startled her."

Andros ignored Nikkis's protest. In Greek, he told the girl to go to the break room and wait for him there.

The girl became silent. Her dark eyes pleaded with Nikkis.

"Really," Nikkis said. "It was my fault."

"Fault has no value," Andros said. "The piece has been damaged."

"Why does it matter?" Nikkis asked. "The piece is a fake. The strike mark only makes it look older."

The girl's eyes grew large and wide. She hissed in breath.

Andros released the girl and rounded on Nikkis.

For a long moment, his angry eyes made her believe he might spit insults and curses at her, too. However, the irrational rage drained from his eyes. His cold smile returned. In English, he said, "How do you know this, Dr. Aristos?"

Nikkis smiled. "Isn't it what you brought me here to do?"

"Yes, but you will pardon me if I ask you again how you know that this piece is a fake. The cleaning is so we can determine if it *might* be a fake. You may have saved this young woman her job and a month or two of salary."

"May I, then?" She smiled past Andros for the benefit of the young woman, whom she hoped had understood the conversation in English.

Andros stepped back.

Nikkis took the girl's seat. She shifted the magnifying lens back to a position that would allow Andros to see the earring. She picked up the abandoned dental tool. "I see several telltale flaws in the piece."

"Please correct me if I'm mistaken, Dr. Aristos, but your expertise is in ancient scripts—specifically Linear-A?"

"Expertise in any writing system requires the study of the culture."

"Of course."

"Here." Nikkis indicated the spiral pattern on the earring. "First, a single spiral path. The palatial Minoans generally laid down double spirals. They used two tones to indicate dualism in the cycles of life."

"Speculation," Andros said, but Nikkis heard admiration in his voice.

"Yes. Alone, significant but not sufficient. Here, also," she went on. "This small, raised nib in the gold shows that this piece was cast in a lost wax mold. Palatial Minoans hand-fashioned gold in cold form. No one knows exactly how, but on even the finest pieces, under proper magnification, a trained eye can find tool marks. Sometimes, the pieces even have Linear-A glyphs."

"Thank you, Doctor," Andros said. To the girl, in Greek, he said, "Continue. You heard what she said. Did you understand?"

The girl nodded.

"You know what to do?"

"Ne," the girl said. She dipped her head so low that it made Nikkis embarrassed for her.

To cover her unease, Nikkis stood.

The girl took her seat again, and again Nikkis saw her dark eyes flash, this time gratitude—gratitude and something else, maybe just nerves. Maybe a question or–

No. Nikkis decided she was making things up now—the warehouse, the artifacts, the tiny little lose-your-job drama played out in front of her. She was being foolish, and she needed to get her focus back, to do what she had come to do. She needed to prove her glyphs existed in order to be free to set the course of her future.

To Andros, Nikkis said. "I'm guessing you didn't bring me here to show me fake earrings. After what I saw at Knossos, I'm guessing I'm here to examine pieces containing Linear-A."

Andros nodded. He walked along the tables.

Nikkis patted the woman's shoulder. "I'm sorry," Nikkis said.

The girl looked up, smiled, and said thank you in Greek, "Efhahreestoh." She glanced after Andros, then at the ceiling, before she picked up her dental pick and hunched over her work.

Nikkis followed the lines of the girl's quick glances.

Andros strode away. Above him, where the container walls neared the ceiling, Nikkis spotted a security camera.

She followed the line of the containers at the ceiling.

Every few feet, cameras looked down, one on each worker's station.

She supposed that even police might be tempted to steal. Or, perhaps—and, yes, that must be it—they had to document every process and procedure for evidentiary reasons.

Andros was a stickler for detail, but she could see that the cameras made the women nervous.

Nerves aside, she admired the discipline and patience that the entire setup demonstrated. This man was concerned for his family name, for history, for his culture, and for his people. In spite of her gut reactions to him, she could appreciate Andros's professionalism.

Nikkis followed him to the last table, one next to the wall of containers at the corner farthest from the entrance to the arena of tables and workers and cameras. A white sheet covered the table and a little pile of whatever it supported.

Andros grasped an edge of the sheet, and with the dramatic flair of a sculptor pulling a cover to reveal a masterwork, he whipped the sheet upward and away. Light from above reflected from fragments of white and black marble. Each fragment was the size of a man's hand placed down flat with the fingers splayed. Their shapes were all different, but their sizes were nearly the same.

Nikkis moved in close. It looked like rows and rows of glyphs covered every fragment. Thousands of glyphs.

She picked up a piece and examined it.

Linear-A. Between the wall at Knossos and the fragments on the table, she'd seen enough Linear-A in one day to make a hundred academic careers. She couldn't believe so much ancient script lay strewn on a police detective's temporary working table in a warehouse on the waterfront of Iraklion.

"*This*," Andros said, "is why I brought you to Crete."

"My God," Nikkis said.

"Are these authentic, Dr. Aristos?" Andros asked. "Is such a thing possible? Carved in marble—not clay?"

Nikkis liked the excitement in his voice. He wanted this to be real. He knew he needed a clear head to make the call—an academic like Nikkis who was, theoretically, not invested in the outcome.

But she *was* invested in the outcome. She wanted the find to be real. It would make her career, her life. It would free her from–

Only if she got it right.

She took a breath and forced down her rising emotions. To give herself a moment, she lifted a folded, white smock from a stack at the end of the table. While putting it on, she searched her heart and found the cold stillness that had served her for so long. Like the women in the arena putting on their white coats, she put on her objectivity and training. "I'll have to examine the pieces closely," she said. "Certainly, I recognize some of the glyphs."

"As do I," Andros said. "But others."

"Yes. I see them."

"Glyphs from your article. The glyphs you said could be predicted to exist if your interpretation was correct."

"Perhaps someone read a pre-production version of my article," she offered. "I have reason to believe that was possible."

"The fragments of stone came from the mountains near here—a site in the hills to the south of Knossos. We thought them fakes until I read your article."

Nikkis pulled a metal chair over to the table. She checked the magnifying lens and light. Both worked fine. "I'll need some time."

"All the time you like," Andros said. "Do you have everything you need?"

"Coffee. Black." She settled in over the first fragment. She would be meticulous. Perfect. This opportunity had two sides. If the stones and glyphs were authentic, she would be first to publish with her interpretation. If fakes, she would be known as the woman who helped break an artifact forgery ring. Either way, she would teach where she wanted and when she wanted. She would have and manage her own digs.

No more Andersons.

No more ambush dinners with the butcher's son.

Finally, her life would be her own.

It would be a life deciphering the messages written in stone from the past. She would spend her days on Earth in that noble quest, in helping whoever had sent these messages across time to find a voice in her world.

~~~

Andros left his useful American, *Professor Nikkis Aristos*, to her work. He headed off into the maze of containers to take care of business best done away from the eyes and ears of workers and guests.

Dr. Aristos was everything he had hoped she would be, and much more. She had precise and useful knowledge in her field, and spending her life focused on gaining that knowledge had ensured that she was inexperienced in other aspects of life. Her blood and face were Kritiki, so she opened doors that would not open for him. Her typical, narrowly focused American ambition kept her from seeing the larger patterns in the world around her.

Except for one disturbing thing, she was perfect for his use.

She was too beautiful. Her face. Her form. Her smell. She haunted him. She clouded his mind and judgment.

For now, he could allow for this small distraction. Soon, he would have to deal with it.

Trying to banish the image of Dr. Aristos's soft chinos tightening as she bent over a table full of marble, he moved out of the warehouse and into the light of day. There, he focused on business.

Yorgos leaned against the Toyota, dwarfing it.
~~~

Men like him were useful as long as they did as they were told, and more and more he had that dangerous feeling that a day would soon come when Yorgos would try to think for himself. He couldn't have that any more than he could tolerate the uncontrolled distraction of Dr. Aristos.

Andros moved close to the big man. "A girl," Andros said.

"The American?"

"No." Though Andros wondered if she might not be the better target for testing Yorgos's loyalty. "Dr. Aristos is a woman."

Yorgos nodded.

"I will send the girl to the break room," Andros said. "One of the workers."

Yorgos nodded again.

"Take her off the payroll."

Yorgos said nothing, but Andros thought he stiffened a little. "Do you understand my meaning, Yorgos? I want this done now. I want it done quietly. Take her out through the dock under the warehouse. We do not want to disturb the work of our Dr. Aristos."

Yorgos nodded and lumbered off toward the warehouse entrance.

Andros didn't like the cold feeling that touched him. His father had once told him that the back-of-the-neck tingle was "a tiger in the grass of tomorrow lying in wait for you." Andros wondered if Yorgos was that tiger.

~~~

Beneath the floor of the waterfront warehouse, Andros hid in the shadows of pilings that supported the building. He mused on what was and what could be while he waited for Yorgos to bring the girl's body down. The stench of harbor seawater, mold, and dying barnacles reminded him that progress meant death for some and success for others.

His father had taught him that, and he had taught himself to be successful rather than dead. So, he waited and watched.

The warehouse trap door opened and closed. After the brief flash of overhead light, two silhouettes climbed down the ladder.

Two shadows—one small and slight, the other huge.

They came to the planked walkways under the warehouse, the small boat docks used by locals for moving small goods or for commuting.
~~~

His first thought gave Yorgos the benefit of the doubt. *Efficient.* He wouldn't have given Yorgos credit for that. He had expected the giant to kill the girl in the break room or the bathroom before carrying her to the water for sinking. This was better—silent, discreet finesse of trust and betrayal, avoiding noise and the effort of carrying a body.

For a moment, Yorgos rose in his estimation. The plan was worthy of Muscus.

Andros relaxed and leaned against a pylon. The planking under his feet rocked, moved by the gentle swells created by distant winds and rocking freighters and ferries.

Yorgos loomed over the girl. The girl was pretty enough. She might have found a good husband and bred Greek wharf rats. Who knew? In the backward way of the modern world, she might have finished her education and built a career for herself. She might have gone off to England or America and gotten high-level degrees. The British and Americans were like that—weak enough to give women voices and knowledge. She might have grown into an ice queen like Dr. Aristos.

Dr. Aristos was back in his mind again. He hated that she haunted him.

Andros tried to dismiss her image.

She had *him* thinking of her as Dr. Aristos, and that annoyed him, even angered him a little. He would use her first name.

Dr. Nikkis. No. That wasn't good enough. He tried to banish the formal title and replace it with the diminutive, little, as if she were a child. *Mikrí Nikkis.*

That was better. He returned his attention to Yorgos and the girl. Andros congratulated himself for giving the problem to Yorgos. The final moment of the girl's life would be terrible but mercifully short. It would be the same as the final moment of a small chicken in the hands of a hungry farmer. Terror, then darkness, then the forever silence of deep water and the whims of Poseidon.

"Take this," Yorgos said.

Andros straightened and peered through the shadows.

Yorgos handed the girl something.

"I've never seen this much money," she said.

"Take it and leave. Go. Never come back here. Don't even come back to Iraklion. Never."

"I don't understand. Why does Andros give me so much money?"

Yorgos glanced around before answering. "I give it. You do not want *his* gift. After receiving it, there would be no more gifts—not ever."

The girl made a scared chicken sound.

"You understand me, then?" Yorgos asked.

"Come with me," she said. "You can't stay. What if he–"

"Go. Others here need me. In the money, there is a note. Take it to a man named Tylissus at the ruins of Knossos."

"But–"

"Do it. Then, run far and fast."

Rage burned in Andros's blood. He began to shake, and he almost stepped into the light where he could be seen. He almost confronted Yorgos right there—right then. But Andros had not come to the power he held by taking rash action. To attack Yorgos in the shadows beneath the warehouse would not end well for Andros.

As if to confirm his thoughts, the big man displayed his strength by grasping the girl, lifting her, and placing her in a little dory, the kind men used to gather urchins along the rocky shores to the east, near Kokkini Hani.

"I can get help," she said. "My brothers."

"Only Tylissus. Go to Knossos, then leave Crete. Go to Athens. Go to Italy. It doesn't matter. Just go."

Andros had seen enough betrayal. Silently, he slipped away, hidden by the shadows of pylons.

It was not the first time the chill on the back of his neck had saved him from disaster. The same feelings had kept him alive when men came for him at the Academy. Hazing, they called it, but for him, a German-Turk, it would have been death.

He had turned the tables then. A terrible accident they all called it.

He called it justice.

Yorgos was like those men, and justice was needed again.

~~~

Nikkis paced. She gripped two ancient fragments in her hand, let their worn edges press into her flesh, tried to feel the age of them—tried to feel the hands that had fashioned them, the mind that had given form to the words encoded there.

She couldn't quite find those hands, that mind. They were just beyond her reach, beyond her ability to see. It was the frustration of her entire career, her studies, her life. Everything meaningful felt hidden to her, secreted behind a shadowy veil of
~~~

flawed memory or perception. It was like reality was meaningless. Only her dreams were real, but too often they were impossible to remember.

She stopped. She dropped one fragment into the pocket of her smock and placed the other fragment under her stereoscope. The fragment of marble couldn't exist. It was wrong in so many ways, but it was right in so many other ways.

When all the possible explanations have been exhausted, the impossible must be correct.

Nancy Drew and Sherlock Homes had said that in the stories she read as a girl, the stories that filled her mind before she met Daed, before she knew that stories were lies—back in the days when she believed in heroes, heroines, and magic.

Daed.

Thoughts of him had come back to her so easily in this place. Since she arrived in Crete, he had come to mind more often than in all the years since high school.

She blinked hard to clear her mind and focus on the impossible artifact under the stereoscope. This was no time to think of *him*. She'd given up such foolishness long ago. She had a Ph.D. now. She had to think and act like an adult if she ever wanted to be in control of her own path through life.

She needed to find Andros. Needed to talk to him.

She grabbed up the fragment, pushed her chair back, stood, and spun around to go find him.

She ran full into Andros's chest. Startled, she rebounded, stepped back, and stumbled.

He caught her.

More solid and much stronger than he appeared, he seemed suddenly taller, and the spice of his hair oil made her flush.

He supported her for a moment then pulled her tighter to him.

She struggled and pressed back. Her hair fell loose.

"Eenay ohrayah," he said. *Herein is beauty.*

She recovered her poise, her balance.

"Let me go."

He did.

Embarrassed, she straightened her hair and brushed herself off as if she'd fallen to the soiled concrete floor.

He looked down on her. "Leaving?"

"Looking for you. Where have you been?"

"You found something important?"

"I don't know," she said. She handed him the shard of marble she'd been gripping. "Look at this."

"Yes. Like the others."

"No," she said. "Not at all." *Of course* he couldn't see the difference. It was quite likely she was the only one who might even look for it. She grabbed the fragment back. Her excitement returned, and she forgot the moment of confusion in his arms. She took his hand and pulled him to her workstation. She put the artifact under the scope. "Sit," she commanded. "Look through here."

He smiled. "You are flushed, my dear Nikkis."

"Oh, for God's sake, just sit down and look."

Confusion flattened his smile. He sat and looked.

"What do you want me to see?" He pressed his eyes to the eye pieces of the stereoscope.

"The edge of the shard. Near the top of your field of view."

"Yes. Glyphs."

"And two other things."

"Part of another glyph. Some sand."

"Half of a Classical Greek letter. Like a delta."

"Perhaps. Perhaps not. Perhaps half of a lybris." Andros stood and faced her.

Letting sarcasm color her words, she said, "The labia of the goddess religion?"

"More likely a double-bladed axe," he said.

"Perhaps," she said. "In palatial times, the battle between male and female religious systems played out. It makes sense that the symbolism of the bull would be offset with serpents, passion flowers, and labia. Some people posit that the symbol is no more than two triangles joined, a dual triad."

"This means nothing," Andros said.

"It means something," she said. "See the eight-petal flower at the joining of the two *blades*? That makes it more than a delta or a mere lybris. That makes it much more likely a personal mark—possibly a name."

Andros shook his head. "I've seen a dozen marks like this at Knossos and other sites. A mason's mark. A signature. An axe. No matter. Just suppositions and sand."

"Not sand. Mortar. This stone came from a larger stonework, a Roman construction—newer than any other Linear-A ever discovered. If there is a delta here, then this could be a shard of the Rosetta Stone for Linear-A."

"I am *only* a detective, Dr. Aristos." His voice had a sharp, icy edge. His dark complexion seemed paler, more stone-like. His eyes became black marble and his lips hard and thin.

She stepped back.

"I know enough of such things," he said, "to express disappointment that you would allow yourself to leap to such amazing conclusions."

It was her turn to smile. She pulled the second piece of stone from her smock pocket.

"And that is?" he asked.

She moved to the stereoscope and carefully fit it, edge to edge, with the first. "A perfect fit," she said. "These two stones were once one. Someone scored the original and broke it. Look."

He bent over the scope.

When he stood, his stone face had become the face of a young boy, a boy filled with hope and joy. "The delta and the epsilon are unmistakable."

"You have more of this material?" she asked.

"They are not forgeries?"

"We'll need tests."

"But?"

She couldn't help her grin. "Based on my observations of composition, tool marks, and edge wear, I think it's safe to say these are at least two thousand years old. I can't imagine why people two thousand years ago would try to forge Linear-A."

Andros beamed. He opened his arms and stepped toward her.

She stepped back and crossed her arms.

He stopped and crossed his. "I'm sorry, Doctor. I know you do not like to be touched, but I *am* Greek."

She nodded. She was beginning to believe she had misunderstood the cultural cues. Perhaps she had simply been an ignorant American after all. Still, she avoided the hug by saying, "There must be more. Where were these found?"

The boy's grin and innocence disappeared from his face. "In the hills," he said

"When can we go? I need to see the site."

"No. Not possible."

"I have to see where these pieces came from."

"You have paid for your trip and more, Dr. Aristos. Tomorrow, I will put you on the plane back to your home."

She couldn't believe what she'd just heard. "You'll *what*?"

"You have done what I brought you here to do. Now, you must go back to your home so I can finish my work."

"But this may be the most important–"

"Doctor, I work to catch forgers and thieves. You have proven to me the authenticity of these stones, but that does not mean that the source from which they came is a safe place for civilians."

"If you mean you brought me here to discover something this important and plan to cut me out of the–"

Andros's face and eyes became stone again.

Yorgos rounded the tables and joined them.

"Yorgos," Andros said.

Yorgos's attention shifted from her to him and back. Something was going on between the two men, something they weren't telling her. She imagined they were playing out some long-term, political game. The ambitions and manipulations of the police of Crete were likely no different than the Machiavellian games of American professors.

It didn't matter. All that mattered now was getting to the site and seeing where the two fragments came from. If, in-situ, there were more fragments, more Roman mortar, more Classical Greek next to Linear-A… *If*, then there could be nothing more important in the world.

"You finished the chore?" Andros asked.

Yorgos nodded.

"I can't be sure," she said. "It might be forged. Testing will take weeks. In-situ examination can confirm in a day."

Andros looked back to her. "You seemed sure a moment ago."

"No. I told you testing was needed. Don't confuse my excitement with certainty," she said. "I could be sure if I saw the site. I can pay for my own flight home later, if it will help."

"She wants to go into the hills?" Yorgos asked.

"Which hills?" she asked.

Andros said, "I will have Yorgos take you to the hotel to pack."

"I won't go," she said.

"You should leave now," Yorgos said. "The hills are not safe."

She glared at the two men.

Andros looked to Yorgos then at her. His eyes softened. The corner of his mouth turned up a bit, just enough to tell her he had come to some decision that pleased him. "Yes," he said. "I think you are right, Dr. Aristos. It would be better if you saw the site of origin."

Nikkis had prepared more arguments. For a moment, confusion clouded her mind. Where Andros had been a stone obstacle a moment before, now he suddenly agreed with her and wanted to help her. She felt like she had just run up a flight of stairs in the dark and tried to climb one more step—a step that wasn't there.

Yorgos frowned for just long enough for Nikkis to catch it before he became once more a stoic statue.

"Yes," Andros said. "It would be better if we are very sure of everything."

She took a breath and nodded, pretending she'd known all long there were no more steps to climb. "When do we leave?"

Andros was already walking away. "Yorgos will return you to your hotel now. Get a good night's sleep. We will leave early tomorrow—before sunrise." At the door, he paused. To Yorgos, he said, "Make sure she has appropriate clothing."

Yorgos, silent once more, nodded.

When the big man turned away and started toward the doors, Nikkis had the impression that he was angry at her.

She followed Yorgos. To avoid fueling his anger, she bit the inside of her lip to keep from showing her elation. She reminded herself that excitement is the enemy of discovery. Many careers had been ended by researchers who reported results too early because they wanted to believe something. She wouldn't be one of those. She would see the stones in-situ. She would document strata, positions, and orientations. She would return and do the appropriate tests. She would–

"Doctor?" Yorgos's deep, gentle voice startled her. He held the door to the parking lot for her. She hadn't realized they had reached it and stopped.

"Yes. I'm sorry. I–"

He cut her off. "We should go."

"Of course."

Ancient Gifts

Daedalus found himself once more in the silk-draped chambers of the queen and surrounded by women who considered her pleasure the divine purpose of their lives.

The last time he had seen her, she had been lithe and vibrant and filled with the dark grace of sensual understandings most people can barely imagine. Her clothing had been sparse or non-existent every time he had seen her. This time, lying nearly motionless in a nest of silk cushions, she hid her face behind dark veils and covered all her flesh with silk skirts.

Servants moved about her lifting cushions, helping her move her head to perfect angles, lifting her wrists and hands when she needed to reach for the fruit arrayed on golden trays all around her nest.

Several of the younger women, likely nubile virgins, came to Daedalus and made it clear that it would please the queen for him to be pleasured.

He stepped past them toward the queen.

"Already, you refuse my gifts, Mason?" Queen Pasiphae's slow, hoarse whisper behind her veil held none of her normal haughty command. "Have you traveled…." She paused and took a labored breath. Her veils billowed and settled before she continued. "…to so many lands… seen so many wonders? Women trained to drive men mad with pleasure bore you?"

"Enough lands," he said, "and enough wonders that I know that gods live in all lands and have many names."

"Speak plainly," she said.

"What you and your king have done will not please your gods, whatever names you give them. Gifts such as that bull are not to be ignored."

"Clever man." She pushed her hands down into her cushions and struggled to sit straight. Her servants rushed to help her, to prop pillows beneath her back. Her veil fell away from her face, revealing the reason for her slow speech. Nearly her entire face was black with bruises. Her gray eyes had swollen to mere slits, and a red cut marked her forehead at the hairline.

Daedalus stiffened.

"No, my mason," she said. "The king did not do this. Nor have I been punished by the gods."

"I'm sorry." He understood exactly how the damage had been done. "I did as you asked."

"Yes," she said. "If not for your skill, I would be dead."

He could not look at her. He looked down at the polished stone of the floor.

"You did well," she said. "I have never been so filled, so satisfied."

He looked up, facing Pasiphae's wounded face again. In Aegypt, Thracia, and in the Far East, he had seen perversions he believed could not be outdone; the joy in the queen's bruise-swollen eyes told him that until now he had only seen the weakest and smallest offences against man and gods.

"I called you here to reward you—to give you the pleasure of my company and the company of my attendants."

"You are kind," he said. "I did what I did to balance power here and perhaps save your people and this island kingdom from the wrath of Poseidon."

"You did what you did to save your son."

"Yes." Denial would gain him nothing. He nodded. "And especially that."

"You will be rewarded for doing as I asked."

"Freedom for myself and my son?"

"I will reward you for trying to save our land."

"Please," he said. "If not my own freedom, then the return of my son to the mainland."

"Your reward shall be a gift that will help you save your son."

"We need only a boat."

She lifted her hand. A girl ran out of the chamber. "I have watched you," she said.

He waited.

She reached for a grape. Her shaking hand grasped the fruit.

Eager hands steadied hers. Other hands snatched up the fruit and delivered it to the queen's mouth. Juice dripped over her swollen lips and battered chin. After she swallowed, she said, "Your hands are clever. Your mind is even more clever."

"Thank you, Queen of the Serpents."

"You know we struggle forever—the King of Bulls and the Queen of Serpents."

"Yes," he said.

"You have seen some of my power."

He shuddered at the memory of the golems.

"No doubt," she said, "you have heard other things. Yes?"

"I have heard...." He paused. "*Things.*"

"Yes," she said. "The power whispered about only in secret places when servants and soldiers believe I will not hear. Tell me the truth, now. Tell me what you have heard."

For the time it takes a flint spark to flash and die, he considered whether it would be safer to lie. Since his life might already be forfeit, he chose the truth and what little honor that could win him in death. "I have heard many things in many lands, and in this land I have heard that you were born of unholy union between a serpent god and a rutting goat. I have heard that you can reach into a man's chest and pull his still beating heart from his flesh. I have heard that you can keep that heart in a box while the man yet walks and lives, and should you ever wish him dead, you need merely stab the heart to kill him. The whisperers say these things and more—that the venom of serpents does not harm you, that a spear cannot kill you, that yours is the power of seeing to far places even when no man or woman has ever been to that place."

Her chuckle was a low, guttural sound deep in her bruised throat. "True, and more," she said. "When I bestow a true gift born of the will of my goddess, it is much like when you build a palace. It is at once rare, beautiful, and terrible."

"I wish no such gift, My Queen."

"Your wish has no weight in this. My goddess demands that you be well-gifted."

Daedalus glanced around the room. No guards appeared, but he was as trapped as if they stood at every split in every silk curtain that made the enclosure.

"Come close to me," she said.

He crossed the remaining distance.

"Kneel."

He knelt, and he prayed Ikarus would live long enough to escape and that Nikkis, who had become the image of his hope, would live well and long.

She reached out for a bowl of golden grapes. She poured the grapes on the ground and settled the bowl on the polished stone at his knees. "Put both your hands in this bowl," she said.

He did.

A servant stepped through the wall of silks and handed her a pale, white-crystal vial. She lifted the vial and poured red wine over his hands. "Now shake them off."

He did.

She smiled.

"Is that all?" he asked.

"One more thing." She gestured to the bowl. He placed his hands once more in the bowl, palms down, one over the other. "Do not remove your hands from the bowl, Mason. Do you understand?"

He did not, but he nodded.

A second servant brought her a golden box. She held it above his hands, opened it, and turned it over. A beating, human heart fell on top of his hands.

Daedalus wanted to pull his hands back, to run, to scream for help. The warm flesh pulsed and throbbed on the back of his hands. He bit his tongue, fearing the worst.

Her hands disappeared beneath her silks then reappeared. She raised her hands above the bowl. Silks slid back from her bruised forearms. She held a long, golden spike. With both hands, she drove the spike downward into the heart, through his hands, and into the base of the bowl.

Ice and fire cut through his hands and spread like flowing, molten stone up his arms and into his chest.

Daedalus opened his mouth to scream. Before sound formed in his throat, one of the two servant women gasped, clutched her chest, and fell forward, dead.

He closed his eyes. His scream gathered in his chest and throat. It rose to his mouth and poured over his lips.

The queen laughed and withdrew the spike.

He wanted to look away, to not see his hands, the maiming of them, the terror of losing his ability to touch, to make. He wondered who he would become without his hands.

"Open your eyes. Look upon my gift, Mason."

Terror shook him, filled him with weakness. Still, he had to look. Had to see.

First, he flexed his fingers, testing. They moved without pain. They felt strong—maybe stronger. He dared open his eyes.

The meat of the heart covered his hands, flat and empty and still. He slid his hands out from beneath it, out from the pool of blood—his and the heart's. He held up his hands.

Bloody, yes, but not maimed.

His fingers responded to his thoughts. He touched the fingers of his right hand to the back of his left where the spike had skewered him.

He touched only warm, blood-slicked skin.

He touched left to right, and again found healthy flesh.

Trickery—he thought. He'd seen false holy men and women perform such tricks to ensure awe, fear, and loyalty.

She said, "Not a trick."

He stared at her bruised face and wondered if he had spoken his thoughts out loud.

"No," she said. "Your thoughts are your thoughts. Your heart holds your fear, and I know your heart. Do you not remember my lovers? Do you think that magic was any less than this?"

"What horror is this?" Daedalus asked. He balled his fingers into fists, opened them, and flexed them. Heat filled his hands, and the skin tingled as though his hands alone had drunken too much wine too quickly.

"A true gift born of my new power," she said. "The gift you have given me has blossomed in my heart. I see new patterns in the hearts of men and women, new thoughts and feelings. The goddess moves. My hands become hers just as yours have been mine. She bids me give you this gift, so I have given your hands more than the cleverness of a man. I've given them the knowing of anything they touch. Only my goddess may give this gift. Given to a woman, no man can refuse her caress. I have never given this gift to a man before, but I believe that of all the men I have known, your hands and heart make you deserving. I suspect you will find uses for this gift that I cannot yet imagine."

"It can't be. I don't understand."

"Nor do I, but it is part of the future my goddess desires. When healed, perhaps I will understand more. Each day brings me new visions. For now, I do as *She* has demanded."

"I don't understand," he said again. He couldn't deny her power, and he feared her words and what she might have done to him. Daedalus shook.

"Touch me, Mason." She opened her silks to him. She cupped a bruised and swollen breast and lifted. "I will teach you the use of this gift."

He stepped back.

"Have no fear of me, Mason."

"I do fear you."

"The marriage of Poseidon's gift and my goddess creates power that will last through many ages."

"Already, I regret what I have done."

"You only gave me what I asked."

"I asked only for freedom. What have you done? My hands?"

Exhausted, she pulled her silks closed and collapsed back into her cushions. "I tire, Mason. If you will not accept my teaching, then be alone in the discovery of the gift of your hands. Leave me."

Servants lifted and carried the dead girl away.

Daedalus backed away from Pasiphae and her insane hungers and ambitions.

~~~

Daedalus understood stone and chisel and wheel and ramp and lever and pulley. To the things he understood, he returned. To gods he could not name, he prayed the queen's magic had not ruined his hands for work. To the encampment of the masons who raised the walls of Knossos, he hurried, and when he arrived, he went to his overlook and his sheet of mica.

The queen's games and appetites clawed at Daedalus's mind. He could still feel the fire and ice where the spike entered each of his hands. He tried to believe it had not happened, that the queen had tricked him with gore, with some drug timed to kill a woman in his presence. He had known her obsession with the white bull. He had seen the trickery she had meant to manipulate her husband.

None of it fit into his knowing of stone, air, fire, and water.

He wanted to finish his work in the caverns, the secret work he began for himself while creating the bull and the cow. He wanted to finish and test his work—to fulfill his hope that he and his son could escape this place, could flee from Crete and be safe once more among their own people on the mainland.
~~~

But first, unwatched, or so he believed, he returned to the mica stone he and Ikarus had been studying when first Nikkis had come to him, when he had first felt his life become driven by forces he could neither see nor name.

He ignored the greetings of the workmen and water women working in the lower quarry and quickly strode up the switchback trail to his overlook. In the shade of his pavilion, he found that the large, layered slab of mica had neither changed nor been moved. He sighed as a wave of relief washed through him. The magic of stone was magic he knew.

Stone.

In stone, he could always find the works of gods: a shell, a leaf, the wings of a bee—the works of gods who could see the whims of a man a thousand, thousand years before that man's birth.

He removed the wire and rod cutting tool from the edges of the stone. He let the layered stone fill his thoughts—layers of time and the thoughts of gods set in motion before time had measure. He marveled at it. His mind returned to old thoughts, to comfortable thoughts. He let the habits of a mason who considers how to use such a stone to enhance a palace enfold him.

Only once before in all his life had he seen such a sheet of stone, and his efforts to use it had ended in disaster. The sheet had been smaller, the length of a man's arm instead of the length of his whole body. He had hoped to cut that stone to fit in a frame of larger stones to bring golden light to an indoor fountain.

He had scored the sheet, set his wedge, and struck.

The sheet cut, but the impact separated the layers of mica and destroyed the edges and the stone's transparency. It ruined the stone and destroyed his plans for the fountain. Instead, he positioned polished bronze reflectors to bring light to the fountain.

This time, he didn't have the luxury of failure.

The king, like the queen, had given Daedalus a gift—the gift of life and additional service. The king had seen the slab of mica, and he had ordered it cut so that it could become the roof over his throne.

To fail with this stone would mean death for him. It would mean he could never return to Nikkis. It might even mean the death of Ikarus. The boy could not long stand against the king and queen alone.

Daedalus put his hands on the sheet of stone and closed his eyes. He savored the cool, smooth surface and let its coldness drive dark memories from his mind.

The hushing sound of his heart touched his ears. The hot, chalk smell of pale marble dust filled his nostrils, and the stone beneath his hand seemed to sigh.

If the stone could speak, he thought, it would tell me how to cut it.

As if the stone did speak, as if it whispered to the flesh of his hand, he knew his answer. He felt the thin lines within the layers, felt and saw them, long and tiny and invisible to the eye, but real and true. Eyes closed, he let his fingers trace those lines. A moment later, certainty filled his heart.

The thought was insane—would have been insane only a week ago.

The idea was impossible, but he *knew*. All the thoughts the gods had set into the stone so many ages ago came to him in a rush of knowing and told him what he must do in this moment.

He lifted his hand high.

Eyes closed, ears ringing with the sound of his own heartbeat, Daedalus struck the stone.

Beneath his blow, the stone cracked. Eyes still closed, he knew that two pieces thudded heavily against the earth at his feet in the same way a man knows when he puts his hand down upon the surface of a table.

Impossible.

Cold terror rushed through him. He had been foolish and rash. He had made the mistake of a child with his first hammer and chisel. His foolishness would end in his death and the death of his son.

He opened his eyes and fell to his knees where the stone rested on its edges in the dust—where it rested on its smooth, perfectly straight edges. It could have been firm meat he had cut with a fine-sharpened blade and placed on a butcher's bench to show off his work. The slab was now two transparent stones. One was as thin as a silk and perfectly cut at its edges.

"How?" A familiar voice behind him.

He turned. Ikarus, young and strong and tall, stood at the entrance to the mason's tent. "How did you do that?"

Daedalus searched beyond his son for others who might have seen. At the first bend in the trail, where the shadow of a tall, thin cedar provided a little relief from the sun, his son's two guards endured the endless boredom known by all guards in all the armies of man. They chatted quietly and watched the water girls in the quarry below.

Daedalus motioned to his son to come closer. He whispered, "You saw?"

"With only your hand—a perfect cut."

The two men stared for some time at the stone. Neither said a word. Finally, Ikarus asked, "How?"

"I don't know," Daedalus said. He knelt and touched his fingertips to the edges, still not convinced the cut was real. "I don't know."

But he did know, and it terrified him.

~~~

There was an old story, Daedalus knew, of a man who turned everything he touched to gold, including his horse, his wife, and his daughter. It was a child's story, but Daedalus suddenly wondered if there might be truth in such stories.

Confused and afraid, he had returned to his chambers after cutting the stone. He'd been careful to touch nothing, but when he had gone to his own cushions and settled himself to sleep, he had touched the fine weave of the blanket on his bed.

Instantly, he knew the intertwining of wool with fiber from crushed plant stems. The threads had been spun together by aging hands, hands filled with aching, throbbing pain—gnarled hands with brittle nails. A woman owned those hands, and she had long past lost her sense of joy in the sun that warmed her skin while she worked. She had even lost the memory of having once known such joy, and Daedalus could feel her emptiness, her patience in waiting for death to come to her and relieve her of the gnawing grief of lost husbands and sons—of lost youth.

He leapt from his bed and paced through the night, his hands out from his sides so he touched nothing.

Eventually, the sun rose over the white ridges above the valley of Knossos, and Daedalus took his two guards, Yorgos and Skatas, the sly, narrow-faced soldier more loyal to ambition and the king than to the country, on the long hike into the highlands above the palace. Daedalus wanted to be alone, or as alone as the king's guards would allow him to be.

They followed the flow of the Vlychia upstream to a waterfall no taller than a man, but it made an effective barrier to any boat that might wish to travel from the Kairatos, up the Vlychia, and finally higher into the hills. Above the falls, the stream
~~~

became a mere rivulet, a creek a man could wade across without trouble. Below the falls, the water became fuller, broader, and only crossable by boat or swimming.

Under the high, late morning sun, Daedalus considered the mystery of the Vlychia. He puzzled at its size above and below the cascade's white spray and rainbow glow. He had often puzzled over this odd stream. Its murmur and mystery had taken his mind off troubles many times.

Even while thinking, he took some pleasure in the sweat and panting of his guards. Yorgos was smart enough to find shade and give Daedalus free movement. Skatas had no such native intelligence. He was a fool's fool, and he stood in the sun sweating and determined to watch Daedalus the way a cat watches a mouse—sniffing at the edge of a hole, waiting, biding its time until the mouse fully reveals body and tail before pouncing.

Skatas believed the moment would come when he would advance himself by catching Daedalus at some activity for which the king would punish the mason and reward the soldier.

Daedalus knew the man was right and wrong. Such men lived in every kingdom. Their fate and future depended on the whims of their king. The little man's ambition might help him catch Daedalus at some treasonous act, but no advancement would come because of it. Not with this king.

And not on this day.

Taking action to escape or to oppose King Minos would have required attention Daedalus could not provide. Puzzles consumed his mind: his hands, the stone, Ikarus, the change in the flow of the stream from trickle to torrent.

The water, he knew, was captured in the mountains above. All water, from snow, from rain, from dew formed in cold nights, flowed into the earth and moved slowly along channels and underground cracks and sometimes even through the maze of caves he used as a workplace.

Water entered the valley of Knossos above the cascade. That water flowed year round, but it was never greater than waist deep, and never fast enough to push a man down except in spring when melting mountain snow and rain caused the swelling that flooded the farmlands below.

Below the falls, water flowed in volume—enough to bring barges up from the sea to the palace itself, enough that no man could cross without a boat, that no man could stand against the current without a rope. It flowed faster than a man could walk, and that meant that much more water came from somewhere.

"Do you plan to stand in the sun all day staring at the water?" Skatas asked.

"If needed," Daedalus said.

"I do not," Skatas said. "Finish your business here."

"You plan to tell the king that you bade me ignore this threat to his palace?"

Skatas turned and looked around for the threat.

"Leave him alone," Yorgos said from his shade. He drank water from a goat skin he had brought. "A rat's thoughts cannot match the mind of the mason."

Skatas turned on Yorgos. "Trickery is a liar's tool. I trust my blade, and I can cut out his tongue. That makes me his match."

Yorgos shook his head slightly, like a father disappointed in a small child. "You believe destroying holds greater power than creating?"

Daedalus let the two argue. He held his hands in front of him and let the sunlight warm them. Remembering his vision of the old woman's hands, he remembered to take pleasure in the sun on his flesh. He wondered if the queen's gift might be a gift after all. To test it, he knelt beside the cascade, placed his hands in the cold water, and touched the flat, bedrock marble below the surface.

He closed his eyes.

Behind him, the men bickered—Yorgos, cool in the shade, taking pleasure in making Skatas angry, agitated, and hotter.

Daedalus let his thoughts move outward through his hands and into the cold stone beneath the stream. The stone became his body, his skin, his bones, and his flesh. Like a man touching his ankle to check for swelling, he touched the folds of layer upon layer of stone beneath the ground, layers of sand laid down on the ancient bed of a sea that became land long before man walked the earth. In folds of rock, he found the answer to the mystery of the stream.

Two streams flowed here—one above the stone streambed and one below. The one above fell off a cliff. The one below welled up from below the rock riverbed to embrace its falling sister. The water in both came from the hills above, but the one below was much broader, much deeper, and carried the heart's blood of the stream that fed the people of the Palace of Knossos, joined the Kairatos, and eventually carried ships from sea to the palace piers and back to sea again.

Daedalus stood. He walked to Yorgos and sat beside him in the shade.

Skatas abandoned his pointless battle with Yorgos. He looked from one man to the other and finally realized that he stood in the hot sun for no reason except to entertain others. He glared at both men for a moment before he followed their lead and settled himself in the shade.

"In legend," Yorgos said, "this is a flow of abundance—a gift to us from Rhea to the Kouretes warriors for having protected Zeus from Kronos."

"Not a gift for us." The little guard's voice held deeper contempt for Yorgos than normal.

"No," Yorgos said. "Not for *us*. Your forefathers were not Kouretes."

"Nobody's were," said Skatas.

"Legends," Daedalus said. "They often have some truth in them. Please, while we rest, tell me the tale."

Yorgos smiled and handed Daedalus the water skin.

Skatas reached for it.

Yorgos pulled it back. "The mason bade me carry this for him. *He* was wise enough to bring water for both of us." Yorgos more carefully and pointedly handed the water to Daedalus.

Skatas frowned, and his gaze held new hatred for Daedalus.

Daedalus drank.

Yorgos said, "Zeus was born of Rhea by Kronos, and his mother sent him to my ancestors, the Kouretes, to protect."

"Ah, yes," Daedalus said. "And this little man comes not from your blood or from the strength of your people."

"No. He does not."

Skatas spat on the earth. "Who would want to be of the blood of cave dwellers?"

"So," Yorgos went on, "in return for protecting her child, she promised us that so long as our people lived in this valley and honored the will of the gods, the stream would flow tenfold for our bounty. And when she said it, the earth lifted up and split in two so that the stream of the water born of the sky above ground would flow over this falls and meet with a stream from the heart of the earth itself, a flow of her heart blood that would forever sustain us."

"Not forever," Skatas said.

"No. I suppose not," Yorgos said. "She said that when the time came that men of foreign blood came to rule this valley, when they corrupted the memory of her and her son, when they insulted the gods by destroying love and the gifts the gods had given them, she said that on that day the stream would return to the heart of Gaea and cease to flow."

"Stories." Skatas stood and turned a nervous circle in the sun. "Water is water. Stone is stone. The sun has addled you both."

Daedalus nodded. "Truth," he said. "Two rivers do flow here."

Yorgos smiled. "Truly?"

"Yes. Exactly as you said. One flows upward from beneath the stone. One flows over the top of the stone."

"Liar," Skatas said. "You can't know such things. No man can see beneath the earth."

Yorgos asked the smaller guard, "Do the walls of the Palace of Knossos shine in the summer sun brightly enough to make a man look away?"

Skatas tried to spit on the ground at Daedalus's feet, but he was too dry. "Mason's tricks. I know the fires of Helios hit the crystals and bounce away because they cannot burn the stone."

"The crystals that only grow beneath the ground," Yorgos said. "The crystals only the mason has been able to find, and that he has always found when they were needed?"

Skatas fell silent. He moved toward the shade.

Yorgos decided at that moment to stretch out and lay down. The big man did not yield even enough space for Skatas's sandaled foot.

Daedalus sipped the water and wondered where the power of gods and the power of men mingled and mixed so that neither could tell which was wielded by which. It was a new thought for him—a thought he would not have pondered at all before the gift of the queen.

Even then, he would not have believed the gods cared about the doings of men, but then there was Nikkis. When he thought of her spirit and her beauty, he could no longer doubt that the will of gods worked in the lives of men.

The two guards still argued, and Daedalus needed to get away from their bickering. He wanted to be truly alone, to stand next to the stream in silence so the ceaseless cacophony of thoughts in his head could slow, could take on the sound of stream and wind and grass.

He started upstream along the goat trail that climbed the rock face of the ridge over which the stream tumbled.

"Mason!" Skatas's shrill voice cut the soft sound of the breeze. "Halt!"

Daedalus froze.

"Let him go," Yorgos said.

"He'll run. The king will kill us both."

"That trail goes from here up to a cliff wall. There, the stream cuts between two canyons. Where will he run to? Let the man have a moment of peace."

"You're not in charge here."

Behind him, Yorgos's leather and armor clattered and creaked.

The little man made a tiny squeak.

"Okay. Okay," Skatas said.

Daedalus paused, but he didn't turn. He didn't want them to see his smile.

"If he runs," Skatas said, "it will be you tossed to the rats or trampled by the king's bull."

"You won't run, will you, Mason?" Yorgos asked.

"No," Daedalus walked on. "I just want to be alone for a moment."

"You see," Yorgos said. "He won't run."

Daedalus continued walking. Yorgos was right. Where could he run even if he wanted to? The upper stretch of stream flowed in a narrow canyon. Even if he climbed the narrow and dangerous goat trails out of that canyon, he wouldn't survive long in the highlands. He would have to come back this way. That meant passing Knossos and certain capture.

An image of Nikkis came to mind. He smiled. Somewhere in the highlands, she lived in a small village. For a warm moment, it was pretty to think that the gods might guide him to her. For a moment, he smelled her musk on the breeze and felt her touch on his arm.

It was silly, and he shook it off.

After climbing up over the edge of the rocks onto a more level path along the side of the stream, he encountered a boy who looked like Ikarus had looked at ten years. Except this boy had dark hair. The boy hunched over something beside the stream. The long, leather of a sling hung over his shoulder. One end dangled in the water, pulling against flowing ripples.

Daedalus approached close enough to see that the boy hunched low over a bird, a jackdaw.

The sling. The bird. The boy.

Daedalus understood, and a sadness grayer and darker than the death of a bird should create crept into his heart. The grayness and darkness came from the death of a bird, the need of a boy to kill, the darkness of a culture that would teach a child to value the power of death. Even more than that, the sadness came to him because he was much like the bird. His life was a toy to be played with by a king until broken and discarded.

The boy heard his approach and turned his head.

Daedalus saw the tears in his eyes and the hopelessness in his face. Suddenly, the idea that the boy had killed the bird seemed absurd.

"What saddens you, boy?"

"I think it will die," the child said.

"What?"

"This bird." The boy stood. Cupped carefully in his hands, he held the jackdaw. The bird's plumage glistened gray and blue-gray in the sun. Its eyes were wide with fear. The boy's gentle grip held the bird's wings against its sides. "A hawk hit it. Right out of the sky, but the hawk didn't get it. I chased it off."

"Perhaps it's only stunned."

"No. It drags its wing. That's why I could catch it."

"What's your name, child?"

The boy stiffened. "No child works the herds."

"I beg your pardon. You have become a man sooner than I did. I was not allowed to work the herds at your age."

The boy relaxed. "Mikos," he said.

As gently as he could, Daedalus said, "Mikos, consider that it might be better if the bird did die. He might suffer less."

"No!" Mikos turned his narrow shoulders away from Daedalus to protect the bird.

"It's all right, Mikos. I won't hurt it. I promise. It is your bird, and you will say what must be done."

"I know you," Mikos said. "The king's mason. You'll kill it. They say you can cut a mountain in half with a hammer."

"Who says such stupid things?"

Mikos looked down at his bird. "Just they," he said.

"Well, *they* are very foolish people." Daedalus smiled for the boy's benefit. "I would need a chisel to go with my hammer."

The boy looked up. Light sparkled in his eyes. He returned the smile.

"You know," Daedalus said, "I have studied birds. I have even tried to build wings that imitate them. Such amazing creatures—delicate and so strong at the same time. If you let me see the bird–"

The boy's smile disappeared. "You won't hurt it?"

"No."

Mikos held up his bird. Daedalus very gently cupped the boy's hands and received the panting animal.

Fear.

Daedalus almost dropped the poor creature.

Terror. Heart-pounding, rib-aching, can't move terror came to him through his hands. It crawled up his arms and tried to grab his heart and tear reason from his head.

"Your bird," Daedalus stammered.

Mikos stared at him. "You're shaking."

"Your bird is very scared."

"You'd be scared too if a hawk hit you and then a giant came and scooped you up."

The truth of the statement was undeniable, but the boy didn't know the half of the fear the bird held in its heart. *Pain.* It feared the hawk's talons and beak. It feared the crush of Daedalus hands. It feared that it would never fly again. It feared the loss of freedom and flock.

Daedalus began to cry. He tried to calm the bird, to give the bird his own confidence, his belief that there would be another breath, a time when pain and fear did not rule the moments of life.

Nikkis came to mind. He saw her there, felt her in his heart as if she stood next to him and rested her warm hand on his forearm.

The bird calmed. Daedalus opened his hands.

"No!" Mikos cried. "It will try to fly. It will hurt itself!"

The bird shook itself then settled into the safety of Daedalus's hands.

"Zeus," Mikos said.

Daedalus closed his eyes. "Shh," he said. "Let me listen to the bird a moment." He let his mind open to the feel of the feathers on his palms, the tiny prick of claws in his flesh. He lifted a finger and stroked the bird's wings. Smooth feathers, warm flesh, pulsing blood, light bones—hollow bones. A shoulder, twisted but not broken—pulled back when the hawk had struck, but the bird would fly again if it survived long enough.

He stroked the bird's shoulder to sooth the animal. When it seemed calm enough, he lifted the wing tip and gently but firmly pressed the tiny shoulder back into position.

The bird turned its head and pecked half-heartedly at his fingers.

By the queen's gift, he knew both the bird's desire for help and the animal's pain.

Daedalus opened his eyes. "Mikos, I think your bird will be fine."

As if his words were all it needed, the bird tested its wings.

Daedalus gasped. In that small flap and flutter, he found the secret he'd been missing. Such a simple secret guarded by jealous gods for so long—the rotation of the shoulder, the rise and scoop, and push of the wing. The shape that made the wind flow over the wing and pull it upward, higher. Hollow bones. Long feathers over locking joints.

His metal rods were too rigid, too hard and heavy. His joints too loose and without locks to allow for effortless glide.

Daedalus laughed.

The bird flew.

"You fixed it!" the boy said. "You healed the bird."

"No," Daedalus said.

"Yes," a woman said. "Go back to Titan and the herd, Mikos."

Daedalus spun. Nikkis, wearing linen wrapped at her waist and pulled beneath and under her legs then tied at the waist again, stood beside the boy.

"You saw, Nikkis?" Mikos asked.

"I saw," she said. "Now, go."

Mikos looked up at them—first one then the other. He giggled and blushed.

Nikkis gave him a stern look.

Mikos forced a frown, and he ran. He looked over his shoulder several times, and he hit the dangerous goat trail up the canyon wall like a mountain goat. He bounded upward and across the face of the canyon like he'd spent every day of his life playing there.

Daedalus imagined that the boy might have. Certainly, Mikos and Nikkis were much more familiar with the lay of this land than Yorgos or Skatas.

"You healed the bird," Nikkis said.

The suspicion in her eyes broke his heart. "No," he said. "I only put its shoulder right."

Her head tilted to the side. A wry smile lit up her face. "That's not healing?"

He imagined it sounded very strange. He returned her smile.

"Your guards will wonder where you've gotten to," she said.

"You know about them?"

"I watched you climb the valley." She gestured toward the top of the canyon wall. "From there, we can see everything from here to the sea."

"And anyone who comes toward the high country."

She nodded. Her smile left, replaced by a puzzled expression. "But," she said.

"Yes?"

"I couldn't see that it was you. I didn't know it was you until I…." Her words fell away. She shook her head. The fire of Helios flashed in her hair.

"I felt you," he said. "Before I helped the bird, I was drawn up the canyon."

"I felt you," she said. "We do not usually bring the herd to the highlands above."

"Something happened to my hands," he said.

She stepped close and took his hands in hers. As soon as they touched, he knew her the way he had known the bird. Inside her, he touched her fear, her suspicion of men, her loneliness.

He pulled her close.

Their arms snaked around one another. She pressed near to him, and he tried to make her part of him, to bring their two skins under such heat and pressure that they would become molten, mix, then cool as one. As he stood there, her fear fell away. Her loneliness, and his, dissipated like a morning mist burned away by the fires of the golden chariot.

They might have stood forever like two statues cut from one stone and entwined in a reverie of love for all of time, but a call echoed in the canyon. "Mason!"

"What magic, this?" Nikkis whispered into his chest. She turned her face upward to his. Tears streaked her face. "What have you done to me that I can find you in my dreams and feel you from the tops of the mountains? How can you undo me like this with your touch?"

He asked, "How can I know you are nearby simply by closing my eyes? Some new magic moves in me."

"The queen," she said. "The new magic?"

"Nikkis," he whispered. "I felt these things for you before the magic came to my hands. Now–"

"Mason!" Yorgos cried.

"I told you he would run," Skatas said.

"Go, Nikkis."

"No."

"Please. I must go back. These men will die if I do not."

"I will die if you leave."

"I promised I would come to you." He gently pushed her away. "I will keep my promise." Breaking their touch was like cutting away his own arm. He felt like she should still be there, still attached in some way, but she was not.

Nikkis stumbled away toward the ridge. Like Mikos before her, she looked back at him over her shoulder. Then, she turned away and each step she took became more stable and graceful than the one before. Each step moved a little faster than the last until she ran with the fast, low gait the mountain people used to tirelessly cross great distances. Only a few heartbeats passed before she melted into the stone and scrub like she had never been there at all.

He closed his eyes and breathed deeply. He found her in heart and mind. She stood very still in the shadow of a small, twisted tree. Her skin and clothing blended with the background so well that as long as she didn't move, she would not be seen.

He opened his eyes. "Nikkis," he whispered.

Finally, he turned and headed downstream toward his guards. "I'm here," he called.

"Ha!" Yorgos said. "He didn't run. You owe me an amphora of raki." A beefy thump followed by the surprised squeak of Skatas made Daedalus smile.

~~~

Days and weeks passed, and only small finishing touches remained to complete work on the palace. Daedalus, Master Mason, designer of the Great Palace of
~~~

Knossos, was a prisoner no more. Minos had moved him and his son into the palace where, so the king said, they would be more comfortable—where, Daedalus knew, the king could keep them watched and safe from wandering off to the docks again.

But Daedalus had built the palace, and the queen had told the truth. The gift was helpful in gaining freedom and taking Ikarus off the island. Of course, not even her goddess could have given her a vision of how he would use the gift. He counted himself blessed that he had come across Mikos and his bird only a day after receiving the queen's gift.

That bird had given him hope. It may have saved his life and the life of his son.

If he had not touched that sad little creature, the means of his escape would have been poorly built. Certainly, the idea had been good. He had built well, and he might have survived his tests; ah, but in the end, he would have died. Worse, he would have killed Ikarus.

He rose from his bedding and from the woman the king kept with him as a spy and the queen kept with him as a double spy. He had mixed just enough extract of hanging cups flower in her wine so that she would sleep the night away. He had thought perhaps he should make love with her to quicken her heart and deepen the effects of his potion, but Nikkis lived in his heart, and he could not bear to place his hands on another woman.

Still, he could not send the courtesan away. Sent away, she would create suspicion. Sent away, she might come to harm for failing to seduce him. He liked the woman, and he wished her no ill. They had come to understand one another, and he believed her relieved to be with a man who did not hunger for her, even if only for a while.

She stirred.

He made a silent prayer to Poseidon that she would not stir so much that she could see him go or know the path of his leaving. She settled back into her sleep, her breathing deep and steady.

He moved as silently as he could. He would take nothing with him—not even his tools. The less he carried, the better his chance of escape. He would take only one thing of value, Ikarus.

Daedalus had built the palace, and he had designed the flow of air within the walls and the flow of water beneath the floors. He had also built in certain tools of statecraft. Some, the king or queen knew about. Some were known only to Daedalus.

He found the corner of his room and took care to place his entire weight on one floor tile. Weight in the right place, he pressed inward on the correct stone at the back corner of his chamber. Finally, he moved to press his weight on the correct edge of the wall.

A vertical crack along the center of the corner appeared. Before opening the gap more, he checked the young lady by the dim, flickering light of his oil lamps.

She still slept, and he had to admit that her beauty belied her treacherous heart. In the morning, he imagined she would flee the palace rather than face the wrath of both the king and queen. In fact, he expected it might be a full day before his absence was discovered. If luck favored him, two.

The dark paths of his escape were designed with unseen exit, entrance, or hidden observation in mind. He knew them in his soul, so he moved through darkness, blind but certain. When he slipped into his son's chambers, he paused to let his eyes adjust to the low light of a low-burning lamp.

Ikarus slept.

Like Daedalus, the boy slept with a spy.

Daedalus had made sure the woman with Ikarus would sleep well too, and he had no worries about her constitution. Youthful Ikarus still lived in his appetites. He would have seen to the quickening of her heart.

Daedalus roused him, one hand over the young man's narrow jaw. Ikarus, of the two of them, was better built for the task at hand. Ikarus had the long, lean strength and stamina of his mountain-raised mother. Daedalus was, and had always been, a mason, and he had the broad shoulders and powerful arms that a man who lives by the hammer eventually grows. Strength and cleverness had done much for him, but in the night ahead stamina would mean survival.

His powerful hands saved them both when Ikarus tried to cry out.

"Silence," he whispered.

Images of confusion, lustful memories, pride, fear, and relief at recognition rose from the flesh of Ikarus and into Daedalus's hands. Daedalus gasped.

Ikarus recognized him and nodded.

He pulled his hand away lest his son's confused thoughts and feelings overwhelm him.

"Father." Ikarus looked at the sleeping girl. "What…what are you doing?"

"We leave, Ikarus."

"Now?"

"This moment. We leave. We will be free and gone before the king rises and the queen's acolytes dance before the rising sun." He lifted the lamp from his son's table and led Ikarus into the dark corridors behind the palace walls.

The secret ways beneath the palace had been laid by the hands of Daedalus himself, and no record of them remained in the king's treasure vaults in the darkest, coldest cellars of the palace and hidden beneath the pithoi, the jars of olive oil and wine so large a man could be drowned in them. No record of the hidden labyrinth existed anywhere, neither in clay nor on Aegyptian papyrus.

Only Daedalus knew the ways from the palace to the high, white mountains not so far from the caves where Zeus had been hidden by Rhea and protected by the Kouretes, and when he had returned to the mainland, he hoped to find friends in courts—friends that envied what he had built for Minos—friends that would return with him and put an end to the cruelty of this king who had betrayed gods, murdered men, killed children, and treated women like cows in his herd.

Father and son passed from cut-stone corridors into caverns, and the caverns twisted and turned beneath the highlands above the palace.

After several hours of dark travels, Ikarus said, "We are lost. The maze of caves is endless."

Daedalus smiled in the darkness they traveled, keeping his hand on the wall of the cavern tunnel, keeping Ikarus near his back, keeping good trim on the wick of his lamp. He smiled because he knew the younger man to be clever and resourceful but prideful as well, and it had taken the boy nearly half the night to finally show he was uncertain about the path his father had chosen.

"Here. Look," Daedalus said.

The narrow, twisted gap opened into the mountain workshop where he had built the bulls. Daedalus led Ikarus through the secret, inner caverns the boy had never seen. There, they came to the mouth of a cave that opened onto mountain scarps.

Daedalus said, "It has been too long, my son, since we have seen the night sky through the eyes of free men."

White fire, stars, turning in the ancient heavens and marking the nights, the months, the years Daedalus had been a servant for this or some other king, spun above them.

Ikarus gasped and stared at the sky.

"You have been very busy in the nights," Daedalus said, "You have not had a good place or a reason to look up and see the will of the gods painted in the night sky."

Ikarus said, "I will bring Cosima here. This will ignite her passions."

"No. We're leaving. This sky will be the roof of the palace in which we live from now on."

"Father, you make poor jokes." He gestured at the shadowy, pre-dawn valley stretching out from the base of the cliff. "We are farther from the coast than we were at the palace. Even if we went back and made our way once more to the river, we have no boat. How can you hope to leave?"

"We fly."

Ikarus laughed.

Daedalus moved back into the cavern. There, he pulled linens back and away from one wall to uncover the wings he had begun building in secret while building the bull and heifer. The wings he had snuck away to rebuild after learning so much from Mikos's bird.

Ikarus stared. "Father, you're mad. You *do* mean to fly."

Daedalus began to arrange the straps and stirrups and pads.

"All these years," Ikarus said, "I thought it just talk. I believed this dream of flying was only one of your thought games, a diversion to sharpen your wits."

"It was that," Daedalus confirmed. "Now, we see how sharp my wits have become. The wings are made, and we will use them." He lifted one set of wings and hung them on a hook set into the stone. "Stand here with your back to this pad. I will strap you into them."

"It's a word game. Father, it's only a game—a way of thinking of new things."

"This *is* a new thing." Daedalus took his son's shoulders and tried to turn his back toward the wings. "We must go quickly."

Ikarus resisted, still staring. "There were days when I believed you thought it possible, but–"

Still holding his son's shoulders, Daedalus made the boy look into his eyes. "But you never believed I had built them."

"The gods cannot let men fly."

The boy was scared, and they didn't have time for scared. Gently, Daedalus said, "The gods let men sail, ride horses, weave, make metal. They let the Phoenicians dye clothing purple."

"But–"

"You don't believe they can work."

Ikarus affirmed his doubt with silence.

"Think of all the things we have built, my son." Daedalus put a palm to the boy's cheek.

The boy glanced at the earth then nodded.

"We can fly, Ikarus," Daedalus couldn't keep the joy from his voice.

Ikarus looked up. "You have done it?"

Daedalus sighed in relief. Curiosity had broken the boy's fear. "I have built the wings and watched hawks, eagles, and black kites. I have soared on wings above this very mountain, and I have turned circles with vultures."

"No." In the lamplight, Ikarus's eyes were wide, dark coins set into his face.

"Yes."

Ikarus shook his head and backed away from his father. Hope and excitement warred with doubt in the boy's face.

"I will show you." Daedalus said. "Help me. Be quick. When the sun first comes to us and strikes this face, the dark stone below will warm. A wind will blow up this rock face to lift the soaring birds into the sky. We must leap into the sky with those birds, or we are lost."

Ikarus at least pretended to trust long enough to be fitted into the apparatus and listen to his father's instructions, but Daedalus knew only one thing could prove to his son that his father had not gone insane.

He hung his own wings on the hook then strapped himself in.

From their high vantage, looking out over the hills and along the coast to the east, they watched the sun split the distant sky from land and sea. Daedalus waited while Helios rode upward, imagining first light now pouring inland and waking the townspeople of Zakros, Gournia, and Malia. The fire of the chariot burned the air of the island of Crete and brought him the first breath of the gods—the first rising wind from the valley floor, the wind that called hawks and black kites to wing and to sky.

Burdened by the apparatus of flight, Daedalus waddled out of the cave and onto the ledge.

"I beg you, Father. Please, do not do this. We can return to–"

Like a hawk, Daedalus leapt from his perch.

Ikarus screamed.

Daedalus fell toward the valley floor.

His son's screams grew thin behind him.

He had watched the hawks and kites do just what he did now, and he knew that from above it looked like he plummeted and nothing could turn his fate away from the rocks below.

Halfway between his son and death on the rocks on the valley floor, he pushed his legs against his stirrups and used that leverage to power the push of his arms—long, toothed rods slid over rolling gears to lift, roll, and flap the wings. The joints locked. The wings snapped rigid, cupping and gathering warm air rising from below.

Daedalus shifted his weight and turned into the sun. He soared along the ridge below Ikarus, and the wind lifted him as easily as it lifted terns and hawks. He turned away from the ridge and back until he soared along the ridge in the other direction. The breath of the gods lifted him up until he flew high above the head of his son.

Wrapped in the awkward looking apparatus of flight, the boy stood flat-footed and staring up at his father.

Daedalus could not help it. He laughed. He rose higher, and he took a moment to look down on the hills and valleys, on the trails and goats.

A flash of light on the next ridge toward Knossos caught his eye.

There, far along the hill slope and now below him, arrayed and armed and armored, marched a ten-man squad of king's soldiers.

He turned hard away from them and soared over his son. "Hurry!" he called. "Leap like you are diving into water. When you have fallen halfway, kick into your stirrups! Push the bar with your arms! Together, push and kick!"

Ikarus stepped to the edge. He looked down. Then, he looked upward. Fear and awe mixed on the boy's face.

Daedalus turned again.

The soldiers had drawn nearer. They pointed at the flying man.

They called out to him by name.

The luck he had hoped for died. They had discovered him missing, and they had somehow followed him or found him, or, perhaps, the gods had merely willed that he be seen and known.

It didn't matter. The why of it and the how of it would only lead to his ruin.

"Soldiers!" he screamed. "Jump!"

The soldiers moved onto the nearer ridge trail.

Ikarus stood still.

Daedalus screamed and turned and careened in the sky.

In only a few heartbeats more, the soldiers would move along the ridge to a point where they could see the cavern mouth and Ikarus on the cliff.

"Jump!"

Like a fledgling hawk, Ikarus jumped.

Daedalus turned his head downward, rolled his wings forward, and shortened them the way a hawk pulls his wings shorter to dive on a sparrow. He matched his son's fall to be near him, to coax and coach.

"NOW!" Daedalus called. "NOW! Kick and push!"

Ikarus kicked. He pushed. His grunt echoed from the cliff wall and brought relief to his father.

The great wings spread, snapped open, locked against the joints taught to Daedalus by the jackdaw. Leather, wax, tar, and feather caught air. The young man curved downward and outward, belly toward the ground. He leveled out over the dark stones and dry grasses of the valley.

Soldiers high on the hill screamed their surprise. Others screamed in fear.

"Now! Pull then push again!" Daedalus called.

And it was so. The great wings flapped.

"Again!"

The young man rose. He shifted his weight and worked his levers and stirrups as he was told. Soon, side-by-side, two men soared along the ridge line high above the king's men. Father and son flew like giant hawks looking down on workers in the vineyards. They rose and turned and lifted ever higher.

Ikarus laughed.

"Save your breath, my son," Daedalus called. "We have a long flight ahead of us."

"Go home, little men!" Ikarus called. "Go home and tell the king that Daedalus and Ikarus have flown away!"

"Don't taunt them."

"We can fly!" Ikarus screamed. "We can fly!" He worked his great wings. He flapped and worked to fly higher. "Tell your tiny king that the magic of Daedalus can break the bonds of any prison and the chains of any tyrant!"

"Let the wind do the work," Daedalus said, "Let the wind carry you! Rest, and let the wind work."

Ikarus kicked again and again. The wings pressed air. He roared with laughter.

"To sea, now!" Daedalus called.

As a pair, Daedalus lower, Ikarus twice as high, the two winged men turned outward over descending ridges. They flew to the north, letting rising, ridge winds carry them over land then out over the sea toward distant, mainland shores.

Daedalus called to his son, instructing while they flew. "Like the vultures and black kites, we must soar. Only flap the wings if we get too close to the sea," Daedalus said. "Soar like the vultures. Soar and save your strength."

"I am no carrion eater!"

"Come down, Ikarus! You fly too hard! Too high!"

"I am no peasant who takes the used women tossed off by kings!" Ikarus laughed like a child. He kicked and pushed and rose ever higher until distance made him a mere speck high above Daedalus.

Hanging from his wings halfway between the heavens and the realm of Poseidon, Daedalus feared both the wind-borne laughter of his son and the patient whisper of Poseidon's waves below.

The laughter stopped.

The waves whispered.

The tiny sound of a small twig breaking froze Daedalus's heart a moment before the long scream began.

He twisted against harness, wings, and air. He searched for Ikarus, and he found him. The boy was above him and falling. One wing bent back and upward, the other flapped pointlessly, pushing him back and around so he spun while he fell.

Daedalus's child called for him. "Father! Help me! Father!"

Daedalus turned hard. He pulled in his wingtips, trying to get beneath his son, to do something, to somehow, by impossible means, catch him.

The boy plummeted, calling, screaming.

He passed in front of Daedalus. For a moment, before the wind and twisted wings spun Ikarus away, their eyes met. His son reached out for him. The boy's eyes were wide with the terror of a child caught in a monstrous dream and hoping his father will come to wake him.

Helpless while the failed work of his hands killed his son, Daedalus watched and listened until the patient waves of Poseidon embraced and silenced Ikarus.

Daedalus turned in long circles, flying low, looking for his son through a weeping haze.

He circled over the place where his son had met the sea. The battered wings floated there for a time, twisted and crumpled. The waters gave no sign that Ikarus had ever been attached to the frail device.

Poseidon had taken his son.

Daedalus circled until the wings finally slipped beneath the surface.

Poseidon embraced his handiwork.

Helios drove his chariot, and he trailed the heat of his passing over the wings of Daedalus. A cracking pop and a shuddering vibration warned Daedalus that his wings might not be stronger than his son's. His wings were merely less abused.

His first thought was to join his son in the darkness of the cold water below. He deserved no better. He had led his son to his death; he had given the boy flight and brought him to the embrace of Poseidon. It was the price men should pay for pride and insults to the gods.

He would join his son, and he would pay Poseidon his due.

His wings creaked and rattled. He looked out along the edge of them, and he saw the fine papyrus layers he had used to anchor his feathers lifting up and folding back.

He closed his eyes and let the knowing of his hands reach out into his wings to feel the heat, the softness, the melting honey, tar, and beeswax he'd used to hold feather, papyrus, wood, and leather in place.

This was not the will of Poseidon. This was an attack by jealous Helios.

But who knew what contracts the gods had with one another?

Perhaps this was all the doing of the queen's serpent goddess, the goddess who had given him the gift of knowing through his hands—she who had lived in the souls of men long before either Poseidon or Helios had names.

Turning in the wind, he wondered if the queen's goddess had known after all that he would use her gift to try to fly. Perhaps she had sent him the power of his hands so he would hold a bird, so he would build wings, so he and his son would die.

Perhaps not the goddess at all—perhaps the queen had known. Her anger and deceit might have been that dark—that violent and corrupt. Perhaps his son had died in the games of court after all.

His wings shook and bucked.

A spread of feathers pulled free from the long taper of the back of one wing. They twisted off and away into the wind.

What matter if the forces against him came from his own heart or from the dark hearts of gods, goddesses, or queens? Ikarus was dead. All that remained of the boy was a father's memory.

His own death would not honor his son's memory.

He turned back toward the island. Feeling the wings through his hands, he carefully kicked and pushed, flapping, striving to gain enough height to move over the headlands and into the hills beyond.

With every flap, his wings tore and tattered more.

He held long glides, and he spoke aloud to both gods and the shade of his son. "Your mercy lives in destiny. If I join my son, I will be glad of it. If preserved to honor his memory in life, I will do so with sadness and gratitude. My hands to your will. This mortal man hangs by the work of his hands between birth and death."

But, being a man, his heart clung to life, and his mind, the formidable mind of the Master Mason, Daedalus, spun and worked to find the balance between gliding, flapping, and loss of feather and fabric.

Finally, he slipped silently over land.

He flew high enough to clear several ridges. He locked his wings and used the rising air over each ridge to gain greater height. He soared again, inland, angling back over land, past the cave from which he had launched, inland and away from Knossos even farther. He passed once more over soldiers, and seeing their faces, he knew they saw his.

Some faces showed anger. Some showed fear. Some showed awe. None showed friendship, kindness, or cause for hope.

He rode higher on yet another push from the breath of Poseidon. Only a perverse god would kill his son then help him fly high enough to get past the soldiers, yet the breath of Poseidon stayed beneath his wings and carried him higher, high enough to force the soldiers to travel long and far to catch him.

Inland. Higher into the mountains he flew—as far as his wings would carry him or until they would not.

He passed over herds and flocks. He passed over a woman in a long, linen shift. She held a long staff, and she wore curved knives crossed on her back.

She looked up.

His heart stopped.

Nikkis. A giant bull, perhaps her Titan, walked beside her.

She recognized him. Her smile came quickly and easily. Her beauty called to him. He craved her touch, her warmth, some safety and relief from his own grief.

Cold fear touched his heart. She was beauty and held his heart, but he had killed his own son. If she knew, she would hate him. There would be no smile for him. No kind touch.

Shame filled him. He had killed his son, and here, hanging in the sky, his thoughts were of this woman.

He couldn't let her see him, talk to him. He had to hide, to fly away.

She called to him.

Far behind, soldiers chased. They trailed many dolichos behind him. Perhaps ten ridges separated the soldiers from Nikkis, but he still could not land near her without bringing ruin to her. If her ruin did not come from the soldiers, then it would come from being with him.

He continued inland to lead the soldiers away. He flapped. Feathers fell. Wax flowed.

He soared onward, but he no longer soared upward. Failing wings gave ever greater power to the earth's promise to embrace him.

The ground came up. He flapped hard to lift himself, to bring his feet under him, to cause his wings to scoop air and slow.

The right wing twisted and made the sound of a woman's palm on a man's cheek.

The long, hollow metal wing bone bent. Like a drunken dancer stepping down from a table to a chair and finding nothing beneath his foot, Daedalus twisted in the air. He fell and rolled onto his back. The brilliant blue bowl of the heavens flashed above him. He thanked whatever god or goddess had given him his days that he had met Nikkis, that he had heard Ikarus laugh and cry, and that he could no longer be a danger to either.

Wrapped in his own wings, he crashed through the branches of an olive tree, crushed a stand of sage, and hit the earth like a clam dropped by gull on seashore rocks.

Pain burned his limbs and set fires in his skull. Dark billows of dream smoke closed around him. He knew only a moment of pleasure during which he believed death had come to him and he would soon be reunited with his son, bowing low before Hades.

~~~

Daedalus woke amid the rubble and splinters of his wings. His head throbbed. Molten bronze pain burned in his shoulder.

He opened his eyes. Bright sunlight stabbed at the darkness of his mind.

He closed his eyes, turned his head, vomited, and the dark clouds covered him again.

When he next opened his eyes, the lightning flashes of pain had become a distant, rumbling storm. Wreckage of feathers, Phoenician cedar, papyrus, leather, and cypress wood surrounded him.

He wondered how long he'd lain here. He wondered where *here* might be. He hoped it was far enough from Nikkis to keep her safe.

He tried to move his arm, to untangle himself from the apparatus.

The lightning storm of pain returned. His right arm would not work at all. His left arm was weak and badly bruised, but he managed to use that hand to free himself.

The gods had battered him. Now, they punished him with life.

The same gods, gods who set their plans in motion a thousand, thousand years before any man was born to see the patterns of their games in mortal lives, had condemned him to live.

To what end, he could not know. Perhaps he now lived only to grieve his son, to know that loss as punishment for his arrogance.

Ikarus had been right. The gods were jealous of flight.

He fought his pain to drag himself from the wreckage, the place where soldiers, if they had seen his fall, would first look for him.
~~~

Through thorns and over broken rocks, he dragged himself. Up-slope, because they would first look for him in the drainages, gullies, and ruts—places where the earth hid the bones of the lost and dead.

Up, he crawled, until he came against a wall of white stone, a rise of limestone the shape of a dolphin's fin. In the scrub and twisted tree landscape, the stone provided the only shelter he could see. He rested his back against it.

He slept. He woke. He slept again.

Perhaps a day passed. Perhaps three.

Finally, thirst drove him to keep his eyes open and look for water.

Across the contour of the ridge and tucked into a cut that made it invisible from any other place on the hill, he found a darker shadow hidden beneath large bushes. Bright green grass grew at the base of the bushes. The bushes meant water, and the darkness within the shadow of the bushes might mean water he could reach.

He dragged himself along the arid ground until he came into the thick of green grasses and brush. A small trickle of water, not even a full rivulet, seeped from the mouth of a cave hidden by the bushes. The mouth of the cave was large enough to let a man enter, and the water trickled away down a cleft in bare rock and disappeared into the valley below.

Here, he could hide and heal.

Daedalus crawled through the brush and into the cave. Inside, the cave opened up to form a small, shadowed room. In the center of the cave floor, a small pool held enough water for him to put his face down and drink.

Thirst slaked, he slept again.

Eventually, he woke with greater presence of mind and some strength. He used his own knowing hands to seek out the cuts and breaks in his body. With the clear, methodical clarity his many years as a mason had taught him, he went about the business of cleaning his open wounds. Finally, slowly, painfully, he built rock cradles to create the leverage to allow him to set the broken bones of one arm and one leg.

He gagged himself to stifle his own screams. He set each bone, then fainted, then bound the limb, set the next bone, and fainted again.

Pain left him swimming in delusions and fading in and out of consciousness.

He opened his eyes and saw only red dust in the entrance of the cave, like veils of red pulled over the light of day. Whether he had traveled to the underworld or the annual hot wind had brought the dust from Afrikae to settle in windless silence over all of Crete, he did not know. If the former, then he would soon see Ikarus. If the latter, then he thanked the goddess that had given him wings for her kindness in hiding his sins beneath desert dust.

When he next opened his eyes, he saw the darkness of a night with no stars in the mouth of the cave.

He closed his eyes tight, trying to clear mind and sight. When he opened his eyes, a bull stood in the mouth of the cave, a giant, dark creature with double-curved horns that swept forward and downward and could have skewered a man and tossed him aside like a leaf struck by winds.

He nodded a greeting, and he closed his eyes.

He did not know how long he languished in the little cave before at last opening his eyes and seeing clearly. When he did, he drank, crawled to the entrance of the cave, and by morning's first light found a stone on which to lay and warm himself like a lizard.

In the first days of his crawling and healing, he gathered herbs and berries. He set deadfalls and ate lizards and rock rats.

When he was strong enough, he made a crutch and hobbled his way back to his wings. Red dust covered their remains. He recovered a few spars, some netting, and some of the torn leather. These things, he used to trap birds and bats.

Weeks passed, and his bones became strong. The cavern became home—home and a shrine to Ikarus.

The cool nights of spring gave way to the hot days of summer. The heat of summer nights surrendered to the chills and rains of winter. Whether to torment his soul or to give him a gift of kindness, the gods sustained his rivulet and allowed his body to heal. By force of the habit of life, he brought in and stored foods for the wetter, colder months.

On foraging trips from time to time, he avoided groups of soldiers. They searched, but he couldn't be sure they searched for him. They might be looking for anyone or for anything—or they might be looking for a man who could give wings to an angry king.

Often, he thought of Nikkis. He wondered if a place existed in the world where such a beautiful creature could live without becoming the prey of some king or petty tribal tyrant. Perhaps, if she stayed strong, Nikkis could be safe in the hills with goats and sheep and bulls. He hoped that for her.

Perhaps hidden in a cavern, he thought. Perhaps, she might be safe in a cavern home.

He caught himself at the game of dreams. No matter where he was, she couldn't be safe with him. She deserved a better life—not the life of a poor man who limps from past injuries and who lives in a cave with the ghostly memories of his son's fall from the skies.

Nobody deserved those memories.

Nobody.

~~~

With the spring, Daedalus came to more fully believe that the fault in the death of his son was not Poseidon's, not Helios's, and not the queen's. The fault lay in his hands alone. What gifts the gods had given him, he had used to create the tools that took his son from the earth.

Within his cavern sanctuary, using his nets, he captured bats, held them, learned their secrets, and freed them.

Outside his sanctuary, he captured birds, held them, and learned their secrets.

Hollow bones.

Thin leather wings.

Locking joints.

Stretch and angle and cup.

He learned, and he decided to once more build wings to put himself truly in the hands of the gods. He would fly either to freedom or to his son. Either way, he would take away any possibility of wings for a king who would steal from the gods.

He traveled far from his cave in search of materials with which he could mimic the wings of the bats and soaring kites.

On a warm morning two months before solstice, he knelt beside an ancient and untended olive tree. In the shadow of the tree's thick and twisted trunk, he had found the carcass of a dead rabbit stripped of belly and bowel—likely by a wildcat.

The kill was fresh, and the skin was thin and strong.

He carefully lifted the skin. Holding it up, he waited for the queen's gift to give him knowledge of the strength of the rabbit's legacy.

A flash of light caught his attention.

Below, on rocky slopes between rowed olive tree shadows, sun glinted off bronze spear points and white bone helmets.
~~~

Soldiers searched the olive groves—three men to a row, three rows at a time.

Soon, they would break from the cover of the groves. If they searched for a man or woman, they would begin a methodical up-slope sweep of the rocky hills and crags.

No matter who or what they searched for, if they found him, they would question him.

As quickly and quietly as a lame man could, he moved from the shadow of the olive tree to the shadow of a boulder. He waited for the soldiers to move into thicker tree cover before he slipped to the shadow of a higher boulder.

He moved upward and across the slope, staying low, keeping to shadows, taking care never to let his silhouette break the horizon of the ridge.

Hobble and wait.

Peer downward.

Check their progress. Be sure none looked upward.

Scrabble from shadow to shadow.

Over and over, he moved. Over and over, until the soldiers broke cover, lined out, and began their own ascent.

He ducked low and tried to keep rock or brush between him and the searching men. Scrambling, crouching, trying to stay above them, to move unseen to the top of the ridge where he hoped to slip over the top. Once he put the ridge between him and the eyes of hunting men, he could stand erect and push his aching leg for greater speed.

The sun rose higher. Daedalus sweated, but he thanked the gods for the heat. He wore no armor, and his pursuers would wither within their rib-bone breast plates and tusk helmets.

Finally, he sighed his relief and slipped over the ridge's spine, where he pulled up short.

Daedalus stood on a white stone shelf. Only a hand's breadth from his foot, the ledge ended, dropping off in a cliff five times high enough to kill a man who fell—or leapt.

His new relief faded into the shadows of hopelessness.

No escape. They would be on him. They would question him. When he did not answer, they would beat him and drag him back to the king. There, if he would not bend his knee and beg to be allowed to serve, they would break his legs and force him to serve or die.

At least Ikarus was beyond this new promise of pain.

A king who would steal from gods would not rest knowing a man lived who could give him the secret of flight.

If soldiers could fly, then Minos's god, the long-horned bull, would have to give way to a new god, an angry, terrible, taloned eagle. Minos and his soldiers would look down on all the world, and it would be because Daedalus had tried to save himself and his son. It would be because Daedalus had loved and promised to leave and return.

In that frozen moment standing on the edge of the cliff, Daedalus realized that if the king and his soldiers could look down on all the world, they would find Nikkis.

The thought brought horror to his heart and determination to his mind.

He had to die.

And if he must die, he would die like his beloved Ikarus, pulled from the sky by the earth.

Standing at the edge of the cliff, he let the breath of the earth rising up the rock face caress his face and lift his wild hair. He stretched out his arms and touched the wind with his splayed fingers. Birds and bats came to mind. The memory of his first flight on dawn winds came to him—the fear of the leap, the rush of the wind, the moment at which wings spread and caught and held and lifted him skyward.

He would die, but he would feel the freedom of riding the wind for a moment before he found his end on the rocks below.

No one else would be hurt because of his work.

Nikkis would never be found by the likes of Minos.

He crouched slightly and closed his eyes. Knowing his last moment was at hand, he once more thanked the gods for the many beautiful things he had seen in his travels. He imagined the one most beautiful thing he had known. He wanted to die with that thought in his mind.

He saw sunlight on the wings of Ikarus—bright wings, still new and strong, skimming across the blue sea and rising. It was beautiful, but he feared to see more, feared he might see the terror and pleading in his son's eyes again. He wanted to let go before that.

The form in the wings turned to look at him. It was not Ikarus.

The wings belonged to Ikarus, but the body attached to them was Nikkis. She flew in wings made by Daedalus, and she laughed, and the wind danced with her hair, and the golden rays of the sun shone from her skin.

He wished he could see her one more time before he died.

A shrill whistle broke the hiss of wind in his ears and forced away the growing image of Nikkis under wing.

Again, the whistle.

Daedalus opened his eyes and searched the curve of the parched ridge line for the source.

Off to his right and upslope from him, beyond where the cliff curved inward and cut into a softer slope, a herd of goats poured along a narrow trail like a long line of soldiers moving in file toward some distant city. Occasional, ambling cattle flanked the goats like scouts.

Silhouetted against the sky, the head and horns of a bull appeared. The noble curve and forward sweep of long, pointed horns made the stone horns on the walls of the palace look foolish.

Daedalus remembered the face of this bull. He had seen it before—in a dream. No. He had seen it in the entrance to his cavern.

Certainly, this image of the bull was the one the king hoped for and failed in achieving—this vision of power, of muscled neck, powerful, flat head, and deadly horns. The glorious bull seemed to rise out of the ground, though Daedalus told himself that could not be. The bull merely strode forward over the lip of the ridge.

Behind the bull came a woman.

Daedalus swallowed a breath of wind. He held it for fear that breathing might make her disappear, for fear that he might already be dead or that the seasons that had passed had been a dream and he might yet be delirious and broken from his fall.

There, about to die, he found the meaning of life.

Nikkis was not just a woman. She was all women. Her skin shone paler than the bull's brown hide, but it glowed with life well-lived under a sun that gifted it with shades of dark honey. Where the bull had been merely a beautiful creature, this woman was the beauty that existed in the whole of life. She was the meaning of the rhythm of his heartbeat.

Her skin knew both the work of the field and the home. Her hair, though bound at forehead by a leather strap, tumbled over her shoulders in long coils of molten bronze and a glistening black that no sculptor's hand could ever capture even had he the skill to work in polished obsidian. The simple, linen shift she wore covered her breasts, belly, hips, and thighs—a much more practical attire than the bare-breasted dresses of the women of court, and more alluring for that.

"Eenay ohrayah," he whispered his respect for such powerful, divine beauty.

Daedalus looked downward. His end waited for him.

He looked at Nikkis, and though she had not yet seen him, he knew that he could no longer think of his end. He had to live long enough to speak to her—to, if she would only gift him thus, hear her voice again.

He held his open hands up in front of himself. He had always, the whole of his life, trusted his hands and their strength to protect him, to help him, to find a way for him.

He would trust them now.

He stepped off the cliff.

He reached.

He grasped stone and held, dangling above the precipice but hidden, he hoped, from above.

He glanced downward, and the vision of his sandaled feet dangling over nothing but talus, cactus, and brush gave him fear, and fear brought him greater strength.

Above and along the curve of the ridge line, he could see the woman that had inspired him to leap and live.

And she could see him.

Nikkis stared, eyes wide, mouth slightly open.

The bull snorted. The hissing grunt echoed from valley walls.

She looked away and whistled twice, very quick and sharp. The bull turned upward and back over the ridgeline, toward the searching soldiers.

Daedalus wondered at such a slight and beautiful creature's ability to control such a powerful giant.

Hanging there, burning pain slowly growing in his arms, watching the movement of beauty and power, hiding from the death of grief and the death of flesh, hoping for an impossible new kind of life, he remembered his lost wonder, awe, and curiosity.

The world was full of mysteries he had not yet seen, full of discoveries that would take a thousand lifetimes to find. Only living well could honor the loss of a son. Living well was the only vengeance a man could truly take against gods and kings.

She disappeared from his view. A new darkness covered his heart—fear for her.

Voices carried over the ridge to him. Men. Tired, winded men. They were no more than a stone's throw from his cliff.

They questioned Nikkis, asked her if she had seen a man, a large man with hands that could kill a girl like her, powerful hands that had done ill to the king.

Daedalus strained to hear, and he wondered at himself for straining to hear not her answer but merely the sound of her voice, the perfect music issuing from an instrument formed by the thoughts of gods.

Her answer came on the wind, and her soft voice caressed his wounded soul. The sound was a balm that gave him hope and brought new strength to his burning arms.

"No," she said.

One of the men made a very rude suggestion about such a beautiful girl alone in the hills. Another agreed. And another.

Daedalus struggled to pull himself up, to climb back onto the hillside and face spears rather than let Nikkis come to harm protecting him.

She whistled.

The earth shook.

Daedalus clung tight to stone. Gravel fell from above. He closed his eyes and shook his head to clear the dust and stone from his face.

The bull's movement carried his rumbling rage through the earth and stone.

A man screamed.

The clatter of spears and armor carried on the breeze. More men screamed.

A moment later, the gentle silence of the hill country breeze returned.

Nikkis whistled again, much nearer now.

He looked up. Against the purest blue sky of Crete, she appeared. She offered him a rope woven of linen, leather, and grass. Her eyes, golden brown and shining, like freshly pressed olive oil, looked down on him.

"Take hold," she said. "Titan will pull you up."

Gladly, Daedalus grasped her line.

She whistled.

Titan pulled.

Daedalus rose.

Modern Legends

Yorgos drove the police van that carried them up the winding, switchback road beyond and southwest of Knossos. As they got farther from the coast, they passed more motorized trikes—machines that looked like they had been cobbled together from cars, lawnmowers, and motorcycles. Nikkis's window became a cinematic scroll of ancient groves of thick-trunked olive trees, ordered rows of twined grape vines, and hectares of desolate, dry alpine terrain where low, green scrub mixed with white stone rubble and tumbling, slowly falling fieldstone walls that might have been a few years old or might have been placed by weathered hands before the birth of Christ.

Finally, the road turned to a narrow, dirt track that gave up pretending to be a road at all. The pavement gave way to broken stone and dust, and the road soon ended in a wide, flat turnabout. Where the road should have continued, a narrow, cobbled trail snaked upward into a maze of hills and scarps.

Yorgos parked the van at the edge of the turnabout. One side of the turnabout overlooked a deep gorge. The other nestled against the base of a steep ridge that rose to a sharp, stone spine against the sky.

Nikkis commented on the absence of guardrails to protect turning cars and walkers from the cliffs. "People drink. They make mistakes," she said.

"Why encourage people to be stupid by protecting them from themselves?" Andros said. "If they plunge to their deaths, they only do it once, and it warns others from such foolishness."

"In my country, we are kinder to the unfortunate."

He chuckled. "Your country is still very young."

Nikkis thought it better not to retort. She opened her door, stretched her legs out, and slid down from the van onto the broken limestone of the turnabout. Her hiking shoes gave her firm footing, and she took a breath of mountain air. The dry air reminded her of a dig she had worked in the American Southwest. And that air had reminded her of some vague memory, perhaps a dream, where the air was cool and dry in the morning and evening but could get hot enough in the day to make a person tired from merely walking and breathing.

The dreams were like that. She'd had them all her life, and the images and feelings sometimes slipped into her day, but she could never resolve them into anything more than fleeting feelings of experiences she could not possibly have ever had.

Like so many feelings, she had learned to ignore the passing dream images.

She inhaled again and smiled. It felt good to be out of the van, and the quality of the air, southwestern, dreamlike, or merely different than she was used to, invigorated her. Her legs wanted to move, and she hoped they would be walking up the cobbled path instead of down or up the steep slopes.

By the time Nikkis got to the rear of the van, Andros and Yorgos had already opened the double doors. They stood with heads bowed together like awed interns over a newly unearthed artifact. Between them, Andros held a military-grade data pad that displayed a topographic map. They ignored her approach.

"Avoiding the village is better," Yorgos said.

Andros shook his head. "No."

Nikkis asked, "Where is the dig?"

Both men looked at her like she had just stepped into their reality from another dimension. She began to believe they wouldn't answer, but Andros finally nodded.

"Here, Dr. Aristos." He pointed to a corner of the screen.

"That's not far." If she read the legend correctly, it wasn't more than ten miles from the parking lot.

Andros frowned.

Yorgos said, "For a jackdaw, it is an hour. Maybe less."

Nikkis understood immediately. Dozens and dozens of isobar lines, often running into and on top of each other, separated the lot and the dig site. A straight line would mean many climbs and many descents. In such mountainous terrain, they would make better time following contours along drainages and ridges.

Andros said, "These mountains are ancient limestone uplifts. You have this understanding, Dr. Aristos?"

She nodded. "What's our path?"

"This mountain," Andros went on, "is like the gods dropped a giant wad of mud on the earth. You have buttes and plateaus in your West. Yes? It's like that, but several thousand feet tall and rounded off on top. Mt. Psiloritis Geopark is just past the west edge of this map."

"Yes," she said. "I understand. I can read the map."

He ignored her and continued lecturing like she was a freshman undergrad. "The main drainage begins high and at one edge of the mound. It almost cuts it in half. As it comes through the mound, it goes straight for many kilometers east-to-west before curving northward toward the sea." He pointed to the ravine below the lot.

"I can read the—"

He interrupted. "Many finger drainages come in from both sides to join the main drainage. Between each drainage is a ridge."

"Yes," she said. "We can't walk up and down the ridges. I get it." Mustering all the sarcasm she could, she said, "It was lucky for me that a man came along to read maps for me on my other digs."

Andros looked up from the display. Shadow hid the man's dark eyes, but Nikkis took some satisfaction in the tight line of his lips.

"Of course, Dr. Aristos. I forget you are American." He touched a point high on the west end and north side of the main drainage. There, two finger valleys converged. "We will go here—to a village. In the morning, we follow old trails along contours to the head of the valley. There, we'll cross south and southwest along the back ridge that makes up the headwall of all the finger valleys. Eventually, we will go north and descend into this valley to the site." He tapped the screen.

In spite of bad experiences rubbing salt in male ego wounds she had inflected over the years, she flashed a triumphant grin and said, "That wasn't so hard, was it?"

Yorgos grunted, turned to the van, and busied himself with equipment.

Andros turned to his own light pack and slipped the data pad inside.

She turned her attention away from the men to the high-side edge of the turnabout. There, a rough-brick pedestal supported a perfect replica of a white, domed church—complete with bell arches and three small bells that swung in the breeze and tinkled out their own call to early sext—midday prayers.

"What is that?" Nikkis asked.

Andros spun away from his packing. "What?"

Yorgos chuckled and continued his work with his pack. Muscus joined him at the rear of the van.

Nikkis crossed to the little church. It was like an elaborate rural mailbox. It could have sheltered very large packages from rains and winds and whatever other weather might come to the mountains. The entire front of the church was a hinged door. On one side, an ornate brass latch in the shape of an odd little serpent with the head of a bull held it shut. "This," she said.

"Ah." Andros said. "Nothing. A shrine. Someone has erected it to honor a dead loved one."

"Somebody died here?"

"Perhaps," he said. "Or maybe someone just liked the view here, so their family erected this to honor them after they died. Either way, it's a sort of home for their soul in case it visits this place." Andros reached past her, unlatched the front of the shrine, and swung the face of the church outward. The gentle tinkle of the bells became a clatter.

"Don't," she said. "It must be personal."

Andros said, "See the serpent with a bull's head? Heathens. Local superstitions. Not even the sacrifice of Christ can shake the ignorance from these people." He held the door open against the breeze.

"Ancient beliefs," Nikkis said. "The bull and serpent had meaning here long before the Christian church ritualized blood sacrifice and cannibalism."

"Of course, Dr. Aristos," Andros said. He started to close the little door.

Nikkis's curiosity got the better of her. She leaned to peer into the little building.

Andros paused, holding the door open.

Inside, an oil lamp's small flame flickered, illuminating two clear plastic Coke bottles filled with colorless liquid and corked with wine corks. Beside the bottle lay a bar of chocolate wrapped in blue—the label, in Greek, said Health Chocolate. There was also a small plastic bottle of unopened mineral water. A gold-framed picture leaned against the back wall of the shrine.

The face that stared out at her drove all thought from her mind. She knew the face.

Daed.

"Dr. Aristos?" Andros said.

It couldn't be. The faded black-and-white photo was at least 50 years old.

"Nikkis?"

Daed hadn't even been born, she told herself.

He had never had a mustache or worn a fedora or a black vest.

She shook off the idea. The thin air was getting to her. They must have gained more altitude than she'd thought, but the man in the picture looked out at her with a very serious expression. He seemed to be concentrating, trying to see something important that might be small or distant.

Andros's touch on her shoulder made her jump away from him and the little church.

"Dr. Aristos, are you well?"

Nikkis stood straight. She almost laughed at herself for making up such things about a man who was likely dead before she was born. "Sorry," she managed. "You startled me."

"Yes," he said.

She gestured to the photo and asked, "Is he the man who died?

"Probably."

"And these things?" She pointed to the bar of chocolate and the flame.

"To help him. To feed him. To light his way in the afterlife. To remind him of his life in the flesh."

"And the bottles full of water?"

"Raki," Andros said. "Not water." He turned away from the shrine and headed back to the van.

Nikkis looked back to the man in the picture and wondered who he had been and who had loved him so much that they had built such a place and kept it nice.

She touched the door of the shrine and began to close it.

Muscus grasped the door and stopped her.

She started. She'd been so engrossed in the picture and intricate beauty of the little shrine that she hadn't heard him come up behind her.

He reached past her and grabbed the water bottle. "Hill people make the best raki," he said. He turned his back on her and headed to the van.

"Put that back," Nikkis said.

At the van, Andros and Yorgos had their backs to Nikkis and Muscus.

The little man strode away from the shrine, opening the bottle and bringing it to his lips.

In the time it took for him to bend his elbow and bring the neck of the bottle to the height of his chin, Nikkis bent, grasped a round stone, stood, and unleashed it with perfect aim.

The stone clipped the little man in the back of his neck.

The stone wasn't a deadly missile, but he dropped the bottle, yelped, cringed, and spun. Faster than Nikkis could see, Muscus's hand dipped beneath his jacket and reappeared with a pistol. For a moment, his eyes searched the hills behind Nikkis. Finding no other enemy, his dark eyes settled on her. They became black slits in the shadow of his heavy brows. The pistol turned toward Nikkis.

A thought came to her from deep in her mind where only dreams and suppressed secrets lived. *I haven't found him yet. Not yet. Not again.*

"No!" Andros's yell had the same effect on Muscus as a choke collar on a guard dog. He jerked. The pistol slipped back under his coat.

Still, Muscus's enraged gaze drilled imaginary holes through Nikkis.

"Put it back," Andros said.

Muscus picked up the bottle, corked it, and moved back to the shrine. He replaced it and slammed the door of the shrine closed. The little bells clattered. "I will dance on your grave, she-goat," Muscus whispered in Greek.

Nikkis almost cursed him in his own language, but she caught herself. This was no place for trouble. She gently latched the shrine closed and apologized to the spirit of the man who had been so well loved.

When she turned back to the van, she found all three men checking weapons.

"What's this?" she asked.

"We walk from here," Andros said.

"Through a war zone?"

Andros held a large, ugly and deadly looking pistol. He pulled on the spine of it, and it made a very decisive click. "I told you that you would not like this place, Dr. Aristos. You insisted on coming."

Nikkis knew it was true. She glanced at Yorgos. Stoic as always, he avoided her eyes by re-checking his pack and equipment. Beside the big man, Muscus looked up at her. His smile and wink chilled her.

Nikkis moved to put the giant between her and the little man.

Yorgos finished his fiddling and hoisted his large day pack onto his back. Andros gave up his suit coat for a dust-gray T-shirt and shoulder holster beneath a multi-pocketed photographer's vest. Muscus climbed into the rear of the van and busied himself in shadows where Nikkis could not see him.

"So, we hike along the contour of the ridge?" Nikkis asked.

"There is a donkey trail." He pointed to the highest edge of the turnabout. "It will take maybe two hours or so to walk to the village," Andros said. "We'll stay there tonight and hike to the site in the morning."

Nikkis nodded.

Andros called Muscus. The little man came into the light from inside the van. He now wore desert camouflage military fatigues and a black harness. He carried a very nasty little automatic weapon.

"Jesus," Nikkis said. "Is it that bad?"

Silently, Muscus trotted away and up the trail.

Andros walked after him.

Yorgos motioned to Nikkis to follow. He handed her a light day pack. "Locals hate police," Yorgos said. "We are safe but careful—for your sake."

Even in the hot sun, Nikkis's skin felt cold. She swallowed the acid lump in her chest. It was much too late to turn back, so she shouldered her pack and fell in behind Andros. Yorgos followed her. Her new nervousness was helped a little by the fact that she could see Andros and knew Muscus was ahead of him. Having Yorgos behind her didn't bother her.

She was a little surprised at herself. Normally, having a man walking behind her on a trail would have bothered her. After a few paces, she realized that she was actually glad Yorgos was behind her. Of the three men, he was the only one that hadn't insulted her or hit on her. She hoped that if weapons were actually needed she would be able to trust Yorgos to point his in the right direction.

Deep in thought, she watched the trail for a few paces. When she looked up, Muscus had disappeared. Nikkis was sure he was up there somewhere, and she even thought that he might be higher up on the side of the mountain, trotting along goat trails so he could look ahead and down on their path.

Within a few minutes, sweat poured down Nikkis's spine, and she was grateful for Yorgos's advice during their shopping trip. She had let him talk her out of her baggy chinos into sweat-wicking synthetic pants with zip-off legs to make shorts.

"This will let you adjust for heat," he said.

With Yorgos's approval, she picked a sleeveless sport top and a short-sleeved cotton button-down.

After a brief pause on the trail where she zipped off the legs of her pants and unbuttoned her shirt half way, she almost laughed at the memory of the big man's gentle influence. It was good that Andros hadn't been there. She would never have let him help her choose.

After fifteen minutes, the broken, twisting trail had also made her grateful for the steel-shank, light hiking boots Yorgos had so carefully tested for fit.

After twenty minutes, the contour-hugging trail rounded one of the many sharp ridge shoulders.

A man and his donkey blocked the trail.

At first glance, the man looked very old. As she got closer to him, Nikkis found something from his pale, brown eyes that suggested the strength and energy of a younger man. In the American West, she'd seen eyes like that on overworked, forty-year-old ranchers who looked seventy. Those same men could rope a calf, jump off a horse, and put the calf down in a few seconds.

He stood in the shade of a rock smoking a cigarette, holding it between thumb and forefinger, letting the smoke drift from his mouth up to his nose and then inhaling it once more into his lungs so that each draw gave him two full breaths of smoke. He wore loose, black britches and high, black-leather boots, and he appeared to be cool and rested in spite of the heat of the high, late morning sun. Life under the mountain sun had cooked the man's skin brown and dried his face to the texture of a hard raisin. Add the toll of cigarettes and the amount of alcohol everyone on Crete seemed to drink, and he might be much younger than he looked. Of course, after a certain age, it was hard to tell how old native Kritikis might be. This man might have been as ancient as the stones of the mountain, or he might have been merely forty. Whatever his age, he had been smoking all his life, and it was clear that he had no fear of cancer either from the smoke or from the sun. It was also clear from his glare and squint that he did not like tourists on *his* trail.

The stoic donkey, burdened by canvas packs, rested on the uphill side of the man. It appeared younger in the skin than the smoking man, but the donkey's dark eyes told Nikkis that it was equally old in heart.

"Is the trail clear to the village?" Andros asked.

Nikkis worked her way past Andros and held her hand out to the donkey. The animal nestled its nose into her open palm. She scratched the soft skin and flesh where its lips met its chin. The donkey shuddered with pleasure. The canvas packs rattled and clanked.

The man ignored Andros and smoked his cigarette.

"Rock fall? Other people?" Andros asked.

"Ask him if the donkey has a name," Nikkis said.

"He's one of the villagers. He won't answer our questions," Andros said.

"Does the donkey have a name?" Nikkis asked the man.

The man smiled at Nikkis but spoke to Andros. "For her beauty," the man said, "I will speak to you, *Fascist*."

The man's words carried venom. She glanced at Andros and Yorgos.

Yorgos stood straight. Nikkis caught the movement of his finger to the trigger guard of his weapon.

Andros held his hand out and closed it into a fist in front of Yorgos. She hoped Muscus, wherever he was, could see—and cared—that the old man was harmless.

Yorgos's finger froze, but it did not return to at-ease.

Nikkis wondered what grudge this old man could possibly hold against the police. Even if he hated the Turk and German in Andros, it didn't explain Yorgos's response.

He pointed his cigarette at Nikkis. "She reminds me of a woman I once knew."

"She is very beautiful, but she is American," Andros said.

"I think not." The old man took a pull on his cigarette. "What do fascists know of the people of Crete?"

"Excuse me." Nikkis said, hoping to interrupt the tension. "What is the donkey's name?"

"Virgil."

"Dante's Virgil?"

"Ours first," the old man said.

Nikkis laughed, and the old man smiled.

"Is it far?" she asked. "Did Virgil have to carry this load all the way from the village?"

"Not far. From here, only two cigarettes," the man said, "My Virgil is used to it. Every week, he carries broken tools for the Bull of the Mountain."

"Cigarettes?" Nikkis asked.

Andros said, "They measure walking distance in the time it takes to smoke a cigarette."

"Broken tools for a bull?"

"Local superstition. Leave broken tools and appliances in the right places in mountains, and a minotaur, a man-bull, comes and fixes them in the night."

"I know what a minotaur is."

Andros shrugged. "Of course."

"Where does he leave them?" Nikkis asked.

"You would call it a dump."

The old man coughed and spit into the dust.

"It's late," Andros said. "You, Nikkis, will need rest for tomorrow's work."

The insult heated Nikkis's blood. The retort rose to her tongue, but the old man spoke directly to her in Greek.

"Such beauty," he said, "should never have left our home. I thank my goddess I have lived long enough to see it return."

Andros tapped his skull to indicate that the old man was addled. In English, he said, "He doesn't understand how far away America is."

Again, Nikkis began a retort, but the man shook his head and chuckled. "Fascists have always underestimated my people."

"Ignore him." Andros pushed on past the old man, and the donkey. "Let's go."

Nikkis glanced behind her. Yorgos was preoccupied with the trail they had already traveled.

Nikkis kissed the donkey's nose. She whispered in Greek to the old man, "Thank you. I will remember your kindness."

He nodded, dropped his cigarette, crushed it under the toe of a black boot, and took up the reins of the donkey. As she passed him, he said, "When you see The Bull again, thank *him* for my kindness."

She didn't know what to say, so she nodded and followed Andros.

Hiking in silence, her mind worked obsessively on the things she had seen and heard. Muscus, in his fatigues, scurried from rock to rock somewhere above them and ahead. That little man respected nothing and no one. He would steal a drink from a shrine. Andros wanted respect, but he was hated by everyone he met, excepting men who worked for him, and she wasn't really sure about them.

The Linear-A script was real. That she was sure of. She was in Crete, which was a dream come true.

To what she did and did not understand, she added the old man who acted like he knew her, like he had seen her before, and who had given her a message to give to an imaginary minotaur. Nikkis dismissed his words as a local parting blessing of some kind.

The academic in her believed that the longer she was in Crete, the stranger her experiences became. Some, she could reconcile with her knowledge. Others, like the old man's familiarity, she could not.

Another part of her, a part she wanted to ignore, tried to ignore, reveled in the sunlight, the perfect colors of the stones, the bushes, and the grass. That part of her, in spite of herself, forced her to look up at the Mediterranean blue sky and sigh—sigh long and slow as if she had just ended a long day of translating, lit a candle, and settled into her favorite chair back at her apartment in the States.

The hike wore on. Small trails joined or split off from their trail, and Nikkis could tell from wear on the stones that each track had carried many thousands of sandaled or booted feet. The more they walked, the less tired she felt. In fact, she realized, since they had talked to the old man, her excitement had grown.

She was about to see her first mountain village, a village where no road had ever gone, where the only traffic that entered or exited was on foot or donkey.

It was all she could do to keep from sprinting ahead of Andros like a child on an outing with stern parents who could do little more than hobble along while she could run and jump and revel in the feel of wind and sun and the touch of her feet on the worn cobbles set on the mountainside over three thousand years ago.

The twenty minutes after leaving the old man seemed like an hour, but according to Nikkis's watch, it was almost exactly twenty minutes when they rounded the contour of the mountain and came into the shadow of a cleft between two great rocks. One, a twenty-foot spire, was pale and white and shone in the sun so brightly that Nikkis had to lift her hand to shade her eyes from the reflection. That spire seemed to guard travelers from falling into the deep, rocky gorge they had followed since just after they met the old man—a gorge that looked like it had never seen a drop of water. The stone on the uphill side was black but equally bright. It extended upward from the slope of the hill, a smooth, curving column that drew her eyes to look into the stone.

The deep, swirling translucence of the stone so fascinated her that she was between them before she realized they were statues—representations of stolid men in bone and tusk armor and helmets. Each held a long javelin, but the points pressed into the ground, each angled inward, point toward the trail and shaft across the body of its owner. For a moment, she wondered why the points would be down rather than held upward like other Greek statues she had seen.

Taking advantage of the shade, Yorgos leaned against the feet of the white statue. Andros leaned against the other. Both men sweated heavily. "The villagers believe these statues protect them," Andros said.

Nikkis broke off from staring at the statues. The two men looked tired. She nodded to Yorgos and said, "Would you like me to carry the pack for a while?"

Andros chuckled.

Yorgos unslung his pack. Muffled, metalic sounds came from within. He unzipped an outer pocket, pulled out a water bottle, unscrewed the cap, and offered it to Nikkis.

She ignored the water and looped an arm though the shoulder harness of Yorgos's pack and lifted. She nearly fell over. The pack was much heavier than she'd guessed. She grabbed with both hands and lifted through her legs and hips in earnest. She couldn't lift it from the ground.

She felt the amused stares of both men.

Silently, Yorgos offered the water again. She accepted and thanked him. Stoic, as always, he nodded.

Andros watched and waited until she had drunk her fill before he took the bottle and drank as well. He drained the bottle and tossed it off the mountainside.

Nikkis started. The casual littering reminded her how far from home she was, and it angered the part of her that revered the ancient history of the land of her ancestors. She was about to call out Andros, but she caught Yorgos watching her.

The man frowned, shook his head slightly, and shrugged.

The bottle tumbled down the stone face, bouncing, and spinning, and flashing in the sun. Finally, it disappeared into the brush and bushes that marked the path of seasonal or subterranean water along the bottom of the ravine.

"Well, Dr. Aristos." Andros gestured at the statues. "What do you make of these?"

Nikkis reminded herself she was out of her culture, and she forced herself to focus on the statues.

Because of their luster, Nikkis had assumed that the sculptures were recent, part of some odd Greek art restoration or improvement project. The modern Greeks were famous for such things, like the restorations at Knossos. Before she'd seen Knossos, she would have condemned restorations as a defiling of artifacts. Now, she was starting to see the value in education and in making the reality of the past more immediate to tourists who like water in bottles.

Given that, she couldn't understand placing monuments like these so far from benefit to the public.

She examined the stone more closely.

Fine, almost imperceptible pitting showed where rainfall and wind had eroded softer limestone pockets out of the raw, native marble. The stone had been carved long ago. She ran a hand along the smooth foot of the white statue. If it was ancient, whoever had carved it had known the stone so well that they had anticipated wear and weather. Rain and wind had actually polished the stone.

Almost breathless, she whispered, "An amazing piece."

Beneath the feet of the statue, Linear-A glyphs covered the polished block face—row after row of clear, sharp glyphs. Her first thought was that so much Linear-A out on an open trail had to be fake because nobody had reported it. Her second thought was that nobody had reported it because everyone believed it fake.

And at the bottom of the inscription, she found the lybris and the flower mark again. It shouldn't have been here—not on male monuments. She had been sure the lybris and flower suggested a feminine interpretation. Perhaps the symbol was merely a mason's mark and had no religious significance, a variation on the flowerless lybris that dominated the ruins of Knossos. In fact, this mark may have been the mark of an apprentice who had added the flower to his master's mark.

No. She could not believe that. *Silliness*, she told herself. Statues in such excellent condition could not possibly have been old enough to be contemporary with the inscriptions she had seen beneath the palace.

Just in case, she asked, "Were these statues unearthed recently?"

"No," Andros said. "They are interesting, are they not?"

"The mark here." She pointed. "The same as the mark in the tunnel at Knossos."

"Yes. And some of your glyphs, also."

"Never buried? You're certain."

He nodded.

"Then," Nikkis said, "they are much too young to be made by the same hands as the artisans of Knossos."

"Yes," Andros said. "Until recently, I thought these statues were mimicked work done after World War II—maybe earlier, but no more than a few hundred years old at the most. I never gave them a second glance. No one did. Now?"

"They are certainly older than a few hundred years. This style and level of skill are lost. Whoever did this planned for the weather pitting. He was a very clever craftsman." She caressed the stone. It warmed beneath her hand. She had the feeling that it arched toward her fingertips like a caressed cat.

"But the text?" Andros said.

Nikkis knelt on the cool, shaded cobbles. She put fingertips to stone and traced the glyphs, trying to recognize patterns repeated from other inscriptions she had seen.

"I don't know," she said. "The stone appears to have been carved maybe…." She paused. "Don't hold me to this."

"No, Doctor," Andros said. "I understand that this is only a preliminary examination."

"I'd guess from the wear on the edges of the glyphs and the pitting in the smooth surfaces, maybe a thousand years ago at the most. Maybe as young as five hundred."

"And, the Linear-A is genuine?"

"Five hundred to a thousand years old?" She shook her head. "You know better."

"I did. Now, I don't. That's why you're here. Every text I've ever read describes Linear-A as an undeciphered, pre-Doric Minoan script—as glyphs likely only understood by a select priest's caste. All known examples come from at least three thousand years ago."

Nikkis's fingertips lingered on the stone, tracing the last glyph, the signature mark. It was somehow familiar. She had a sudden unnatural urge to put her face to the stone, to press her cheek into the glyph, to kiss it.

The irrational feeling couldn't be explained by having seen the glyph before.

A chill crawled over her skin.

She was going insane. *Dehydration?* She ignored the absurd feeling and stood. "Do we have any more water, Yorgos?" she asked.

The man produced a new bottle, and Nikkis drank.

"Then, I read your article," Andros said. "I recognized these glyphs, the ones you posited as likely if your theories about the language were correct." He pointed to the stone: the stylized bull's horns over the circle shield that she had suggested might represent a priest warrior, the crossed serpent and circle that she had suggested might represent the maternal aspect of life-creation and goddess.

Nikkis wiped water from her lips. She swallowed. "It can't be right," she said. "A clever forgery, maybe. Someone found an artifact we've never seen, and they copied it."

"Perhaps." His tone told her he had other theories—and perhaps hopes. "Let's get to our lodgings, and then we'll discuss it." Andros continued along the path.

Yorgos hoisted his pack and waited for Nikkis to follow Andros.

Nikkis still stared at the stone. She let her hand trace the mason's signature again. "Who were you?" she asked in a Greek whisper. "Who the hell were you that you predicted the same glyphs so long ago?"

Yorgos tapped her shoulder. "Maybe he knew them. We walk in an ancient land of secrets and mysteries."

Startled, she looked up.

Yorgos smiled and nodded. "We should go," he said.

The last thing she had expected to encounter on this trail was a romantic ideal from a warrior giant.

She tore herself away and followed Andros, her mind reeling with possibilities, fears, and more than a few hopes of her own.

~~~

Andros called it a bed-and-breakfast when he spoke English to Nikkis. When he spoke in Greek, he called it something much less kind.

Muscus called it hell in both Greek and English.

Yorgos treated it like home, and Nikkis called it local color.

The frail, old woman who owned the rust-stained stucco and stone block building seemed to be made of sticks and weathered leather. At the warped-plank, blue-framed front door, she greeted Andros with a stern face and an outstretched palm.

After Andros paid her, she crossed her arms and stepped back from her sentry's position in the blue doorway. From the shadows, the old woman stared silently at the little troupe of outsiders.
~~~

When Nikkis stepped up to her and said hello, the old woman's wrinkled, oil-paper skin paled. Her chapped lips formed a little O and revealed gaps between stained teeth. She crossed herself then spit in the street.

Nikkis moved past her quickly. Inside, in the cool embrace of a shaded hallway, Nikkis asked Andros, "What was that all about?"

"They spit like that for luck and to drive away evil. Old women like her don't like western ways. Your shorts, unbuttoned shirt, and boots—and the fact that you look men in the eye—marks you as a fallen woman in this world. If you remember, even I mistook your American directness for interest."

She didn't like the way he smiled when he said it.

"American women have a reputation here," he added.

"As do Greek men," Nikkis said, "Everywhere."

"Perhaps both are myths." Andros led her down a dim corridor to a plank door. He handed her a key and opened the door for her. "Your room, Dr. Aristos."

He held the door so that she had to pass very close to him to enter. She took the door in hand to close it.

Casually, he held it open against her effort.

"We eat dinner in one hour," he said. "The old woman will cook for us. We will sit at tables in the street and enjoy the cooling evening."

She tugged on the door. It wouldn't budge against his grip. "And tomorrow the site?" she asked, more to cover her frustration and discomfort than to get information.

"Yes. Tomorrow, I will show you where we found the pieces."

She pulled the door once more. He smiled, deliberately holding it for just a moment. A sudden sense of just how far from home and friends she was transformed her frustration into vulnerability and rising panic.

Apparently satisfied by what he saw in her eyes, he released the door.

Too quickly, she closed the door and checked for a lock. The door had more than a lock. It had the deadbolt worked by her key, and hinged iron bars could be folded out and dropped into braces bolted into the concrete floor on either side of the doorway.

Partly to listen, and partly to steady herself, she pressed her ear to the door.

His footsteps moved away.

She wouldn't give him the satisfaction of hearing her lock the door. When she was sure he was out of earshot, she breathed deeply to steady her hand, put the key in the lock, and threw the bolt. She didn't want to take the chance he might come back. He had said that he understood that her directness was not interest, but she had met men before who saw refusal as a challenge. The incident with the door had not been the first little power game she had endured.

For good measure, she set the braces, too. Tired and safe, she took a deep breath, turned and looked at her overnight home.

Quaint, rural, and historical—a vintner might have lived there a hundred years ago. The room was white-washed plaster over stone and barely large enough to sleep, think, and pray. An olive wood, hand-hewn bed dominated the room. One edge of the bed pressed against the wall, and the spindle headboard and footboard each touched their respective walls. Over the head of the bed, blue wooden shutters covered a wood-frame window that held no glass or screen. Beside the headboard, two olivewood shelves, one above the other, supported the room's amenities. The top shelf held three candles. The bottom held a basin, pitcher, and a folded towel. A small nightstand beside the bed supported a golden candle. She touched the deep, golden wax—real beeswax. Beside it, she found a sleeve-box of Ohio Blue Tip matches.

She chuckled to see those matches so far from home.

Above the shelves hung an elaborate, triptych icon. The center image was a man the size of Yorgos. He was bare to the waist and from there down wore only a sort of leather apron. His skin glistened with sweat, and his muscles strained under the effort of wrestling a dragon in the mouth of a deep, dark cavern. The image to the left showed the Minoan priestess holding her serpents. The image on the right showed a bull's head with flaming red eyes.

Nikkis moved to collapse onto the bed, but the ornate hand-tatted duvet caught her eye and stopped her. The rounded, down mattress was covered with the most exquisite linen handwork she had ever seen. The bed linens were so beautiful she was afraid her touch would soil them.

She pulled the pitcher and basin from their shelf and set them next to the candle. After pouring, she splashed water on her face and set to cleaning herself.

While she stripped trail dust and the feeling of Andros from her skin, her mind jumped from image to thought to fear and back. The events of the week and day were a storm she wanted to calm. She had left her job in a fit of anger. She had traveled to Crete to work with a man she didn't like and wasn't sure she could trust, but she had touched ancient stones and glyphs. The job was real. The artifacts were real.

It was all impossible. It was someone else's life. Something was wrong with her—had to be wrong with her. She had even believed for a moment that she saw Daed's face in a shrine. That was impossible, and the certainty she had felt in that moment terrified her.

In the swirl of thoughts and feelings, the old man on the trail returned to her mind. He'd talked about returning beauty—spoke like he knew her.

The glyphs of her article came to her. Always, along with them came the mason's mark, the lybris and flower, as if it were a glyph she should have predicted, one that she knew but had simply forgotten to include in the paper. It was a common mark. The double axe, the open labia, the two triads… A thousand articles had been written about that connected triangle symbol.

But the flower? The lybris and flower triggered a memory, a shadowy, fleeting feeling in her the same way the light on the statues had, the same way the air at the airport had. There was something more that she was missing, that she should be able to remember.

Other memories chased away the glyphs, memories of Anderson and her father, of the ugly feeling that came from just being near Muscus, of the resentful desire she feared she saw smoldering behind Andros's dark, sardonic eyes.

She grabbed up the hand towel and wiped her hands and face as if a vigorous rubbing could scour away the haunting memories of the world she'd left behind and the confusing, overwhelming world she wandered in now.

She washed her hands, face, and legs, then she took off both shirts and her shorts, sponged herself clean, and finally toweled dry. Even then, she carefully tested her skin against the linens to be sure she did no harm to the delicate work.

Satisfied, she climbed over the bed to the window, reached out and pulled the solid plank shutters closed. The shutters had their own pivoting locking bar. She rotated it across the seam between the shutters and settled it into its wall-mounted cradles.

Certain she was as safe from intrusion as she could be in such a place, she let herself collapse into the mattress. It accepted her with all the caring of a mother's first embrace of a newborn, wrapping her in the smell of fresh linen washed in mountain spring water.

A little nap before dinner would clear her mind of shadows.

The light scent of melted beeswax lingered in the room. Her heart calmed. Her breath slowed. Her ever-reaching and searching mind still grasped weakly for thoughts she should have had, things she should think through, images she should pay attention to.

Behind closed eyelids, the memory of Daed came to her—his face lit by a shooting star. Eyes filled with lover for her, he moved closer. The storm in her mind and heart stilled. Nikkis slept.

~~~

In her dream, Nikkis watched herself and was herself in the same moment. The part that watched knew she would wake up and forget, and that part raged against the loss even while she slept and dreamed.

The dreams began before her earliest memories. While dreaming, she suspected the dreams had begun before she was born.

Her dreams had always been a refuge from her life of parents and teachers—and later colleagues and politics.

Refuge.

In dreams, she watched and was a Nikkis she'd never seen in the mirror. Certainly, Nikkis looked much like Dream Nikkis, but Dream Nikkis was stronger. She was stronger in ways that weren't about muscle, though Dream Nikkis had that strength, too. Dream Nikkis was a girl who had lived a life nearer the vine, as her father would have said—a life that included bare feet and hard earth. Dream Nikkis was a goat herder. She was a young woman, and all the young men and women of her village were goat herders.

And in the dreams, two things were always true—even in the new dreams, the horrible ones, the terrifying dreams that woke her in cold sweats and filled her with cold fears—the dreams that had started on the plane.

She loved a man. She loved a bull.

This time, she found Dream Nikkis lying in a fabulous bed made of silk cushions in reds and blacks. Precisely painted geometric patterns and spirals covered the
~~~

walls of her room. Along the ceiling at intervals, an elaborate flower blossomed in bas-relief.

She lay death still among the silks. A group of women had left her arranged just so—her hair long and flowing out over the silks, her head propped up and turned just so to one side, and her bare shoulders peeking up out from under the sheerest and reddest of silks, a red that she, a woman from a mountain village, had never seen before.

Her dreaming self watched and wondered what fabulous man she loved that he had such opulence in his life, that he could treat her so well. Such men certainly had never been a part of her waking life. This, her watching-the-dream self said, was why she loved her dreams so much.

The self she watched tried to move her head and could not—tried to lift a hand and could not. It was like the silk that covered her was wet wool wrapped around her to hold her arms, legs, and head in place.

It wasn't the helplessness of being tied to a stake and burned. That was another dream that made no sense. In that dream, helplessness and fear mixed with hope and love.

This was a different helplessness and a different vulnerability. No love or hope lived in this dream. Worse, both her watching self and her dream self fought rising panic.

She tried to scream for help, but her mouth only opened a crack. Only a drop of drool and the tiniest of whispers escaped.

The women had drugged her and arranged her like a doll.

Both of her minds knew it, and neither knew what to do.

When he entered the room, horror filled her.

He was a king, and he was not her lover. Her lover was a strong man, a clean-shaven man with broad shoulders and powerful hands, a man whose mind could fly through thought like a soaring kite on the high winds and whose hands could feel the delicate texture of a flower or the strength of the grain of wood or stone.

Daedalus.

Her lover's name was Daedalus.

Like the ship. The giant ship. Bright. Powerful.

Daedalus.

She wished for him—to hear his whispered love in her ear, to be wrapped in his powerful arms.

Nikkis. She imagined Daedalus's voice.

Nikkis, he whispered.

It was his voice. It came to her from the air that sighed through cracks between the stones of her room.

Nikkis, I love you.

This king, this oiled, bearded madman who thought himself a bull, who tried to live like a bull, who would never meet another man in battle save after his guards had gutted the opponent, strode forward, bare feet slapping at the stone, his black hair dripping olive oil, his fat lips and bearded chin making him look more goat than man. He strode forward, and he smiled. "This is my due," he said. "As your bull, I choose you this night from my herd."

I love you, Nikkis, the stones sighed, and those stones warmed beneath her pillows.

The king, Minos, tyrant of the island of Crete, the man who sent his bone-clad guards to kill and pillage as he pleased, lifted his kilt and took his member in one oiled hand. "I have brought you my passion, pretty little cow."

Dreaming Nikkis, watching Nikkis, now fully understood the hopeless, loveless horror of this dream.

She was trapped again.

She was trapped by a man who would rape her while she was drugged.

"Shake it off," she tried to call to herself.

Nikkis, the stones said. *I'm with you.*

"Daedalus," she mumbled to the stones through her drool. "Help."

I love you. The stones warmed.

The king looked down. He stepped forward onto one of her draped silks.

"Shake it off, Nikkis," she told herself. "Wake up!" She reached a hand into her own dream—reached for herself and took her own hand and slapped it.

"Aahhhh," the dream self, the drugged self, said. "Nuadasalus."

The king flopped down on the cushions next to her. He put his flaccid, oiled fingers—fingers that had not done useful work in years, if ever—against her cheek. "You will bear me sons," he said. "I will show the arrogant mason how a king creates the future."

Terrible desperation gripped her. She tried to wake, to leave the dream, but she couldn't.

Nikkis, she told herself, you earned your Ph.D. Stop this silliness. If you can't run, face it. Go into it.

The dreamer pushed the dream self aside and took her place. The dreamer took the body and sat up and pushed the king back. Surprised, the man tumbled onto the hot stone floor.

He jumped up and yelped. He landed once more on the cushions, this time on his knees before her.

"This is the pride and power of the Bull-King of Knossos, then," she said. "All my life, I have been told that the great king is a man who is honorable and powerful. Now, I see only a man who must drug women to bed them."

The king's eyes went wide. "Sorcery? Pasiphae? She has done this?"

"I do not know your wife," Nikkis said. "I only know the tales on which little girls are raised, and you are not a king worthy of my bed."

At this, the king smiled. His eyes became dark and predatory. His head tilted like a cat fascinated by a bug crossing the floor. From his curled beard, a tiny rain of oil dripped to the cushions. "You are of my herd, and I will take my bull's portion."

"You will not," Nikkis said. "This is not the act of a king favored by Poseidon."

The king straightened. "No. Not Pasiphae. She has no respect for my gods."

"I am Dr. Nikkis Aristos, and I would die before insulting my family by bearing your child!"

"You speak insolent gibberish." The king raised a hand to strike.

Nikkis pushed him hard.

Unbalanced, he fell back onto the hot stone floor.

He yelped like a kicked dog. He tried to stand, to lunge for her.

As if the stones of the palace lived, the floor bucked.

The king fell back and again landed hard on the stone. He jumped up, but the floor moved beneath him and knocked him down again. Like water set to rippling, the floor rolled upward and downward, the gaps between stones opening and closing.

The king sputtered through his mustache, rolled, crawled, and struggled to find footing. All the while, the hot stones burned him and he screamed.

Protected by her cushions, Nikkis smiled and laughed. "Run, little king. My lover comes for you!"

"Sorceress," he hissed. He scrambled across the hot, rolling stones and made his escape from her presence.

As soon as he was gone, the stones calmed, cooled, and settled.

Nikkis, the stones whispered, cooling to the touch, *I love you.*

"I hear you," she said. "Where are you? I need to see you. Come to me. Daedalus, please come to me."

In her dream, she knew he could not. In her dream, she knew she was waking.

Her dreaming self swore to remember—to remember Daedalus and his love. Her dreaming self knew she had made that promise a thousand times and never kept it.

~~~

Nikkis woke to a chuffing, puffing sound. It reminded her of a steam locomotive she'd seen when she was very young.

Sunlight had not come into the room during sunset, but it came full into her room at sunrise.

Sunrise. She had missed dinner—slept through the night.

She lifted her head. Her hair covered her eyes.

She reminded herself to remember the dream, but it was already too late. It had already faded into the dark fog of the passing night.

She blinked and peered at her window.

The window framed the lover from her dreams. His bare shoulders glistened bronze in the morning sun.

The triptych. She realized she must be seeing the triptych. It was the same man.

Nikkis blinked and took a breath. When she looked again, the man was still there, and he was real, and he was at her window—her open window. She was sure she had closed and locked it.

For a moment of sheer vertigo, her head spun. He was both a memory from a hundred dreams, dreams that crashed in on her now, and he was the very real face at her window.

His face, the face of a man who lived in the weather, who embraced the sun and the night sky, who could look into a flower and see the same beauty he saw when he looked into the starry night, hovered at her window, framed there by the brilliant blue wood and the burning sky of the sun's rising.
~~~

Back-lit, his dark, curly hair shone like a delicate, gold-laced, obsidian crown. His shoulders filled the window from frame to frame, and his shirt, or what was left of it, barely covered the muscles of his upper arms in a net of home-weave cotton.

But the eyes.

His were the eyes of the bull in her room in Iraklion—wide, brown, and burning with the confusion of some unknowable torment.

She brushed the hair from her eyes.

The sound of the locomotive came from him. The panting, hissing, and puffing came from deep in his massive chest.

He stared at her, into her, through her glare, through the hard set of her jaw, past the tight clamping of her teeth, and into her chest, her very heart. His eyes cut into her like a bull's horns and opened her to him and to herself.

His gaze found her small, scared, naked core, and it warmed and excited her.

She clasped the linens and pulled them up to cover herself.

His huge hands hovered over the sill, his fingers twitching as if turning something unseen over in his hands. He seemed confused, uncertain.

An insane desire to reach for him, to cover his searching hands in hers and calm him, took over her thoughts and fears. Heat rose to her cheeks, and she looked down and bit her lip. When she looked up again, he was gone, and like her dreams, his memory became a series of questions to which she had no answers.

Someone outside yelled.

A large bell rang—a church bell.

Nikkis, holding her covers wrapped around her, went to the window and looked out.

Andros and Yorgos ran past her window. Both carried pistols. In Greek, Andros commanded, "Stop! Halt!" He stopped and took aim.

Yorgos ran into him from behind.

Off-balance, Andros fired into the ground. "Fool!" Andros screamed at Yorgos.

Nikkis screamed.

Andros looked up and barked commands like he owned her. "Get inside! Close the shutters!"

"He's unarmed," Nikkis said.

As if surprised she had not already closed the shutters, Andros stood and stared. His cold eyes fixed on her chest where she clutched the linens to her. In calm English, he said, "A madman is loose."

To cover her sudden sense of exposure, she said, "You'll shoot him for being mad?"

"This is not America," Andros holstered his gun under his arm, faced Yorgos, and commanded, "Go!"

Yorgos sprinted away.

Nikkis glared at Andros.

He stared back in open admiration. "You are blushing, Doctor," he said. "I'm pleased to see that I affect you after all."

Cool air on her skin reminded her that she was naked under the blanket she clutched. One-handed, she reached out and closed the shutters. Once closed, she set the bar in place. In the act, she again remembered latching the shutters the night before.

The window had been closed and locked.

She was sure.

She thought she was sure.

She examined the bar. Tiny, fresh scratches scored the center of the bar where the madman had used some tool to lift it free. He had jimmied her windows.

Nikkis leapt from the bed and gathered her clothes. She dressed, watching the shutters the whole while. No matter how her dreams had made her feel, she knew she wouldn't be safe again until she finished the job she came to do and returned to America.

Ancient Grief and Hope

After escaping the king's soldiers, he had only lived and worked in the village for a year, but Daedalus was sure he'd met everyone. However, on the day he and Nikkis were to wed, he discovered he had only met perhaps a third of the people who lived in and supported the village. Women, middle-aged and older, carrying linen bags of olives and nuts, arrived in the early morning. One woman, a stout old matron trailed by six children, arrived with an already dressed goat carcass slung over her shoulder like it was only a shock of dry field grass.

As he watched the arrivals being taken in by families who dwelled in village houses, it became clear that some people had walked two or three days to attend the wedding.

They came and they came until the village overflowed with squealing children, laughter, music, and dancing.

He hadn't been allowed to see Nikkis for two days, and he wouldn't be allowed to see her until the Village Mother and Father brought her out to tie her hand to Daedalus's and wed them heart-and-soul for all of time.

He let Nikkis's friend Mikos, the goat boy who had shown kindness to a bird, trim his hair. He would be clean-shaven and well-groomed for his wedding night, for his first unfettered love making with the woman who had saved his life thrice: once in rebirth of spirit before the death of his son, once hanging from a precipice and near his mortal end, and a third time when she resurrected his love from the ashes of her despair.

Nikkis.

Eternity would not be enough time to show her his love and gratitude.

"There is still time to run away, Traveler." His father-in-law sat on a short stool chewing leather strips then using the wet leather to bind together a carrying basket, a gift meant to hold their first-born child. Daedalus admired the man's strength, clever fingers, and optimism. He could see Nikkis's spirit in the old man.

"Where would I run that her love would not follow?"

"You once lived in the palace." Brown leather juice dripped along a white streak in his otherwise black beard. The juice dripped from the tip of his beard onto the floor between his legs. "I don't think she would follow you there."

"Too long in too many palaces," Daedalus said.

"What was it like?" Mikos asked. His cold knife nicked Daedalus's neck.

"Take care, there, boy," the old man said. "If you bleed him dead, who knows what Nikkis will do to you?"

In response, the knife shook in earnest in Mikos's hand. Its edge scraped at Daedalus's neck.

Daedalus wondered what terror his new wife might hold for Mikos. He could only imagine what the children of this village might fear. A sling? More likely a deft hand with a sharp blade on a dark night. He already knew that Nikkis could bring a blade to a man's flesh if needed. He had never heard the story of that horror from anyone in the village, but Gask would have whined to any who would listen. Mikos must have heard that tale.

Daedalus wrapped Mikos's hands in his own to steady the blade. He closed his eyes, and he let the feel of the boy's fear come to him, come to him in images of blade and flesh and the castration of a goat. "She has said how much she favors you, Mikos." Daedalus said. "She has said that you are good with the animals and with your blades. I know it is true. I saw you with the bird by the stream. Do you remember?" He spoke the truth, and the fear cleared from Mikos's mind and heart.

Mikos's hands stilled.

"She has said," Daedalus continued, "that you dream of distant places."

"I have traveled," Mikos said. "I've seen the magic walls of the shining palace you built."

"Not magic." Daedalus released the boy's hands to let him continue cutting.

"Not magic like the bird? Will you tell me how you did it?"

"The walls are merely made of stone found deep in the ground, beneath the other stones of the quarry. We look for places, tiny caves in the deep stone. There, we cut blocks as hard at core as any granite but soft and scaled on the outside like the scales of a viper. The scales are small and golden. When Helios passes above, the glorious fires of his chariot are captured and cast outward toward the piers on the river and any boats that might arrive. From the riverside, the palace looks like a home built of the fires of Helios."

"And from the mountains at sunset," Mikos said.

"I hadn't thought of that, but I'm sure you are right," Daedalus said.

The old man spit leather juice on the floor. "No good will come of filling the head of a goat boy with visions of shining palaces."

"Who can say?" Daedalus said. "I was once the son of a village tinsmith. I have traveled the world and walked in the halls of many kings."

"Spoken like a man whose ambitions will take him away from us."

The pull and cut of Mikos's blade stopped.

Daedalus smiled. "You need not fear for your daughter's happiness. I have seen enough of the world, and I have come full circle. My only ambition in this life is to deserve the love of your daughter, raise your grandchildren, and to spend my days giving the gifts of my hands to this village."

"I will see other palaces," Mikos said. "Someday, I will. I swear it."

"We do not want to displease my daughter." The old man laughed. "Before you leave to see the world, finish shearing this madman who would become my son." The smile and the sparkle in his eyes told Daedalus that these words made him family more than the coming ceremony ever could.

"My blade is sharp and my hand steady." Mikos stood straighter, and his blade was steady. "I'll have him ready in time."

"Sooner," the old man said. "I have the father's duty to tell him a man's secrets before his wedding night."

"I'm old enough to hear," Mikos said.

"So you say, but when I tell your mother you have heard, will she agree or will she sharpen her blade and look for me?"

The trio laughed together and chatted easily of distant lands and goats and gods until Mikos finished cutting and left.

"Secrets?" Daedalus brushed the hair from the linen cape and belted apron he wore for his wedding.

"Promises." The old man put aside his leather work, stood, and crossed to Daedalus.

He had once seen Nikkis's blade appear at Ikarus's neck as if from the air itself. Her father must have taught her that trick. A long, thin blade touched tip to Daedalus's throat.

He spoke slow and low. "Take good care of my brightest treasure, Foreigner." The love and sparkle had left his face and voice—no promise of family. "Tarnish her, lose her, or betray her—let her come to harm in any way before you die trying to protect her, and I will make a drum from your world-weary heart. For the rest of my life, I will beat out my grief upon it daily, and I will hand it down through generations. Do you understand?"

Daedalus whispered, "She is your brightest treasure, but she has become the only light in my dark soul. Without her, I would be lost and worse. I promise you, new Father, that I will kill or die before I see any shadow cover her light."

Daedalus held the old man's black eyed gaze and allowed the blade at his throat. Though he was sure he could disarm the old man, he waited while Nikkis's father satisfied himself that he could see the truth-light, the spark in eye and soul, that confirmed Daedalus's words.

Finally, the old man smiled. "Ah, my son, I never doubted you." He put the knife away.

"Now," Daedalus said, "I have a gift for you."

The old man raised a graying eyebrow.

Daedalus fetched his gift from the next room. He unwrapped the linens covering his work.

The old man frowned. "The head of a bull? What gift is this for a wedding day?"

"A helmet," Daedalus said. "Each year, the red dust comes from across the sea. Each year, it takes the lives of goats and cattle and sometimes dust-blinded, lost men who fall from cliffs to their deaths."

"And I'm to wear this in case I fall?" The old man smiled.

"To let you find the lost. I made the eyes of thinly sliced amber. They will protect your eyes, and the color will let you see better in the haze. The nose has linens within to clear your breath. I hollowed each horn to catch distant sound and bring it to you. The neck closes to keep the dust from your face."

"Your hands are a wonder." Nikkis's father embraced Daedalus, accepted the gift, and left. The light in his father-in-law's eyes and in the strength of his embrace told Daedalus that his gift had spoken well of his understanding of family and village.

Finally alone with his thoughts, Daedalus sat and counted himself lucky to have found a home with these fiercely loyal people. The old man's blade had not scared Daedalus so much as reminded him of the value of the love he had found. His heart pounded and his hands shook from anticipation of seeing his bride soon—of being bound to her.

The gods had granted him many gifts in his life, but for the first time he knew without doubt that the gods had given him a gift of which he would never be worthy, a gift that would force him to work every day to become worthy.

He breathed deeply to quiet his heart and steady his hands. Finally, as calm as he could become, Daedalus rose, arranged his apron and cape, and went out of the house into the village to join the festivities of his wedding.

~~~

So many times for so many years away from his home, Daedalus had wished for things not at hand. In northern climes, chilled by winter rains and shadows inside stone houses waiting for a time when he could go out and put hands to stone again, he had wished for the feel of spring sun on the flesh of his face. In the Nubian quarries of Aegypt, he had wished for clouds, cold, and rain. In deserts, where he had stayed in the stone city of Ur, he had built terraced towers and elaborate catches for water to feed growing plants. There, he had wished to feel mud between his toes.

In Crete, standing in the middle of a circle of villagers, he lifted his face to the spring sun and knew he would never again wish for anything except to stand in that sun, to be surrounded by these people, and to love the woman who stood beside him.

Nikkis's mother and father stood beside the couple.

"Join hands," her father said.

This was the most serious moment of the day, but Daedalus could not stop the little boy's grin that stretched his face. He lifted his hand and looked deeply into Nikkis's eyes, the eyes that had loved him, held him in the world, taught him that he could honor his lost son by living and helping others rather than by seeking reunion in realms of darkness.

She looked up into his eyes, and in her he saw himself as more than he could ever hope to be, more than he had ever been.

They clasped hands. Flesh pressed flesh. His heart leapt in his chest, tried to escape his body to seek and embrace her heart.
~~~

The magic the queen had given him, that strange power to know beyond knowing, could not be contained. It moved through him, a wave of heat, a seeking that dove into her hand and ran up her arm and found her spirit and heart.

His grin grew. Only love lived inside her—only visions of contentment together and with family and village. He had found his home and his future.

Her father clasped his hands over theirs. "I bind you now, one to the other, in heart and soul."

Her mother wrapped their wrists together with a small band of leather. "For this time," she said, "and for all time."

Nikkis's mother and father joined hands, left-to-right and right-to-left, so Nikkis and Daedalus stood face to face within the circle of their embrace.

Her mother said, "When one calls, the other shall come."

Her father said, "When one weeps, the other shall comfort."

"When one rejoices, the other shall dance."

"From this time until the end of time, you shall be one."

"We shall be your family…"

All around them, the voices of the hundreds gathered continued the refrain of the wedding, "…your village, and your protectors."

Nikkis's parents released one another. Her mother twisted a long band of woven goat's hair into the leather around their wrists. A long, loose strand dangled in the slight breeze.

Daedalus lifted the dangling string and handed it to her father. "And we shall be, forever, a part of your family…"

Nikkis continued, "and this village…"

Together, they said, "And we shall be protectors of all who witness this day. From this time for all of time, we are one."

Her father's smile appeared, and he took up the twine in one hand. With the other, he reached out. His wife took up his hand. A village man took her other. Within moments, every hand of every person in the village had connected in an unbroken chain that snaked up and around the cooking fires, between tents and homes, and finally back to Nikkis, who took up the hand of Mikos.

A horn sounded in the hills above the village.

A current of anger and fear ran into Daedalus's hands from the assembled and connected village. The fear grew to rage so overwhelming that he pulled his hands free from the link to wife and family and village.

The moment of bliss was broken. Daedalus knew the horn was not meant to mark their union. It was an alarm.

All eyes looked to the hills, to a stone spire where one man stood in silhouette against the sky, horn to lips.

The horn sounded again.

"What?" he began.

Chaos erupted. People ran in every direction.

Nikkis's parents ran for their home.

"Invaders!" Nikkis said.

From beyond the edge of the village, a loud metallic pounding echoed in the valley and among the buildings.

Daedalus took Nikkis in his arms. He kissed her quickly to seal their vows. "My wife," he said.

"Husband," she said. "We must run. We're unarmed."

"Who?"

His answer came in the form of king's soldiers moving in units of six, two-by-three, bone-over-tin shields protecting flanks, fronts, and rears, marching inward from every direction. They marched through the rows of tents, through the alleys between stone buildings, and inward toward the open area at the village center.

Daedalus and Nikkis held one another. Surrounded, they had no place to run.

The clamor in the distance stopped. The marching soldiers froze.

Silence filled the village so completely that it was more deafening than the roar of stone falling from a quarry rim.

Behind the soldiers, men and women began to appear. At first, they stepped from shadows and doorways in ones and twos. Then, they appeared more quickly. After a few minutes, every man and woman who had been at the wedding stood crowded around the soldiers. Just as Nikkis and Daedalus had no route of escape, the soldiers were also surrounded.

Each villager held a long, razor-sharp blade, a blade that could slip between bone breastplates and pierce thin tin or thick leather, a blade used for killing men and goats alike, a blade they knew like they knew their own fingers.

"What do you want?" Daedalus called.

From one rank of six, a large, Herculean man stepped forward.

Daedalus recognized Yorgos—as large as Daedalus himself, the man towered over the other soldiers. Sweat dripped from the roped sinews of arms that glistened in the morning sun. Daedalus wondered at the speed and effort of the march that had been needed to surround the village so quickly and completely.

Yorgos stopped in front of Nikkis and Daedalus. "You are the Master Mason, Daedalus," he said.

"You know me," Daedalus said.

Yorgos nodded.

Daedalus said, "You are Yorgos, third in command at the Palace of Knossos."

"By the king's will, we must escort you to the judgment chamber of The Bull and Ruler of all Crete."

The people behind the soldiers tapped their blades together lightly. The ticking sound of blades, metal on metal, was the sound of a thousand scorpion claws opening and closing—the promise of death.

Yorgos shifted his weight. Sweat dripped from his nose. In the shadows of his helmet, his wide eyes shifted from side to side, taking in the masses of men and women and knives surrounding him and his men.

Someone deep in the crowd spoke, "Protect from this time to the end of time."

Again, the scorpion's promise sounded from the assembled.

"Yorgos," Daedalus said. "A bad situation for you."

"The king's soldiers have sworn themselves dead in his service," Yorgos said.

"Such a choice," Daedalus said, "pretending to be dead for the vanity of a king or accepting a herder's blade in your throat."

"I regret that gods and kings use us poorly today, Mason. We have no choice. You have no choice."

"We all have choices, Yorgos. Even today. Even here."

"We are sent to succeed or die. This was the great king's promise to us. You have hidden much too long from him."

"These are good people. You are a good man."

The scorpion claws chattered. The armor of the nervous soldiers rattled. A chill breeze carried the hot smell of sun-bleached dust through the village streets.

"I must protect my men. You must come, or none of us can return. Any who return without you will die by fire, by the teeth of rats, or torn in two between oxen. Worse, the village of each man who fails and lives will be put to death. These are not good deaths for soldiers."

"The village will fight," Nikkis said.

"My men will fight," Yorgos said.

"Too many will die," Nikkis said. "The village will die."

Daedalus nodded. He pulled her close to his side and held her. He reached inward to share her fear. He knew her vision of a village empty of mothers and fathers, filled only with old people and the very young, parentless children. He knew her fear of more soldiers coming to kill even the children and old as examples to others.

Daedalus put his hands on her shoulders. "I will send for you when I can," he said.

The scorpion tapping grew loud.

"NO!" he called so all could hear. "Hear me!"

The tapping stopped.

"I have within the hour sworn to protect wife, family, and village." He watched Yorgos's eyes sweeping the crowd.

"To stay would be to kill people I'm sworn to protect," Daedalus said. "I will go with these soldiers. They will leave in peace and never return."

"No." Nikkis broke away from his embrace.

"Yes," he said.

"Then I go with you."

"No," Yorgos said.

Nikkis turned on the giant man. She put a work-sculpted hand on his shield and pushed. "I will go where my husband goes, or you will kill me here in the center of my village in front of my family and friends so they know I did not abandon him of my own will."

"Nikkis," Daedalus whispered, "this does not help me or the village."

"Choose," Nikkis said. "Choose now, soldier of the coward king who cannot build his own house."

"Please," Daedalus pleaded.

"I cannot stop you, Goat Woman. I can only warn you. I was there in the quarry the day Gask searched for you. Do not put yourself in front of the king."

"Nikkis," Daedalus said. "I know this soldier. He is honorable. Please listen to him."

Yorgos lifted a hand. Two men broke ranks, trotted forward, and flanked Daedalus. Nikkis grasped Daedalus's arm and wedged herself between her lover and one of the soldiers.

Again, the air filled with the calls of a thousand scorpions ready to sting and kill.

"As you will, Goat Woman," Yorgos said. He called out, "They choose this! We need shed no blood."

Daedalus called out, "Let us do this for you. We will return to you. I swear it. We will honor our vows. We are joined for all of time."

He and Nikkis, arm-in-arm, stepped forward. Yorgos and the flanking soldiers followed. The ranks parted to give them passage and fell in behind them as they passed.

The scorpions rattled, but the crowd opened a path for soldiers and lovers.

Nikkis and Daedalus led Yorgos and the king's soldiers onto the trails to the lowlands and the palace Daedalus had escaped only the year before.

~~~

As soon as the column cleared the village, Yorgos ordered his captives' hands tied. Once that was done, two-by-two, the column of soldiers moved in double-time along the goat and donkey tracks of the hills. In the center of the column, Nikkis and Daedalus took the places of two center-rank soldiers.

The column of soldiers and their two captives snaked along narrow trails toward Knossos. Even surrounded by steep hills and deep, narrow canyons, escape might have been possible if Daedalus had been alone, but escape would endanger Nikkis and the village. He knew this king, and he had no wish to be the cause of the death of either Nikkis or her village. Walking quickly under the high sun, he wondered if the gifts he had so recently counted as his weren't merely the gods' entertainment, the spice that made his capture so much the sweeter for his disappointment.

Perhaps he would, after all, reunite with his son in the darkness rather than honor him in life and works.

In spite of the soldiers' discipline, the winding mountain tracks broke their ranks from time to time; but each time a cleft or a boulder or a vale separated the soldiers
~~~

from one another, at least two pairs of men moved as a unit to keep Nikkis and Daedalus flanked.

The ranks broke and came together time and again.

They marched on until Helios reached the highest point in his race across the sky. Daedalus imagined that changes in terrain made the line of soldiers seem shorter. He imagined that the soldiers pulled together more tightly.

No. That couldn't be right. He began to pay attention to the numbers of soldiers ahead of him. After several quick counts and recounts, he became very sure that each time terrain broke the ranks, fewer men reformed their lines.

Still, the disciplined soldiers silently closed ranks and reordered themselves.

"Are your men so unhappy that they desert?" he asked Yorgos.

Yorgos ignored him and moved more quickly. His head turned incessantly from side to side, searching the hills, the rocks, the swales and hummocks. His normal calm steadiness faded, and Daedalus took that as answer enough to his questions about the missing men.

"Our people," Nikkis said.

"It won't go well for them," Yorgos said. "They must know what Minos will do."

"Yes," Nikkis said. "They know."

Yorgos nodded. "I should have known that any bride the mason took would be a woman to inspire such passion and loyalty."

The rubble and scrub of parched hills gave no sign of man, woman, or beast. Still, soldiers disappeared and Yorgos became more and more nervous. He ordered the men to a faster pace.

Helios rode across the sky, and the day that should have led to their wedding night became a long, hot, sweaty march of death.

Their crooked trail turned down the shoulder of a ridge and twisted into switchbacks along the valley wall of stone and rubble.

From above, a man screamed.

Daedalus froze and looked up.

A man leapt from the rocks above. Like a hawk diving from the sky, he crashed onto Yorgos.

Both men fell, rolled down the slope to the valley floor, and stilled.

Yorgos stood.

He pulled his blade from the chest of the man who had leapt from the cliffs.

"Mikos," Nikkis gasped. "Just a boy."

Nikkis's eyes held the same contempt Daedalus had seen the day Gask died. Her skin paled, and she shook.

Yorgos hooked a toe under Mikos's limp arm and lifted. His hand pulled out from beneath his back. In a death grip, he still held a goat-butcher's blade. "Old enough to kill is old enough to die," Yorgos said.

Daedalus scrambled to the valley floor and knelt next to the boy. Hands tied, he couldn't reach the boy's head, but he leaned low to listen for breath.

"Mason," the boy whispered. "I see the palaces." His breath rattled. His eyes glazed, and he stared forever more at distant palaces and kings.

"The gods frown on the work of this day," Daedalus said. "How can you give your loyalty to a king who claims to protect his people but would cause such a thing?"

"The king has no blame in this, Mason. *You* are cursed," Yorgos said. "Cursed by all the gods, and good men die of your curse."

"This morning, he cut my hair with this blade," Daedalus said. "A child."

Soldiers gathered close together on the valley floor, standing back-to-back with comrades, all poised to defend should other herders leap from the sky or rise from the earth to attack.

Yorgos pulled up a tall tuft of dried grass and cleaned his blade.

Nikkis struggled to get at Yorgos. Soldiers held her back. She spat in Yorgos's face.

Yorgos ignored her. To Daedalus, he said, "You sought to escape, and the king's soldiers saw you. Only a day's march north and east of here, you leapt from a cliff to fly. Your son cursed the soldiers and died in the sea."

Looking at the pale face on the ground, Daedalus said, "I wanted to save him."

"You hid," Yorgos said, "until songs of your gifts to villagers came to us in the palace. The king sent us for you on your wedding day."

Daedalus stood and faced Yorgos. "The curse is this mad king."

Yorgos frowned. "If the gods wished the gifts of your hands to come to men, the king could not find you."

Nikkis said, "If men did not serve the king, it would not matter what he found."

"The gods made this king. Had you served him, your son would live. My men would not be dying. You are cursed, Mason, and I weep for the people close to you."

"Slaughter," Daedalus said, "is the work of men; only men can stop it."

"What use to us," Nikkis asked, "is a king who kills us or enslaves us? A thief of lives. He steals from us all."

"Born to a village like yours," Yorgos said, "I serve the king to serve my village just as you did in the quarry."

"Then you knew our village would come for us," Nikkis said. "It's our way."

"This child chose death."

"You chose," Nikkis said. "I was forced. Daedalus was forced. As you said, they choose, and your men die one by one."

Yorgos's eyes glistened. He nodded. "If we return without you, our villages will die." He lifted his spear from the ground, raised the tip, and rotated it in a circle.

The soldiers moved quickly, closing ranks around him. Yorgos led the men downslope, along the valley floor to a dolphin fin ridge of limestone cutting upward through the scrub.

The men pressed Nikkis and Daedalus against the pale stone ridge then surrounded their captives.

"We will die here," Yorgos said. "You will die with us. The killing will end with us in this place."

From every rock, nook, cranny, shadow, and bush, scorpion claws clattered and snapped. The sound echoed through the mountainous terrain.

Soldiers moved nervously, their bone armor clacking and their breath coming in short, quick gasps.

Daedalus recognized the place. It was the same stone ridge where he had found his cave. Not far from the semicircle of soldiers, he found the dark shadow behind concealing bushes. Beside him, Nikkis radiated the heat of rage as if she were a bonfire.

"Nikkis," he said.

The murderous flame in her eyes turned from her friend's killer toward him.

"Nikkis, we can stop this. We can save these people." He stood close to her, close enough to feel her breath on his chest, to hold her eyes with his. "Whole villages depend on what we do here."

He waited while her eyes cleared, while her breath slowed, while her heartbeat matched his own.

Finally, he turned to Yorgos and said, "I can save the villages and your men."

"For the honor of our villages and our families," Yorgos said, "we will die. Because of your curse, we will die. But if we must die far from our homes, we will hold against this rock so that we at least see the faces of the men who come to kill us, and we will take many of them to meet Hades with us."

"Papu!" Nikkis called out.

Yorgos moved to slap her.

Daedalus thrust his shoulder into the soldier, caught the man's breastplate, lifted Yorgos from the ground, upward, and back against the ridge of limestone. The soldier's training was good, and his spear point came to Daedalus's neck.

Daedalus froze. "If you kill me, what will stop them from killing you all?"

"She calls to her family, to the murdering villagers."

"So, you wish to live," Daedalus said.

"I call to them," Nikkis said, "to stop the slaughter of your men, fool."

"Let us help you," Daedalus said. "Let us help them. You can live. The villages can live. The horrors of this day do not yet include mass carnage and suicide."

For the second time in the day, a man, Yorgos this time, looked into Daedalus's eyes—looked deep and long, seeking something, some hope or truth or promise.

Yorgos cut Daedalus's hands free.

Daedalus rubbed his wrists. "Cut her free as well."

"You go and speak to them. She stays with us," Yorgos said.

"Will they believe a man whose new wife you hold at the tip of a blade?"

"They did not believe you in the village."

"No," Daedalus said. "There, your spears and shields gave you advantage on flat ground. Here, they have you if they want you."

"We will keep her," Yorgos said.

Daedalus said, "Yorgos, if you want to live through the day, show them Nikkis's freedom. Show them that we choose to go with you. If they see that we choose freely here and now, they will follow, but they will not kill."

Yorgos shook his head then cast about, looking for something.

When his searching stopped, Daedalus followed his gaze. The soldier had spied the cave in which Daedalus had once lived.

"There," Yorgos said. "That cave." He pointed to one of his men. "Go. See if it is big enough for all of us inside."

"Wait," Nikkis said. "I know that place."

Yorgos said, "We are not beaten yet, Mason."

Nikkis chuckled and asked, "Will you make that hole in the earth your tomb?"

"I see only one approach, and we are trained and armed."

Nikkis said, "You may be from a village, but you are not from a village like mine. These mountains are filled with caverns, tunnels, cracks, pits, and underground rivers and rivulets."

"You know other ways in?" Yorgos asked.

"Two that I know of, and I found those because goats fell in. Some of the men and boys, boys like the one you killed, make sport of exploring these caverns. They will find you there, and there, in the darkness beneath the earth, you'll die."

Daedalus pointed at the cave. A man moved from the shadow of the bushes into the light at the cave entrance. He sat on a rock, bent, picked up a small stone, and began to sharpen his long, curved knife.

Another man appeared from the shadows beside him, then a third.

"At least they show themselves now," Yorgos said.

"What does that tell you, Soldier?" Daedalus asked. "In our march from the village, how many have you seen? Why do they show themselves now?"

Yorgos frowned. He nodded. He cut Nikkis's bonds.

She stepped away from the soldiers and held up her hands so anyone who looked could see that she was free.

Daedalus joined her.

"Enough!" she called.

"Go home!" Daedalus called.

"We are free!" they called together.

"Then come away from the soldiers," a voice very near them called.

The soldiers jumped. They turned in every direction.

As if born whole as a man from bush and stone, a man appeared from hiding near the cave. His clothing was the same blue-green and brown as the land and brush. His face, covered in dried mud, was as pale as the dust of the trail. "Come to the cave and join your father," he said.

A soldier moved toward him.

"Hold!" Yorgos ordered.

The soldier stopped.

The man smiled. Flakes of mud fell away from his face.

The soldier glanced at Yorgos.

"Ranks," Yorgos said.

The man backed up into his place in the defensive line.

Five more men stood up on the hillside, suddenly appearing from crevices, folds in the hill, and bushes.

"Go," Yorgos said. "I trust you, Mason. I once watched you in the darkness making a deal with your son. I have seen your heart and believe you an honest man."

"I once saw you," Daedalus said, "silent in the darkness pretending to have seen nothing. We are much alike, my friend." He took Nikkis's hand, and they walked halfway to the cavern entrance.

"We are free to do as we choose," he said.

"Then come home with us," Nikkis's father said.

"In the village," Daedalus said, "we chose to go to Knossos. We chose life for the village and for the soldiers."

"Soldiers," Nikkis said, "who are only men from other villages."

A man cried out. "Soldiers who killed Mikos!" His was the voice of grief and sorrow.

A keening went up from many mouths and spread outward into the valleys and knolls. The mountains echoed grief and rage and fear—the cry of hundreds of mothers and fathers for the loss of a favored child.

"Papu!" Nikkis cried. "I am with Daedalus. We are born to be together. I cannot leave him. Never. Be happy for me, Papu! I have known joy and love!"

Again the cry of grief. The horrible sound echoed in the mountains.

Soldiers turned in circles, searching for the invisible source of so many voices.

The wailing faded like sunset wind that has come and then trails away to the stillness of a clear night.

When the echoes died away, the men at the cavern mouth were gone. The men on the hillside above the soldiers were gone.

Only Daedalus, Nikkis, and the soldiers remained.

Daedalus embraced Nikkis. They kissed. The kiss was long, and joyful, and sad, and when they parted, they looked into one another's eyes and knew that if all they ever shared in life was that one kiss, it would be enough.

Finally, they turned to the soldiers and joined them for the long march to Knossos and false judgment.

Modern Pitfalls

Detective Andros and Yorgos were gone for some time before returning—enough time that Nikkis could eat a breakfast of honey, yogurt, eggs, and fruit. Each time the woman who ran the little boarding house came back to fill Nikkis's water glass or to offer some new morsel, she paused a moment to cross herself and stare.

After a half hour, another woman appeared, an even older one, which Nikkis had thought impossible.

Stooped with bent back, the newcomer wore the black dress and shawl that most of the old women of the villages wore.

The housekeeper pointed at Nikkis.

Nikkis expected another crossing and spitting session.

Instead, silent tears poured freely down creased, leather cheeks, but the new woman stood steady, her gaze holding Nikkis's face as if blinking might make Nikkis disappear.

Uncomfortable with the woman's tears and naked stare, Nikkis glanced around, hoping Andros would return so they could begin their hike.

The policemen were nowhere to be seen, and the crying woman blocked her return to her room.

Nikkis met the ancient woman's gaze, and in it she saw something familiar about her eyes, about the way she cried without sobbing, without breathing hard, without moving her head or losing her composure. Nikkis admired the hard-won dignity of her sadness.

In Greek, Nikkis asked, "Why such tears… "She hesitated to use the word that came to mind, but it felt right. She hoped the old woman wouldn't take offense. "… Grandmother?"

"Yiayia," *Grandmother*, the old woman said. "Ne! Yiayia!" *Yes, Grandmother.*

"Excuse me?"

"You know me." The old woman moved to stand before Nikkis at the table.

"I don't think we've met."

"You *have* come back, just as she said." The woman nodded in the direction of the housekeeper, who slipped out of the room and into her kitchen. "Even without us, you have learned the secrets of priestesses."

Nikkis stood. "You've confused me with someone else." She extended her hand. "Doctor Nikkis Aristos. Pleased to meet you."

Nikkis's name did what the tears could not. As though struck in the chest, the woman collapsed into a chair. The housekeeper, hidden behind a door, moaned loud and long like she had just heard that her brother or son had been killed.

Nikkis didn't want to hurt them more than she already had, but she had no idea what she had done to them. It might be one of those little cultural things like holding up your hand palm-out to signal a high-five or *talk to the hand*. In Greece, she knew, to hold the hand palm out was a grievous insult.

She reviewed her words and actions. Nothing she remembered provided any insight into this odd behavior.

Staying in the little room with the old women became unbearable. "Excuse me," she said. "I have to go."

"No," the old woman swiped away her tears and looked up. "Please. Let me look at you, Dr. Nikkis Aristos."

"I'm sorry if I've offended." Nikkis turned toward the hallway and the refuge of her room.

One hard, gnarled hand shot out and grasped Nikkis's wrist.

"No," the old woman said. "Please."

Nikkis tried to pull away, but the ancient hag, who couldn't have weighed more than eighty pounds, held her as if her claw-like hand were a handcuff and her body part of the stone floor.

"What do you want?" Nikkis asked.

"You are not her, then?"

"Who?"

"Not Cliantha?"

"Oh my God." Nikkis fell back into her own chair. "How do you know my mother's name?"

The woman's grip tightened. "Look at my face, child. Long years and the gods have writ in lines the life I have lived. Look into my face and know me."

Nikkis stared long and hard. The haunting familiarity in the eyes became clear to her. This woman had her mother's eyes. The face was her mother's face. The face was Nikkis's face—Nikkis's face if she lived and worked in the sun for sixty or seventy more years. "Who are you?"

"I know your mother's name because I gave that name to her the day I brought her from my womb."

They sat for some time simply staring at each other—staring and mapping the features of one another's faces. The woman's grip loosened. Her palm turned up. Nikkis's hand grasped the hand of her past.

Stamping feet and grumbles preceded the return of Andros and Yorgos.

The old woman stood.

"Wait," Nikkis said. "We need to–"

"Fascists," the old woman said. "We will talk again." She pulled free and walked to the open door.

Andros appeared outside the door frame. Yorgos followed behind. Andros pushed into the doorway and came up short in the face of the old woman. "Look out," Andros said.

The old woman held her ground and coolly peered into Andros's eyes.

A long, thorny moment passed. Andros looked away.

The old woman stepped forward.

Andros and Yorgos backed out of the doorway to let her pass.

"Peasants," Andros said.

Nikkis tried to see where her grandmother went, but the men stood in her way.

Andros snapped at her. "Pack. We leave in ten minutes."

Nikkis asked, "What happened to that man?"

Andros glared at her. "Pack for the hike to the site," he said.

She understood instantly that the man had escaped. She didn't know the man, but her relief was deep enough that she thanked the gods of this place for his safety. Whatever he had done, she was very sure he didn't deserve to be shot. Rather, she believed in her heart, even if it was only a foolish, sheltered, middle-class American ideal, that the man needed help.

~~~

Nikkis hated to leave her grandmother behind. She had so many questions, but she also had a job to do. She told herself she would come back when the work was done, and she was packed and ready when Andros and Yorgos emerged for the hike. This time, they wore their pistols on the outside of their vest jackets, and this time their clothing was much more military.

"You look like a couple of commandos," Nikkis said.

Neither man laughed. "No law rules in this area," Andros said.

"What does that mean?" Nikkis asked. "The people I've met seem nice enough."

"They know a tourist when they see one," Andros said. "They see only a pretty woman they don't know, and they believe you probably have money. They would steal you blind if we weren't with you. It would be best if you don't speak to them alone. Some are very dangerous."

"Like the madman at my window?"

"He broke into your room. He might have killed you. He might have kidnapped you. You have no idea what he wanted."

She asked, "What do *you* think he wanted?"

"I think he was one of the forgers I want to catch."

"You think he wanted to make a forgery of me?"

"My dear Dr. Aristos," Andros said, and his face took on the smirking expression she was learning to loathe. "Even a criminal can see beauty."

"Not an answer," she said.

"Enough," Andros said. "We're leaving,"

"Where's Muscus?"

"In the hills," Andros said. "He is near enough, but we won't see him unless something goes wrong."

"So, what?" she asked. "He's a ninja?"

"Ninjas wish they had his skills." The hard, icy smile Andros flashed answered her more than his words.

Nikkis could only imagine what might go wrong. She suddenly wished she could leave, could find her way back down the mountain to the van; of course, that might mean encountering Muscus alone. She suspected that both Yorgos and Andros were
~~~

restrained by professional training; whereas, unless leashed by Andros's authority, she suspected Muscus did as his animal nature moved him.

Nikkis preferred facing danger consciously and with preparation. Animals, especially male hominids, were unpredictable.

She gathered her own small pack and once more hiked with Andros ahead and Yorgos behind. Before they left the village and stepped onto goat trails into the hill country, Andros's normal sardonic smirk twisted and reset into a thin-lipped, bloodless line of stony determination. On the trail to the site, the two men fell into wary, uneasy silence.

Nikkis decided silence was for the best. She wanted to get to the site, find something to make this insane trip worthwhile, and get out.

They meandered along goat trails and alongside ancient, tumble-down rock walls. She watched her footing and tried to drink in the peace and sharp beauty of the sky and hills surrounding her. She remembered being on campus, a place she had worked so hard to be, a place where her job should have made her feel secure and where no matter how long her resume and how strong her CV, she never felt quite right. Here, surrounded by guns, madmen, and ghosts from her past, a place that should have unnerved her completely, she couldn't help feeling at home. Some part of her knew this strange, barren hillside was where she should be, where she had always wanted to be.

The mystery of her feelings in this place sustained her through the march up ridges and over hills. The feelings couldn't come from meeting a woman who was possibly her grandmother. They had started long before that. For a while, she told herself she was having subconscious responses to stories her parents told her when she was young. Then, she convinced herself that dreams and memories from her studies had combined to create feelings of false connection. Eventually, tired and hot, she began to entertain the absurd idea that genetic memory might be at work.

When she began to believe it impossible that they could climb higher into the mountains without meeting the gods or at least cutting a hole in the perfect curtain of blue sky, they topped a ridge and started down the other side.

The valley floor beneath them wasn't more than fifty meters below the long headwall ridge line they had been walking on. Maybe a kilometer long and half a kilometer wide, lush green grasses spotted with barren patches of pale stone covered the valley floor. The floor curved away from the bottom in gentle slopes that ended against brown, rocky steeps. The south ridge, the higher by a hundred or more meters, looked like a line of castle towers and minarets, sharp spires poking into the sky. The more rounded north ridge reminded her of pictures she had seen, or perhaps dreams she once had, in which fat, lazy goats grazed on sparse brush. At the far end of the valley, the floor ended in an abrupt line. Beyond that line, through pale haze, she made out another stone scarp opposite the valley.

Nikkis remembered the map. That sharp line marked a cliff. Beyond it, the main drainage that cut northwest toward Iraklion and Knossos. This valley was one of the many finger valleys that poured into it.

In the verdant curve of the valley floor, a cluster of several tents made a circle. The "site" looked more like a small Boy Scout campout than any archaeological dig she had seen.

As they walked down toward the camp, Nikkis searched the valley and surrounding hills for the telltale piles of sifted dirt and the grid of lines and pits that marked most digs. Instead, she found men in tan-and-brown camo fatigues—two sitting at a low table outside a tent, two pairs standing at opposite ends of the little camp. A pair stood up the valley drainage and another pair stood down-slope. Finally, near the valley spill-out, she found one mound of debris that might have qualified as siftings, though it looked more like a dump. Near it, she could make out a dark hole in the earth, more of a well than a pit. Over the well, someone had set up a silver tripod and winch.

For the first time, it occurred to her that the dig might be in a cave complex. The limestone bedrock of Crete certainly contained caves and labyrinthine cavern systems.

The six visible men wore the same fatigues as Andros and Yorgos. The two pairs standing at the head and foot of the little valley held stubby, automatic weapons.

Nikkis had seen enough images of paranoia in the statistically stupid, security-controlled world to know the difference between men who held unfamiliar weapons and men who held familiar weapons they could and would use.

These men were the latter.

Their weapons hung from strap harnesses, and the stocks of the weapons nestled near their shoulders. One hand rested on the weapon's handle, one long finger ready over the trigger guard and touching the safety.

She knew these sentries should make her feel safer, but she found herself wondering why Greek police needed this kind of firepower in the mountains of a civilized country—the country where, in fact, Western Civilization had been born.

"What are they afraid of?" she asked.

"Thieves and forgers." Andros followed his words with whistles—three long, sharp tweets and one lower, shorter one.

"And madmen," Yorgos said.

Nikkis turned and looked at the normally quiet Yorgos. His face was hard, and his eyes moved constantly, scanning the hills, looking everywhere except where the armed men stood.

The gunmen raised their free hands to acknowledge the signal.

The sitting men stood and looked up the trail.

She followed her guides into the valley and up to the men at the table. As they approached, the mountain smells of sun-warmed stone and sage gave way to the smell of unwashed men, kerosene, and gun oil.

The two men moved to meet them. One was blond, tall, and muscled. There was more of Northern Europe about him than Greece, and he was certainly not Kritiki. The second man, darker and shorter by nearly a foot and half, was rail hard and thin. He reminded her of an Egyptologist she had known, a man who had survived at least three wars. That man had once told her that the men to fear in war are never tall. He had not smiled when he said, "Tall men died quickly." His words came to her, and she saw the truth of them in the man before her. His dark skin, narrow face, and ropy neck muscles made him seem dangerous. She guessed he was perhaps Egyptian or Syrian—an odd mix for a policeman on Crete. Of course, it might make sense that Andros would be more comfortable with mixed bloods like himself.

"What have you brought us?" The blond man's accented Greek confirmed his Germanic roots. "She's amazing!" He licked his lips and reached for Nikkis.

Andros reacted before she did. His hand moved faster than her thoughts. The smack echoed in the canyon between the two ridges. The man's head snapped back. Surprised and unprepared for the attack, he failed to defend against Andros's vicious following kick, a kick that caught the man just beneath his ribs and sent him sprawling on his back and gasping for air in the dust.

The man's total look of surprise was not lost on Nikkis. Deep in her belly, she knew with cold certainty that the soldier had expected to maul Nikkis with impunity.

"I didn't know," the man said in Greek. He gasped for breath. "I'm sorry. I didn't know she was yours."

In sharp English, Andros said, "You will address our *guest* as Dr. Aristos, and out of respect, you will speak English in front of her." He glanced at Nikkis. His hard, cold eyes made Nikkis want to run.

The man crabbed backward away from Andros. In English, he said, "Yes, sir."

The darker, scarier man stood straight as a rod, saluted, and waited at attention for Andros's commands. "At ease," Andros said.

The man stepped out and clasped his hands behind his back, but as near as Nikkis could see, he did not come close to relaxing. She didn't blame him.

Andros switched to German. "Where's Borstin?"

The thin man glanced at Nikkis.

"Speak," Andros barked.

In English, the man said, "We do not know."

"Something wrong?" Nikkis asked. She hoped something was wrong. She hoped something was wrong enough that they would have to go back to Iraklion or at least back to the village where people pretended to know her and like her.

"A man went missing," Andros made no attempt to pretend something else had happened, and his casual confidence in telling her the truth made Nikkis even more nervous.

"Disappeared?" she asked. "Quit or something?"

"Dr. Aristos, I told you I was dealing with criminals."

"But he might have–"

He interrupted her. "Thieves who steal millions of dollars rarely concern themselves over taking a few lives. Do you understand?"

"I do," she said. "But it had not occurred to me that your men might be involved."

Everyone became very still.

Nikkis knew she had said something wrong. She didn't know what she had said that upset them, but she wished she could pull the words out of the air and swallow them so they had never been spoken or heard.

Andros broke the awkward silence. "The missing man has been kidnapped or killed."

Loudly, Yorgos sighed.

"When someone kills a policeman," Andros said, "my men become very involved."

Andros turned to Yorgos. "Drop pack. Check in with Idas and Christos. Find out what happened."

"Sir," the shorter man said, "we know what happened."

Andros gestured for Yorgos to hold his ground.

"Minotaur, Sir. Last night."

"And Borstin went after him." Andros said.

The soldier nodded.

"Against my orders."

Neither soldier said anything.

"Damn American cowboy idiots." Andros handed his pack to the blonde man. "Take this."

Nikkis bit her lip. She had a hard time believing Americans would be policemen in Crete.

Andros turned to Nikkis. "The man did a foolish thing. He left camp alone in the night. He should have known better."

Nikkis nodded. "Minotaur? A smuggler? Dangerous?" She hoped her feint showed the right level of concern and confusion. She knew she had just been warned to stay in camp, especially at night.

"Please, Dr. Aristos," Andros's smooth, silky voice was back, but it no longer soothed Nikkis to hear it. "Believe me when I tell you that you are safe here."

"Where are the other archeologists?"

"No others will see this place until you validate the site."

"I see," she said. "Then let's get to work." The sooner she gave Andros what he wanted, the sooner she could leave. And there was still a chance she could salvage something from this mess, a paper or some recognition or reputation. What she was sure of was that the volume of material she'd seen at the warehouse didn't come from this valley. This dig was too small and underdeveloped. She was also now quite certain that the men in this valley were not regular police.

In spite of her doubts, she had to deal with the moment. She was here now, and she'd be damned if she were going to go through all this and go home with nothing.

"Yes. Come, then." Andros strode off toward the lower end of the valley, toward the hole in the valley floor.

Yorgos came up beside Nikkis. He touched her elbow.

She allowed him to guide her after Andros.

~~~

At the edge of the hole, Andros and his people had set up a tool box and the battery-driven winch and tripod arrangement Nikkis had seen from the ridge. From the ridge, the hole had seemed more like a circular well. Up close, it was clearly an irregular circle made of angular, blocked edges—very regular edges, like circled concrete blocks covered in local debris and vegetation.

"This isn't a dig at all," she said.

"No," he said. "Right now, only a discovery. As I said, you are here to validate the nature of our finds. Later, someone will dig." His grim smile widened until white teeth showed. "Perhaps you will have this dig, Nikkis?"

She ignored the use of her first name, the chilling smile, and sideways promise. "The edges are masonry of some kind. From the looks of the exposed brickwork, it's likely Roman-period construction." Excitement warmed her blood. She wanted to laugh out loud, but she breathed more deeply and tried to suppress the surge of joy. She had to stay calm, to prove herself professional. She reminded herself that the fragments at the warehouse had told her as much.

"Very good, Dr. Aristos," he said. "I had initially thought it Venetian, but it didn't take us long to validate the Roman brick-making techniques."

"The Linear-A came from here? That doesn't make sense."

"If this situation fit into the current beliefs about the divisions between pre-Doric, Roman, and modern artifacts, we would not have need of you, Dr. Aristos."

Nikkis suddenly felt very glad they needed her. She was beginning to think these men might be very intolerant of people they didn't need.

"Shall we go down?" he asked. He pulled the line from the tripod and winch. There was a military-issue climbing harness attached to it. He gestured to her hips with the harness. "I'll help you."

She took the harness from him. "I know how it works." She put the sling on herself, stepping into the leg holes, slipping the harness up over her thighs, settling her rear into it so the heavier, under-slung straps would support her like a swing.

While she cinched in the waist of the harness, she wanted to turn her back on the leering Andros. In spite of her clothes, his gaze left her feeling immodest, almost
~~~

naked. For the first time, she cursed the shirts and zip-shorts Yorgos had made her buy.

Even so, she knew better than to show that he affected her in any way.

She forced herself to take a breath in spite of her desire to hurry and get down the hole to see the inside of the brickwork. She methodically checked each fitting, strap, and buckle. When she was ready, she grabbed the winch, shook it to test its anchors, and, satisfied that it would hold her, she turned her back to the hole, leaned into the harness, and let her weight settle out and back over the dark maw in the earth. "Light?" she asked.

From an equipment box near the winch, Andros produced a battery-operated, fluorescent hand-held.

He reached for a D-ring on her hip.

She intercepted his hand and took the light. She hooked its safety lanyard to the D-ring herself. Then, holding the light in her left hand, she grasped the line to the winch in her right.

The last thing she checked was Yorgos. Behind Andros, he stood like one of the statues she had seen on the trail to the village. Only his eyes moved, scanning the surrounding hills. Briefly, their eyes met. He nodded slightly.

Settling her weight fully into her harness, she said, "On belay."

"I'll be here," Andros said. "When you want to come up, whistle once."

She nodded.

"You know how to whistle, don't you?"

She cut off his clumsy attempt at flirtation. "Lower me," she said.

Andros pulled a lever on the side of the winch.

The line played out. She leaned back against the line until she hung over the edge at a thirty-five-degree angle and could walk down the broken-block lip of the hole. Carefully, she moved step-over-step. After about a meter, she came to the edge of the broken dirt and masonry. Beneath her, darkness opened up under the lip of what now appeared to be a domed and vaulted roof. Nikkis's heart pounded faster. It wasn't a cave. It was a structure. A large one.

She let the line come on, leaning back farther to prepare to dangle from the line. Finally, she bent deep at her knees, braced a hand against the Roman brick so she could move her feet below the dome without swinging and smashing into the bricks.

Once below the dome, sitting in her harness like a swing, dangling in mid-air darkness, she turned on the fluorescent.

Light flooded the interior of the house-sized chamber.

Dr. Nikkis Aristos went to work.

Quickly, she defined the space. It was Roman brick-work making up an interior-vaulted dome, and the dome had been situated above a natural chamber of native limestone and marble.

Temple? Burial vault?

Deep in natural rock, many glittering sparks flashed up at her.

She looked down into a black cavern full of sparkling fairies.

This was gypsum crystal, a subterranean form of calcium made of the same stuff as limestone and marble, only softer and newer and, because it was so fragile, never found anywhere except in pockets and caverns deep underground. This was the material that had once covered the walls of Knossos, once caught the light and flashed it outward so that any who approached the palace would see giant, blinding, shining walls.

She couldn't help being overwhelmed by the sheer glory of the sparkling light in the heart of the earth.

It didn't take much longer for her to touch down inside the domed cavern. Weight once more on her feet, she stepped toward the gypsum-crystal walls. The crystals looked like a thousand butterfly wings frozen on stone and waiting for sunlight to touch them, melt them, and set them free.

She pulled up hard against her line. It threatened to lift her if she pushed against it. Backing off a bit and fiddling with her harness, her light swept and flashed in the cavernous space.

Her eye caught another sight, the sight she had been sent into the earth to examine.

Fragments of marble like the ones she had seen in the warehouse littered the sparkling floor of the cavern. If the gypsum crystal was a nest of butterfly wings, then the white marble was a cruel joke of man or gods—mysterious stones tossed from the heavens to crush the helpless butterflies.

She looked up. Rays of sunlight streamed through the hole in the roof of the chamber, the source of the fallen stone.

"Andros! I'm down. Slack!"

Another half meter of line played out. When the line stopped, she unhooked her harness, focused her light, and moved to examine the walls and fragments.

The exterior of the dome was made of Roman brick. Inside the Roman brick, a lining layer of very carefully cut-and-fitted stones made smooth walls. She bent to touch a broken liner stone. Slick marble.

She picked up a fragment of liner and found something as wondrous as the gypsum crystals.

Linear-A.

She picked up another fragment.

More Linear-A.

Every fragment of liner stone was covered in it.

She flashed her light upward and strained her eyes to see the walls of the vaulted chamber.

The walls were covered it in. Every stone was inscribed with Linear-A.

She laughed. There was no doubt in her mind that the find was authentic. Andros had been right to call her in, and it was no wonder that the archeologists in Crete had chosen to ignore him. The stones had mortar on them from the Roman period. They had fragments of Roman brick attached to them.

Roman brick had protected the Linear-A from the elements for two thousand years.

The Romans had quarried the older stone from somewhere. That somewhere was the true source of the glyphs. The Romans had used the scripted stones to line the roof and walls of a cistern. *Of course*, she thought, *Linear-A had less value to the Romans than the stone.* She laughed out loud. Inside the domed chamber, her laugh echoed. The reverberations brought a light rain of dust from the ceiling.

She revised her considerations. *Not a temple. Not a burial vault.* The circular chamber at the low end of the valley drainage was a Roman cistern, a catch for water to be sent by aqueduct to lower lands.

"Dr. Aristos?" Andros called. "Are you alright?"

"Fine, Andros," she called back. "In fact, wonderful!" She had fulfilled her dream, and suddenly all the travel, the indignity, the humiliation, the leering men, the fears and foolishness of the town, all of it was meaningless. She had found a cache of Linear-A carved by some hand over three thousand years ago, carved into marble and later used to seal the inside of a Roman cistern.

And, if the stone at the warehouse were an indicator, somewhere inside this ruin she'd find stones that also had Ancient Greek on them. At the least, her name would be associated with the largest cache of Linear-A ever found. If she were very lucky, her next paper might be about the new Rosetta Stone that let her completely decipher Linear-A.

How like the Romans to destroy the artifacts of the culture on which their civilization had been built.

She turned a slow circle, her light passing along the chamber walls like a lighthouse beacon.

Her feet crushed fragile stone butterflies.

She froze. She gripped the fragments in her hand harder. She pressed her fingertips against the sharp, clean edges, smiled, and warmed to the visions of publication, of fame, of respect, of walking away from Crete and Andros and never again tolerating manipulative people like Karin Anderson in her life.

She ran her fingers along the edges, and then she stopped and all her fantasies dropped away. Her fingers rested on the mason's mark—the same mason's mark.

The lybris again.

The lybris with the eight-petal flower—the same mark as at Knossos. The same mark as the statues. It was the same mark again, but it couldn't be. The same man couldn't have carved all the various artifacts.

The artifacts holding the mark came from periods spanning at least three thousand years.

So, she told herself, it wasn't a mason's mark at all. It was a symbol. It meant something she hadn't yet understood. A career could be made on that mark alone.

She put several fragments of stone into her belt pouch. Returning to the center of the chamber, she hooked into the slack line and whistled sharply.

She braced for the line's pull.

Nothing happened.

She whistled again.

Muffled by the hole, gunfire answered her whistle.

~~~

A sharp whistle from the surrounding hills caught Andros's attention. He looked up from the dark hole that had swallowed Nikkis. Like water spilling over
~~~

the battlements of a sandcastle, red dust poured from the cuts and crags above the valley—the cloying, killing red fog of the sirocco, the wind that carried dust clouds from the Sahara over the Mediterranean to Crete where it moved like a slow, hot fog.

In minutes, the valley would fill with it.

In minutes, a man would not be able to see more than a few meters.

"Shit."

He abandoned the winch and hurried to his own tent. There, he gathered his weapons. The tent flap opened. Muscus came in. "You're late," Andros said.

"From the change in the weather, I'd say I'm just in time."

"They'll come now." Andros pulled back the slide of his PPQ.

"You mean *he'll* come."

"He won't be alone." He put a single round in the chamber and closed the slide.

"No. But some of them didn't make it here. I found them gathering."

"Damn them," Andros said. "They knew the dust would come." He slid a full magazine into the weapon, flicked up the safety, and holstered it.

"They've lived here a very long time." Muscus mocked him.

Andros only nodded. He put extra magazines in the pockets of his vest.

"You want me to work from camp or in the hills?"

"I have other work for you." He reached into his pack, pulled out a small piece of paper, and handed it to Muscus.

Muscus read the note Yorgos had given to the working girl under the warehouse. "Tylissus's man," he said. "You should have given him to me the first day."

"He served a purpose. Now," Andros said, "is the time and place."

"Some of the other men like him."

"Do it during the attack. It will make them hate the locals more."

As if his words were prophecy come true, gunfire erupted in the little valley.

"Use this." Andros pulled a traditional, curved dagger from his pack and handed it to Muscus.

The little man raised an eyebrow in question.

"Later," Andros said, "there will be sympathy and support for bringing our men and equipment into the valley."

"You have the key to the script, then?"

"I think so," Andros said. "Go."

The little man vibrated with unwholesome excitement. He turned and almost danced out into the red cloud and firefight.

Andros looked forward to the day when he would be rid of association with such uncouth monsters.

~~~

She stared at the sky, mouth open. The blue above her seemed to know that violence was happening outside. It changed from the brilliant blue of a hot, late morning sky to an eerie, dusky red. It was like the perfect blue paint on the sky had suddenly turned to blood and rust.

Another shot sounded.

Nikkis called for Andros.

Another.

"Andros!"

A staccato burst of automatic gunfire answered her. To her, it sounded more like a string of children's firecrackers than deadly force, but she knew better.

For a terrifying moment, she wondered if she should yell again or stay silent.

Yorgos's face appeared over the hole. "Stay where you are. Kill your light. Hide!"

His voice carried desperation and fear—fear for her.

She started to ask why, but his massive head and shoulders jerked. His huge body fell forward and wedged in the opening for a terrible moment before it broke through. Backlit by the red light, she watched him tumble through space like a limp scarecrow someone had stuffed though the hole and into her cistern.

She jumped back, but she was hooked to the line. Her lunge used up the slack. Momentum lifted her feet from the earth and turned her into a pendulum.

Yorgos hit the ground hard and made three horrible sounds all at once: a hissing moan from his lips, a crunching sound from his ribs, and the ripe melon sound of his skull cracking.

A wave of horror and nausea washed through her. She vomited, swung, and twisted on the line, lifting her feet so she didn't touch him. She swung and struggled to see above her and below her at the same time, trying to wipe off her face, catch her breath, and find a place to set her feet and release her harness.

Finally, she got one foot on the ground, lunged upward, and released herself.
~~~

The line snapped loose. She fell on her back, crystal butterflies crushed beneath her and her face next to Yorgos's.

She gasped in dry, ancient air, trying to fill lungs suddenly emptied. Precious heartbeats passed before she breathed well enough to speak. "Yorgos. Can you hear me?"

He only stared, his pupils fixed and dilated, his breath no longer moving—his lungs no longer able to move it.

She sat up, grabbed him, and shook him. "Yorgos!"

His massive head lolled to one side. Blood trickled along the line of his neck.

Nikkis pulled her hands away. She slapped at her harness until she found her light. Shining it on his head and neck, she found a red line below his ear. The wound was so tiny—no more than two inches long, but it had sent the huge man into her hole. He'd been knifed—cut beneath the ear in one fast strike.

She couldn't wrap her mind around it. Such a huge man couldn't have been killed so quickly. So much life simply couldn't be gone that fast.

Breathing deeply to get control, she reminded herself that she knew enough physiology from her study of ancient bladed weapons to know that the knife had severed his carotid. While it was an expert blow and would have killed him, it was the fall that had actually killed him. The gush of blood would have been tremendous unless his heart had stopped pumping it, and there wasn't nearly enough blood on the floor for him to be dead of loss.

She swallowed hard, trying to keep from vomiting again. She swallowed again and again before she spoke to herself by name. "Dr. Aristos," she said. "Focus. You need to focus and move forward, here." In a way, in her shock-induced, surreal, objectively clinical moment, she believed Yorgos lucky to have not had to stare at the useless interior of the cistern while his lifeblood pumped out through helpless fingers grasping at his own throat.

Shadows moved above her.

She looked up and saw a man's shadow, this time with his back to her. In the darkening, red light above, she saw a flash of a man wearing fatigues, then someone dressed all in black and wearing a head-covering black hood bolted past the opening.

Thieves or terrorists.

She switched off her light and rolled away from Yorgos as silently she could. She rolled until she hit the wall, where she crawled quickly to a shadowed space between the bed of gypsum and the thick base support for the vaulting of the Roman dome. Turning her face into the wall, she hoped for invisibility in the shadows.

Men called out in several languages: German, Greek, something guttural and dark.

Silence.

A scream.

More gunfire.

Silence.

She waited, counting like a child playing hide-and-seek, telling herself she would count to 500. If the gunfire stopped for that long, she would call for help.

Sounds of combat continued, and she started over several times before she managed the full count in silence. When she finally reached 500, she held her breath and listened. The cistern seemed to echo a hissing, scratching sound.

She couldn't place it—didn't recognize it. It might have been anything.

Five hundred wasn't even ten minutes, she told herself. She had no idea how long a firefight could last. Adrenaline made it seem longer. She had probably counted too fast.

She began her count again.

At fifteen-hundred, she had calmed enough to realize that the hissing sound was too regular to be made by a man's movements or even the movements of monsters imagined in the dreams of the child that wanted to scream and cry inside her.

The hissing was too rhythmic and random to be the sound of equipment or burning fuses or any of the many dangers she imagined.

She lifted her head and peered through the dim red light bathing the interior of the cistern. Through the hole above, where she should have been able to see high sun and blue, she found only dark red, as if some god-like photographer had covered the sun with a red filter so thick that it obscured everything beyond ten meters.

She got up, moved to Yorgos's body, grasped the cable and tugged tentatively. The line held. She yanked hard.

It still held.

She didn't want to call for help, and she didn't want to stay in the cistern.

Yorgos didn't need help; but if she stayed with him, it wouldn't be long before she'd need help. She had no water or food. She didn't know who, if anyone, would be waiting for her above or looking for her.

She pulled herself up the cable, hand-over-hand, cable wrapped around a leg and ankle to act as a lock and leverage like an acrobat. She'd never done such a thing before, but her body knew the trick. It was like her muscles remembered performing in a circus long ago—before her conscious memories began.

Insane. She was going insane.

The silly, vomit-acid laugh that wanted to rise from her belly into her mouth told her just how terrified she was.

At the rim, her arms and shoulders burned and ached from the effort. She held her breath and peeked out into the camp. Thick red dust covered everything. The dust floated in the air. It was the air. It was so fine she could feel it going into her nostrils, but she couldn't actually see it in the air. The redness and deep alien nature of a landscape that had only hours before felt so right in so many tiny, indescribable ways, now confused and terrified her.

In the couple of meters or so she could see, nothing moved.

She looked down. Yorgos and her light lay at the bottom of the hole. Too late, she realized he still wore the pistol on his hip. That and the light might have been useful, but her arms burned from the climb. If she went back, she'd never be able to climb out again.

She crawled out of the hole onto her stomach.

No gun. No light.

She clawed at her pockets for her cell. She found it and pulled it out. A spider web of white cracks covered the dark face. She shook it, but it was as dead as Yorgos. She let it fall from her fingers. It bounced on the lip of the hole and fell away into Yorgos's grave.

Remembering the cliff downslope and afraid of being seen by going near the tents, she stayed on her belly and crawled up the valley and toward the north ridge.

After crawling fifty meters or so, the red dust completely covered her—completely.

It covered everything—every blade of grass, bush, stone, and inch of her flesh and clothing.

She stifled a cough and pulled her sunglasses and a bandana from her shorts pocket. She tied the bandana around her nose and mouth like a TV bandito. In spite of the dim light, she put on the sunglasses, hoping they would keep dust from her burning eyes.

Finally, as prepared for the unknown as she could be under the circumstances, Nikkis Aristos stood and ran as fast as she could. She ran from a dig that would make her career and life. She ran from thieves and murderers. She ran from people who did not respect the law.

While she ran, she promised herself that she would apologize to Andros for doubting him, for believing him melodramatic, for actually, at one point, thinking perhaps he was a crooked cop engaged in some scam she couldn't understand. The attack had proven the truth of his tales of violent smugglers and bandits.

She hoped Andros was alive, that he, like her—at least for now—had escaped.

The initial adrenaline surge that drove her to her feet and into a run quickly gave way to exhaustion and fear of falling.

Escape from masked gunmen and knives was only a relief as long as she had someplace to escape to, and after running for two minutes, Nikkis realized she had no place to run. In fact, she had already lost track of where she had run from.

Tears poured from her eyes.

Like the old woman in the taverna, she neither sobbed nor heaved. She told herself she wasn't panicked or grieving.

Scared, yes.

She told herself she wasn't crying. It would only be crying if she broke her stoic silence and sobbed out loud.

It was the dust.

The dust made her tears pour out.

She told herself the tears were good. Their free flow protected the soft tissue of her eyes. It was the body protecting itself from primal conditions.

A small, choking sound escaped her mouth.

She swallowed and forced herself to breathe normally. She would not cry. She would not!

The camp and south ridge should be to her right. The vague circle of red brightness in the sky over her right shoulder had to be the sun. It had to.

Climb. She decided to climb. As long as she climbed, she couldn't stumble over a cliff. As long as she climbed, she had to be moving away from the valley floor and the scene of the battle. As long as she climbed, she was putting difficult terrain between herself and any pursuing death.

Keeping the sky-glow behind and to her right and the slope in front of her as much as possible, she went on, reciting one of her many mantras of determination, the same mantras that had helped her in grad school, that had gotten her through the politics of academia, and that had brought her to Crete.

Action creates change. Action creates change.

Between mantras, just in case, she also prayed to whatever gods still held sway in Crete. She prayed for help.

Her mind scrambled for a pattern, for a way to make sense of things, a way to find her way back to the village. She'd even settle for the vile Muscus. At least he was a policeman.

She'd been so wrong about Andros. No wonder he and his men carried guns. No wonder Andros's moods could move so quickly from flirtatious to cold and grim.

She'd been so wrong about everything.

Dust inside her shirt, her shorts, and her ears ground against her skin. It covered her skin and made her red, which she hoped turned her into a ghost on the hills of Crete. She smelled like burned sand. The world smelled like burned sand, like hell must smell on a very bad day.

As if thinking of a ghost created one, a long, low moan came from the shifting dust.

Nikkis froze and crouched low.

Only the hiss of dust moving over rocks and plants came to her ears.

She crept forward.

The wailing came again—a deep, bass voice like a bear in agony, or perhaps it sounded like a man who had been shot. She thought of Yorgos and the other men. She wondered what kind of men would attack an armed camp of police.

There would be time to find people when the red dust cleared—if it cleared. She had no desire to meet moaning friends or foes under these conditions. She angled still higher and away from the voice. She slowed and lifted her feet and placed them down more deliberately, as cautiously and quietly as she could, trying to use silence and the cover of the dust storm to keep her hidden.

A dust storm. Like a sand storm.

For the first time, she became fully conscious of the fact that she was in a dust storm.

Of course. She'd heard of this. The sirocco sifted and lifted the fine sands of the Sahara, took them aloft, swept them across the Mediterranean, let them settle from above in a windless, drifting haze of red.

She almost laughed, but she was afraid to open her mouth. Fear had made her a child. Some superstitious part of her thought that the dust had a supernatural explanation and that maybe, just maybe, the ancient ghosts, shades sent by Hades, had come in the blood wind to kill the defilers of history.

It was funny—her, a rational, trained Ph.D., believing in such things even on a subliminal level when she understood perfectly well that a wind superstitious old women believed carried sickness and called the big tongue had carried fine dust over to Crete and covered probably the whole island and not just her little part of it.

The hooded men had used it to cover their attack, and they had probably never known she was in the hole.

She silently thanked Yorgos. He had died to protect her.

She'd been afraid of superstitions that probably came from stories put in her head before she could remember by her parents.

Only superstitions.

She smiled. Gritty dust reminded her to close her lips.

A shadow appeared in front of her.

She froze.

A tall, narrow boulder, she told herself.

It moved.

A man. A big man.

The shadow was a man's, but his head was huge. He turned.

Not a man. In silhouette, long, curved horns swept out and forward over a snout.

A monster. A minotaur.

Terror stripped her of her rationalizations and turned her into a child.

She crouched low. She held her breath, afraid he might hear.

He's a man, she told herself, but she remembered Yorgos and Andros talking about The Minotaur as if he were something more than a man—something to be feared.

No. No such thing. This had to be a man. The dust made his head seem misshapen. Maybe he wore a helmet with something stuck on it.

The top of her own head might have come to his chin, but his strange head made him easily two feet taller than her, and his shoulders were wider than two of her, and his waist narrowed to the size of her shoulders.

God, he was huge. Bigger than Yorgos. But his head....

The dust thinned between them.

His black, thick head began at his shoulders with no narrowing at the neck. Atop that head, horns, broad, dark, and pointed spread outward and forward.

He *was* a minotaur.

The Minotaur. The Minotaur the guards had talked about. She had thought it was some police codename, maybe the name of a known thief.

But it—he stood here in front of her, a creature of shadow and myth, and the dust storm had brought him out of his dark labyrinth.

This was no apparition. The creature turned first left then right, searching for something in the dust. It was real. It was a thing from the past, from childhood dreams of helplessness.

Instinctively, she hugged a boulder and prayed to the gods and goddesses of this terrible land, prayed for the gift of invisibility.

Ancient Tested Love

One hundred of King Minos's soldiers, each sworn to do the king's will or to die in the attempt, had left the shining palace at Knossos to attend the wedding of Daedalus and Nikkis. Fifty-seven returned, and all of them knew they owed their lives to the master mason and his wife.

Daedalus held Nikkis close, knowing that soon they would be parted and that quite possibly they would never see one another again.

Tall, broad, and grim, Yorgos walked beside them.

The trio, side-by-side as equals, strode the paved way to Knossos. Behind them, soldiers lined out in triple columns, swords sheathed, lances reversed, and helmets off, marking step with the leader of each column. The soldiers did all they could to show their respect for the man and woman they had been sent to capture.

Daedalus understood the tribute the soldiers showed, and he hoped that in some way it would help, but hope was a hard thing to keep alive when tested against his knowledge of this king and queen and their jealousies and appetites.

"I give you my sorrow, Lord of Stone and Men," Yorgos said.

"We have known each other too long, Yorgos. Let me be Daedalus to you, if I am worthy of that name on any man's lips."

Nikkis, one arm around her husband's waist, laid her other hand on the huge forearm of the soldier. "This is not your doing, Yorgos. In the village, you spoke wisdom. You do this because to do otherwise would cause death in your own village."

"Truth," Yorgos said, "does not take the taste of cowardice from my mouth, nor does it free me of the debt I owe. If my people would be spared and it were my life alone, I would die for you before letting those who rule here bring you under their roof."

"My roof," Daedalus said.

Yorgos nodded. "I pray that the magic of your hands is stronger than fate, Daedalus."

Nikkis squeezed Daedalus's waist. "Ah," she said. "A fine day to return to our house!" She stepped forward and danced a turn in the sunlight. She began to sing a song of bringing home grapes to be crushed, a song that every man, woman, or child of the island knew. It was both joyous and sad. It spoke of growth and life and death and resurrection in the bounty of wine.

She danced ahead of the column, hands high in the sunlight, hips swaying and feet stepping high and quick. She spun and swayed and played the part of vine in the wind, naked grape crusher, and finally joyful drinker.

Daedalus laughed and took up her song.

And Yorgos.

Soon, all the soldiers, each and every one from a distant village where grapes were grown, had joined the song. Feet kept time. The shining walls of the palace Daedalus had built came closer, and the road widened to accept more and more traffic from the hills and valleys in all directions.

The song grew louder and louder until Daedalus was sure a thousand voices sang as one. He looked around. Behind him, the road was choked with soldiers and carts and men and women.

Some, he recognized instantly. They had followed in secret all the way from the village. Some, he had never met.

He wondered at the magic of the people who work the land. Word traveled in the hills faster than a hunting kite can sail the skies from one side of Crete to the other. Here they were, spilling like water from tributaries, flowing from road and trail to join the mainstream of soldiers and villagers from Nikkis's home. As if word had been carried across all of Crete on the wind, they came to walk with Nikkis and Daedalus. All had come to parade up to the gates of the shining palace.

Daedalus sang. He sang from the deepest part of his soul. He sang his fear and his love and his meager hope. He sang for the glory of the people who followed, and he sang for the memory of his lost son. In his song, where grapes are crushed and juice saved and sadness rises into hope, he moved quickly forward and began to dance with his wife.

They sang and danced their way into captivity, and all who walked the road with them that day lived forever proud of having seen the sight and sung the song. All who walked with them remembered and told the tale of the mason who had built the shining palace and the herding girl he loved. Soldiers told of being saved. Herders told of being spared. Midwives spoke a tale of love. They told the tale to children, and they told it to lovers, and they told it to strangers in shaded tavernas. Within a week, the glory and honor of Daedalus and Nikkis became legend from one end of Crete to the other and even beyond.

~~~

Queen Pasiphae stroked the long, sleek side of one of her asps. The creature coiled around her forearm, taking advantage of the warmth of her body and the heat of the sun shining down on her balcony.

To the south, the palace road echoed with a song of sadness and joy. She knew the song. It was an old song, a song of her goddess and the land. It brought tears to her eyes to hear so many voices singing—so many. How long had it been since such tribute had been paid to her goddess? Too long. Not since before the Bull-King had invaded her home.

Like an army of ants pouring forth from a single hole, the throng of singers crested a rise and appeared on the road.

She gasped at the sight.

The serpent tightened around her arm.

At the head of the column, two figures capered like young goats. They swung, and danced, and swayed, and in the sunlight, their dark hair flashed copper lights. Their work-darkened skins glistened with sweat.

She knew the master mason instantly. She imagined his bride, the herd girl she had heard about, danced beside him.

Behind them, the king's Death Army marched, spear-points reversed and helmets off.

Surrounding all, a thousand hill people ran, danced, and sang.

She wondered at the spectacle of the people of the hills dancing with soldiers on the road to the north entrance to the palace. She searched her memory for some holy day or heroic festival she had somehow forgotten, but she found nothing.

No. She was sure. Whatever this procession was, it was a new thing—a thing of gods and goddess moving the hearts of men and women upon the earth.

She stared in wonder at the sight.

The asp bit her at the wrist. Venom burned in her flesh.
~~~

She had no fear of the venom, but she wondered that the serpent should bite without ritual or warning.

The song grew. The people came on.

The goddess came to her in the vision brought by the serpent's fangs.

Queen Pasiphae turned from the parade and entered her chambers. Before the vision came full upon her, she returned the asp to its basket.

She reclined on her cushions. Silks behind her bed parted, and a servant appeared with a jug of wine.

"Pour," she said. "Then, I will be alone."

The servant poured.

Pasiphae drank. The distant song mingled with the wine, and she smelled the crushing of grapes and the sweat of harvest days. Within the euphoria of the wine and venom, the song of the people rose and fell. Her body wanted to move with that sound, to undulate, to move and be a part of the song.

The servant left, and Pasiphae lay back to accept the full blossoming of her vision, of the will of her goddess.

The song grew louder. The voices caressed her skin. Thousands walked behind Daedalus and Nikkis. In the hills of Crete, thousands and thousands more thought of them. *The spirits of Daedalus and Nikkis became one, a golden serpent undulating through the hills, pressing forward toward the palace—a two-headed serpent with one voice.*

They were the will of the goddess.

The two of them together had become the will of the people and the land.

Pasiphae stood before the advancing serpent. She tried to join the song.

The serpent's tongue lashed out and swept her aside. The great beast of song moved past her.

She jumped up. She called after it. "I am Pasiphae! I am first priestess!"

The serpent paid no heed.

Alone beside the road the mason had built, she wept.

The song grew stronger. It gathered in voices the way the crushing vat gathers in grapes.

She looked up, and the tail of the serpent was passing. Quickly, she wiped away her tears, rushed forward, and grasped the tip of the tail.

It coiled around her hand and embraced her arm. It pulled her along at the serpent's tail. Least among the legion of singers, she gratefully joined the song.

~~~

The singing legion passed the outdoor theater Daedalus had built and danced up to the northern-most entrance of the shining palace of Knossos. There, before red pillars and cypress plank doors, Daedalus and Nikkis stopped dancing and singing.

Above them shone the terraced roofs and brilliant walls. Higher still rose the red pillars and covered terrace where the king and queen could stand to look out over the road.

Nikkis's arm snaked around Daedalus's waist.

He pulled her close. In the heat of her hip against him, he found the courage to face the coming trials.

Yorgos stood beside them. "We've come far, Daedalus. The road is flat, but I see no easy path from here."

Daedalus nodded. He looked up. Above the palace doors and beneath the balcony of the king loomed the giant, stone horns he had fashioned with his own hands, the horns meant to symbolize the power of the king, meant to remind all who approached that within the maze of the palace was an arena. In that arena, the bull, the symbol of the king's power, chose life or death for anyone who dared stand before it.

The song of the people trailed away on the wind. A jackdaw, high in a cypress, cried out, hoarse and shrill.

"I sense no easy paths," Daedalus said, "but, perhaps, I can find a path the king does not expect."

Yorgos smiled. He set his feet apart, squared his shoulders, and settled the point of his javelin in the earth. "Show me your path, Daedalus," he said.

Behind them, a rippling rattle of armor and bronze weapons rolled away from them and back to the farthest ranks.

Daedalus glanced back. Every soldier stood in rank and file, matching their captain in stolid form. Daedalus promised himself that if he lived through this day, he would one day carve statues to show the world the hearts of these men, these guardians of honor.

He and Nikkis faced the palace.

"King of Knossos! Strength of the Bull! Herdsman of all of the People of Crete! I am Daedalus, Master Mason, who raised the walls of your palace for the glory of your nation!"
~~~

His words echoed off silent walls then followed the people's song away on the breeze.

Helios whipped his horses. Shadows moved the width of a man's finger.

"He will not speak to you thus," Yorgos said.

"A king who hopes to fly might speak so to a man who can give him wings," Daedalus said. "If you and your men hold, he will speak to me."

Behind them, another ripple of sound rolled from the rear ranks forward—a gasp, the hiss of air pressed from a hundred chests through surprised lips. The gasp came from the farthest tail of the serpent of men, and it gathered strength and volume until it swept over Daedalus and died against the walls of Knossos.

Yorgos turned. "I see nothing," he said.

"The king comes," Daedalus said. "Those in the rear can see him first."

Yorgos turned back and nodded.

As Daedalus expected, King Minos appeared on the balcony above the stone horns. Framed in the sky between red columns, he spoke. "Your army has no weapons against these walls, Daedalus, Fool of Stone."

"I have no army, King of Knossos. I come of my free will. My wife walks beside me. We seek the legendary justice of the wise King of Knossos."

"I have sent for you, and my men have brought you. There is no more." The king turned away to leave.

"No!" Yorgos cried.

The king turned back.

"The mason and his wife led us home!"

The king frowned down on his captain.

Daedalus saw Yorgos marked for death in that look from the king.

The king spoke. "You were lost?"

"Doomed," Yorgos said.

"King of Knossos," Daedalus called so all could hear, "who was given the gift of the White Bull, who commanded that stones be brought from the earth to create this palace, who keeps peace and prosperity for all in this empire, I ask for the justice of your bull!"

Nikkis gasped. "No!"

"Mason, this–" Yorgos began.

The howls and clattering of soldiers and hill folk drowned out all sound.

After a long moment of cacophony, the king roared, "Silence!"

The assembled hissed and stomped and howled.

"Silence!"

The din grew.

Daedalus stepped forward and mounted the first steps up to the gate. He turned and held his hands up. The sea of people calmed. Their howling and hissing died off.

The king's withering gaze shifted from Yorgos to Daedalus. A smile spread across his face. "Face the bull. The gods shall decide your fate!" The king chuckled and turned.

Again, Daedalus called him back. "Should I survive the justice of the bull, the king's boon shall be mine?"

For the second time, Minos turned. Daedalus waited while the king looked out over the thousands assembled below him, while he glanced at Yorgos and the columns of soldiers who were supposed to be loyal only to Minos.

Daedalus waited for the king's answer. Kings like Minos, who had taken their power rather than inherited it, were seldom complete fools. He would answer, and he would use this moment to secure his power over the people of Knossos and all of Crete.

The answer came. "Ask."

It was neither promise nor commitment, but Daedalus answered as if it were both. "Freedom for myself and my wife. We wish only to be together forever, to love one another until time ends. We ask no more."

The answer came too quick.

"*Done!*" the king bellowed. "In six weeks! On the turn of the season!"

King Minos turned and strode into the shadows of the palace. His laughter echoed from the terrace for a moment before following him into the darkness of Knossos.

A thousand mouths sent forth cheers and screams and whistles of joy.

Amid the chaos, Nikkis put her hand on his wrist. "I don't trust–"

"A king's promise," Yorgos said. "Made in front of thousands."

"A king's promise." Daedalus wrapped her hands in his. "A lie and a truth. It is all we have."

"Six weeks," Yorgos said. "Six weeks before the festival of the changing year. He will hurt you before then. He will covet your wings and rape your wife."

"I will die first," Nikkis said.

"No." Daedalus took her in his arms. He surrounded her with his strength. He willed his love to touch her, and he found her fear and soothed it. "As long as you live, I live," he said. "As long as you breathe, I have hope. As long as the king believes he and his soldiers might one day fly, you will be safe."

"A dangerous path," Yorgos said, "to play at the games of kings."

"Yes," Daedalus said. "But not a path he expected."

The heavy doors opened.

Daedalus, hand-in-hand with Nikkis, waved to the assembled. Amid their cheers, he and Nikkis walked into the Bull's Labyrinth of Knossos.

~~~

Daedalus had built the palace down the side of a west-facing hill overlooking the Vlychia and the valley of the Kairatos into which it flowed. Thus, the face of the palace, canted slightly to the south, took in the warmth of the sun from dawn to dusk. The rooftops of the palace towered several levels above the crest of the hill. Using the tricks he had learned to gather water in Ur, he had created catches and sluices and angles in the surrounding hilltop and in the roof so that captured rainwater channeled into stone cisterns high on the hill. Those cisterns, in their turn, were covered in stone vaults. The design was very clever. Even though the cisterns were uphill from the main palace, any unwary visitor who somehow stumbled through the maze of the palace into the cistern vaults would believe themselves deep in the dark, damp, cool bowels of the palace.

Separated from Nikkis since they set foot in the halls of the palace, he had spent four weeks keeping her safe by teasing the king with progress on his wings.

At the end of the fourth week of his captivity, he found himself between two guards following Minos, a few retainers, and several torch-bearing soldiers along the narrow, dark hallways to the cisterns. One of the men carried a linen bag full of scraps of dripping, rotted meat. The stench filled the corridor.

He had heard that King Minos had ordered men drowned in the cisterns or in one of the pithoi, the giant urns of olive oil kept in deeper levels of the palace. Either way, men went into the cistern vaults or the cellars and never emerged into the light of day again. The why of it depended on the whims of Minos.
~~~

Four of his guards carried long planks of wood. Daedalus could not guess what use the king had for them, but he could not imagine that such an odd and deliberate item meant good for him or for Nikkis.

Walking in the cool, damp corridors, Daedalus feared that Nikkis might soon be alone in her struggle with the king and queen of Knossos.

The retinue halted. Water dropping from the vault arches into the cisterns made an echoing dripping sound.

The king spoke, his voice filling the vaulted chambers. "I will show you something of the craft of kings, Mason."

"As you please, Lord of Knossos," Daedalus said.

Daedalus had designed the pits to hold enough water to last a season for three hundred people. Six pits in all, he was proud of his cleverness in them, and all were now filled with water save one.

The king stood near the fourth pit, the empty one. He stroked his beard.

"I think," Minos said, "that you believe you have no Lord. I think you have the sickness of all men who travel widely. You've come to believe yourself beyond the laws of any land—beyond the power of any king."

"I am, as I have been since first I came to this island, at your service."

"I cannot fly," the King said. "I do not have the wings you promised me four weeks ago when I brought you and your bride back from the mountains—the wings I know you can build, wings like those you shattered and scattered high in the mountains."

"Lord Minos, I beg that you remember the bull I built for you. To trick the gods into believing in the death of a bull was the inspiration that let me believe I could trick them into allowing me to fly." It was a lie, but it was all the protection for Nikkis that he could find here in the bowels of Knossos.

"So you have said." The king kicked at a bit of gravel at the side of the empty pit. A pebble fell and clattered in the dry bottom.

Guards and retainers shuffled nervously, spread out along the narrow lip around the pits. The torch-bearers, dressed in belted aprons and nothing else, shook in the chill.

"I work in your service," Daedalus said.

"You serve your bride. You count the daily races of Helios and pray for your day in the arena."

Daedalus took a breath to hide his stiffening neck. He dared not show fear or weakness. The king had spoken the exact truth of his weeks of building failures to create shows of broken wings and torn leather so the king would believe in his efforts.

The King said, "My promise gives you your day in the arena. The day is set. I have accepted your offering of wings in return for denying your wife the privilege of bearing my sons."

It had occurred to Daedalus to teach the king to fly and let him fall to the sea. Certainly, Poseidon would thank him. Of course, the king would not fly himself until many men had died proving the wings. "I have not broken my promise, My King. I would see you safely in the skies rather than dashed to the sea like my son."

The king seemed to consider this new thought. After a long, uncomfortable moment, he said, "King's craft is about the land and the people."

"Of course," Daedalus said.

Minos motioned to a guard. The man stepped to the edge of the pit. He held up the linen bag of meat scraps. Blood and rotted stench dripped from the thing into the pit. Each drop of blood raised a small puff of dust and left a dark spot on the floor below.

"See in this pit my island kingdom." Minos pointed. "In this kingdom, my people believe themselves free." He nodded to the guard.

The man tossed the bag into the center of the pit.

"They have no true freedom," Minos said, "Just as the walls surround this pit, my people are jailed by the sea."

"My Lord," Daedalus said, "The meat will sour the water when this pit fills."

"This pit has never held water, Mason. Your hands failed in its building."

"All the more reason for care in building wings," Daedalus said.

"Once this pit is repaired, the water will be fouled, but not by *this* meat," Minos said. "Think of this pit, my truculent mason, as my island kingdom."

"I don't understand."

The king pointed to the pit floor. "My subjects will soon appear. Watch them, clever mason. Watch and learn the wisdom of the craft of kings."

Four guards moved close to the pit. They held torches high. Below, the reeking bag of garbage lay in the dust, undisturbed. At each of the four points of the Earth, the walls near the pit floor held holes for the exit of water to the many tunnels and tubes that would carry it to kitchens for use, or to baths for cleansing, or to sluices to clear away waste. Each small hole resembled the mouth of a round, dark cave.

"On my island," Minos said, "I have only so much grass for sheep and goats and cattle. On my island, olives and grapes grow between cracks in the stone. I have high mountains and an abundance of coastal villages and fish. I have other foods: tubers and fruits that grow in the highlands of Lasithi and nowhere else."

A scratching sound echoed within the circular walls of the cistern.

"My subjects approach." Minos's oiled beard glistened in the torchlight.

The same flickering light playing over the bag of meats cast jumping shadows in the bottom of the pit. Scratching and hissing made the sound of a sword scraped against a stone. From the holes came the high, grating screech of thousands of…

"Rats," Daedalus said.

"When goats and cattle eat the grass, they grow and breed and feed my people. Olives and grapes feed my people. Lasithi, the high plateau, feeds my people. Even with this abundance, I cannot give enough food to all my people, so my ships go to the sea to bring fish to the shores. I send my ships for trade to Athens, Troy, Cyprus, and Aegypt."

From the tiny caves set in the cistern at the four corners of the earth, black-and-gray rats poured like water. They gushed and flowed. The tide of fur, teeth, and claws inundated the bag of meat.

Still more rats poured into the pit. And more.

When the bottom of the pit was full, and when the flow of rats had subsided, Minos raised his hand, a gesture to a guard. The guard nodded to four others. Each stood above one of the stone holes from which the rats had come. Each slipped a long plank into the pit to cover the sluice holes and block the rats' escape.

The sea of mangy fur rippled. The ripple became a wave. It rolled one way and then the other, always a knot of boiling hunger roiling around the bag of meats.

Daedalus believed he watched his end. He believed he would soon replace the bag of meat at the bottom of the pit. He had failed Nikkis. His battle now was to hold his heaving belly and shaking knees in check. If the story of his end ever came to Nikkis, he wanted her to be proud. He wanted her to know that he had died with no other shame in his heart than that he failed to save her.

The knot in the center of the pit seethed, rolled, and boiled. A thousand hungry rat voices screamed their fear and desperation.

"In good seasons, Mason," Minos said, "the people live fat and happy and clean. They breed. Men fight, as they always do, but they fight over women.

"In bad seasons, the people become lean and angry. They send their sons to other villages to steal food. When the grass is dry, cattle die. When blight shrivels the olives, men fight over who owns the stronger trees. When the grapes are small and hard, men fight over who owns which row of vines."

The rats boiled, even though the bag of meat had been consumed. Still, the frenzy continued. Blooded fur and desperate hunger drove them to eat one another alive.

"In famine," Minos said, "men of peace will kill for a goat." He chuckled. "Your pale face tells me that you begin to see the craft of the king. See these, my subjects, eating one another in an island kingdom where there is this much but no more. See my subjects, who have grown fat and have bred and have come to the bad seasons when they have not enough of anything."

"No," Daedalus said. "Rats cannot think. Men are stronger in mind and heart."

Minos ignored him. "The wisdom of a strong king is the only thing that keeps men from consuming one another like rats. I stand before them as strength, a bull at the head of the herd, and I dispense justice. I decide who owns which tree, which vine, which woman."

Daedalus realized the king did not intend to kill him here. He meant to create fear. He meant to manipulate. "Why show me this?"

The king gestured to a guard.

The guard shoved one of the torch bearers into the pit.

Rats screamed and swarmed.

The man leapt up, rats clinging by tiny teeth to legs and arms. He still held his torch, and it still burned. Valiantly, he swung it like a branch. Rats screamed and burned—but not enough rats.

Soldiers shuffled nervously. They glanced at one another. They glanced at the king.

The man's screams for help joined the hungry, wailing din of the rats.

Veteran soldiers averted their eyes.

Daedalus did not.

Screams echoed in the chamber and rolled upward into the halls of the palace. The screams went on and on, the sound rising and falling and taking no breath.

The hapless man swung his torch. He begged for help.

"The craft of kings," Minos said. "Show strength so no man doubts that he will die if he is fool enough to lie or challenge or steal or fight when the will of the people and good of the kingdom are at stake. No man will dare bring the attention of the king to his home and family for fear he will be judged and treated thus.

"Choose, Mason. Give me wings that fly, or in chains you shall see my child cut from your wife's belly in the center of the market. The child will live. The bull shall trample you and what remains of your goat woman. Your remains shall be brought here so that you can be together forever. Thus, I shall keep my promise. Choose."

The king and his retinue left.

Daedalus turned to follow, but the soldiers barred his way. One pointed at the pit.

Alone with two soldiers, Daedalus faced the pit, the stench of death, and the echoing cries of rats consuming a man and one another.

The man in the pit stopped fighting the flood of fur and fang. He fell and covered his eyes with hands that bled and showed bone. He whimpered, writhed, and twisted under a coat of fur and blood.

Daedalus had no choice. He watched until the man's screaming and writhing ended. When the chaos of feeding was over, the surviving rats searched the walls for the covered exits.

One of his guards poured oil into the pit. The oil covered the thousands of tiny, clean rat bones mixed with the bones of a man. The rats licked at the oil, and the oil covered the bodies of half-eaten rats and coated the fur of the remaining rats.

The second soldier tossed a torch into the oil.

The pit erupted in flame. A wave of heat rolled upward and outward, pushing Daedalus and the guards back into a hallway. The spouts that fed the cisterns became chimneys. Smoke and flame rushed upward and outward. When the wave of heat had passed, the three men moved back to the pit and watched the leaping, screaming rats burn.

After the fire died, the guards took Daedalus to the deeps of the palace instead of his chambers or his workshop. They took him to the storerooms where, rumor said, the king sometimes ordered men drowned in olive oil.

Daedalus told himself that drowning would not give Minos his wings.

The guards placed him in a cold, stone storage pit in the palace belly, a pit he had built to keep fruits and tubers cool, a pit that could also be used to hide riches. The soldiers slid a stone slab over him. In the darkness he heard the scraping sound of a giant pithoi being placed on the stone above him, and he knew his death would not be so kind as being tossed to rats. He would be worked, starved, and weakened until he gave the king wings or died.

Once again, he found himself praying to Poseidon for time—time to find a way to save Nikkis.

~~~

Weeks passed. Each day, guards brought Daedalus out of his hole and marched him to his workshop. Each night, they returned him to the hole, a dark pit only large enough for a man to curl into a ball. It was like being pushed back into a womb made of rocks. The insult was all the greater because Daedalus had cut the stones with his own hands and set them in place according to his own design.

Each day, he labored on the wings for the king, and at the end of each day, the king himself inspected those wings. In the king's dark eyes, Daedalus watched the growth of lust for power and the growth of resentment and anger toward Daedalus. Each day, Daedalus remembered the lesson of the rats, and his fear grew—fear that Minos would never allow him to face the bull. Worse, he feared that Nikkis might never escape the king's plans for her.

At night, his womb of darkness both welcomed him and tormented him. When the stone had sealed him in, he breathed deeply to calm himself, and he set himself the task of working through the puzzle of his trap, of Nikkis's trap.

Each night, he failed.

The wings were nearly finished, and the changing of the seasons would come soon.

He rolled in his prison so that his face and hands lay flat against the stone belly of the tiny world he had built with no thought that it might one day be used for a prison for him or anyone else.

He pressed his cheek against familiar stone, and he whispered his despair, "I'm sorry, Nikkis."

The stone warmed beneath him. His hands knew the stone by the gift of the queen, the gift that would now become the bane of the entire world, for Daedalus knew he would finish the wings before he would let Nikkis die; and if he finished the
~~~

wings, she would die. Either way, the king would fly. His soldiers would fly, and his ships would sail, and it would be the end of the world.

Sunlight heated parts of the palace; shadow cooled other parts. As he had meant for it to do, the palace breathed. He listened to the breath of the stone. Fall air, the air of the hills, hissed through the stone. Soon, all of Crete would celebrate the bounty of the land.

His own breath matched the breath of the stones, and he let his heart move through his hands to seek his love.

Each night, he used the queen's gift to seek her. Each night, he found her in her chambers, locked in, cared for like a cow being prepared to sire a sacrificial calf.

Tonight, he reached for her through his sadness and found her. She breathed slowly.

At first, he thought she slept, but then he felt the footsteps of the king, footsteps he knew better than any other save those of Nikkis. The king's tread insulted the stone, and the stone cooled under his feet.

The king came to Nikkis's chamber.

Daedalus tried to wake her. *Nikkis. Nikkis.*

She did not stir. She merely breathed.

He gathered his mind and heart. He reached through the stones to far corners of the palace. He willed the movement of air through corners, through windows, beneath the floors so that the sound of the air would call her name.

Nikkis, the palace whispered.

She did not stir.

Her shallow breath came slow and deep. She didn't sleep. She had been drugged. The six weeks they had bargained for neared its end, and the king had not come to her, had not taken her. She had no reason to test her food or drink. She had not seen the rats. She had not seen Daedalus's fear.

Now, while Nikkis lay helpless, drugged, the king who fancied himself a bull came to her chambers.

Daedalus's anger grew. His blood heated. He rolled in his tomb and pressed his hands against the floor beneath which he had been sealed. He arched his back and pushed against the flat stone that sealed him in. He pressed until muscles in his back, shoulders, and thighs popped, until he collapsed, spent, into a mass of despair in the darks of the earth.

"Nikkis," he whispered.

"*Daedalus.*" He heard her voice in his mind and knew it to be true in his heart. "*Where are you?*"

He had tried to escape, to press the stones upward and to lift the many stone-weights of olive oil that rested in a giant urn above him, but he had never withdrawn his consciousness from the stone. And now, from her heart, she spoke to him. An impossible thing, but who was he to say a thing could or could not be? Too many things that could not be had passed in his life.

"Here," he said aloud. "I'm here."

"I can't move."

The king's footsteps entered her chamber. Daedalus heard avarice, lust, and vengeance in the man's voice.

A coward.

Daedalus raged. His rage moved through his hands and outward into the stone. The stone warmed where it had been cold beneath the bare feet of the king. It welcomed the rage of the mason who had cut and placed each slab.

The stone heated as if it had been in high summer sun all day. It heated like the stones over the great fires that heated the queen's baths.

The king danced and fell. He fell onto Nikkis's bed of cushions. To touch stone would be to feel the wrath of Daedalus.

Daedalus flexed his hands. He sought to move his stone prison, to bend or break it, but he had built it too well. Helpless, he listened and reached for the knowing of a moment he dreaded, the moment when the king moved to take Nikkis.

Nikkis stirred. She moved.

"Yes, my love," Daedalus said. "Wake."

In spite of the drugs, she woke. With heavy limbs, she attacked the surprised king. Though her body was slow, her will was as strong as the stones of Knossos. No man Daedalus had met could stand against her wrath.

He reveled in her will. He sent his own to help her, and when the king had fallen to the stones, leapt up and away from the burns, and retreated in terror, Daedalus hissed his love through the corridors of the palace.

"Forever, Nikkis."

"*Forever,*" she whispered, and she fell to her cushions, exhausted, still drugged, but safe for another night.

While Nikkis slept, Daedalus stared into darkness. Safety for one night was not enough.

The king's fear would give way to rage. He would come again, and he would bring soldiers, ropes, and chains. Daedalus needed help.

If his anger could heat the stones of the palace, perhaps he could do more.

He set his heart and mind to the task of seeking. He reached through the stones, but beyond the palace, beyond the stones he had cut and placed, his seeking felt like reaching into dark waters and groping for frogs in muck. He felt nothing and found nothing.

If the stones he had cut would respond, then perhaps the stones he had cut them from…

He searched the darkness beyond the palace for his quarry—for his quarry and his quarrymen.

Far beyond the cold and dark, he found both quarry and men. They still toiled, though their joy had fled beneath club and lash.

~~~

When Helios had raced to his highest point in the sky, the king's men came for Pasiphae like she was some concubine, a mere heifer in his herd. From that act, she understood how far her lusts had let her fall and how fearless her husband had become in the years since the mason had arrived on her island home.

Her guards, her women and eunuchs, stood tall and proud and ready to spill their blood for her and for the Serpent Goddess. They would, if she let them, stain the flat, smooth stones of the new palace with lives given for her pleasure or protection.

With a gesture, she calmed them and freed them from death on her behalf.

While the king's guards might not have won, battle would have given her husband greater reason to hate, more reason to send assassins to her chambers one night.

Her death and the deaths of her loyal servants were a matter of time, but she need not hasten the coming of that darkness. If she were shrewd, perhaps her goddess and her craft would stand between her people and death.

The guards marched her to the arena then across the open ground until she stood, barefoot in the dust, beneath the king's pavilion.

Surrounded by walls, by nervous men in bone armor, and by the sky above, she felt more alone than at any time since she had married the invading Bull to gather
~~~

in his power and spare the lives of the people of her island who would have fought him.

Suddenly, for the first time, she understood the power of the palace the master mason had built. Anyone who came here would see not only the glory of a people, they would see the power of earth and sky tamed by the mind and hands of a man, and they would feel small in the face of that effort, that control.

Now, she felt small just as her husband intended that she should.

"My wife." He sat above her in a stone chair behind a low, stone rail. He looked down on her. A slave girl combed and oiled his hair and beard. She was a nubile, a girl that should never be allowed to be alone in the presence of any man—certainly not Minos.

"I am brought by your trained hunting dogs," she said.

Muscles in the soldiers' bare shoulders rippled. Teeth ground.

She smiled. It was good to make dogs angry while they were tethered. It was especially good to make them think less clearly in case they were loosed.

The king frowned and waved off his nubile. She gathered combs and oils and retreated into a dark hallway. "Your skills are rare in this world," Minos said.

She nodded. "Good that you remember who and what I am."

"My wife."

"Servant of the most ancient goddess who is the life in us all."

The king laughed. He stood and with a dramatic wave dismissed the guards.

The men turned, each away from her. In unison, with precision that comes of training, they marched away into the belly of the maze of the palace of Knossos.

She stood alone under the hot sun.

The king stood alone in the shade above her.

That he would be alone with her was further proof of how little he feared her.

"Viper Bites the Bull," he said. "A child's game. No one ever wins. We need not play it here."

"If the bull did not seek to trample the viper, the viper would have no need to bite the bull," she said. "As in the game, so in the battles of life. Both die."

He leaned forward, hands on the short wall. "I remember why you set fire to my blood when first we met."

"If that were true," she said, "your dogs would have marched me naked to your chambers. Instead, I stand in the arena so you can look down on me like you look down on some sad Athenian child brought to die as tribute on the horns of your bulls."

"Or like one of the heroes of our own land," he said, "who face death and leap, and tumble with glee over the heads of the same bulls that kill the foreigners."

"Your tricks and foolishness mean little to me. The Athenians are children who have never seen a bull, and your acrobats are men and women raised with cattle and trained to leap for your pleasure."

"And you? What are you to me?"

"The soul of this land, usurper. In me, your own fear faces you and tells you that you lie. Men and gods know this no matter how you wrap yourself in the skins of lies."

"Beware, woman, or you will face the wrath of my horns now and here."

She raised her hands to the sky and set her feet apart in the earth. "Release your liar's wrath on me, Husband. See how your rule fares under my anger."

He stared down at her. His face drained of what color it had. His beard looked like the shadow of blackest cavern darkness framing his pale cheeks and nose.

So, she thought, he does still fear my goddess and her power.

His color returned, and he smiled.

Helios rode on. His rays burned on her shoulders. The air filled with a small breeze and lifted dust from the arena floor, baked and parched and smelling of struck flint.

"We need not fight, my wife."

"Then come down and stand with your feet in the dust of the earth to speak to me."

He walked back into the dark labyrinth of the palace. Moments later, he appeared from an entrance into the arena. "I apologize for sending my soldiers to find you. They did not understand my request."

"You spoke. They obeyed. Who do you blame if they misunderstood?"

He crossed the arena until he stood before her. Eye to eye, he smiled. His white teeth glinted. A jackdaw on the palace roof above them cried out.

"We should be allies," he said, "even if no love yet lives between us."

"To what end?"

"To create peace. To preserve your land. To save your people."

"War. A man's game. It has no place in my heart."

"Not war. For that, I have men and the clever machines of Daedalus."

"So, now you can fly?"

Her reminder of his failure to coerce Daedalus had the effect of a hornet's sting. The king winced. His face hardened.

"I see you cannot," she said.

"No. And no man shall have what I cannot have."

This was it. He had played out his game. He had angered her intentionally. He had baited her from above. He had joined her in the arena sands at the center of the palace at the center of the kingdom.

What he wanted, he wanted badly.

"You need me," she said.

She waited. The jackdaw cried. The breeze died.

Finally, he spoke. "Yes."

"To what end?"

"Our people love these two."

"What two?"

"My love," he said, "you have long held the blade in waiting for my loins. Let us speak as we once did, before our anger, before our daughter was lost to us."

"Before you let her run away with the Athenian."

"He stole her."

"She chose. She was my daughter as much as yours."

For a moment, she thought the rage of the bull would overcome Minos, but he shook his head and said, "Yes."

"What two?" she repeated. She knew he meant Nikkis and Daedalus. What other two could there be? The people spoke their names together as one. Not even the king and queen were spoken of as if they were one person.

"The trickster mason and his vile goat girl."

She nodded. "You made your promise. The day comes. It will be done. He will leap the bull, or the bull will kill him."

"I do not know how," Minos said, "but I believe the mason will leap the bull."

"And you cannot stop it?"

"He is clever. Some god whose name I do not know favors the mason. Whoever he is, he is a powerful god."

"Or she."

He paled.

She waited, wondering if she knew all his spies in her retinue and if any spies she did know might know her heart in this matter. She dismissed the fleeting thought as the foolishness it was. He had not the craft of mind for such double and triple thinking. He was a man of goals and actions rather than a man of hearts and souls.

"Perhaps," he said. "The man's flesh weakens, but the fire of his spirit burns bright, and the people already gather to see his trial in the arena."

"He has not been trained," she said. "You will kill him and lose everything he might bring you because you threaten a man who should be embraced and because you lust after one woman where you have many."

"I know this man." The king spit on the earth. "He is strong and clever, but his mind is bewitched by a woman. In that, he is weak."

"Love," she said. "That magic is forever lost to you."

"Somehow, he will leap the bull to save this girl from my bed. This is a man who built wings to escape me and free his son."

She laughed. "You covet the thing that killed his son. Perhaps his madness and refusal save your life."

"It is not his son he tries to free now. It is the witch, this woman who beguiles all who meet her. She feeds the passion in his heart. How small a thing for a man who has flown to merely leap a bull?"

"A small thing, I think," she said. "You should have let him leave when he first attempted to sail to Athens."

"A man who can build ships of war like his, who can build wings and fly, who can fool the gods with craft, who knows the thoughts of stone—I cannot let such a man go to my enemies."

She could not suppress her smile. "Perhaps to have fewer enemies would be prudent?"

He closed his eyes. His face colored a deep red.

She set her feet and waited to see if his legendary rage would unman him or if his desire for power and control would best his rage. If the former, the blow of a king's fist was nothing when compared to her experience inside Daedalus's cow. She would hold her ground and take what came. If the latter, she would know that his need was greater than even she could imagine. Much might be gained before this meeting ended.

After a long moment, the color drained from his face. He opened his eyes. "The past has passed."

And there it was, she thought, *opportunity*. "And the future is a thing you wish to control."

"Now, you are the clever woman I married."

"I have always been, much to your dismay."

"If he beats the bull, the people will have hope that they too can beat the bull."

"You," she said. "Beat you."

"The bull is my power here."

"You claim you have no power except if the cattle follow, and the cattle only follow as long as they believe the bull stronger than any other."

Silence.

The jackdaw's taunting cry.

The breeze came and went and came again.

The smell of flint rose from the dust of the arena. Like the breeze on her skin, red rage rose and fell in his face.

Finally, Minos said, "When he finishes his leap, he will repeat his request for my boon."

"You fear breaking your promise?"

"No. I will grant it."

"You brought me from my chambers to tell me what every servant in our service knows—that Daedalus will leap the bull and you will free him as he asks. My husband, you have depths of mystery I have not understood."

"You know the way of curses as well as I know the way of war."

"Ah. I see. You need my goddess to help you turn your honesty into a lie."

A cruel and familiar smile stretched the king's face. "I need a curse that will give him the horror of his granted request."

She laughed. Her mirth echoed in the circle of the arena. "What horror can hide in love and freedom?"

"Eternal love," Minos said. "The madness that brings grief. I wish to give them that gift."

Her own regrets rose and threatened to ignite into resentful rage. His words reminded her of the days when they were young, of the nights before Ariadne was taken from her, nights when the mere smell of him made her insane with desire.

Yes. For her and for him, love had been a terrible madness.

She breathed deeply and called on her goddess for peace. Her violent, lust-driven mistakes with Minos were not the mistakes of Nikkis and Daedalus. For Nikkis and Daedalus, love was a different thing. It burned in their eyes. Those eyes shone, but they shone with more than mere lustful madness. These two were mated heart and soul. They lived what she had once believed might one day exist for her. They made manifest what the goddess of serpents promised to all who lived near the earth, who renewed themselves in the sight of another by ever shedding their past and coming to a new skin, to a new self, to a new vision of hope.

He nodded. "You agree. I hear it in your silence. Love is madness. I will give them that curse. I will free them. I will give them one to the other. For all of time, they will be bound. For all of time, they will be born again over and over. In every life of flesh, they will be fated to come together. They will love."

"Done," she said. "By their hearts. I had no hand in it."

"And their first passionate kiss will send him into madness—fill him with the memories of every tortured life they have lived, with the fears and frustrations of the past. He will see no sense in his life, and he will become like the enraged bull, terrified and filled with a maelstrom of remembered moments and unable to think like a man."

"For the mason," she said, "to strip him of his mind is a terrible thing. Still, Nikkis's love is strong. She will stand by him."

"No," he said. "For her, there will be no memory of their lives. She will love no other, but she will be coveted by all, used by any who can. She will never be able to wed a madman. They will go through all of time coming together and being torn apart and tormented because of the madness of love."

This was a curse worthy of the black soul of her husband. Now, she knew his rage and how it had come to take him. This was a deeper, meaner anger than she had ever seen in him. He could neither control the mason nor, for some reason she did not know, could he drug and abuse the herd girl. Worse, he could not turn the faces of the people from them to him. Inside, she shuddered, but she showed none of her fear and contempt to her husband. "Such a terrible curse," she said. "You ask me to condemn their love?"

"I ask you to preserve it through your art. I will free them. We, you and I, will curse them. The people will see the promise kept, and the people will fear the curses of the gods of their rulers—the Bull and the Serpent Goddess. The Bull and the Serpent can kill with a gift. The people will follow."

"It will take much power, much magic to make your curse true."

"Whatever you need, you shall have."

That was what she wanted. She understood why she was here now, why she had the serpent vision during the arrival of the mason and his wife. For her goddess's will, she now had advantage in the doings of men.

"I will need the girl—Nikkis—before you take her and use her as you have so often used others."

He blinked. Fear flashed in his eyes for just a moment before they turned to sharp, black obsidian. "She is a witch," he said. "I will not have her near me again. Bind her to him in this curse, and I promise you that we shall rule together again as we once did, side-by-side."

His rage had gone far beyond the rage of a bull. She saw in his eyes the rage and vengeance of a man who has seen himself in the eyes of a young woman and hated what he has seen. In his voice, she heard desperation to be free of his mortality and the haunts of his own past.

"I will bind your words in blood, my husband," she said. "Beware my wrath. Do not think to play at words and promises with me and my goddess."

"No," he said. "We will have peace if you make her love only him and make her suffer in her loneliness because of his madness. I want her beauty to live on." Spittle flew from his mustache and beard. It spattered the dry earth between them and disappeared in tiny puffs of dust. "I want men and women to adore her, desire her as a possession. I want her to be able to love no other, and I want her to be possessed by many."

Her husband was insane.

"No," the Queen said. "No woman deserves endless servitude and terror."

"We must do this together," he said. "We must be united, your power and mine, in this, or the people will revolt, the crops will be lost, and the land will no longer feed your people."

His words of rage and vengeance held both promise for her and wisdom for the island. She could lay this curse into clay with blood. Nikkis and Daedalus could be set free to love and live. The people would be at peace in their fear, and the land would be fruitful.

In her chambers, she had condemned many men to lives of torment within husks of clay or wood or bronze. She had no pity for the lusts of men, their lies, or their thirst for power.

Though his desire was to create pain, she hoped that peace could come from condemning the lovers. Peace for her people, for the land, and for the worshipers of her goddess was a dream she held dear—redemption for allowing the King of Bulls to rule beside her.

But the price.

She could not trust her husband even if she did as he asked.

Watching Daedalus's love for Nikkis, she had grown to hope such love could still live. Now, to help to turn that love into a curse…

Pasiphae remembered the vision she had on the day of the return of Nikkis and Daedalus. She remembered her gratitude in being allowed to hold the tail of the serpent.

The goddess had given her the vision of the power of the serpent that was their love.

She said, "If my goddess wills this revenge of yours, I will do it."

Closing her eyes, Pasiphae bowed her head and sought the voice of the goddess within. Almost before she began her seeking, the goddess opened her mind to her husband's deceit. *There* was the game. *There* was the reason for the guards, for the arena, for his descent from on high to the dust of the earth to face her.

Minos had thought through his words most carefully. *He* had played on her anger and her hope. He would keep his word, and she believed she knew what that meant for her, for Daedalus, for Nikkis, and for the hope in the hearts of the people of her land.

She opened her eyes and faced her husband. "Yes," she said. "I will do this for my goddess and my people."

"And for me?"

On another man's lips, the words might have been honeyed dates to savor. On his, they were barbed hooks to be avoided. She turned and walked away, leaving him standing alone in the heat and dust of the arena of the bull.

~~~

Fall winds had come to the quarry, and the men there had long toiled day and night without benefit of the master mason's wisdom. All were certain he was dead, for though the king had promised he would live to face the bull, none had seen the mason since he had entered the shining labyrinth palace he had built.

Men and women in the hills whispered tales of a monster, a minotaur that had been born of the queen's mating with the white bull. Some stories had the monster eating human flesh to survive. Some said the monster was Daedalus himself, doomed for his affronts against the gods.

Superstitious tales swept the land, and people toiled in the darkness of their hearts where men such as Daedalus and women such as Nikkis died at the hands of tyrants.

The winds of the changing season came. They swept over the highlands and brought dust and dried grasses over the lips of stone quarry walls many times the height of a man. The dust settled to the ground, and the men looked up, even under torchlight and fear of whip.

Some said the mason still haunted the quarry. Some said he would forever—always calling for water from his love, Nikkis.

The wind blew, and it whipped, and it slid between stones and around slabs. It caught at straw near the mortar pits.

A stone cutter paused, his hammer high. He held. He listened.

"To the chisel with that hammer!" a soldier ordered. The soldier raised his lash. Hand high, he froze. He heard the voice. Terrified, he let his lash fall limp to the ground. He turned in a circle to see who had spoken, but no one was there.

The cutters dropped their chisels. They gripped their hammers. They looked at one another. None spoke. They strode past the guard, and he fell in behind them.

Water women joined them.

Other cutters, carriers, and soldiers joined them. Those few who could not hear the whisper in the stone and wind of the quarry tried briefly to stop the flow of men and women moving up the long, winding road out of the pit. They failed, overwhelmed by the rising tide of flesh.
~~~

~~~

Darkness can salve the torn heart, especially if a man has lived a full life within the palace of his own mind. Sages have said that a man's fears are shadows. With enough time in the dark, those shadows can become as nothing within the blackness of solitude.

Each night, Daedalus calmed himself and welcomed the darkness of his cell, and he quickly found the place in mind and heart where time neither passes nor holds. There, he found only moving images, recurring memories, and the flicker of hope that lives in a future where the sun once again brings day and night.

One day, the guards did not come for him, nor did they come the next. His only knowledge of night and day came from the working of his body, the knowledge of the stone, and the movement of air through the palace.

In his mind, building from the image stones of memory, he constructed a temple to the future, a future where his meager hope lived.

He found Nikkis's face there.

He found his memory of the scent of her sweet breath, the filling inhalations of love when he put his face into her hair, his lips to her neck, his nose to her ear. He embraced his memory of the sound of her sigh when he whispered his love to her.

Even imprisoned in darkness, a man can hope to see light once more.

The hope of Daedalus was more than the mere desire to see the sun again. His hope was a heartbeat, a moment spent in the arms of a woman whom gods and kings conspired to keep from him.

In the darkness, the master mason listed his tools: tattered clothing, fingernails, hair, patience, mind, heart, stone, small splinters of wood, straw, darkness, hands, desire, love.

Among his tools were two that he thought he might use together, the gift of the queen and love.

He would see Nikkis again. He would honor his vow to her, her family, and her village. He would save her, or he would die trying.

Using the queen's gift, he set his will and spent his heart's guttering flame in the darkness by calling out through the stone. He searched for his love. In his mind, he walked his memory of the labyrinth he had been made to build by king and queen, the palace of Knossos, the place foreigners called the maze of the bull.
~~~

By the gift of the queen and his knowing of the palace, by his trust that the palace would speak to him in a million tiny ways of its experience, and by his trust that the movement of dust across floors carried all the knowledge of the movement of air and breath throughout the labyrinth, he would seek and find her.

Up toward the light, he sent his mind. He moved his thoughts into warmer corridors where men and women, some terrified and lost, some purposeful and ambitious, worked in the service of the living palace. He sent his mind outward to the walls of the outside, the south walls, the walls where thin stone, nearly transparent, fit into moving frames of wood fashioned by his hands.

The panels stood open, and air hot with the fire of Helios flowed inward, warming the palace halls.

Along with the heat, he let his knowing flow inward, and he followed it up again, and through a twisting maze of passages, rooms where visitors stayed and where important men were sent to take pleasure from women who might or might not survive the night and for whom Daedalus felt sympathy and fear.

Had he his way, this palace would become rubble. He cursed his own pride for letting the rulers here make him build it. He should have run. Ikarus could have lived.

Even in his self-condemnation, he searched for her. Out again, he sent his mind to the broad expanse of the courtyard where bulls roared and charged and people watched Athenian children die beneath sharp hooves or on twisting, tossing horns.

Love guided him. He felt her presence ever there, beyond his reach. Her love and the memories in the stones pulled his mind and soul toward her.

Through the king's chambers, he followed the sighs of stones, sighs that might have been his spirit in the stones themselves, sighs that flowed like a lover's whisper and carried his spirit, his vision, his hope onward.

When he found her, she was not in the king's wing. She was farther east, nearer the chambers of the queen, nearer the queen's baths.

Relief washed through him like fresh water poured across the amber face of dusty mica. "Nikkis," he whispered.

She lay in a dimly-lit chamber walled in by the labyrinth of rooms and corridors. Her door was made of thick planks of olive cross-banded with ornate copper. It was a door to keep men out, and it was a door to keep Nikkis in.

Alone on silken cushions and covered only by sheer silks of red and black, the colors of the king, he could sense the movement and strength of her breath. Because of his gift, he could even feel the steady, slow rhythm of her heart.

She wept, but she was healthy and whole.

"Nikkis," he whispered again. The palace heard him, and his spirit moved in the stone, and air through cracks in the stone mimicked his whisper.

Her heartbeat quickened. "Daedalus?" she asked. "Where?"

"Shhh," he said. "Shhhh, Nikkis. I'm with you. I live."

"I love you," she said.

"I love you," he said.

Brilliant light—a white explosion of pain—tore him from his love, from his concentration. He covered his eyes with his forearm. A long slit of brightness shone from the crack of the stone that had sealed him into his tiny pit. A woman stood above him, made silhouette by bright light, her hips and thighs deeper shadows within floating layers of linen and silk.

"How long?" he asked.

Pasiphae, Queen of the People of Crete, said, "Since they last took you out to work, two days."

"Only two," he said. "Two days."

"You thought it more?"

"I feared it more," he said. "Nikkis?"

"Well, for now. She has refused the king. He calls her a witch. He fears her almost as much as he fears you."

"I want to see her." He tried to move his arms and legs, but they would not obey.

"I protect her," Pasiphae said. "You will see her soon."

"He knows you've come to me?"

She laughed. "Get up, my mason. Rise, and come with me. I will make use of you, and you will make use of me."

Daedalus considered her possible meanings for a heartbeat. In the pit, he had only the magic of his hands and mind. Outside, he had both of those and freedom to move. He willed life into bloodless, frozen muscles. Groaning, he crawled up from his pit.

The queen stooped to help him stand. She steadied him on his cramped legs, and she helped him stretch and move beside her down long corridors, up stairways, and finally into the light of day.

Modern Minotaur

Escaping from the firefight and Andros's dig had only gotten Nikkis lost. Now, hiding amid rocks and scrub from an impossible monster, she thought of her mother and father at dinner the night before she had run away to Crete. They loved her. Anderson may have tricked them, but they loved her so much that they wanted her to feel it even if Anderson's lies had been true.

Dust burned her eyes. She tried to blink it away.

The monster turned toward her. In spite of the blinding red curtain of the dust storm, its massive snout and bright red eyes found her.

The heat of its awareness, the consciousness behind the eyes making her the center of the monster's attention, paralyzed her. She shrank lower against the solidity of the rock.

This thing couldn't exist, and yet it was coming through the storm after her. Her rational mind reeled under the assault of recent days. Flight from work and family. Impossible artifacts. Ancient animosities between policemen and restaurant owners. Murder.

The minotaur stood over her, huge, a man-statue of fur, deadly, sweeping horns, and wild eyes.

She made a small noise like a child trapped in night terrors where fear froze her diaphragm and turned terrified screams for help into small croaking sounds.

In the maelstrom of strange thoughts that swim in the dark night of terror, her mother reminded her to wear clean underwear in case she had to go to the hospital, Daed screamed at the sky—eyes wide and red and rolling in his skull, Yorgos tumbled through space to the cistern floor, a confused giant stood at her window asking silent questions through sad eyes, Anderson sneered at her rejection, and Andros's silken voice brought more uncertainty while trying to console her.

All these thoughts swept through her like some deep mental dam had broken, unleashing a swirling, chaotic wave of uncertainties and fears.

She fought the currents and eddies, but it was too much. Her mind spun and reeled and could not finish the thoughts it began. Only the red eyes of the monster held constant in her moment of indecision.

She willed herself to become part of her sheltering rock, to be even smaller than she felt under the gaze of this creature.

Powerful hands reached forward.

Again, she tried to scream and nothing came out. She willed her legs to push, to run, but she didn't move.

The hands hesitated. Then, the monster pulled at its own skin. What she had believed was fur peeled away to become a large, square cape. It held the cape out over her, pressed it down onto her, and wrapped her in it.

She twisted, but she only succeeded in helping him wrap her in the cape. She kicked his thigh. It was like kicking stone.

The thing deftly wrapped her in the woolen cape. Like a swaddled child, the cape pinned her arms and legs. It draped a loose corner of the blanket over her head, grasped her shoulders, and lifted her from the ground. Gently, the monster turned her helpless form and cradled her in his arms.

She wanted to fight, but she was too exhausted to fight, to kick, to thrash about. Inside the cape, held safely in powerful arms, unexpected relief washed over her. At least for a while, the dust no longer pressed against her eyes, fought her will, and challenged her spirit.

Cocooned in the darkness of the blanket, she felt him walking easily, carrying her. In the steady rise and fall of his gait, she felt purpose and direction. His strength and certainty surrounded her where hers had failed.

In his strength, she found hope. He could have killed her with one hand. He might have gored her with those horns. In the storm after the attack on the camp, she would just be one more body.

She inhaled the scent of him. He was at least part man, and his dank smell somehow spoke to her of things she could never have understood from his red eyes, his powerful hands, or the dour shape of his bull's mouth. The smell combined with the certainty of his gait and the confidence of his hands to convince her that for a moment she was safe from thieves, gunmen, knives, and holes in the earth. His smell and strength let her believe he had fought the storm to find her and make her safe.

She pressed her swaddled face to his chest, closed her eyes, and held on to the mythic creature that had saved her from sand devils and men.

The tears that she had tried to believe only protected her eyes from dust now poured cleansing relief down her cheeks.

~~~

Her minotaur placed her gently on the ground. He unwrapped her head and loosened the cape so that she could move.

She sat, still loosely wrapped in his cape. Near her legs, a clay bowl filled with oil supported a burning wick and provided low, flickering light. She sat in the dirt just inside the entrance of a cave.

Outside the entrance, the red dust swirled. Some trick of the cave kept it out as if it dared not enter *his* home.

Freed of the dust outside she looked up at the monster. In the low light and clear air of the cave, he was a man wearing a mask shaped like the head of a bull.

"Thank you," she said.

Turning away from her like she was a bag of groceries set temporarily on a kitchen counter, he ducked low under the cavern entrance and walked away into the red storm again.

In the moment before he vanished, the lamp's light caught the curve of his shoulders where his bronze flesh disappeared beneath the mask. The man at her window turning away came to mind, and she was almost sure this man was the same man Andros and Yorgos had chased in the village.

She sat in the silence of the cave, searching her mind for some thought that would make sense of combined fear and relief. Finally, she shook herself. Fear and relief couldn't help her. She could do better.

Dr. Nikkis Aristos would do better.

She took a deep breath and forced her mind to focus on concrete, useful things. First, she willed her hands, still clutching the cape, to relax. Then, she turned her gaze to the lamp.

The oil lamp's light danced and flickered, but it allowed her to focus and calm herself. After a few breaths, she peeled away the cape and began to take stock of the cave. She discovered several volleyball-sized pottery urns and plastic bottles lined up against one wall of the cave.
~~~

Carefully, she checked their contents.

Water. She drank. The water tasted sweet, sweeter than any drink she could remember in all of her life. When she'd had enough, she shook out her bandana, dipped a corner in the water, and washed her eyes.

The effort left her exhausted but relieved.

She rested in the cool cave. Eventually, water and rest resurrected thought. She wondered at the thing that had brought her there.

Think, Nikkis. That's what you do best. That's what you're trained to do. Think it through.

She stood and moved to the entrance of the cave. Kneeling, she peered out into the red fog. The dust stayed out because air moved in the cave and created positive pressure. It was like a sterile white-room. Since the dust was fine and not driven by wind so much as dropped in hot stillness, it stayed outside.

She smiled and reached a hand out into the gritty, moving dust then brought it back in.

It felt right that the dust should stay out there. It gave her a sense that some control had been returned to her.

The irrational flood of emotions that had swept over her while her monster carried her subsided, but the memory of lost control haunted her.

Exhaustion, fear, and possible shock were not good foundations for irrational, insane trust in a man who wandered about in a dust storm wearing a bull's head.

She'd never felt so helpless before; she'd never felt so grateful, and she'd never been so sure of her safety.

It was all wrong.

Irrational. Crazy. Wrong.

Yorgos was dead.

Someone—someone who was not a policeman—had killed him.

No matter what fear and exhaustion had made her feel, this could not be a good situation.

The minotaur man had gone. He'd left like he had nothing to fear from the dust or from men. She was sure he'd come back.

The masked gunmen were still out there.

In spite of the fact that the minotaur had saved her, he might be one of those terrorists. He might be the one that killed Yorgos, and nobody but the minotaur knew her location.

She did not like the growing certainty that her savior was the man Andros's men had been so afraid of.

Peering out into the slow, red swirl of fine Sahara dust settling over the landscape, she decided that hiking away from shelter would be folly. She hoped she had time to come up with a better plan, a way to gain advantage or at least knowledge.

She moved back into the cave, picked up the lamp, and held it as high as the low ceiling would allow.

For a moment, the oil rippled up against the wick. The flame guttered. Then, the flame strengthened on freshened oil. The chamber just inside the cave entrance spread out to the size of her mother's dining room, though the walls were made of limestone strata canted at angles by ancient, geologic forces. Farther back, the chamber narrowed, and the cave became a long, sloped corridor. In the low light, the walls there seemed to be whiter and smoother.

She moved toward the white walls, hoping to find a place to hide, a place where she might see who entered the cave before they saw her.

Pitted limestone walls closed in around her. The roof became lower. She had to crouch, but she found what she'd hoped for. The main tunnel split away in three directions. Each tunnel disappeared deeper into the earth. Her little cave shelter was more than a mere cave. It was a cavern system.

Nikkis looked behind her. The red light of the storm still shone on the cavern walls, and she still saw no means of escape near the entrance.

The whiter walls around her were covered in slick, damp lime deposits common in such caverns.

She peered down the three passages. One looked slick and steep and headed off to her left. The center passage looked even less inviting, and she thought she could hear moving water in that direction. The third appeared to slope downward only slightly, and it had the advantage that it might come to surface sooner—or at least move toward the back wall of the ridge.

If the dust stayed outside because of air pressure, the air had to come from somewhere. She held her weak flame up before each tunnel. It was hard to tell, but she thought the flame wavered more when she moved it close to the gently sloping tunnel.

At least the tunnel would let her move farther from where she'd been put. With luck, it would lead to another opening.

She had no intention of staying where a man Andros feared put her—a man who wore a bull's head.

She had gone fifty or sixty meters deeper when she realized her light had gotten brighter.

She stopped and examined her wick and flame. Neither had changed.

Movement caught her eye.

She became animal still.

After a long moment listening for movement and feeling for threat, she realized she'd seen her own reflected image on the slick walls. Touching her hand to the slick wall confirmed that she had moved out of the relatively soft, surface limestone and into a stratum of hard, striated marble like the marble of the white statues guarding the village.

Sharp edges in the pale surface met her touch. She moved her light closer.

The edges became visible, carved characters.

Unbelieving, she rubbed at the stone as if her hand could wipe away an illusion. Nothing changed. The stone held meticulously carved, perfectly preserved Linear-A.

The walls were covered in it. This cavern corridor held more Linear-A than existed in all the museums in the world—even if she counted Andros's finds.

She held up her lamp and turned a circle.

Everywhere, endless rows and rows of glyphs. She peered deeper into the tunnel. The glyphs continued as far as the lamplight let her see. When she moved deeper, the moving light lit more and more rows of glyphs.

She put the lamp down at the base of one wall. Once more, she found herself chilled by the thrill of her fingers tracing familiar patterns of glyphs—tracing, and trying to remember some pattern, some key just beyond mind and memory.

Once more, she found that mark—the lybris and flower.

Her heart soared—until she found tools leaning against the cavern wall.

Steel tools. Sharp. Made in America. Made in Germany. Made in Japan. Made in Greece.

Her heart stilled, chilled, and sank into her belly.

Fake.

All of it.

She'd been fooled.

She'd found the source of all the Linear-A, and it was fake. The sherds, the stones in the warehouse, the Roman cistern, the fragments, and now this, the source of all the old marble and Linear-A.

She'd spent her life studying the languages of Crete, and a ham-fisted bully in a bull mask had fooled her.

She wanted to scream and curse, to cry out the names of all the gods ever named by mankind. The only word that came out was a quiet, despairing, "Shit."

She traced the lines again. She had come to Crete and nearly been killed—*for this*.

"Just, shit," she said.

~~~

Exploring the cavern, Nikkis mused that the forger's choice of the minotaur mask was fitting. The cavern tunnels might well have been part of the labyrinth of mythic Crete, though academic speculation on the nature of the truth behind the myths of Minos, Daedalus, and the labyrinth suggested that the original maze was the palace of Knossos itself—or, perhaps, some destroyed complex on the island of Thera.

Regardless of what truths lived at the core of the myths, the man who wore the bull's head and walked in the dust storm knew enough of the legends of Crete to make use of them for scaring people away from his illegal work.

She almost laughed at his Scooby-Doo choice of masks. If Yorgos's death hadn't been so fresh in her mind, she might have.

The Minotaur was certainly part of the group of thieves and forgers who had killed Yorgos. If they could create carefully aged forgeries as good as the ones she'd seen, they could certainly use the bull and the myth to keep superstitious locals like her grandmother scared.

After all, her grandmother had been willing to believe Nikkis was some kind of magical priestess, able to stay young forever. Fooling ignorant people was easy.

Now, she understood Andros better—his anger with the villagers, his guns, his contempt for men who failed to follow orders. Thinking it through, she decided she
~~~

admired Andros's bravery and courage. He was a misunderstood man in difficult circumstances.

The walls, though.

Something didn't fit.

Lamp high, she moved deeper into the cavern labyrinth. Further on, lime accretion coated some of the carvings. Archaeological training kicked in. For such thick layers of accretion to have occluded the text, the text had to be at the very least hundreds of years old—more likely thousands of years old, but the tools suggested otherwise.

The forgers were clever, but the cavern tunnels and galleries weren't manmade. The accretion couldn't have been faked, at least she didn't know of a way to fake layered lime deposits.

Of course, they had fooled her at the warehouse. They had fooled Andros sufficiently with the cistern that he had flown her halfway around the world.

The carvings continued, and she followed them deeper.

Meter after meter of Linear-A covered the walls of the cavern.

There was too much of it to be the work of one man, and the lime accretion had taken many lifetimes. The deeper she went, the thicker the accretion became.

She finally stopped when she found a stalagmite as tall as her knee. Embedded low in the column of accumulated lime and minerals, she found a fragment of marble with both Roman Latin and Linear-A engraved in the surface.

It looked so real. It could be her Rosetta.

No. she told herself. It's all a lie. Modern tools did this. They must have found a way to increase the speed of accretion.

But the stalagmite had to be more than a couple thousand years old. It had to be.

So much script couldn't be the work of one man—not even one generation or even ten. That was clear enough.

She shook her head. She had to get a grip. She reminded herself of one of the axioms of her discipline. She whispered, "Proximity does not imply causality."

Just because the script deep in the cavern system was similar to and relatively near the script at the mouth did not mean the same hand had created it. Dozens of generations of mimics had done this.

These forgers couldn't possible know the ancient language. They merely copied what had been done before. They copied the script they found deep in the cavern.

Nobody completely understood Linear-A. If someone had deciphered all of it, they couldn't long keep that secret in an age of satellites, cell phones, and the web.

Mesmerized by a mystery that spanned generations, she wandered—turned now right, then left, then right—raising her pathetic little oil lamp to show her more and more of the carvings.

In places, dripping water left calcium deposits that covered over the glyphs. In other places, the glyphs appeared to be sharp and new. In several places, she found glyphs cut into calcium plaque that had covered old glyphs—almost like someone had come and tried to repair the carving of past generations.

It made her laugh, the idea of someone trying to preserve a record of nonsense; and that's what it was, she was sure. *Nonsense.* It had to be.

But the nonsense held her eye and mind. Once more, she traced a finger along the slick surface of glazed lime and cut stone. Certainly, the glyphs she had predicted were in the stone here, but they made no sense. Someone had simply tossed them together. If her theories on the grouping of Linear-A glyphs were correct, then–

She caught herself actually thinking about the possibility that these mountain men, or this one man and whoever had taught him to mimic Linear-A, had some relationship to the original, living use of the language.

The flame in her little lamp guttered.

Ominous, undefined shadows jumped all around her.

Suddenly, she realized she'd been wandering a long time. She had been mesmerized by the glyphs, consumed by fantasies. Her oil burned low.

Panic pulled her chest tight and grasped her throat. If the little lamp went out, she would be in the dark. Cavern dark was not the dark of a starry night. She'd be in the pitch blackness of the grave, the realm of Hades, the land where no man has eyes.

Her flame quivered and licked again as if gasping for air and oil.

She pulled it down closer to her body and tilted it to protect it from her breath and to feed more oil to the wick. The tiny tongue of life and light leaned, pointing away from the deeps of the cavern.

Airflow.

She had forgotten the positive pressure in the cavern.

A thousand Nancy Drew-type stories she'd read had used the lighted match trick to escape caverns. Light the match and watch the bend of the flame. Find the source of the air flow.

Maybe.

The idea of heading to the cavern mouth chilled her. Even if she were willing to face dust and minotaur again, she might have passed a dozen twists or turns and side tunnels.

The finger of flame pointed back toward the mouth of the caverns, but there might be many draft holes in a system like this one. She didn't dare use that pointer and hope for the best.

The moving air had to come from somewhere. Standing still here would mean darkness soon, and that meant death by thirst or, more likely, from a panicked, stumbling fall into some unseen chasm.

Nikkis decided that if she were to die in the dark, she would at least die moving toward hope. She headed deeper into the maze.

The flame guttered again. This time the hairs on her arms stood up. Goose flesh. Moving air. A breeze she could feel.

She turned and walked against the breeze. The fresh scent of sea rode that breeze.

The cave narrowed to a low crawl hole. The tight crawl created a venturi effect, and the breeze came through strong and steady. She crouched low and pushed her lamp into the hole.

The breeze blew out her lamp before she could see inside.

The darkness of the grave had her, but she'd seen enough to hope her shoulders might barely fit in the hole.

She dropped the useless lamp and crawled into the hole, fingers stretched out in front of her. She pulled herself forward, sliding her belly along the slick stone floor, pushing with the tips of the hiking boots Yorgos had bought for her. She found herself praying to an unnamed goddess that she might find light before she wedged herself in this vent and turned it into an unmarked grave where she would be slowly covered in lime crust.

Suddenly, the dark, tiny tube of rock closed in on her. It seemed to grab her chest. She gasped, and she was stuck.

Panic took her. She clawed at the earth and stone. She kicked.

She screamed and emptied her lungs in one long, wail of fear and despair, and when her lungs were empty, her clawing and kicking moved her forward a foot. Desperate, screaming silently from empty lungs, she clawed again.

Another foot.

She blinked. Points of light appeared before her.

Exhaustion and asphyxiation, she thought.

A slow motion certainty that death was coming passed through her, and, in that moment of peace and certainty, the beauty of the sparkling lights hit her as perfect, exactly what she should be seeing as she died.

A streak of light crossed the other sparkling lights, making them momentarily invisible.

A shooting star.

She realized that her narrow passage of stone was like a long, slanted telescope tube. From inside, she looked up the slope toward a field of stars.

The night sky. Beautiful, perfect night sky!

Hope renewed her will, and Nikkis pulled, struggled, and breathed her way out of the tube of stone and onto a steep, rocky slope.

Either the dust storm had moved on, or she came out in an unaffected valley. It didn't matter to her. She lay on the slope sucking in fresh, cool air. Each breath cleared the fog of panic from her mind.

By pale starlight, she made out rocky, scrub-covered terrain covering a rough, steep slope. Too exhausted to trust her footing at night and with no idea which direction she should travel, Nikkis simply rolled onto her back and stared at the circling of the constellations, the endless drama of gods and heroes.

Her head pillowed on stone, she slept.

~~~

Early rays of sunlight woke Nikkis. She blinked and shaded her face with her hand. The rays broke through a saddle cleft in a ridge on the opposite side of the valley into which Nikkis had emerged. Nikkis had seen beautiful sunrises before, but the brilliant crimson, purple, and gold of this one made up the most beautiful she had ever seen. Vaguely, she knew that the colors probably came from dust in the air, but it didn't matter. She was alive, and this sunrise contrasted against her memory of the darkness of the underworld from which she had escaped.

She turned and looked at the impossibly tiny hole from which she had emerged. She started to giggle. After a few deep breaths, her giggles of relief turned to crying for the second time in two days—for the second time since Daed had disappeared.

She had to get a grip on herself.
~~~

She sat and wept and watched the sunrise, the perfect, amazing, wonderful sunrise. Her heart told her that the whole world celebrated her return to the land of the living.

Eventually, her sobbing slowed and the fancies of her heart gave way to thought. She reminded herself that the dust of the moving storm reflected long rays of light, creating a red and golden effect, a unique Greek alpenglow, a surreal, living flow of light along the silhouetted eastern ridge.

East.

She smiled. Nancy Drew would be proud of her. She had freed herself from the cave, and she had a bearing.

She stood to let the new sunlight cover her—warming chilled clothing and flesh. She turned a slow circle in the sun, trying to get a sense of where she might be, where she might go.

She stood on the shoulder of a ridge on the west side of a valley. Up the valley, the two ridges closed together to make a vertical wall.

Along the contour of the ridge toward the low end of the valley, the slope on which she stood became steeper, almost a sheer scarp—much too steep to walk safely.

She congratulated herself for having chosen to wait for daylight.

Directly below her, the bottom of her valley promised better footing. A blue-green carpet of grass, flowers, and heavy foliage snaked along the valley bottom and marked deep ground water, probably the underground flow that captured the seep that had formed the cavern.

Above, Helios set his whip to work, and his fiery horses pulled the golden chariot up the slope of blue, island sky until his fire illuminated the humps and stones of the eastern ridge. Pale limestone rubble and brighter bits of marble flashed amid the greens and browns of arid, mid-alpine plants only goats could eat.

Nikkis smiled at the thought. She'd been on Crete too long. When she'd arrived, the ground had only been a stony cover for antiquities. Now, she thought about the landscape as either alive or as fodder for grazing.

She pushed useless thoughts away.

Her reality right now was that this land was a trap that could kill her if she didn't find help.

She looked for a trail—or at least a goat path. She followed the drainage line at the valley bottom until the inviting carpet of deeper, more succulent greens disappeared to her right around the ridge shoulder and, she imagined, down another slope. Where the lower valley turned, the far ridgeline dipped. Beyond that ridge rose another. Beyond that, another, and then another ridge, lower, and another beyond that and another, until the ridges became an endless series of descending blue-green ripples spreading away from her and eventually disappearing into a haze of red that blurred the distinction between earth, sky, and hell.

Helios whipped his horses, and the red grew brighter, became the deep rusty, luminous color of grapes before full ripeness.

Grapes.

Exactly, she thought. The distant haze had the same translucent quality of ripening red grapes when morning sunlight passes through the skins and the meat. Even the swirls and seams in the distant dust storm looked like the lines traced by dripping night dew across the skins.

For the second time, she shook her head and pushed away useless thoughts.

Gone too long. Not enough water. Not enough food. Not enough sleep. She'd never even seen grapes like the ones she'd been thinking about.

Raspberries. That was the color. She'd made up the grapes out of her memories of washing raspberries she'd picked back home in the States.

It didn't matter. She was alive. It was beautiful. "Eenay ohrayah," she whispered, and for the first time she truly understood the deep, soulful, divinity of beauty described by the idiom that had no true English translation.

She glanced up at the sun.

Beautiful, but soon enough it would just be hot.

She needed water. She had to find the village. At least, she needed to find help.

A wisp of lazy upslope breeze carried a distant metal-on-metal clank.

She strained to hear.

It sounded again, and she recognized the sound.

A bell. A cow bell.

When she'd been younger, she had hiked with her father. She remembered something he'd said, "Never fight a mountain. Follow the goats. They know what they are about."

"There aren't any goats," she had said.

He had laughed and suggested that in America deer would do.

She missed the sound of his laughter. It had been a long time since she'd heard it.

Here, there were definitely goats. She doubted there were any deer.

She imagined what a goat would do, how it might walk on such a slope. She picked her way along the contour of the slope, following a groove cut into the earth, some kind of animal trail—maybe even her father's goat trail.

She hoped whatever had cut such a zigzagging and crisscrossing series of grooves in the hillside wasn't something that ate people.

She didn't think anything on Crete ate people—at least nothing in modern times.

There had been lions in the old stories.

The Minotaur had eaten human flesh.

That thought gave her a shudder. She had just escaped the Minotaur.

She slipped, scrambled in loose stones, and regained her footing.

To keep her mind clear and to keep panic at a distance, she tried to remember all the ancient tales she knew. Some memories came to her that made no sense at all—memories of men hunting cats in hills like these. Some of the stories came from books. Other stories came from her parents, though they were all told to her in English and changed so they took place in America. Still, she was pretty sure the stories came from Crete.

She found herself wishing she were at her parents' house waking to the smell of her mother's abused American cuisine and the sound of her father bellowing pop songs in the shower, his Greek accent making them sound like curses instead of the old Billy Joel and Harry Chapin ballads he loved.

The metallic clang echoed in the valley.

A bell—definitely a goat bell.

She laughed out loud. Or a cow. Or a sheep. Or maybe just a piece of metal hitting another piece of metal in the morning breeze.

It didn't matter. Metal meant people.

She rounded a rib in the valley wall. Below her, she could see more of the valley. She searched upslope for the goats. The valley was a short box canyon, maybe only a hundred meters from where she stood to headwall ridge. She imagined that she had spent much of yesterday either beneath that valley floor or behind the wall of the canyon's head. She wondered if the cavern system's entrance were beyond her ridge or perhaps over the canyon headwall.

She dismissed her fantasy ideas of understanding the cavern's topography. She could not know how the cavern tunnels had twisted and turned. Crete was an uplift—a tectonic outcast sailing on molten undercurrents in geologic time toward a cataclysmic meeting with Africa. Crete had never had glaciers, at least she didn't think it had, but this box canyon reminded her of the U-shaped, glacial valleys of the Rocky Mountains.

No glaciers—at least not big ones that cut out U-shaped valleys.

Maybe she remembered wrong. Maybe that geology was some other island.

Lately, her memories tricked her. She remembered things that made no sense: the familiar smell of the minotaur man, spinning star stories, familiar glyphs, and the fragments of dreams.

She told herself that water and food would clear her thinking.

The ground shook. Pebbles dislodged and rolled down the slope.

Another strange memory moved through her exhaustion and tried to make itself a part of her reality.

Moving earth meant love.

A child's song came to mind. *When Rhea moves to love…*

She was losing it. She was pretty sure she'd just made that up. She couldn't remember more of it—couldn't remember ever learning such a song.

Shaking her head and biting her lip, she took a deep breath of warm, chalky air. Weakness took her knees. Dizziness made her sit down on a rock.

She closed her eyes and waited for the spinning to pass and for her head to clear. After a few more deep breaths, she opened her eyes. Still, she sat quietly for a few minutes. Breathing deeply, she watched the line of sunlight move along the valley floor. She listened to birdsong and to the dry skitter of a lizard running across stones.

Following the sound, she found the lizard and watched its long, green shape move between the stones and cactus. He took a few lizardy steps then stopped and flicked his tongue to taste the air. Convinced of his safety, he moved again.

It was the same thing she was doing, she guessed.

The bell sounded again, closer.

Nikkis lifted her gaze from the friendly, cautious reptile.

Across the valley, a line of goats marched along the far ridgetop like a furry train, nose-to-tail, moving steadily. While she watched, they moved downward onto the ridge face and along one of the long, crisscrossing trails. The lead goat wore a bell around his neck. Brown, black, and white, he moved with his head high and alert while the others followed along behind sniffing at tufts of grass and stone.

Above them, dancing along as if the nearly vertical wall were a taverna's flat dance floor, baby goats capered and butted heads. One ran up the wall of the slope like a sprinter on a track. Another chased. A third dove down the slope then bleated pitifully for having been separated from his brothers and sisters.

The adults moved stolidly onward and downward, demonstrating the patience learned by parents throughout time.

The capering joy of the kids contrasted against the ancient, stark beauty of the landscape made Nikkis laugh. She laughed for joy because of the capering of the goats, and she laughed in relief because if a goat wore a bell, someone took care of it.

She fought off her dizziness and forced herself to stand.

The lizard darted away into the shadows of stones.

She picked her way along the contour, still following goat trails, angling downward toward the valley floor and, she hoped, a meeting with the goats and their herder.

She slipped sideways between the close faces of a boulder long ago split in half by a fall from high above. When she cleared the narrow cut between the stones, she quickly managed the last short descent over a two-meter-tall scarp wall to the valley floor. There, she easily walked across the flat meadow on soft, green grass. Brilliant orange flowers filled the meadow—Flanders Poppies—thousands of them. She waded through them, in no hurry to turn toward a fieldstone fence that crossed the meadow near where she expected the goats to arrive.

The verdant valley bottom was an oasis within the dry hills. Somewhere here, she might find water—perhaps a spring, an upwelling, or just the movement of water underground.

She imagined that this little valley might even have once have cradled a small pond that had silted in over time. She had seen such meadows in the Rockies and the Cascades.

Finally, she turned toward the fence across the valley mouth.

The ground shook again. It vibrated like a pile driver pounded at the bedrock beneath the grass.

Behind her, something hissed like a steam locomotive.

The bull-man came to mind—the flesh-eating Minotaur.

She didn't want to turn. She didn't want to see a monster. She didn't want to believe that she might be taken underground again.

Still, she turned.

An actual bull stood among the poppies.

Only a bull. She sighed with relief that the bull-man was nowhere to be seen.

The bull's eyes focused on her.

With the focusing of his attention came the realization that he was a huge creature, easily taller than her at the shoulder. His narrow hips were low behind his massive back. His rear legs tightened and bunched beneath his body. The head of the thing was as broad as the shoulders of the bull-masked man, and that made the tiny, brown-red eyes seem impossibly far apart.

Instincts took over her muscles. She became as still as the pale stones on the hillsides.

The bull's shining horns reflected chariot fire. Long, deadly double-curves pushed outward from forehead roots thicker than Nikkis's arm. The horns curved forward, and their curve sloped parallel to and out over its snout. She'd never seen a bull like it before, but that nagging, ghostly dream-feeling hit her again.

She saw something familiar in this bull's face. He lived in her head in some forgotten image or memory.

The glistening, horn swords flashed sunlight, and the strange déjà-vu feeling made her sure she had stood just there and seen this same bull before.

He shook his head, as if to say she shouldn't be there, as if to warn her that he would come and drive his horns into her soft flesh and tear her into bits that could be trampled.

He drove a front hoof into the ground.

The ground shook.

Nikkis kept her eyes on the monster, and she carefully stepped back.

One step.

Another.

The giant's shoulders quivered. Clouds pushed outward from flared nostrils like some giant steam engine lived in the thing's chest driving muscles and heart. Hissing puffs caught the morning sun and lifted upward like glowing clouds made of the very spirit of power.

"Eenay ohrayah," Nikkis whispered.

The bull shook its massive head.

Nikkis's trained mind turned the vision of beauty and power into knowledge. She found her advantage. The sunlight that lit the bull's breath also shone in his eyes, and from the look of his tiny, brown-red eyes, he didn't see so well.

Her foot struck a loose stone. Slowly, eyes on the bull, ever-so-slowly, she bent at the knees, grasped the rock, and lifted it.

The bull shook its head again. While it shook, she threw the stone off toward the edge of the canyon meadow. It clattered against the canyon wall.

The bull turned. He charged a few meters in that direction.

Nikkis quickly moved backward through the grass, still watching the bull.

He stopped his charge, shook his head, and turned toward her.

She froze. The up-slope breeze carried her scent. He must be able to smell her. And, if she felt his movement through the ground, he might feel hers.

Clearly, he knew someone trespassed in his valley, or maybe he merely protected himself from something he couldn't really see. A part of her pitied the poor creature. She was suddenly sure he was as scared as her. Trapped in a cage of stone, literally back against a wall, he only protected himself.

Of course, her sympathy wouldn't stop him from killing her if she didn't do something quickly.

She remembered the stone fence behind her. It made a corral of the valley by stretching from one wall of the canyon to the other.

She'd climbed down through a cleft of stone too narrow for the bull to escape, and she'd stumbled into his pen. She was on the wrong side of his fence. She glanced over her shoulder.

Not far.

All she had to do was get over that fence and join the goat with the bell on its neck where he grazed on the other side.

As if it heard her thinking, the goat lifted its head and looked right at her.

The bell clanged.

The earth shook.

Nikkis turned from the goat and faced the bull.

He lowered his head and charged toward the sound—toward Nikkis.

The bell echoed in the canyon.

The bull stopped. He lifted his head and spun, facing the echo from the rear of the canyon.

Nikkis backed up quickly.

The bull spun again and faced her.

The poor thing, she thought.

She wondered at herself for that thought. The bull would kill her if it could. There was no doubt in her mind that it would. Still, it was so frustrated and confused. Sadness pulled at her heart, and a part of her wanted to walk to the bull and stroke its head until it calmed and knelt and laid down in the grass to sleep.

The bull moved slowly toward her. Glowing mist shrouded its head.

Instinct took her muscles again. She put her fingers to her lips. She pinched her lower lip and sucked in through the pinched gap she made between lip and teeth.

A short and sharp whistle erupted from her lips.

The sound surprised her. It also echoed in the canyon.

The bull spun in a circle.

Nikkis turned and sprinted for the fence.

Every footfall of her mad dash felt like self-betrayal. Each time her feet touched the ground they signaled the bull, called him to chase her and kill her, to take out his frustration on her, to drive his sharp horns into her and throw her high into the air, and to crush her beneath powerful, sharp hooves.

She ran faster than she had ever run in her life.

The ground shook.

Weeds, grass, and poppies grasped at her ankles, pulled at her, dragged at her, aiding the bull in his efforts to catch her and end her.

At the fence, the goat stared at her from slit-pupil, golden eyes. He bleated. His bell rang.

The thunder of confused and angry bull protecting his realm echoed from the canyon wall and mixed with the goat bell. As if in one of her dreams, the sounds and smells and thoughts mixed together in a surreal moment. Sadness for the bull merged with hissing huffing, galloping thunder, which mixed with the distant and helpless sound of Nikkis's own panting, agonizingly slow breath.

Almost to the fence, she imagined the heat of bull's breath on the back of her leg. One thought filled her mind, the kind of random, silly thought that makes the gods laugh. *Not yet. Not again.*

She leapt.

Beyond thought, her hands reached for the top of the wall. Like the gymnasts she had admired on television, she upended herself. Her hands cupped sharp stones on the top of the wall. Her shoulders and elbows became springs coiling, loading, and then exploding when she snapped hard at hip and thigh.

She cleared the wall, but she spun too fast to do the gymnast trick of landing on her feet. Instead, she hit the ground hard, tripped, spun, and tumbled into the grass near the goat, rolling, falling, and thumping on hard earth and soft grass.

The whole while her body performed to save her, she felt like she watched from a distant place, amazed at her own impossible leap.

She came to a halt in the grass, and for a moment the thundering in the canyon continued. Lying very still, she waited, praying the bull couldn't or wouldn't leap the fence—or simply crash through the rock wall.

Tall grass framed the blue sky overhead. Her heart did more gymnastics in her chest. Her breath made its own cloud of mist rising in the morning air.

Once more, the sky struck her as somehow bluer and more right than the skies of her home in America.

The head of a goat appeared above her, filling the circle of blue sky. She'd seen goats before, in the States. She'd seen goats since she'd come to Crete. There were the goats near Knossos and there were goats in the fenced yards right in Iraklion, but she had never see one so close, and she had never seen one loose in the wild or after barely escaping death on the horns of a bull.

His bell tinkled, and his short, sharp horns made Nikkis hold her breath. Only six inches long, they were still every bit as sharp and dangerous as the bull's.

The goat horns reminded her of curved knives, and the very sharp tips glistened. She'd never thought about how sharp a goat's horns might be. She'd never really thought about why a goat needed horns. Suddenly, both things seemed very important.

He was bony and lanky—not like a farm-raised goat. He belonged in this landscape, and the way he looked at her told her she did not.

The head dipped.

Nikkis, tired, bruised, unable to sit up, and held by the thick grasses from rolling away, closed her eyes and tensed for the tearing of horns that would come to her flesh after all, after so many years, after everything.

The goat licked her face.

It licked her again.

The fear left her, drained out of her into the ground, into the dark labyrinths beneath the surface of the world.

Nikkis giggled.

The goat gave her face a thorough cleaning.

Nikkis squirmed in the grass, but the animal was insistent. Laughing, she finally relaxed and let the animal work until he was satisfied that her face was presentable. Then, he returned to grazing.

Smiling, wet, and sore, Nikkis managed to sit up enough to peer over the grass and poppies. The fence she had leapt now protected him from her and her from the bull.

Nikkis wondered at herself, at her own ability to climb down the narrow track in the cliff, to run in the tall grass, to leap and vault the wall, which now seemed impossibly high, high enough that the bull's shoulders came to its top.

He lifted his head from grazing and hung it over the wall. His dark eyes had lost their red sheen and the narrowness of his rage and frustration.

Now, he was the picture of contentment. Huge, damp eyes seemed to be asking her for something.

Everybody wanted something.

Exhausted and relieved, she fell back into the grass. She only wanted to lie in the grass, to listen to the soothing clank and clang of the goat bell, to watch the blue sky change hues slowly through the course of the day.

Too much had happened to her. *Too much.* She needed to sit perfectly still for a long while.

Her parents wanted her to marry and make babies for them. That insult had been manageable until they had decided that even Anderson would be okay if their lesbian daughter would adopt.

She shuddered at the thought of Anderson touching her.

Andros. He wanted things—the same things so many men wanted from her, the things they lied for, cheated for, and seemed willing to do almost anything to get.

Men. They all seemed like the bull to her. They couldn't think, couldn't remember their own experiences long enough to act like they had one, solid, thinking brain instead of two tiny, hard, and very confused brain nuts.

Andros wanted that, but he wanted more than most men. He wanted respect for his work, he'd said. He wanted the restoration of honor for his family, and he somehow wanted that from her.

The way he'd said those things, she was sure of their truth. Another part of her was equally sure that there was more to it than the Linear-A and forgery rings.

But she'd seen Yorgos killed right in front of her.

Andros might be dead too.

The image of Yorgos in the pit, dead from trying to protect her, filled her head. Her heart caught and cramped.

The goat bell rang.

The camouflaged form of the sly and dangerous Muscus came to her. That image pushed adrenaline into her blood. That little man had cold and empty eyes. When Muscus looked at her and the edge of his narrow little mouth creased into what for him must have been a smile, she had the same feeling as when the bull had started to charge—the overwhelming desire to turn and run.

The villagers didn't help. They had stared at her and whispered like they had never seen an American before or like she was the Whore of Babylon come to town on a golden chariot. They all whispered—all except the old woman, her grandmother. Even she wanted something from Nikkis—reunion and healing of lost family.

She supposed her random thoughts about the villagers might be near the truth. It was possible they had never seen an American before. It was possible they'd never seen men like Yorgos and Andros before.

Except, she knew Andros had been there before. They knew him and didn't like him at all.

Even the man in the bull mask wanted something, the man who had saved her from the dust storm, but who had taken her to a cave filled with the forged artifacts Andros hunted.

A policeman had died for her, and the very man Andros hunted had saved her life, but her giant savior was a thief, a forger of antiquities, and only the gods knew what else.

Certainly, he was big enough and powerful enough to terrify anyone she had seen in the hills of Crete. He certainly might have killed Yorgos.

But when she saw him at the window—when he had picked her up—there was more to this. There was something else that just didn't make sense.

Muscus, a policeman, made her want to run away and hide, but a known criminal picked her up and carried her like a small bag of groceries, and she felt safe, protected—somehow right in the same way that she felt at home under this incredible, perfect blue sky.

She shook her head in the grass. Shoots and leaves tugged at her tangled hair.

She was afraid of a short, wiry policeman, and she felt safe in the arms of a giant thief, forger, and murderer.

Too much had happened. She'd lost her mind.

She closed her eyes. Behind her lids, she easily drew his image from memory—broad and huge and powerful even engulfed by the blinding dust sent by the gods to confuse her. He loomed above her, his huge shoulders glistening with sweat and powdered with the red dust brought to Crete by the hot Sahara winds.

In her memory, he caught her and lifted her again.

From the mouth of the bull-head mask he wore, she thought she heard her name—her name in a thick, Greek accent—her name, spoken so softly, gently, and reverently that it might have been the sound of a prayer or of Sahara sand sliding along his smooth skin.

"*Nikkis*." The wind found voice in the leaves of grass. "*Nikkis*."

She let the safe sounds of the goat's bell and the imagined susurration of her name on his lips lull her into a needed, healing sleep.

~~~

"Who are you?" A girl asked in Greek.

Nikkis shook her head to clear sleepy shadows from her mind. She rolled to her belly and got up to her knees, ready to run. Fiery aches in every joint and muscle reminded her of her ordeals.

"I'm sorry," the girl said. "You were living in a bad dream. You called out for someone."

The pain kept Nikkis from leaping up and running. The girl's words sank in. Her young voice carried sincere concern.

Nikkis's heart slowed. She looked around.

Goats surrounded her. The bull stood at the stone fence, watching. A herd girl stood near the belled goat.
~~~

The girl wore tall, black boots and baggy work pants. She filled out her man's work shirt and vest too well. Otherwise, Nikkis might have taken her for a man. She rested one hand on the hilt of a curved knife set into a sash at her waist. In her other hand, she held a long staff made of some nearly black wood. Smooth from use, it shone under the mid-day sun.

"You aren't from around here," the girl said.

"No." Nikkis's lips cracked and her tongue caught against the dry tissue inside her mouth. "Do you have water? I can pay."

The girl took her hand off her knife. She stabbed her stick into the sod and left it standing upright. "Who are you?" she asked again.

"Nikkis."

"The ghost." The girl smiled. Dark eyes caught the sun. Light danced in them. "I know of you," she said. "The old ladies whisper your name."

"No. That's someone else."

"Perhaps, but only a ghost or a goat can travel so far and so fast over these hills. They say you went away with the fascists two days ago. They say you went to their camp and will never be seen alive again."

"I live. Barely."

"Perhaps. That I can see you does not mean you are not dead."

Nikkis stood. Muscles she didn't know she had complained, popped, and burned. She gasped.

The girl was at her side instantly, helping her, steadying her. "You're hurt."

"No," Nikkis said. "Not really. I'm just sore, tired, and thirsty."

The girl settled Nikkis back into the grass then knelt and pulled on a shoulder strap. A net bag slid from behind her back, along her hip, and around to her belly. The herd girl, in her traditional mountain herder's garb, pulled a very modern, plastic bottle of water from the bag and handed it to Nikkis. The blue label said, "Mythos."

Nikkis smiled when she realized she'd been expecting a goat skin from this child. She unscrewed the lid and drank deeply. The lukewarm water felt like ice cooling her throat and belly. She drank half the bottle before she realized she might be drinking the poor girl's entire water supply for the day.

She capped the bottle and handed it back.

"Go ahead," the girl said. "Your cracked, dry lips and red face tell me your outside has dried too much. You must be worse on the inside."

Nikkis touched her forehead. Where she touched, it stung.

Wind burn.

"Yesterday," she said. "The dust. I got lost."

"Lost?" The girl shook her head then tapped the water bottle. "Drink," she said. "Your confusion will pass."

Nikkis didn't understand, so she obliged.

While Nikkis drank, the girl said, "My name is Lígokrasí."

To give herself a moment to recover and to confirm the odd name, Nikkis repeated it with a more American pronunciation, "Leehograssi? Little wine?"

The girl laughed. "Yes," she said. "You have good Greek for an American."

"Greek parents."

"Ah. My mother says my father said my name to her just before I was conceived."

Nikkis laughed and returned the bottle.

The girl drank the last of the water. "Most people call me Leeho." She slipped the bottle back into her pouch and rotated the pouch around to her back.

Nikkis extended a hand. "I'm pleased to meet you, Leeho."

Leeho grasped Nikkis's hand.

The goat herder's skin felt like a glove made of soft wood. The girl had lived a hard life. Touching her hand, feeling the strength there, the years of work, and then looking at the valley, the bull wandering in the stone corral, the goats, the steep and unforgiving terrain—it all washed in on Nikkis, flowed over her, hit her that these people had lived like this for thousands of years.

In four thousand years, only the pottery and goat skins had given way to the convenience and pervasive presence of plastic.

"Where are we?" Nikkis released the girl's hand and tried to stand.

"Titan's canyon." The girl grasped Nikkis's hand again and helped her up.

The name fit the place. It fit the bull. It felt like a place she should know—like perhaps some myth she'd read or some story she didn't quite remember might have included this place.

"Is it far to a village?" Nikkis brushed dried lime mud and red Sahara dust from her shorts and shirt.

"You should rest a while. Let the water soak in. Then, I will show you the way."

"I'm fine," Nikkis said. "I need to get to a village."

"Why not fly?"

"What?"

"The fascist camp is difficult cliffs and three valleys west of here. You must have flown."

Nikkis shook her head. "No. I can't fly. I'm not a ghost. I was lost in a cavern."

The girl pursed her lips and narrowed her eyes, apparently deciding whether to believe Nikkis's more practical explanation of her method of travel.

Nikkis said, "Which way?"

The girl apparently came to a decision. She pointed at the canyon mouth. "Five cigarettes," she said.

Nikkis stared at the girl. "Five packs of cigarettes?"

"No. Down the valley, across the main valley, up the other side, and down to the village."

Nikkis rebuilt her mental map. She had gone to the head of the main valley with Andros and Yorgos.

Yorgos. She shook off the memory of his face and forced herself to concentrate.

The monster must have taken her over at least one ridge—maybe a couple. The cavern system had brought her under at least one more ridge. She had come all the way around the fingertips of the valleys to a finger valley nearly opposite the village.

Nikkis pretended to be confident of her bearings. She nodded and took a shaky step toward the valley mouth.

The girl pinched her lower lip between thumb and index finger then sucked sharply. The shrill, sharp whistle blasted out twice.

The goat bell rattled and clanged. The bull chuffed and stomped. Without a word, the girl turned, pulled her staff from the earth, and started down the valley floor.

Goats filed in behind her—the belled billy first and the others behind. The little goats dashed ahead, danced around the girl, butted heads, and dashed back to Nikkis.

Every living thing in the valley seemed to follow the girl. Even the great bull in his pen followed as far as he could before the stone wall stopped him.

Given the clarity of purpose presented by moving girl and marching goats, Nikkis figured she had all the answers she'd get for now. She found a place in line with the goats.

Ancient Faith

The palace corridors hissed with the life of the stones, and every step filled Daedalus with new fear. The corridors the queen and her guards escorted him through took them into the queen's wing, into the queen's labyrinth, and finally to the room where Daedalus had witnessed the horror of the living souls trapped in clay and stone golems. It had been over two years since that night, but no man could forget that night.

Where he had nurtured hope when he saw the light of day, he now imagined himself a clay-faced toy of this twisted woman.

They walked into the chambers. The guards escorting them stayed outside.

The queen moved off to one side, and Daedalus stood at the door, peering across the room and past the stone circle, the same stone circle in which the fire that did not burn flesh had roared, the same stone circle against which he had seen the queen mounted by a murdered man.

The cold stones showed no sign of recent fire.

The balcony beyond shone under the late morning fire of Helios. A woman stood on the balcony. Sunlight through her diaphanous skirts highlighted her familiar shape and told him that his hopes had not been in vain.

Nikkis.

She stood well and hale, and she turned from the sunlight to face him.

For a long moment, they looked at one another, expressions blank, uncertain. He felt the water on his cheek before he knew he had let it loose from his eye. "Nikkis," he whispered.

He had no sense of either of them moving, but the distance between them became nothing. They held one another. Tenderly, they touched one another's faces. Tears flowed. They smiled. They chuckled. He kissed her, and he kissed her again. He put his nose to the soft flesh beneath and behind her ear and inhaled the scent of her.

"Nikkis."

"Daedalus."

He didn't know how long they simply held one another, how long they stared and touched and kissed. He forgot all sense of time and place. He forgot that he had been brought to this place by a woman who could kill a man and trap his soul in mud and stone. Even so, they eventually believed in one another, and Daedalus, still hugging Nikkis as if letting her go would mean to lose her forever, turned to the queen.

Pasiphae stood, silent, waiting and watching.

"Why?" he asked. "What do you want?"

"To serve my goddess." She pointed to the archway into the room beyond, the room where the bath lay and golems hid behind a curtain.

Daedalus pushed Nikkis back, protecting her with his body. "No," he said.

"Please," Pasiphae said. "You need a bath."

"You do," Nikkis said.

Daedalus looked at his wife again. "How long have you been here?"

"Two days since she brought me out of the king's wing."

"Has she–" He stopped himself. He didn't know how to explain to Nikkis what he had seen in this room.

"Please, Mason," Pasiphae said. "Come and see for yourself. It is safe. The Goddess demands that I do this." The Queen said it like it explained all—the cruelty, the hollow cow, the golems, the power in his hands.

Cautiously, he crossed to the arch. Beyond, in the room with the bath, he saw the curtain that had covered the golems. It hung to one side, open, revealing the wall against which the golems had stood. There, where tortured men had stood in rows, only gray rubble, torn fur, and scattered gems remained. No single piece of stone resembled any bit or part of a man.

"Released." Queen Pasiphae came to stand beside him. "Please," she said. "We will bathe you, and I will tell you what we must do."

Nikkis led him to the water. She stripped away his soiled clothes. Then, she stripped away her own and led him down into the queen's bath.

Queen Pasiphae followed. She took up a sponge, and she and Nikkis washed Daedalus's bruised and soiled flesh.

~~~

For two days before the Festival of Bulls, Pasiphae and Daedalus made preparations. Together, they gathered clay from the tidelands where river and ocean meet, where the rhythm of life ebbs and flows, and where salt and fresh water mix to create the cycle of water and rain. From her serpents, they drew venom containing both the power of life renewed and the power of death.

From Nikkis and Daedalus, they drew blood to mix with clay and venom.

"Now, clever Daedalus," the Queen said. "We will use your hands to record the words and make the promises here that must be made. The king requires a curse, and if you wish to live through your ordeal with the bull, I must give him the curse he has asked for."

"You do not need me for this," he said.

"No. To curse you is an easy thing. To give you freedom to break the curse yourself, your hand must press the curse to the clay. Then, my craft shall make the clay both cage and key."

He asked her, "What is this curse?"

A pained look creased her brow and darkened her eyes, but she answered him. "If you die, then your soul shall rise again in flesh, and the new flesh shall be condemned to love only Nikkis, and she will love only you."

"If this goes badly," he said, "my greatest hope is that the gods will smile on us and let us love in the afterlife or in another life."

Queen Pasiphae caressed his cheek.

He grasped her wrist to check her touch.

Nikkis hissed and stepped forward.

The queen pulled her hand away. "Don't worry, Nikkis. I have tested his love. He is more loyal to you than any man ever was to woman, wealth, blade, or horse."

"I do not fear his love will fade," Nikkis said. "I fear your hand will harm."

Daedalus slipped his arm around Nikkis. His hand rested on her hip and knew the strength of her spirit and body. He shared her anger and soothed her at the same time.

Sadly, Pasiphae said, "He would die for you. Would you also die for him?"

Under his comforting touch, Nikkis's muscles knotted and quivered, ready to leap, to kill, or to die. "If need be," she said.
~~~

"Good," the Queen said. "Because Minos must harden this tablet in a fire sprinkled with your blood. I will do what I can to keep that from happening, but if Daedalus succeeds, I doubt you will be set free until that fire has burned."

"An empty curse," Nikkis said. "I would gladly fire the clay myself to be so cursed."

The queen shook her head. "Hear the rest. You will not think it so kind a fate once you understand. Heed me. Know that if the clay is fired, I shall contrive to keep this clay in a cavern where once Daedalus and I met. With the help of the gods, perhaps he will there find and crush this tablet. Because it is made by his hand, he will be able to break the curse."

"Eternity together is no curse," Nikkis said.

Pasiphae said, "Oh, but it is."

"You taunt us for your own pleasure," Daedalus said.

"No. My husband does. He has bargained with me. If I will curse you, Daedalus, damn you to eternal torment, he will restore my place by his side in the judgment chambers."

"Sad, petty power," Nikkis said. "It is meaningless."

"Everything is about power," Pasiphae said.

"Only," Daedalus said, "for those who refuse to see the world in other ways."

Queen Pasiphae held up the disk. "Look closely, my children of innocence and love. Look at the power of my goddess, the creations of the mother of serpents. See the spiral I have set in the clay made from the waters of your lives and the mingled blood of your hearts? Within this spiral, Daedalus, you shall press the words of your curse. This spiral is the path of eternal renewals. See the flower at the center? See that both sides match, but neither side touches the other?"

"Red clay," Nikkis waved a hand in dismissal. "Mud and scratches."

"One side is your curse, Daedalus. The other side is Nikkis's."

"Help us or kill us," Nikkis said.

Daedalus had seen the golems and their use before they were smashed. Nikkis had not. He pulled his bride closer, told her by his touch and his silence that they were safe for now. He listened carefully to the queen.

"See the spiral coming to the edge, coming to the forking place, to the moment of decisions? That place is wide. To trace the path of life on the disk, you must choose between circling the edge or crossing over and moving toward the center."

"What does it mean?" Nikkis asked.

"As long as the disk is your curse, the decision is made for you. Instead of living on the spiral of life, you shall forever come together. Forever, you will love. Forever, you will be lost to one another."

"Again," Daedalus said, "you promise bliss but warn against tortures."

"Forever," Pasiphae said, "is a very long time. Every time you come together, you will know one kiss of passion—a first kiss." She touched the split in the spiral path and traced the circle at the edge. "Here, in that moment, you, Daedalus, will lose your mind."

"I will still love him," Nikkis said.

"Yes, my dear. You will." She turned the disk over. "You will love no other. That is your curse. You will love no other, but many will desire you. You will be used by those who confuse power and possession with love for all of time. Now, you know my husband's revenge for your rejection."

"I'll kill myself before the kiss," Daedalus said. "I won't allow her to be tormented."

"I'll care for him," Nikkis said. "Again and again through eternity."

The queen ignored them both. "You will become like the bull, Daedalus. You will have strength of will and power of body, and you will remember every moment of every life you have lived. You will remember her kiss once, twice, in a thousand lives; no memory will make sense. Your memories will not fit together in the mosaic of time. They will be like a shattered crystal urn—still an urn, but never to hold water again or look like an urn to any eye. You will wander aimlessly. You will rage and fight and die."

Nikkis reached for the disk. "I'll help him."

Queen Pasiphae held it away. To Nikkis, she said, "You will want love. You will want to love again, but you will forever fear his madness. You can only find peace and love with him, but he will be driven by his madness, and you will be terrified by it."

"He will leap the bull," Nikkis said. "There will be no death. No curse."

"If he does not?" Pasiphae tapped a fingernail on the clay.

Daedalus pulled Nikkis close. She buried her face in his chest.

"If," he said, "my memories will survive but make no sense, then I want this moment to live among them as a balm." He leaned down to her and kissed her. Her arms came up around his neck. They held one another for a long moment, tongues and lips searching, flesh warming, hearts pounding, testing each other's love, trying to feel the fire that would need to burn so long—to burn forever if they failed in their gambit.

"So easy for you," Pasiphae said. "Love is so easy for you."

Daedalus and Nikkis separated and looked at the queen.

Pasiphae's face betrayed the depth of her sadness, her emptiness, and her pain.

"To lead is often to be alone," Daedalus said. "Who in this life might a queen trust?"

Nikkis touched the queen's cheek. "I'm sorry," she said.

Pasiphae gently pushed Nikkis's hand away. "I have made my choices."

"What if something happens?" Daedalus asked. "What if I can't get to the disk? The king might have a third treachery. He may let us go and still kill me or Nikkis by assassin or by poison."

"He would dare not. His herd of men and women would revolt against him were he to harm you once you have leapt the bull."

"Still," Daedalus said. "I would be easier in my heart if we changed the curse so Nikkis could love another, could have her fate separated from mine."

"No," Nikkis said. "I wish no other destiny."

Pasiphae frowned and said, "Nor could I make one for you, child."

"All of this means nothing," Nikkis said, "if Daedalus leaps the bull. He will succeed."

"I have my own magic." Daedalus held up his hands. "I will not fail. But should I, or should there be some treachery we have not divined, I know at least one god Minos has slighted so direly that he might avenge us."

Queen Pasiphae set the disk down. "I do not doubt you, Mason. I do not doubt you. And I think there may be two."

~~~

Naked at the center of the arena floor, Daedalus searched the seated crowd, especially the queen's attendants and soldiers. He hoped to find Nikkis. He hoped, in spite of all that the queen had arranged, for Nikkis to witness this, to see him either win her freedom or die. If he died, he wanted his last vision in life to be of her. He knew it was a selfish thought, but he could not help his desire to add to his many memories of her love.
~~~

All the seats were full in all the rows surrounding the arena. People even stood on the roofs and on the overhangs of higher rooms and chambers where rooftop perches let them look down into even the smallest part of the arena.

On the west side, beneath an awning, King Minos sat surrounded by his servants, concubines, and nubiles, whose valuable pale skins should never have been touched by the sun. All had come to see the gods judge the man who loved Nikkis, the man from far away, the man who could fly and build palaces that blinded travelers with light stolen from Helios himself.

All had come to see him die or win the favors of the king.

He couldn't find Nikkis. She was not even among the pale, sad lovers of the king.

The ground shook, and Daedalus turned his full attention to the cause of the tiny earthquake.

Titan appeared from the maw of one of the four tunnels into the palace deeps.

Titan. His test would be by the hooves and horns of glorious Titan, Nikkis's sweet bull.

The once gentle bull's dark hide showed marks of torture—red welts, burns, and cuts. Titan had been well-goaded before entering the arena.

Daedalus's belly threatened revolt at the sign of such abuse heaped upon so gentle and noble a creature.

Titan showed no sign of recognition. In his tiny eyes, Daedalus found the red, hard center of hatred that only King Minos could inspire.

As one voice, the crowd gasped.

Titan stabbed one massive hoof into the earth. He lowered his head then flipped it upward, twisting and turning in agony. His eyes, narrow and tiny, showed how little of his life in the hills he remembered, how far from his heart the peace of his time with Nikkis and the people of the village had fled, how broken Daedalus's mind would be if ever the king's curse were placed upon him.

Daedalus pulled in a long breath to calm and prepare himself.

The low shuffle and chatter of the spectators began again.

Titan snorted and stamped. His head stilled. Froth dripped from his mouth. For the first time since he had been ushered into the arena, Titan's eyes focused on the moment instead of on pain.

His eyes focused on Daedalus.

Daedalus cursed the king and this unjust irony.

The shuffling, breathing, and nervous chattering of the crowd died. For a moment, only the heartbeat of Daedalus and the breathing of the bull echoed in the confines of the arena.

Now.

The moment of choice of freedom in life or death had come to Daedalus.

On the roof of the palace, free to come and go as it pleased, a gray and black jackdaw mimicked the snort of the bull, mocking Daedalus, Titan, and the court of Knossos.

Titan jerked like a new, hot iron had been set to his hide. He charged.

Daedalus remembered his nights near the village with Nikkis and the bull. She played this game with Titan. She had tried to teach Daedalus, but he had not been born to it. He had not learned well. Now, it was not a game.

The earth shook. Dust danced on the arena floor.

Nikkis's life depended on this.

Titan bellowed.

Now, tortured Titan would gore him, trample him, and use him to sate the rage the king's men had put into his giant's soul.

"Charge him like a bull," Nikkis had said. "To play with a bull, you must be one too. Know his mind, and he will treat you as an equal."

Daedalus stomped his own foot in the dust. A cloud rose around his ankles. He snorted and shook his head.

Men and women in the crowd laughed. The king laughed loudest of all.

Titan closed the distance.

Daedalus charged the bull, sprinting toward the deadly horns.

People cheered.

The jackdaw cackled.

Titan's head was high—too high. He came too fast. If Daedalus leapt and reached the horns, they would drop down instead of rising to lift him.

By a trick of the gods, time slowed and Daedalus seemed to be looking down on himself, seeing his failure, his own death coming. Daedalus despaired. He had failed Nikkis.

Too late to turn. Too late to run. Either meant goring, trampling, and death.

The crowd cheered. The king laughed.

Daedalus chose to face the creature and display a brave death. At least he could leave the watchers with the knowledge of his love of Nikkis and defiance of Minos.

Gods willing, the memory of his love and honor would drive others to defy the king.

Daedalus's death charged toward him from only a heartbeat away.

He prepared to leap, to take the bull's horns full in his chest, to–

A shrill double-whistle echoed in the arena.

Daedalus leapt.

Titan lifted his head upward and left. He turned and shook his horns at the sky.

Daedalus missed Titan's head. He hit the bull's massive shoulder and bounced away like a pebble from a tortoise shell.

Turning still, Titan plummeted past Daedalus, pulling a rush of dust and wind over the fallen man.

Daedalus fell, rolled, and came to his knees, then to his feet.

The bull spun. Titan searched sky and earth for the sound of the whistle.

Nikkis's whistle.

She *was* in the arena. Somewhere.

Men and women of the pavilion searched among themselves, but the whistle had come too fast. It had echoed from too many walls. No matter how many echoes there had been, the sound told Daedalus that Nikkis watched. She was safe.

His heart roared its joy, and with the joy came a memory—Nikkis in the moonlight, beautiful, dark hair reflecting the silver shine of the night mistress. She held her head low, mimicking the horns of the bull with fists, one finger extended from each, pressed against her temples.

She stamped and charged him. She ran fast, dipping her head low. At the last second, just as he bent to catch her charge, she lifted her head and leapt high. Her hands touched his shoulders, and then she was over him, behind him, and laughing at him.

"Be like the bull," she had said. "Set your horns low, and he will match you."

Titan spun, crazed, seeking the safety of his mistress. He came to a halt, frustrated. Again, his raging eyes found Daedalus. Again, he stomped and charged.

Daedalus lowered his head and charged.

The crowd roared. Women screamed.

Daedalus kept his head low and tried to match the bull, to become the rage of Titan, the weight of anger and pain, the movement of boulders down the side of a mountain, the crushing power of the hand of a god.

He charged, eyes on the earth, heart filled with fear and love.

When the ground beneath his rushing feet danced in dust from the wind running before Titan, he dipped his head lower, a feint to draw down the monster's horns. Trusting his memory of Nikkis at play, he lifted his head and leapt upward and forward.

Titan came too fast. The bull had no time to react.

Daedalus caught the bull's horns safely and squarely in the palms of his powerful hands.

Tricked, terrified, and confused, Titan lifted his head against the man's grip and weight.

Daedalus rose on the horns of the bull, no more weight to Titan than a hummingbird on the finger of a man. He rose and he heaved himself upward, bending and lifting his legs.

Titan lifted, and when the bull's head reached its zenith, before the mighty head could shake, Daedalus snapped at the hips, driving his legs upward and over himself and the head of the bull. He released the horns, rose through the air, tucked into a ball, and let himself spin with the speed Titan had given him.

High in the air, he opened up from his ball. His hands seemed to belong to someone else, perhaps to Nikkis or to some other goddess as they touched the rump of the passing bull and launched him once more into the air.

His feet were still his, and he landed badly, twisting an ankle, falling, rolling. Still, he recovered from his roll and stood upright before the pavilion of the king.

A roar of triumph and approval erupted and filled the arena. The bird that had mocked him flapped its wings and fled.

Minos glared.

Daedalus bowed. For his hidden Nikkis, he bowed. For Titan, he bowed.

The ground shook.

Minos smiled.

Daedalus turned.

Titan came again. No handlers appeared to stop him, to keep him from charging again, and again.

"No," Daedalus said. "No, Titan. Please."

The crowd became silent.

Minos laughed.

Daedalus set his feet, lowered his head, and charged again. White lightning pain flashed in his foot and up his leg. He screamed to give himself strength. Again, he made his leap. Again, he vaulted his old friend.

All around him, the assembled throng screamed and cheered.

His landing was worse. His ankle would not support him. He fell to the earth, face in the dust.

The earth shook from Titan's raging hoof beats.

Daedalus heard only the king's laughter.

He managed to get to his knees, to face Titan and the king.

"This," Daedalus called, "King Minos, is how you keep your promises?"

Save for the snort of Titan and the whisper of dust in the breeze, silence filled the arena.

Someone in the crowd broke that silence with an angry hiss. Another hiss joined the first. And another. Soon, the entire arena shook with the hissing and hoots of the assembled.

Titan charged.

The king lifted his hand.

Handlers poured from the arches of the arena, distracted the bull, harried him, and herded him back into the dark maze beneath the palace.

Exhausted and gasping, Daedalus bent low, hands in the dust. His whole body shook. His head hurt and his ankle pulsed with fiery pain. He wanted to fall to the dust and lie limp until he had slept and lost all memory of the death he had nearly embraced.

"Daedalus!" The king's bellow was a distant voice, no more than a whisper after the sound of Titan's breath and hooves. "Hear the king's promise! You have done what no other foreigner could do, and you have my boon."

Daedalus would not fall before the king. He would not show weakness now. Ignoring his pain, he struggled to his feet.

Somewhere up there, Nikkis watched. She had saved him again, and now he would save her again.

"Name your boon once more, clever one," Minos said.

Daedalus swallowed his own bile. He straightened his spine. Looking the king in the eye. "That the thrones of Crete, the High Priest of the Bull and the Priestess of the Mother of Serpents, acknowledge the love Nikkis and I hold for one another, that we be freed of our bondage to you and allowed our love for all time." He took a breath and added, "And that Titan be freed to his hills once more that he might live to his age in peace."

"Done!" the King bellowed. Minos sat, smiling.

The assembled cheered and screamed and danced.

Under the king's steady gaze, the sweat on Daedalus's back became an icy mountain stream. He saw Titan's madness in the king's eyes.

But the king had granted his boon before gods and men. Any treachery of royalty that came now would come at great cost to the king, for all the world would hear of it, and gods would curse him for it.

But Minos smiled, and his eyes shone red under the high sun. He lifted a hand.

Twenty soldiers carrying armfuls of wood streamed from the tunnels into the arena. Four more followed, carrying a bronze pole.

Daedalus knew his ordeal had not yet ended.

Modern Sense

The high sun had grown very hot by the time Nikkis, the goats, and the girl had worked their way down the valley, across the larger main valley, up into another valley, over a ridge top, and finally down to the high end of the village. During the journey, Nikkis saw no sign of a dig, of Andros, of caves, or of the forger who had saved her from the storm. She tried to talk to Leeho, but the terrain and the goats kept both of them too occupied to allow more than a few words.

She did learn that Leeho was an orphan, that the girl made her living watching other people's goats, and that she liked the behavior of her goats a lot better than the behavior of the occasional tourist and her village's boys.

They came into the village behind one of the ubiquitous, white-stucco, tile-roofed, blue-domed churches. A middle-aged, bearded priest wearing a black cassock worked on grape vines in the yard surrounding the church. As they approached, he looked up. After a moment, he went back to his grapes. A heartbeat later, his head snapped back up, and he stared open-mouthed at Nikkis.

Many men had stared at her like that before, but never a priest, and certainly not after she had spent half a day and a night underground and running for her life from a minotaur and a bull.

The priest walked to the edge of the wall around the grape vines. "Leeho!" he called. "You found the ghost."

"I'm not a ghost," Nikkis said in Greek.

"A good Greek ghost in American clothing," the priest said. "Such a find!"

Leeho laughed, and the sound of it made Nikkis smile. She liked the priest already because he made her troubled friend laugh. That was the kind of priest to have around.

"What will you do with your ghost?" the priest asked.

"I don't know," Leeho said. "She's too big to put in a raki bottle."

It was the priest's turn to laugh. His svelte frame shook. His sparkling eyes reminded Nikkis of her father on his good days.

"Perhaps," the priest said, "You should take her to Papu. I think maybe he can help you with this ghost."

The girl nodded and continued along the churchyard wall into the sloped, cobbled main street of the village. The herd of goats trailed along behind her.

Nikkis spoke to the priest. "I'm a linguist from the United States," she said. "I got lost."

"I'm a priest from Athens," he said. "Until we must be someplace, how can we be lost?"

Nikkis smiled. "I need to get back to Iraklion. Could I use your phone?"

The priest laughed again. "You *are* from America."

"And I need a phone."

"So do I," he said.

"You don't have a phone? Not even a cell?"

"Truly, little ghost, Papu is the one to help you."

"He has a phone?"

The priest shook his head. It was more than just a "no." His eyes seemed saddened by the idea of a phone. His head shake judged, dismissed, and projected disappointment.

She had seen *that* look from other priests. Her good humor drained away into the ground.

He turned back to his vines.

Even if her mere existence and nationality offended, she still needed a phone. "Will you at least point me toward a phone?"

He worked on his grapes. "Papu," he said.

"Then he *does* have a phone?"

He left his vines and walked away toward the church.

Nikkis looked around for an ally, somebody that would show her to a phone. She had to contact Andros. The last of the goats trailed past her into the village street. From the blue-painted doorway of a nearby building, a very old, leathery woman wearing a black dress and scarf stared at Nikkis. She crossed herself and spit on the ground. She backed into the shadows of her house and closed the blue door.

When Nikkis looked back for the priest, she found only vines and the blue-domed church.

Leeho had gotten her this far, and it didn't look like any of the other locals were going to be of much use. For all she knew, the people she saw in the doorways and windows might be thieves or terrorists. The only person she knew she could trust was the one that her gut told her not to trust—Andros.

She followed the goats onto the cobbled street and realized that Leeho's trail had joined the same trail into the village that she, Yorgos, Muscus, and Andros had used to leave after spending the night.

At least she sort of knew where she was. That was something.

~~~

When Leeho turned the goats into a stone-fenced enclosure, Nikkis instinctively helped herd them. When they turned back toward the slat gate, she stepped forward and clucked her tongue and hissed a bit. She waved her hands, and the goats responded as if they shared a language.

Leeho closed the rickety, olivewood gate and looped a wire over the post. She turned to Nikkis. "Thank you, Nikkis. You herd American goats, then. Are they different?"

Nikkis laughed, but the girl's serious expression made her stop. She didn't want to insult this girl who had given her water and helped her find her way out of the maze of the mountains. "No," she said. "This is the first time I've really been around goats."

"You have the knack of it." Leeho tilted her head to one side. "The goats know you. They listen to you and trust you."

Nikkis told herself that she knew better than to believe that goats favored one herder over another. Animals responded to waving hands and noises. She changed the subject rather than offend.

"Where is this Papu? I have to get back to Iraklion."

Leeho shrugged. "We can look for him now, if you like."

Nikkis wondered how hard they would have to look, and she was relieved when Leeho led her to a low, wide warehouse only twenty meters or so from the goat pen.

Inside the warehouse, the stone floor sloped back and to the right away from the door. In places, a thin layer of concrete, cracked and broken, covered older stone
~~~

work like someone had tried to level the floor by building up. The floor had clearly protested, shrugged, and rejected the artificial layer by breaking it into rubble.

Long rays of sunlight came through several broken tiles in the roof.

The light cut through dusty, dry air, illuminating the interior in distorted squares, casting the rest of the warehouse in darker shadows than if there had been no light at all. Three bare light bulbs hung from aging, cloth-insulated wires nailed to the ceiling. Two lit bulbs did nothing to change the shadows and darkness in the corners of the warehouse.

The third bulb dangled from its cord like a shock of herbs hung to die and dry. Gray dust coated it. Beneath the dust, once white glass was charred black from some long ago flare of tungsten and electricity.

By the time Nikkis's eyes had adjusted and she had taken in her surroundings, Leeho had disappeared down the slope of the floor along one wall and into deep shadows.

Nikkis tried to follow, but a motorized tricycle blocked her way. She'd seen them before, these tricycles. Once she'd gotten out of Iraklion into the vineyard and olive country, she'd seen a lot of them. All seemed ancient—no two exactly alike. Each seemed cobbled together from other machines: lawnmowers, bicycles, horse-drawn carts, or tiny hay wagons. The front wheel of this one was missing. Where others had a motorcycle wheel on a motorcycle fork and long handle bars that swept back toward a bench seat or a tractor seat, this one had concrete blocks and a mass of mangled metal that had more in common with modern sculpture than farm equipment.

Like the burned out bulb, the bench seat of this trike wore a coat of thick dust. The low platform mounted over a rear axle and two wheels showed gaping holes where boards had been removed. Through the gaps, the axle and differential made dark lines and masses of hard shadows.

"Leeho?" Nikkis called.

The echo of her voice sounded like it had gathered dust in its short travels from wall to wall.

She turned left to go around the trike. Another one blocked her. Another turn, and another trike. Surrounded by the little machines, all of them in various states of repair or disrepair, she felt like she'd stumbled into a crypt filled with dead and dying Greek farm machines.

She took a deep breath to settle rising waves of claustrophobia, but the shadows and frustrating obstacles made her heart race.

She breathed slowly and deliberately, telling herself she'd had a rough couple days. The dig, the men, the pit, the storm, the manbull, the cavern, the Linear-A, the climb down the mountain, the bull, the goats, the girl.

Yorgos's vacant eyes.

In the crypt of dead machines, Yorgos's eyes haunted her, filled her mind. The dark closed around her. Each breath filled her lungs with the weighted dust of the ages.

She wanted to scream, but she refused to let herself become hysterical. She hated hysterical women.

She wanted to cry, but that had never helped her.

Never.

It wouldn't help her now.

A phone would help. She wanted a damn phone!

Suddenly too exhausted to stand, she sat heavily on one of the trike seats. It squeaked in protest.

"I didn't believe the old women," a man's voice said from the shadows.

Leeho and an old man moved into the slants of sunlight, expertly navigating the maze of machine corpses.

A shaft of sunlight struck the man full on the face. He smiled. Creases cut by sun and habit framed bright, straight teeth and warm, dun eyes. His face shone with kindness and humor.

Automatically, Nikkis brushed back her hair and straightened to greet him.

"You *have* come back from the dead," he said, but he laughed after he said it.

"Excuse me?"

"It's really her?" Leeho asked.

"Of course not." He stepped up to Nikkis. He wrung his hands inside the pale, red cover of a cotton shop rag. He pulled his right hand free and offered it to her.

She tried to stand.

"No," he said. "Don't get up. You look tired."

Nikkis nodded gratefully and took his offered hand. "Dr. Nikkis Aristos," she said.

"Papu," he said.

Though he had wiped his hand clean, a thin layer of warm oil covered the sharp edges of dry calluses. His solid, careful grip told her of a man who lived by his hands and mind.

He let go of her hand.

It struck her that he had held her hand exactly the right length of time to let her know he was her friend and could be trusted. Not too long. Not too short. Not like most men.

Her vision blurred. She swiped at her eyes and willed dignity into her face. She offered him what she imagined must have been a very worn and tired smile.

"You have your mother's eyes," he said. "And smile, though I don't think I ever saw her so tired as you."

She stiffened. "My mother?"

"Nikkis Aristos, yes?" the man said.

"Yes."

"And your father? Alexander Aristos?"

She nodded. "I don't know you," she said.

"And your mother? Cliantha, yes?"

Nikkis slipped her feet to the floor. Leeho stepped in to steady her.

The man stepped back to give her room.

"She is beautiful," Leeho said. "Was Cliantha this pretty, too?"

The man said, "The beauty in Dr. Aristos is a gift from forgotten gods. It does not come from her bloodline."

"It is *her*, then," Leeho said.

Nikkis didn't like the way Leeho emphasized *her*. She asked, "You know my parents?"

"Your mother better than your father." The smile lines at the corners of his eyes appeared again, but the dun softness deeper in his eyes betrayed an old sadness. "I knew your mother very well," he said. "She and I slept in the same house for seventeen years."

"Papu!" Leeho laughed.

Papu laughed with her, and Nikkis couldn't help but smile, though she was sure the joke was at her expense.

"I'm sorry," Papu said, "Come with me. Come to my house. You can clean up. We will fill you with water, food, and raki. Yiayia always has food. She will be very glad to see you."

"No," Nikkis said. "I'm fine. I just need a phone."

"I will make a deal with you, Doctor Nikkis Aristos. You tell me the truth, and I will tell you the truth." Papu said, "I will start. We have no phone in this village."

"I haven't lied to you. I don't know you." *Had he just called her a liar? Really? This old man in the middle of nowhere?* Her blood heated, and she pushed back hard. "You have no right to call me–"

"Nikkis." He grinned and winked. "If your grandfather can't call you a liar, who can?"

For a long exhausted moment, she stood in the silent, dusty shadows and stared at the old man. Finally, she said, "My what?"

"Look at me," he said. "Think of your mother's face and look at me."

She stared. His kind eyes held sympathy. His patient, gentle smile told her he would wait as long as needed.

Her mother smiled like that. She had a way of settling into a moment, into a place—a way of simply becoming part of the scenery and knowing that all the time she needed was hers right then, right now.

Nikkis blinked and suddenly saw her mother's face if she'd been a man.

"No," she said.

"Yes, Nikkis. Welcome home."

"I'm tired," she said. "I could use some water. Maybe a bite."

"Good," he said. "Now we are family. While you clean yourself and eat, I will send a message down the mountain for you."

"But…." She tried to protest, but she was too tired. She wanted him to send word first. She wanted to tell him to call Andros and tell him she'd found the forgers, but she couldn't. Even if these people were family, she wasn't sure they weren't the thieves—maybe even Yorgos's murderer.

"Your mother was born here," Papu said. He put his hard hand on Leeho's shoulder, and they turned. Over his shoulder, he said, "You have Kritiki blood and soul, but you have an American mind. So, I suppose you will do what you want to do no matter who offers advice."

If her grandmother was in this village… If he was her grandfather and he was one of the forgers, then…

They walked away from Nikkis, making their way through trikes and shadows.

Her thoughts spun like a tired, ancient mote of dust caught in one of the shafts of light shining through the broken roof.

Andros. Yorgos was dead. Bull-headed man. Grandfather. Grandmother. Linear-A.

Her mother's voice came to her. "No matter what the problem, it will be easier to solve after you have a bath and dinner."

The retreating pair made their second turn in the dimly lit maze.

Nikkis made her decision. Staying in the dark wasn't so smart. Wandering the streets wasn't so smart. She'd had quite enough of the twists and turns of ridges, valleys, and caverns in the mountains. She needed food and water, and he was offering. Even if he wasn't her grandfather, she'd have to trust him for a little while—at least until she could contact Andros.

~~~

"Yiayia," Papu called. He stood in the hot sun just outside a blue-painted wooden threshold set into pale, native stone blocks. The house wall met with the walls of the next house, and the next. Like giant stairs set into the hills, the houses marched up slope, curving along the cobbled path the villagers called "The Street." At the top of the curve, The Street ended at the church and beyond that gave way to dust and trails splitting off in all directions and disappearing into the hills.

"Yiayia!" Papu called again.

Leeho and Nikkis stood behind him just outside the open door. Inside, the little house looked cool, bright, and inviting. Unlike Papu's world of shadows and machines, this was a world of open windows, sunlight, flowers, and statuettes of goddesses and saints.

"Yiayia! We have a guest!" He wrung his hands in his shop rag, and then he tossed it across the threshold into a small basket on the floor beside the door.

"Don't yell, old man!" a woman called from a rear room. "I heard your fat feet on the stones of the street ten minutes before you touched the door."

"She probably did," he said to Nikkis.

"You live here? Are we going in?" Nikkis asked.
~~~

Papu shrugged.

"And you bring people to my house for food." She called. "Two women, no less. So where will you find me, old fool?"

"Kitchen," he called. "Only the magic of your food and wine and kisses have kept me alive so long."

Silence followed. Then, in an archway at the back of the room, a woman appeared. She was the same woman Nikkis had met at the Inn. She was shorter than Papu—maybe only five foot—and she was as old as the stones of the mountain. Like Papu, her smile used the whole of her face, and Nikkis thought she could see the woman's heart through her eyes.

"You are a snake, you old turd," Yiayia said through her smile. "To charm an old woman like me and put a little blood in her face. *That* takes some magic. Don't just stand there in the street. Come in! Come in!"

"She likes you," Papu said. He gestured for Nikkis to enter first.

Where the warehouse was clearly Papu's domain and the center of a community of men's work and equipment, Yiayia's house was her palace, and Nikkis doubted that any man would dare oppose her there.

Nikkis stepped up and over the blue threshold.

Like Papu, Yiayia wiped her hands in a linen towel, though her towel was tucked into a man's leather belt around her waist. The belt pulled tight the folds of a long, black dress. On her head, she wore a black scarf tied down behind her neck beneath long, loose, gray hair.

She crossed the room, sturdy black shoes clapping on the white stone floor.

"It is my shame," she said, "that I love an old goat."

"In front of company," he said, "you embarrass me."

He didn't sound or look embarrassed. The warmth of the home wrapped Nikkis like a thick quilt bundled around her to keep out the chill of storms and darkness. She was surprised to feel a thin smile of relief stretching her lips and wind-chapped cheeks. No thieves, forgers, or murderers would dare set foot in Yiayia's home.

Papu put his hands out to the old woman, and they held one another's eyes and hands for a long moment before she nodded slightly and turned to look at Nikkis.

"I knew," she said. "You had to come here eventually."

"I'm lost," Nikkis said. "Your husband and Leeho were kind enough to help me."

"Nonsense!" the woman said.

"They did," Nikkis said.

"You are not lost," Yiayia said, "And all the gods of antiquity could not help you if you took directions from these two." She laughed, turned, and headed back toward her kitchen. "Sit for food, wine, and raki. We will talk."

"Please," Nikkis said. "If I could just use the phone."

The woman disappeared into the kitchen, but her laughter drifted through the house.

Again, Nikkis found herself smiling.

Papu moved into the main room. He sat on an ornately carved black chair at the head of a matching, black-lacquered table. Leeho gestured to a chair at Papu's right. Nikkis moved around the table. Grateful to take weight off her feet, she sat.

Leeho sat opposite her, to Papu's left.

"Really," Nikkis said. "No joking around. This village doesn't have a single phone? Not one?"

"None," Papu said.

Nikkis's pulse pounded in her abused feet. She wanted to take her shoes off, to free her flesh to expand after days of being trapped and pressed and bruised inside Gore-Tex and leather. She made do with rubbing her thighs to push blood into her calves and feet. She shook her head.

"You are tired," he said. "It has been a long time since you walked these hills. You aren't used to it."

Nikkis stopped rubbing and looked up.

"She knows the goats," Leeho said.

"This is my first time on Crete." Nikkis tried to stand, but her legs refused to lift her weight. In spite of Papu's disarming smile and the warmth of the house, Nikkis was starting to worry again, to feel a little trapped.

"The wine will help your legs," Papu said. "Leeho will help you clean up."

"I can't stay."

The old man nodded and smiled. "Might as well clean up and rest. You are in Yiayia's home, and she will feed you for a while now. Then she will talk. And talk. Nothing you can do will stop it. You would do better to tell the spring to go back to winter than to oppose Yiayia when she cooks or talks."

Leeho's warm laugh swept away Nikkis's worries. She couldn't help her own chuckle. Food and rest would be good. A clean face would be luxurious. She'd make the best of it. The old man might or might not be related to her, but he certainly understood her mother's habits of home and hearth. Nikkis resigned herself to her fate as pampered guest in the home of Yiayia and Papu.

Leeho helped her to a small bathroom in the back of the house.

Nikkis washed and returned to the table. The washing hadn't changed her exhaustion, but it left her feeling safe and more relaxed than she had since arriving in Crete.

Yiayia appeared from the kitchen with a tray piled high with plates and bowls of chicken, olives, fruits, and breads. The old woman must have been cooking all day.

"Yiayia!" Papu stood to help unburden his wife. "You knew she was coming, you old witch, you."

Yiayia only smiled and went back to the kitchen.

Nikkis couldn't believe any of these simple, village people were involved in anything so elaborate as the forgery ring Andros hunted.

~~~

Andros remembered many dark mornings before sunrise when he walked with his father on the dusty roads of their village, when he and his father talked quietly under stars that were the same whether over Crete, Turkey, or Germany. Long before the birds awakened, he and his father spoke in quiet voices of family and honor.

Those cold nights, like this one, filled him with admiration and hope. In the small, dark hours his father relaxed, his father's memory cleared, and the tales of family history, of the insults of the Greeks against his mother, rose into words and entered the heart of a boy who would one day make things right.

In the pre-dawn light, he would make things right. Today, he would renew the name of his family, of his mother, of his father, and he would make these backward Greeks pay for their insults.

~~~

Yiayia served them a hearty, late lunch, and late lunch ran on into dinner, and dinner ran on into an evening party. Villagers came and went, and darkness came to the village. Yiayia's home was lit by the flickering yellow glows of oil lamps set on shelves, in sconces, or on the table itself. One lamp, the one at the center of the table, was very much like the shallow, clay bowl lamp Nikkis had used in the Bull's cavern.

Several times during the evening, she resolved to have a closer look at it. Each time, some new arrival accosted her.

Apparently, Yiayia *had* known Nikkis was coming. Nikkis imagined some herdsman in the hills had seen her and signaled ahead. She imagined gossip moved like the wind here, spreading swiftly and touching every ear. Yiayia had *only* told a few dozen of her most intimate old-lady friends, all of whom came and went through the evening.

Some crossed themselves when they met Nikkis. Those women, almost all wearing the same black dresses as Yiayia, quickly made excuses and slipped away into the night. Each time one did, Yiayia went to the threshold, spit in the street, then laughed into the darkness.

Because of Yiayia's spitting and laughing, Nikkis imagined family and village rivalries playing out over her presence, but she couldn't imagine what or why or how. When she asked Yiayia, the old woman smiled and offered her dolmades. She tried Leeho, and the girl said, "They don't believe in Yiayia, but Yiayia doesn't believe in them either, so it's okay."

That was all the answer she got.

One woman called Nikkis a devil. Yiayia heard that. She turned and gave the old lady such a look that the woman became very quiet and seemed to shrink into herself.

The rest of the women who arrived treated Nikkis like royalty. They competed to sit next to her or to bring her grapes or olives. They fawned over her, complimented her beauty, gently touched her hair or cheeks the way they might touch an icon of sainthood before crossing themselves—and a few did cross themselves.

No matter what the locals called Nikkis, everyone called her newly discovered, or temporarily adopted, grandparents Yiayia and Papu.

Eventually, Nikkis got tired of explaining her presence and arguing to convince people she was not her mother. She came to believe that everyone in the village and from miles around had come to meet Yiayia's granddaughter.

Through the long afternoon and into the night, she'd been careful to only sip from the top of her shot glass of raki. She had learned that emptying the glass would only lead to someone refilling it. During a brief moment alone with Papu, Leeho, and Yiayia, she asked, "Are the children not allowed to come to a dinner like this?"

Yiayia and Papu both looked into their glasses.

Leeho picked at a small plate of fruit. "No other children. I'm the last one."

"Where did they go?" Nikkis asked. "Did something happen?"

"They leave." Yiayia's voice shook like she had just lit the lamp in her best friend's shrine. "They leave as soon as they can—like your mother and father."

Papu wrapped his wife's shaking hands in his.

"The parents," Leeho said, "The people who raised the children get old. No more children."

"Why would young people stay?" Papu said.

Because, like her father, Papu seemed to need his hands to speak, he let go of Yiayia's hands before he went on. "No automobiles. No telephones. No computing machines. The village is small. Seven cigarettes, they can walk to the road. Eventually, they do."

"There could be phones," Nikkis said.

The three locals all sipped their raki at once. When the glasses came back to the table, silence ruled for a long, awkward moment.

Nikkis tried to find meaning in the depths of the silence, tried to understand what she had said that had caused the three Greeks to act like she had just walked into church singing loud rap and shedding dog crap from her shoes.

Finally, Yiayia said, "Look at us! Our granddaughter comes to our home—our granddaughter who has never even seen us before, who was sent by the gods themselves—and we show her sad and tired old people instead of the happy and young we feel in our hearts for her." She raised a glass. "More raki, Old Snake! Sti-yamas!"

"Sti-yamas!" Papu said, and he and Yiayia and Leeho all threw back a full shot of the potent grape-mash moonshine.

Nikkis sipped. She tried to mentally claw up through her muddle of thoughts and feelings. "We're not so far from the coast," she said. "The road could be cut into the village. If phone lines can't be strung, a cell tower could be built on the ridge. At the very least, a satellite dish could be brought in by donkey. You could connect to the world."

"No." Yiayia's eyes became hard, black crystals in her narrow, dry face. Her gray hair and scarf suddenly reminded Nikkis of storm clouds, and her thin lips tightened and darkened.

"Why?" Nikkis asked.

Papu fiddled with his glass.

Leeho looked from Yiayia to Papu and back.

"Why did you stay, Leeho?" Nikkis asked.

"I belong here." Leeho answered Nikkis, but her eyes watched Yiayia.

"Belong more than the young who left? Why?"

To Nikkis, Yiayia said, "You have less respect for your elders than your mother had." She picked up the raki bottle and her glass and turned for the kitchen. "We are done," she said.

"Tell her," Papu said. "Tell her why no road and no lines. Tell your granddaughter why no computing machines and no phones and no children."

Yiayia stopped at the kitchen archway.

"Please," Leeho said. "Or she will leave."

"I have to leave," Nikkis said. "People are looking for me."

Yiayia spun, her eyes wide and dark. The raki bottle fell from her hand. Her glass followed the bottle and shattered. The sound wrapped the first word she spoke. "Fascists! *They* look for you. They hunt you like a cat hunts a rat in mountain rubble."

She seemed crazed—stung by swarming memories. Of what, Nikkis could only guess.

"No," Nikkis said. "I came up the mountain with the policeman named Andros. *He* looks for me. A policeman."

"Turk!" Yiayia spat on the broken glass at her feet.

"He's Greek," Nikkis said. "His parents were Turkish and German, but he's Greek. I'm helping him preserve Greek culture."

Yiayia crushed glass under her solid, dark shoes. She came back to the table and took up Nikkis's hands. Her aged flesh was cold and her dry skin rough. "Child." Her eyes had cleared. Her voice sounded sane again. The darkness of the shadows hidden in her aging mind had passed. "This policeman—your policeman. When he left, he threatened us. When he comes back, he will keep his threats."

"We were attacked in the hills."

"He is Turkish and German, and his parents were Turkish and German, and when he comes back, he will come back like a Turk or a German. He will come with guns and men to find you."

"He's got a temper," Nikkis said, "but I don't think he'd hurt anyone except thieves or forgers who shot at him."

Still holding Nikkis's hand, Yiayia sat. "We live under a curse. Your mother knew it. She didn't want to believe it, but she knew. She found a man that would take her as far from here as she could get. America—to the farthest side of America."

"I'm a scientist, Yiayia. I don't believe in curses."

Papu snorted. Raki came out his nose. Leeho passed him a napkin. When he'd recovered, he said, "You knew where we lived, so you came to our village?"

"Andros brought me here. It's a coincidence."

"No," Leeho said. "I knew as soon as I saw you. It's the curse."

"You believe this stuff, too?" Nikkis said.

"So do you," Yiayia said. "So does the bull in the labyrinth."

"What does the Minotaur have to do with any of this? That myth grew out of the misunderstood experiences of people who lived here over three thousand years ago."

Yiayia squeezed Nikkis's hand hard. "This village has guarded secrets for thirty-five hundred years. We keep the gifts of the gods safe until love and justice play out and free us from the curse."

Nikkis pulled her hands away. "I'm tired. I need sleep. In the morning, I'll walk out to the road and find my way down the mountain."

Yiayia shook her head. "The fascists will come before dawn," she said. "That is the way of fascists."

"Thank you for your kindness." Nikkis stood. "I'm very glad to have found you, to have been able to get to know you, to hear of my mother's childhood, but the world has moved on."

"Movement is not progress," Papu said.

Nikkis shook her head. In ways, these people were very much like her parents. "I can see why the children left. In ignorance, there is no hope."

"There is no hope for the children of this village anywhere," Leeho said.

Because of the certainty in the girl's voice, Nikkis looked long and hard at Leeho. She was not a parrot of her parents or the old people of the village. Leeho had carefully thought it through and come to a clear conclusion.

"They can get jobs out in the world," Nikkis said. "Look at me. I did. I'm educated, and I'm respected. Your government called me here to help them discover forgers. Bad men make false artifacts and sell them on the black market. They work in hidden caverns in these hills. They have lived here for a very long time and have probably been making forgeries for generations."

Papu whispered, "No forgers."

"One of them caught me in the dust storm. He was huge and wore a bull head mask to scare people. He–"

Yiayia grabbed Nikkis's hand. "You met *him*? Touched The Bull?"

Startled, Nikkis pulled away. "Who?"

Papu poured himself another drink.

Leeho said, "The Bull of the Mountain. Our Minotaur."

"Not a bull," Nikkis said. "A man. He wore a mask—a bull's head. He took me to a cave."

"How did you find him?" Yiayia asked. "I know him. I know he is there, but I have never found his place, nor has anyone seen him except if he showed himself to them."

"In the dust storm. He put me in a cave. I escaped."

Papu pulled a circle of amber beads from his trousers pocket and began flipping them in his hand and sliding them back and forth between his thumb and forefinger. After a long silence, he said, "Escaped?"

"I found a way out. I crawled through a tunnel."

The old man kissed his beads and said, "No, Nikkis. He saved you, and you came home."

Sudden uncertainty clouded Nikkis's mind and heart. A moment before, she had been sure of her knowledge, of what she knew about the hills and the people and the police. She had been sure the bull man had taken her and held her. Now, she remembered that he had left her in a safe place with water. No door locked her in. No rope bound her.

She had chosen to wander deeper into the caverns.

"I think sleep would be best," Yiayia said. "Yes. And I will make you breakfast tomorrow. Then, we will help you find your way home. Papu can take you part way down the mountain on his trike."

"Old woman," Papu said. "The fasci–"

"Hush, Papu," she said. "This woman, our granddaughter, has come home. She is done with the stories of our island. Leave her to rest now." To Nikkis, she said, "Come, child. I will put you to bed."

Exhausted and grateful, Nikkis followed her grandmother to a tiny bedroom filled with a huge, feather bed. When the old woman had left, she fell into the mattress and let herself sink slowly into comfort, warmth, and sleep.

Coincidences danced in her skull while the curtains of shadow closed around her. A man in a bull mask found her in a red dust storm. A cop hunted the bull. She had found her grandparents. She knew where the forgeries came from. The ideograms in her paper matched the oldest of the cavern forgeries. The village children were gone—shadow memories in old hearts. They were all gone. Gone. Somehow, while falling asleep, it all made sense in her heart, but the pattern, the logic, the organizational strategy that would connect it all up, remained hidden around a corner just beyond her conscious grasp.

Dehydration, she told herself. *Exhaustion.* Her body ached, and even though she'd only sipped, she had more alcohol over the long reception than she'd probably had in the last two years combined.

Sleep. She just needed one good night's sleep.

~~~

The sun still hid behind hills, though it touched the tops of ridges. Andros's men moved like silent, mountain cats. Tan, gray, and black camo fatigues made them wraiths in the pre-light.

He and nine men would subdue the village in half an hour. It wouldn't take long. Some of his men would die. These mountain people hated uniforms and guns, but experience had taught him that uniforms and guns would get this job done.

"Everything is ready," Muscus said.

"Good," Andros said. "We will be heroes by the end of the day. We'll rescue the lovely American academic from this hot-bed of godless terrorists. Expect resistance."

"Deadly force." The little man grinned.

"Authorized," Andros said. "Tell the men."

Andros stepped past the statues guarding the approach to the village. Standing tall, he raised a hand in a fist so all his hand-picked, bribed, or blackmailed men could see his confidence and determination. The shadows among the rocks and scrub became very still. Even the birds became quiet in awe of the power he was about to unleash on these peasants in the village.
~~~

~~~

Mourning doves called for the coming of dawn, and Nikkis kept her eyes closed. She woke to the memory of enough of the night before to know that moving would bring the pain of too much drinking. Even once she had realized that she didn't have to drink the whole shot of raki, she still sipped to be polite. Papu had made the raki himself, using his own grape rinds, seeds, and mash. He'd added wild fennel to the mash, aged it in a fifty-five-gallon drum in the sun for a full, late summer month. Finally, he poured the sludge into a copper kettle large enough to put Nikkis and the Bull of the Mountain inside together. Finally, he had sealed a copper kettle top onto the drum and boiled it until the pure alcoholic extract of the mash dripped from the copper tubing at the top.

Kritiki moonshine—raki.

Of course, these people had never known prohibition, so they had no concept of moonshine. To them, this raki brew was an old family recipe. For them, it was like tollhouse cookies in the States.

Them. Her family.

She opened her eyes, forgetting that she had meant to keep them shut.

Mercifully, no pain shot through her head. Tentatively, she flexed a hand—a foot—her jaw.

No pain at all.

She sat up. She should have been in terrible pain. She should have been more hung over than she'd ever been in her whole life. At the very least, her muscles should have screamed from the exertion of the last few days.

Instead, she felt good—light and open to the world of the new day.

A quiet knock came at the door to her tiny room.

"Yes?" Her hushed voice matched the quiet of the knock.

"Come with me," Yiayia said.

Nikkis got up. "Come in."

Yiayia entered. She carried heavy boots and clothing, the same as the other women of the village wore: a loose, white blouse, loose white knee pants, and a long black dress to cover all. "Put these on, child. It's time for you to leave."

"But I have questions."

"Last night, all you had were answers. Now, you have questions? You try me the same as your mother did."
~~~

"I can leave later in the day."

"No," Yiayia said. "You leave now, or you never leave at all."

Puzzled, Nikkis took the clothes and put them on. "What are you talking about?"

"The fascists come for you. They will be here by sunrise. We told you last night."

"Lieutenant Andros?"

"Ne, Nikkis." *Yes.*

"I told you, Andros is not a fascist."

"Any man who imposes his political will by force is a fascist," Yiayia said. "You are an American. Did they teach nothing in your schools?"

"The Nazis were fascists." Nikkis tied the black scarf on her head.

"Fascists walked the earth long before the Nazis. There have been fascists since the Nazis left Crete. You don't have to be a Nazi to use force to get your way."

"Andros wouldn't–"

"Come, child. We go. You did not grow up here. You don't know what the Turks did. You don't know what we did to the Turks—or the Italians and the Germans. These are old wounds, but none of them are as old as the wounds in your soul."

"Yiayia, I'm glad I met you and Papu, but–"

"But I'm a crazy old woman."

Embarrassed, Nikkis looked down and brushed uselessly at her clothes. "I wasn't going to say that."

The old woman forced a thin smile. "No matter, child. Come." Yiayia led her into the main room. Fruit and bread sat on plates at the table. Leeho had eaten, and she was slipping out the door.

Nikkis called to her. "Good morning, my friend."

Leeho turned at the door. She nodded and held a finger to her lips.

Lamplight flashed on the jeweled hilts of several knives—long, long knives with curved sheathes that fit snuggly in Leeho's leather belt and curved back over her hip. The hilt of each knife angled forward above the girl's hips. Crossing her arms, each hand could grasp a hilt.

To Nikkis, the girl looked like a gunfighter. The words of the man on the plane came to her, "Crete. I never go there. Those people know seventeen ways to kill you with a knife." The tiny, efficient, bleeding wound in Yorgos's neck flashed in Nikkis's mind. Even a child could have done that, if she knew how, if she had the right knife, if her hand were steady and her eye cold.

Nikkis heard the screams of women before the gunfire, but the gunfire caught her full attention and drove adrenaline into her blood.

Leeho disappeared into the dark, cold morning. Yiayia ran out into the street and disappeared as well.

Nikkis followed, but when she reached the street, it was empty. There was a light on in Papu's warehouse. She dashed across the street to the warehouse. "Papu," she called through the open double door of the building.

Her voice echoed from the darkness.

"Fascists!" a woman screamed. "Fascists!"

The voices came from the down slope side of town, the place where the trail entered town from the cleft in the rocks. Another gunshot cracked, echoed, and fled the stone-cobbled street. More shots.

She moved inside. "Papu!" she called into the darkness.

"Here!" he said.

A church bell rang. Then another. And a third. She thought she remembered only two bells hanging in the arch of the old church. A fourth bell joined the first two. The tiny village seemed to be surrounded by bells. The clanging chorus rolled inward from all four corners of the village. It rose up into the hills; then, as if sound could be caught by gravity, the ringing of the bells turned back on itself and crashed into the village streets, slamming into a new wave of bell-song.

Nikkis covered her ears. "Where, Papu?"

"Here, Nikkis. Come to my voice."

She stumbled through the darkness. A rough hand took her wrist and pulled. "Quickly," Papu said. "Fascists! You are too pretty for the streets. The old women will fight."

"Fascists?" She pulled against his grip, but it was the hold of a man who had wielded axe, hammer, and wrench all day every day of a very long life. He tugged, and she followed. "There are no fascists in Crete. Not since–"

"There are always fascists," Papu said. A rusty hinge screamed, and dirt and grit ground under foot. The hinge protested again. "They have guns. They wear uniforms. Fascists."

"Police, Papu. My friends."

He laughed, but the laugh was low in his throat like a growl, and he coughed at the end.

The bells faded. A metallic click sounded behind her. She turned. A match erupted, lighting Papu's white-whiskered face. Shadows deepened the wrinkles of his forehead and eyes, making him look much older than she imagined he must be.

She wondered then how old he might be. She couldn't be sure. He might be very old—old enough to have fought real fascists in the streets of his village.

The match moved to the chimney of a kerosene lantern. He lifted the glass, lit the wick, and settled the chimney. He adjusted the flame, and Nikkis's eyes adjusted to the dim, yellow light.

Guns.

Racks and stacks and rows of guns. Crates of guns. Guns wrapped in oilskins. Guns covered in wax. Guns stacked against walls, tucked into shelves, and racked like wine. She stood by a closed, metal door at one end of a long, uphill corridor made of guns. A boardwalk made of wooden pallets separated the two walls of guns.

Some, she recognized from World War II movies and pictures. She didn't know the names of them, but she recognized tripod machine guns, mortars, and hand-held machine guns. Others looked brand new, like they had been bought in the last few years. They looked like the Uzi-kind of guns popular in American TV crime dramas.

The place reeked of oils and solvents.

"Is the lantern fire safe?" she whispered, forgetting for the moment about Papu's fascists.

He nodded. "We go," he said.

"Where?"

"The top of the village. The church. To the hills from there." He slipped quickly past her and up the narrow way between the walls of weapons.

After a few dozen meters, the guns gave way to shelves of knives and racks of swords.

The walls behind the weapons and racks became natural, slick cavern walls. "More caves," she said. "Is this whole island one big cave system?"

"You remember," Papu said.

"Remember?"

"I am keeper when *he* is gone," Papu said. "When I die, you will be keeper."

"Keeper of what? He, who?"

"This." He gestured with the lamp, but he kept his pace. "The safety of the village." He hustled along. The palette boardwalk between the walls of weapons gave way to stone and earth floor. The cavern ended abruptly at a wooden door with a solid, black iron bolt run across it and into the stone.

Papu put his ear to the door. The lamp flickered. Shadows jumped on the irregular rock of the walls.

"Who *is* he?" she asked again.

"The Bull. Your minotaur. He protects us. Your heart's blood comes from this village. It is why he saved you."

"But that's not–"

He shushed her and doused the lamp.

Darkness again. Distant, muted ringing bells reminded her of the dangers outside. The walls closed in on her. She held her breath, afraid that if she let it out she would never be able to inhale again.

When he lifted the bolt, it made a small, slow grinding sound.

His hand, warm from holding the lamp, gripped her wrist again. She let herself be led this time. Again, a squeaking hinge, but not so loud as before. Under foot, the floor changed from grit and dirt to something smooth and cold.

From the darkness came another squeak of hinges and another sliding grind.

Blinding light shone through an open door.

The ringing bells became so loud they hurt her head.

She blinked to clear her sight.

Giants. Huge, round shapes surrounded her.

She stepped back, but Papu held her wrist. Her eyes watered, and the shapes turned into barrels so big that ten men might have hidden inside each. The blinding light came from rows of overhead incandescent fixtures that looked like huge versions of the hanging, tin-coned shop lights her father used in his garage.

The room smelled of wood, wine, and stone dust. Pale molds covered some of the old seams of the dark wooden barrels.

Dust on the floor danced each time a bell clanged. The resonance made Nikkis's skin itch.

"Quiet, Nikkis," Papu whispered between clangs. He led her between the barrels. She looked behind her and found no sign of the door they had used—not even a space between the barrels that might be large enough to hold a door.

They moved quickly up a flight of sagging wooden stairs and through another wooden door into daylight streaming through narrow, clear glass windows set into the stucco wall of a corridor. Papu pulled her along to the end of the hallway. There, they turned a corner into a larger, shadowy space.

Papu froze.

Nikkis recognized the space around her. She'd never been there before, but the back of a church was the back of a church in familiar ways. Pews filled the nave, and an ornate marble altar sat beneath the dome over the sanctuary.

In front of the altar, the priest who had joked with Leeho prayed.

He prayed on his knees between Andros and Muscus.

The two policemen looked down on him. They wore black uniforms, like the riot suits she'd seen on TV. They also wore dull, black helmets. Their combat vests bulged with knives, grenades, and weapon magazines.

Nikkis realized that priest wasn't praying. The police stood, one on each side of the terrified kneeling man, eyes and automatic weapons trained on his head.

"Fascists," Papu whispered. "Quickly." He pulled on Nikkis's wrist, tugging her toward the front door of the church.

She pulled back. "Andros," Nikkis said. "What are you doing?"

Surprised, Andros twisted, bringing his gun up to point at Nikkis and Papu. Face framed by the black helmet, he looked like cold, gray stone. A thin, false smile slowly cut across his face. "Thank God, you're safe, Nikkis." He stepped away from the priest, who turned a little. Muscus slammed the metal stock of his weapon into the side of the priest's head.

The priest fell and covered his head with his arms.

"Andros!" Nikkis tore free from Papu's grip and ran, leaving Papu at the entrance to the church.

The priest struggled up to his hands and knees.

She tried to reach the priest.

Andros caught her and held her. His gun poked at her ribs. His hands bruised her arms. She shook and tried to spin away from him. "Let go," she said. "You're hurting me."

"Fascists." Papu's voice echoed in the dim, emptiness of the church.

"Shut up, Old Man," Muscus said. "What have you told her?"

"Run, Papu!" the priest called. From all fours, he surged into Muscus. His shoulder caught the nasty little man hard in the side of the knee. Muscus grunted and crumbled.

Andros released Nikkis and trained his gun on the priest. His finger wrapped around the trigger.

Nikkis lunged for Andros.

He fired.

A heartbeat too late, she hit Andros as hard as she could with her whole body.

The priest fell, face down on the stones.

Andros pivoted away from her weight. As he turned, he slammed his weapon into the side of Nikkis's head.

Her world became red and black. The dome above her, a mural of heaven and the many saints that blessed the church, spun and melted and darkened. She looked for Papu, but he was gone, or perhaps he was one of the saints. It didn't matter to Nikkis. She was falling, and she wondered as if she watched herself from far away—as if still in the caverns of the mad man in the bull's mask—if she would land soon or if she would just keep falling until she died.

Ancient Curses

The angry roar of thousands of men and women inside and outside the palace swept in waves through the arena. The guards had mounted the pole at the center of the arena, and they had built a pyre around the pole and chained Daedalus to that pole. He stood on faggots meant to burn him to death, and he listened to the rage of a nation, a rage he knew would consume Minos, if not on this day, then soon.

Suddenly, the crowd quieted. All eyes turned.

Daedalus followed the gazes of those he could see.

Nikkis walked into the arena.

No glory of man or the world of men could rival the grandeur and dignity of Nikkis's entrance into the arena. Six guards, bone helms and breast plates shining white under the glare of high summer sun, marched at her side, but none dared touch her. Her strength shone from her like noon sun burning through a hole in black storm clouds. Daedalus could see that those men feared that if they even looked at Nikkis, they might die rather than commit her to flames.

He waited for his love, and Minos smiled from on high, sitting in the shade, enjoying the treacherous spectacle of pain he had devised to be a symbol to all who would defy him.

Nikkis stood straight between the men in bone armor. She turned her face. Her eyes caught morning light and shone with love for Daedalus.

He embraced her gaze with his own. Through his eyes alone, he tried to give her the love she had won, the life they would have shared. She, in turn, he knew, gave to him her love and life. In her gift, even facing death, he found courage and gratitude.

The guards helped her up onto a wooden ladder they had laid over the pyre, the pile of blessed sticks and timbers that would soon be lit to give a false sacrifice to Poseidon, to give a sacrifice the king claimed was a worthy trade for the great white bull Poseidon had sent him.

Hands chained around the bronze pole at the center of the pyre, Daedalus faced her while the guards chained her as well, her arms around him and the pole in a parody of embrace.

One of the guards, a man Daedalus might have known if he had allowed himself to take his eyes away from Nikkis's, whispered, "I am sorry, Mason. I am sorry." Another affirmed his sorrow—and another after that.

Daedalus nodded.

Nikkis smiled and pulled her arms tight around him. "If we are to die," she said, "then I would have this embrace."

The guards retreated at a clattering trot to the curved, stone walls of the arena of Knossos.

Daedalus leaned forward as far as he could, pressing the side of his head against the bronze pole. Nikkis matched his action, and their lips touched.

The crowd screamed in anger.

The guards, men whose families and villages would die if they defied the king, faced the crowds, rattled their shields, and stomped their feet.

King Minos bellowed.

All eyes turned to him save the eyes of the lovers who could not spare a moment of life out of one another's sight.

"This is the promise I have made," King Minos crowed like a jackdaw. "That their love should be acknowledged, and so I acknowledge it! This I have promised, that they should be together for the rest of their lives, and so they shall be. This I have promised, to set them free!"

The people of the palace booed and hissed. Voices beyond the palace took up the calls of rage.

All knew who had built the palace—their temple. All knew whose mind designed the warships that kept them safe. All understood the powerful love of Nikkis and Daedalus, their Master Mason.

As one voice, the Minoan people called for justice from the king who treated them as cattle. Down to the last child and concubine, down to the sewer boys who crawled in filth to keep the sluices free of debris, down to the jackdaws on the roof, all hissed and booed.

Nikkis held him. Their lips touched again, and the love in that kiss silenced the men and women of the palace. The silence of respect moved outward into the lands beyond, and the silence reigned for the length of their kiss.

"And for running from me!" Minos cried. "For betraying me and conspiring against me, I curse this Daedalus of Mycenae. I curse him to love Nikkis for all of time, in life after life! I curse him to find her, to fall in love again, to know the madness of passion. In every life, their first kiss shall tear away his mind and make him as a maddened bull. His mind shall be filled with all the moments of all his lives but never make sense of them. I curse him thus!"

The crowd railed.

Nervous guards set a line between king and crowd. Others filed from dark tunnels into the arena, creating a circle around the pyre in case some fool leapt from the crowd into the arena.

Minos waited for the rage of the crowd to ebb like receding surf.

To Nikkis, Daedalus said, "We shall love each other for all of time. For one of your kisses, I gladly face an eternity of madness."

"No," she said. "Please."

"And her," the King called out, "for denying me. For taking my Master Mason from me. She, I condemn to an eternity of loving only this man who in every life for all of time shall be mad!"

"Only you," Nikkis said.

"Always you," Daedalus said.

Pasiphae, breasts bare, wearing her goddess's many-colored, many-tiered dress, strode from the darkness of an arena tunnel. She carried the writhing vipers of her rites. "Wait!" she cried.

Her loyals followed her, men and women in armor and equal to the soldiers of the king. They circled the arena, and each faced off against a king's soldier.

The assembled people cheered.

She held the serpents high. "This treachery does not keep the promise you made!"

"Set the fire!" Minos commanded. "Free them!"

Three soldiers, burning torches in hand, trotted up from the shadowed halls and into the arena. They entered the arena in the bedlam. They saw the queen's and king's soldiers facing off.

The crowd cursed the soldiers.

The flame-bearers slowed, stopped, and shuffled. Each held his ground at the arena edges. The torches hovered nearer stone walls than oiled wood and flesh.

Daedalus saw the reluctance in the soldiers. He saw the regret and fear on their faces. He called out. "King Minos! Free my wife, or in my death I will bring the news of your ambitions and deceits to the gods. In my death, I will end the flow of the Vlychia's waters to Knossos. Even the Kairatos will weaken and fail the land. In my death, I will destroy all I have built for you. The gods shall punish your folly. I swear to you that I will open the earth and bring fire from the sky. I will fold the stone beneath your palace and bring your chambers back to the earth from which I made them. I will break the foundations of stream and river and let the waters of the sky and earth flow into the ground to be drunk by demons rather than men."

The king raged. "I am King of Knossos!"

"You are a slave of death," Pasiphae said.

"I am your future," Minos said. "Step back, witch, or I will put an end to you and your vile religion of women now."

The viper in her left hand writhed. It opened its mouth and spit venom onto the earth. "I curse your curse," she called. She dropped the snakes. They moved toward the pyre.

The king screamed, "Kill them!"

The soldiers stared at one another for a heartbeat. In all the history of men, there is no telling the who or when of the first blow, the first wrong done that leads to so many others. So it was in the arena. A nameless soldier struck another soldier. Battle was joined. The chaos of the rat pit filled the arena.

People leapt from their seats into the arena to join the fray.

Minos leapt from his pavilion to the arena dust. He tore a torch from the grip of the nearest torch bearer. Huge and terrible, he fought his way to the pyre.

The queen tried to cut him off, but battle and her vestments slowed her.

The serpents neared the pyre.

The king touched torch to oiled branches.

Flame erupted around Nikkis and Daedalus.

Women in the crowd screamed. Men cursed.

The din of battle raged.

The king laughed.

Daedalus locked eyes with Minos and said, "You have chosen."

Daedalus looked down into the flames. The clay disk holding their curse had been placed at his feet to be fired in the same fire that killed them. This was how Minos had planned all along to sprinkle the clay with the blood of the lovers.

Pasiphae's serpents crawled beneath the burning faggots. The queen finally reached the lovers, but the high, hot flames pushed her back.

She raised her arms to cover her face, struggled forward, then fell back again.

"Join them, my wife!" Minos said. "Join them!"

Pasiphae pushed into the fires. Her vestments took flame. She pressed forward, climbing into the flames until she could gather up the disk. Hair and clothing on fire, her eyes burned only with determination.

"Save yourself," Daedalus said. "The people will need you."

She scored the disk with her fingernail, etched three symbols: the hand, the lybris, and the unfolding flower. She tossed it near Daedalus's foot. "Blood," she said.

Daedalus understood what she had done for them.

He would be insane, perhaps. His mind would be the mind of a bull, but his hands would remember. His hands would be their hope. One day, his hands would find a way to break the curse, to move past the endless spiral and back into the cycle of life and love. She had impressed his symbol in the clay—the lybris centered on the passion flower. One day, in spite of all, Nikkis would find him and give herself to a madman. On that day, their lives would begin again.

The queen burned. One of her loyal guardswomen leapt into the fire, grabbed her, dragged her from the fire onto the ground, and rolled her in the dust to extinguish the flames.

A king's guard buried his sword in the loyal, and she collapsed on top of the queen.

Like the waves of rats in the cistern, the waves of fighting rolled from wall to wall in the arena and swept the guard away.

The serpents' heads rose from the faggots. One bit Nikkis. One bit Daedalus. Both turned to the disk and set their blooded fangs to clay. There, they died.

Nikkis's arms tight around him, Daedalus closed his eyes. His fingers closed around his chains.

She pressed her head to his shoulder. The sound of her coughing breath in his ear gave him strength.

Through his chains, he let the knowing of the chain's anchor come to him. Through it, he found its root in stone and then paths into the living rock foundation of the palace he had built. Through the foundations, he sought the craft of gods, the slow, ancient making of stone and lava and lime. He let his love of Nikkis, his grief for Ikarus, and his anger move outward into the earth, seeking Poseidon's realm, seeking older gods, seeking the mother of all gods, the very heart of love hidden deep in the living world. He put on the stone of the palace as if it were a golem made for his spirit. Within the stone, his mind and soul grew and reached and donned the stone of the island of Crete. He dipped his mind into the fire deep in the earth, the very blood of Rhea, and she helped him find the path upward through her skin to another island, the island of Thera.

Daedalus prayed to Poseidon for strength. Within Rhea's skin, the skin she willingly lent him, he flexed arms and legs. He pushed the beating of his heart, and the blood beneath him broke free of the earth, exploded upward, and sent gouts of fire into the sky.

On Crete, the marble of the mountain above Knossos folded. The Vlychia and Kairatos, life water to Knossos, the gifts of Rhea, sank into the earth. The ground beneath the palace shook, bucked, and buckled.

Flame and ash rained from the sky. Flames rose from the pyre. Through the flames, he saw Titan run free from broken rubble hallways. The great bull, followed closely by Poseidon's white bull, night and day running side-by-side, dashed frantically about the broken arena, seeking some target for their rage.

Flames licked at Daedalus's legs. Heat seared his lungs. Nikkis, holding him, head buried in his shoulder, went limp in his arms, and he thanked the gods for their mercy to her.

Into his mighty lungs, he pulled scalding air, his last breath in this life, he was sure. To the gods themselves and to the king and Queen of Crete, he gave voice to the last of his magic. "This palace, built of blood and forced hearts, will fall. I call on whatever grace with the gods remains to me to bring it down, to burn it, and to wash its remains from the pure earth from which I cut these stones!"

He let his head fall, his nose on Nikkis's neck. Eyes open, he watched the clay disk at their feet beginning to change color, to darken, to harden, to become the endless curse he would endure for the sake of her love. The spiral in the clay spread outward, and at the edge where the charred heads of the serpents held the clay, the glyph, hand-fashioned by Queen Pasiphae, marked the hope for his future with Nikkis.

For a moment, he found himself with Nikkis, above the pyre, their love buoying them like empty amphora upon a receding tide.

The twisted, charred bodies beneath them meant nothing. Battling soldiers, fleeing men and women, the court, the bulls, the queen and king—all these memories rose away from them like the smoke rising from the pyre. Nikkis and Daedalus, ethereal, pure, turned to one another, embraced, and melted into one another until neither could tell one from the other.

Subjects and soldiers ran from the palace in fear.

Minos ran from the wrath of the dead, but two bulls found him and tore him into equal pieces.

Queen Pasiphae, on her knees in the middle of the arena, held aloft her hands. She prayed to her creator goddess, and she wept for her people.

Nikkis and Daedalus, chained soul-to-soul by love, died together. With them passed the glory of Minos. The glory Poseidon and Daedalus had created, Daedalus, Rhea, and Poseidon destroyed.

All was as nothing beneath Daedalus and Nikkis, who were perfect love entwined for a moment, for a breath, for less time than it takes for two mothers high in a mountain village to scream and for two babes to take their first breaths, babes destined to grow strong and beautiful and to fall in love and to kiss and…

~~~

Pasiphae's serpents had died for her.

The palace crumbled and burned around her.

The lovers became memory and ash.

Pasiphae, once the High Queen of Creation on the island of Crete, lay in hot dust breathing the scent of bulls and burned men.

Burned herself, she yet lived, and she thanked her goddess for the torment of her pain.

"I forgot," she whispered to the earth from which all great things come and to which all great things return. "I forgot. Daedalus reminded me. Only creation balances the lust for conquest. I failed you, Goddess."

Eyes burned blind, she rose to hands and knees and crawled like a babe.
~~~

She knew no direction, and direction mattered little to her. The pain was important. Grit cut into her knees. White heat seared her blinded eyes. Burned, oozing flesh ground away from her hands into the dirt of the arena.

Her groping hand struck something hard and hot, hard as stone but round. She picked it up. Charred fingers grasped the disk, the curse of the mason and his lover, Nikkis.

She sat back on her heels, resting like a tired child playing in dust. She clutched the hot, fired clay to her breast. She thanked Poseidon, the mason, the shepherd girl, and the goddess. "I understand," she cried. "I know what I must do!"

"My Queen," a gentle voice spoke from the bright, white pain all around her. "My Queen, you are hurt."

"No," she said.

"Yes. Burned."

"No. Burned, but your Queen no more."

"Let me help you."

"Your name, Child?"

"They call me Redimae. We saw the fires. We felt the gods shake the earth. The river is gone."

"The gift." Pasiphae laughed, and in her own ears her laugh sounded like an old woman's cackling.

Gentle hands grasped the disk. "It burns you, my Queen."

"No." She pulled it back. "It heals me!"

"Please," the young voice pleaded. "Your skin falls away."

"I have outgrown it. It offends me. I shed it."

"Let me help you to the cisterns. The palace has fallen, and they are open to the air. We can wash your wounds."

"The others?"

"No others. Not now. Only you and I breathe in this ruined place."

"Yes," Pasiphae said. "Yes. I must live. The Goddess has given me a trust."

Gentle hands grasped her shoulders. Pasiphae wobbled upright onto burned feet, the disk, now merely warm, clasped to her bare, blistered breast.

Standing, Pasiphae could tell the girl was shorter than she. The girl steadied Pasiphae and moved them carefully along, telling Pasiphae when to lift foot, when to walk steady, when to turn.

"Your age, Child?"

"Twelve," she answered. "Here. Sit. I have linens on my donkey. I was bringing them to the palace market. I'll wet them. Sit and be still, my Queen."

"Only Pasiphae," she said. "You must call me Pasiphae. The queen died in the palace."

"But you–"

"Pasiphae, and you will swear on your life that you will never say otherwise."

"But–"

"On your life, Child!" In spite of her pain, Pasiphae straightened to her full height. She reached for what power she still possessed, and she found relief in the flow of it up from the earth and into her veins. The Goddess had not abandoned her. The magics of reciprocal joys still flowed for her. "The voice of the Goddess speaks through me, and you will swear!"

The child stuttered, stammered, and then said, "Pasiphae. I so swear."

In spite of the screaming pain of her skin, Pasiphae relaxed, cradled the disk, and let the child wash her burns. In time, cool water soothing her face, she spoke again, "Child, do you know the caverns of the highlands over Knossos?"

"I do, my—Pasiphae."

"It is time for me to teach a new priestess. I know a cave. There, I once danced and sang the sacred rituals. There, I learned, and there I shall teach."

"I know the place," the girl said.

"You've been there?"

"No, Pasiphae. Never. It is a place of death. None dare go near it."

Pasiphae laughed. "No, child. It *was* a place of death. Now, it will be a place of birth and rebirth. Take me there."

"I'm afraid."

"Be at peace, child. The Goddess has set me the task of protecting that place for all of time, and I will do it by teaching you my craft."

"I'm a weaver. I'm a child."

"Do you bleed each month?"

"Only twice, and three months between."

"A woman, then. You will learn if you desire. If you do not, then at least take me to the caverns so I can begin my work."

"It isn't that I don't want...." The girl's voice held sadness.

"Then what?"

"I'm not worthy. I'm only good for bringing wares to the market."

"I hear the voices of men in your soul. Come close to me, Child. I will tell you a great secret."

The girl's warm breath carried the scent of olives and garlic. It heated the cool water dripping from Pasiphae' bandages. "Very close, Child. Good. We are born of earth and to earth we return. We live by the gifts of women, and we thrive by the hands of women. Women create from the dust left by the destruction of men." She placed her burned hands on the child, one on the back of her neck and one on her nose and mouth. The girl tried to pull away, but Pasiphae held tight. She willed her heart into the child, into her soul, into the damage to her spirit; and Pasiphae, once Queen of the Island of Crete and now merely a priestess of earth, smoothed and caressed and embraced and healed the spirit of a child.

When she freed the child, Pasiphae smelled the richness of a woman's flowing blood.

"Now, young woman," Pasiphae said. "Do you wish to know the power of women to heal across the ages of men?"

The girl wept tears of fear and joy. Where they fell on Pasiphae' hands, they cooled her wounds and healed her burns. "Please," the girl said.

"And you will keep this trust I give you and pass it to another like you and she to another and so through time so that the places I show you will be always held and protected by one of our priestesses?"

"I will," the girl said. "For my life and all the lives granted to me until the goddess returns me to her bosom."

The two priestesses embraced.

Timeless Love

Nikkis woke to aching, white-hot pain in her head and jaw.

Andros.

He had hit her. He shot the priest and hit her.

"Ahhphoo?" She had tried to ask after Papu, but her tongue barely moved. Her head and jaw hurt too much.

Someone laughed.

She tried to lift her head and peer through the darkness to see who, but the movement filled her with dizzying nausea. She tried to reach for her face. Her hand refused to move. It felt like a car had parked on top of her.

For a moment, in darkness, she panicked, suddenly sure her hand was paralyzed, that she could feel nothing and could not will her fingers to wiggle.

She moaned.

Light flared. The room swam in flickering, yellow glare. Nikkis welcomed the light, but she didn't welcome what she saw—pale, chipped stucco walls, barred windows, a single match flame held under a long cigarette extending from Muscus's mangle-tooth smile.

To her, that tiny flame was as bright and painful as staring directly at the sun. His long nose cast a narrow shadow over his brow ridge and forehead, making his features more rat-like. He was a pale ghost-rat with a black stain up the middle of his face.

The little man lit his long, skinny cigarette. The room filled with the stench of anise and cloves. The throbbing ache in Nikkis's head and jaw mixed with the smell of Muscus's cigarette. Nausea rolled in her belly. She moaned.

The match went out, but the coal of the burning cigarette marked the little man's place in the darkness.

"Awake, then," he said. "Good. I hoped you would wake before he came back. I wanted some time together—just the two of us."

The glowing coal rose in the darkness. Nikkis pulled at her numb hands and feet. She struggled, and through the nausea and the pain, she finally realized they had tied her down on a hard board or a table. She couldn't pull herself free.

A memory of a dream flashed through her: chained, helpless, a fire… and someone else. Who?

She tried to gather breath to scream, but something filled her mouth, pressed her tongue back.

"Yes." the little man's breath washed over her face. Olive oil, garlic, alcohol, and his sickly sweet cigarette smoke choked her. She tried to turn away. The coal on the cigarette glowed, and the pale orange light showed his tiny, black eyes. "Fight to get away," he said. "Fight. Squirm. Struggle. Scream. These are the things I've waited for. Now, pretty American Doctor, try to look down your nose at me from that plank. Try to pretend you are above me when I bring you to pleasure in spite of how much you loathe me."

He laughed.

She inhaled, coughed, and choked. Her belly rolled and bucked and sent what little it held up into her gagged mouth. She choked on her own vomit. The gag kept her from clearing her mouth. She shook her head back and forth, retched, pulled on her bonds, and knew she was about to die tied to this table choking on her own bile and the breath of this vile little man.

He tore tape free from her gag, tearing at the soft skin of her cheeks and yanking hair from her temples.

Freed from the gag, her vomit erupted from her throat. In a final act of defiance, she aimed for him. Her spew hit his face. The burning coal hissed and went out.

For a moment, the darkness returned. Then, brighter, white overhead light filled the room.

She closed her eyes against the eruption of pain. She shook her head, trying to clear her mouth and nose, trying to shake away the acid stench of her own vomit, struggling to get free of the choking and to gather in a breath.

Desperate, she opened her eyes.

Andros loomed above her. "What are you doing?" He struck the little man, knocking him away.

The man gasped and cursed. From the floor, he said, "Saving her life for you. She's puking."

Andros leaned over her. "Nikkis?"

She tried to answer. She tried to breathe. She pulled at her bound hands, trying to point to her mouth.

He raised a fist high overhead.

She winced and closed her eyes tightly.

The fist came down hard beneath and between her breasts.

Something wet popped in her chest.

She opened her eyes wide. For a surreal, dying moment, she thought it odd that the world became black-and-white while you were dying.

He hit her again.

What little air she had exploded from her lungs. A gob of green spat upward from her, narrowly missing Andros's face.

Nikkis coughed and gasped. She inhaled deeply, and the entire surreal scene shifted from fuzzy black-and-white to high-definition, full-spectrum color. The ruined room around her intensified, filled with white-washed walls, blue window frames, and a faded triptych of a man wrestling a dragon. Andros's face shifted from bloodless gray to the golden color she now knew came from mixing German and Turkish blood—the color of menace.

She coughed, spat and pulled at her bonds.

Andros produced a handkerchief from his coat pocket. He stroked her cheek, wiping away the slime on her face. "Nikkis," he cooed. "This could be better for us. It could be so much better for you."

She fought for breath. "No," she managed.

"Yes." He caressed her neck. He used his handkerchief to push back the hair matted to her forehead. "We can do this together—you and I."

Nikkis wished he would look away from her, even for a moment. She was sick of the merciless ice in his eyes—the emptiness she had once taken for wounded, mysterious depth.

"She's a witch," Muscus said. "She's put a spell on you, Andros. She has you wanting her. Too much. Too much. Take others. Any other. You can have all of them."

"Shut up," Andros said.

"Think of the money."

Andros ignored the little man. "My Nikkis," he said. "I have almost everything I want from you." He put a finger to her lips.

She tried to bite him.

He laughed and easily pulled back. He traced the line of her jaw. His finger lingered over the throbbing pain where he had hit her. "You've bruised yourself," he said. He leaned low. Warm breath spread over the side of her face. "I will show you how to be a good Greek woman, Dr. Nikkis Aristos."

She tried to turn away—struggled against numbness, rope, sickness, and wood.

The table creaked, her ropes stretched but held.

His cold lips touched her jaw.

Her empty belly convulsed again. She wished she had something to eat, anything, so she could reload and cover Andros with vomit the way she had covered Muscus.

"She's trouble." the little man said. "The stones. The buyers. Your new history of Crete."

"She is a rare treasure." Andros held up a fragment of stone where Nikkis could see it. "Look what she has brought me."

Nikkis recognized the piece of marble as the fragment she'd broken from the stalagmite in the Minotaur's cavern—her Rosetta. It held Linear-A and Ancient Greek together on one face.

"What is it?" Muscus asked.

"It is why she must live. She will tell the world that the Turks taught the Greeks to write. She will be famous." He smiled down at her. "We will be famous together."

"Kill her and tell them yourself," Muscus said. "Kill her and get someone else to tell them."

This time Andros turned away from her. "Get a bucket of water. Bring a sponge. Make the water warm but not hot."

"I'll kill her for you."

"Perhaps I'll strap *you* to the table."

Nikkis lost sight of the little man, but she heard quick feet leaving the room.

She hated that she ever admired the tortured heart and intellect she had imagined lived behind Andros's eyes. He was sick. Her mind had failed her. Her education was nothing against a megalomaniacal psychopath. She'd been his puppet.

He leaned close, brushing her cheek with his lips. "Now, we will have time together," he said. "First, you will hurt. Then, you will hide inside yourself. Finally, you will feel once more. I will teach you to feel. I will teach you what to feel and when. Eventually, I will give you freedom again, but you will not want it."

In Greek, she spoke words that would have made her father blush.

He laughed. "We will become rich and restore the things these Greeks stole from my family. And you, Nikkis, will be the thing most envied by other men—the Greek beauty that returns honor to my family."

Nikkis closed her eyes, turned her head, and wished she were someplace else—wished for the university and Anderson, for her parents' house and awkward dinners, even for the old station wagon and Daed screaming at the sky.

Anything would be better than this.

Death would be better.

He kissed her hard and mercilessly on the mouth.

In answer to her prayer, the small and dizzy death of unconsciousness overwhelmed her.

~~~

In warm, sharp sunlight, she stood tall in her sandals. Her staff set on a white stone and her goats around her, she put her fingers to her lips, pinched her lower lip, and sucked in sharply. Long and clear, the shrill tone went out from the rage of her heart, from the crease in her lips—out and over the hills and stones and to the ears of Titan. She called the bull, and she knew he would come.

~~~

She woke to the warm slide of a sponge across her skin, skin that rebelled as best it could. But weak and tied, she could do little but squirm. Her boots and dark peasant dress were gone. Only the loose, black pants and blood-stained blouse remained. Yiayia's blouse had been torn open to her waist, and the sponge dabbed and caressed. Andros spoke to her in low tones, saying things, terrible things—promising her feelings she swore she would never feel from his touch.

Andros's voice became a rich, dulcet, lying, distant drone.

She watched herself from far away, and she faded in and out of consciousness. All the while, he worked with sponge and voice to clean her, to treat her gently, to sooth wounds he blamed on her—wounds he had inflicted.

When she could, she pulled on her bonds.

Far away…

She watched herself from a distant hillside, from a land of sage and grasses where the goats knew her and trusted her, where the stony earth had caressed her feet a thousand times, and where, in a box canyon, Titan, the bull of her village, grazed.

She watched from that distant place, and in horror she heard what Andros promised to do to her.

Nikkis came back to herself from the mountain dream. Tied to the table, rage cleared her mind for a moment. Driven to that rage by terror, by cold, and by the humiliating touch of the beast above her, a name appeared from deep in her heart. It rose from red darkness and formed in clear center of her rage.

She cried out the name—not Titan's name. Another name. An ancient name in an ancient tongue.

Even having spoken it, she couldn't say whose name it was, but she cried it out again. And again.

Andros laughed.

Exhausted, she closed her eyes and let the man touch her, clean her, say vile things to her.

Exhausted and in shock, she hallucinated.

The girl on the hill. The great, black bull with the sparkling horns charging down the mountain, charging and churning up stone and turf and dust.

The ground shook.

Her table rattled.

Andros's voice stopped. The sponge lifted. Water on her skin chilled.

Nikkis opened her eyes.

Dust rained from the ceiling.

Even with her eyes wide open, images filled her mind.

The red eyes of the bull came to her. The eyes of the bull in her hotel bedroom. The mark of the mason on the stones in the warehouse, another bull, except this one was a bull shaped like a man.

Minotaur.

The building shook.

Earthquake.

A familiar earthquake. A welcome earthquake.

Shock.

Yes. Only a person in shock could think that an earthquake could be good.

She told herself she had to be in shock. She had read that victims of torture often went into shock—that they reported the sensation of viewing themselves from afar.

Someone screamed—someone far away beyond the walls and beyond time. Someone, a man she thought, screamed. Another man screamed—and another.

Silence.

Warmth grew in her chest. The shaking earth brought her a sense of warmth, of safety and in the distant part of her mind where dreams live while she walked her days, where they hid beneath impenetrable layers of velvety blackness, curiosity rose and a voice spoke in Greek, in old Greek, in Greek from her garbled dreams.

She recognized it as her own voice speaking in her fevered mind. *I wonder who he will crush?*

The building shook like it had been hit by a freight train.

Wood splintered.

A gunshot.

Nikkis lifted her head and strained to see.

She saw Andros's back. He ran to the door of the room.

The door slammed opened. Muscus ran in. He slammed the door closed and braced himself against it. "He's com–"

The door exploded inward, shattering into splinters and spinning the little man across the floor like a doll-shaped child's top.

Both in her dream and waking, Nikkis laughed.

Someone filled the doorway—shoulders as wide as the door—a head as large as a bull's.

Yes. A bull.

Titan.

No. Only a man. She laughed harder.

Shock. Yes. She told herself she was going into shock.

She had gone insane. Titan was a bull. The man was a man. She'd never known a man named Titan.

Shock and delirium, she knew.

Her laugh sounded insane.

Now, hysteria.

The bull roared.

Not Titan. Not *that* roar.

Him. He had come.

She strained to see. The man, the Minotaur, stood in the doorway, bare-chested and torn linen pants fluttering like wraiths clawing at his muscled legs. His eyes shone like the eyes of the bull in her room at the hotel. He roared again. Ancient, primal rage shook the walls.

Andros stumbled backward. He grasped at his vest for his weapon.

Muscus stood, turned, and pulled his pistol.

The Minotaur charged.

Muscus looked so funny twisting, turning, trying to find a good way to land. He hit the wall hard. His skull slapped concrete and stucco. He came to rest on the floor like a stuffed rag doll tossed aside.

Nikkis's laughter was high and far away. Hot tears poured from the corners of her eyes and drenched her temples.

Andros freed his pistol, but the Minotaur was on him. The shot cracked in the room, but Andros, like the little rat man, became a wingless flier and found himself against the wall then draped over the form of Muscus.

Safe.

Nikkis knew she was safe.

Still, a small part of her, Dr. Nikkis Aristos, wanted to scream that she was being kidnapped by a madman or a monster. That part struggled for voice for only a heartbeat before it gave up, exhausted, and let her heart's knowledge of safety soothe her mind into silence.

The Minotaur came to her.

Dark curls glistened on his forehead. *Like horns*, she thought. His broad solid shoulder tensed, and he tore at the ropes that held her. Wood snapped and cracked.

Numb and limp, her hands came free. Her bare feet came loose.

Then she was in his arms, *again*. Holding her, protecting her, he ran, *again*—through the house, out onto the cobbled street, then into the hills and the moon-silvered darkness of night.

Men yelled behind them. Gunshots echoed against the hills in the night.

The man, the Minotaur, took no heed. He became a warm, enveloping night wind carrying her upward into a moonlit sky.

No. He would not fly again, she told herself. He only took her higher into the hill country beyond the village.

She put her face into his chest, closed her eyes, and inhaled his Minotaur's scent. In his rocking, running embrace, she let herself slip into peaceful darkness.

~~~

Morning sunlight, pure, golden, and as bright as the ancient walls of the Palace of Knossos, slanted through the small opening to his cavern home.

Nikkis wondered at her first thought of the morning. Knossos was a ruin. She'd seen it. There was nothing bright about the broken stones, failed walls, and dark pits.

Still, she savored the reassuring light. Though the air in the cavern was cool, she felt warm and contented.

Suddenly, it dawned on her that she was under a sleeping bag—nestled up against someone's body—someone who had an arm over her, holding her protectively.

Him.

The events of the previous day drove from her mind the dream images of shining walls, bull's-horn monuments, and spiral paths to blossoming love and peace.

Carefully and quietly, she lifted his arm from her shoulder and slipped out and away from him.

He moaned.

The man was not the giant she had thought. He was large and clearly strong. His tattered linen pants barely covered his scratched and bruised thighs—scratches and bruises he had gotten saving her. His hands and arms looked like they had been painstakingly fashioned from red-bronze. The fine, dark hair on his arms glistened in the morning light, and Nikkis wanted to kneel beside him and touch those fine hairs.

She stopped herself.

This man, if the man who had worn the bull's head mask, if the storied man of the caverns, was probably insane.

Andros was insane.

She shook her head. Her whole life was insane.

The man moaned again—a low, growling groan of pain that rattled in his chest and rolled up through his powerful neck, the neck that, when combined with his beard and the wild mass of dark, curly hair on his head, made him look like a bull when he had burst through Andros's door.

He had come through that door like a stunt man bursting through a cheap movie prop made of balsa wood, and he'd done it to save her.
~~~

To save *her.*

But this man, this bull, couldn't have known. He couldn't have known unless he knew Andros and knew what he planned.

Logic told her that this man must have worked for Andros.

If he did, he had betrayed Andros.

That didn't make sense. Why would a man like this, a man who didn't know her, betray Andros?

Nothing made sense anymore. She struggled to think it through, to use her mind, her training—to figure out the relationships between these people. She tried to remember more of the night before.

She'd seen a bull in her mind. She had felt him coming—known somehow that a bull would save her.

Impossible.

Maybe it was impossible, but she remembered her fear and her certainty that he was coming. Even when she told herself she was in shock, she hadn't quite believed herself.

Impossible. All impossible. Get a grip. You have a fucking Ph.D.!

Home. She had to find her way home.

She had to get out of these hills.

Somehow, she'd get back to the airport. Somehow, she'd get home.

She turned toward the cave entrance, moving as quietly as possible, telling herself that if he woke, she might never escape.

He moaned.

The sound cut into her gut and tore at her heart. It made her want to cry for him.

Against her logic and reason, she turned back.

Sunlight struck his dusty sleeping bag. He rolled onto his back. A dark, wet stain on the bag glistened under an intruding sunbeam.

Nikkis went back and knelt next to him. She touched her fingers to the stain.

Blood.

She pulled the sleeping bag away from the man's muscled chest and abdomen. Low on his belly and near the left where most men had love handles and where this man had ropes of steel-cable muscle, an open wound seeped blood.

He'd been shot.

A new fear chilled her. This time, her fear was not for herself. It was for this strange man.

Dark, shifting mental shadows, curtains that only barely covered the despair that lay beyond them, whipped and threatened to tear under the attacking tempest of this new terror.

If he died, she'd be alone *again.*

But she didn't know him. He didn't know her.

But if he died, she couldn't bear it. Not *again.*

Again. Always *again*, when she thought of this man. But she didn't know him. There had been no before. There couldn't be an again. It was just another déjà-vu attack—some weird false intimacy because her life was upside down. She could beat it.

She searched the cavern for something, anything that would let her help him. It didn't matter what she thought. It didn't matter if he was as loony as the cat that drank transmission fluid in her father's garage. It only mattered that he had saved her from Andros's horrible promises. He was a human being, and she owed him her life. She couldn't walk away and let him die.

He would need water at the very least. She found the row of jars and bottles along the wall of the cave.

The wall above the jars was seamless, pale stone containing row after row of intricate designs.

Linear-A. Linear-A and *her* glyphs.

She ran her hand over the wall, over the tiny, perfectly cut glyphs. She pulled her hand back and looked at her fingertips. Stone dust. Grime. She looked higher on the wall. There, sharp, new ideograms had appeared since she had last been in the cave. Her eyes settled on the mason's mark, the lybris and flower.

Her heart pumped liquid fire. Chilled goose flesh rose in a running wave across her back, shoulders, and arms.

He moaned.

She turned.

His eyes opened. He stared. His dark eyes filled with something liquid and warm, something very different than the bull's rage she'd seen when he picked Andros up and tossed him across the room.

Very different.

Nikkis's knees threatened to buckle. A warm flood tide moved in her belly, and she licked her suddenly dry lips and swallowed.

He closed his eyes and groaned.

She shook off the impossible warm feelings and knelt to the jars. Water. She needed to find water.

She moved a jar to his side, and she found a pile of cloth and rags that might have once been his clothes or might have been rags he used in his work. She used the cleanest one to wash his wound as best she could.

The bleeding had nearly stopped. She thanked unnamed gods for that.

The bullet had passed through the edge of his abdomen just above his hip bone and the waist tie of his linen pants. She didn't know if it had passed through muscle alone or if it might have cut into the peritoneal cavity. If it had, without medical attention and antibiotics, his gut would slowly poison him to death. Even if it hadn't, infection might kill him anyway.

She'd taken anatomy as part of her studies, but it wasn't aimed at first aid or healing. If she'd been a bone hunter instead of a linguist, she might have been able to help him more. He needed a real doctor.

After she cleaned the wound, she did her best to cover and bind it. Then, she soaked a rag in water and set it on his shoulder so if he woke he could suck on it. She did her best to bind her feet with rags and tie Yiayia's blouse closed, and she fashioned a sort of cap to protect her head from the sun.

"I have to go," she told him in Greek, hoping he would understand and not sure he would. She'd never actually heard him speak Greek, or at least not a dialect she knew. "I've done what I can. I need to get help for you."

His eyes remained closed.

She stood to leave, to find her way down the mountain to someone, to anyone who could help her save him.

His hand grasped her ankle. The calluses of his fingers and palms scratched at her soft flesh, but his grip wasn't cruel or angry. Through his touch, she imagined she felt a current of his desperation and fear.

No.

Not fear.

Terror. Terrible, confused, desperate, soul-tearing terror.

His hand fell away, and the feeling faded away.

She knelt again. Caressing his cheek, she said, "I have to go for help. You'll die. I can't stay here and watch you die." She almost added that impossible word, "*Again*."

"Ohi," *No*, he whispered in Greek.

"You do understand," she said.

"Ne." *Yes*.

"You need a doctor."

He whispered something, but his thick accent made it sound like he said snake woman. *Gibberish*.

His neck muscles went limp, and she didn't think he was conscious. She hoped he hadn't lost too much blood carrying her up the mountain.

Up the mountain.

My God, he had broken the door open like it was made of cardboard. He had tossed Andros like a doll. He had picked her up and run up a mountain carrying her—and all of that while shot.

Only a drugged or insane man had strength like that.

She wondered at herself. She should be afraid of him. Instead, she was cleaning and binding his wounds, touching him gently, feeling fears and ripples of warmth and distant thoughts like shadows of a dream filled with a shifting image or a wafting smell or a color rife with emotions without context.

When she had done as much as she could, she set out in search of help in her makeshift cap, torn blouse, loose pants, and rag-wrapped feet. She couldn't be far from the village, and the people there had seemed to know her. She'd follow the valley downward, past the big shark fin rock and across the main valley. The village had to be on the other side. *Five cigarettes*, she told herself. Only five.

She had to find Yiayia or Papu, if he was alive—find them and avoid Andros.

The ridge of limestone shaped like a shark's fin in sight the whole time, she struggled with the broken terrain for what seemed like an hour or two. The going was tortuous and slow. Rocks, cactus, and thorn bushes tore at rags and flesh. Only an occasional bird, lizard, or spider suggested that anything other than struggling plants could live in this dry valley: a green lizard as long as her forearm, a brown one the size of her finger, a few spiders, a scarab, a jackdaw—gray and black and flying low. The vultures that flew above her didn't seem interested, but she kept an eye on them anyway.

Finally, she came to the stone shark fin. Once again, she experienced the strange rush of familiarity with her surroundings, the déjà-vu she had come to accept as normal in this strange place. She turned back and found the shadowed mouth of the cave partially hidden by bushes.

How many hours had she spent traveling no more than 200 meters?

She surveyed the ridges surrounding her. Somewhere up there, she knew a well-traveled dirt and stone trail ran along the headwall ridge and around the finger valleys to the village.

She turned back to the shark fin. Downslope past the fin was the deeper valley. A smaller valley, maybe the one where she had met Leeho, spilled out at the very bottom of her valley—almost spilling into the main valley, too.

She leaned against the limestone. The face of the fin was a twice as tall as her, but the stone had cuts and cracks in it she could use for grips. Hoping for a view of something more than ridges, stone, scrub, and lizards, she climbed the rock face.

Pulling her head up over the ledge of the ridge, feet blistered and bleeding, beginning to fear that she might not find anyone at all, and wondering exactly how the man had gotten so far so fast in the night while shot and carrying her, she came face-to-face with a familiar, brown goat.

Her nose and the goat's nose hovered only inches apart on each side of a tuft of green, thorny scrub dotted with small red berries.

The goat's slit, golden eyes focused on her.

"Easy." She moved her feet around below her, searching for leverage and finding nothing better than the tiniest of toeholds.

The goat stepped back on the white rock. It lowered its head. The tips of the otherwise black horns were worn and sharpened to a cream color that almost glowed in the sun.

Her hands sweated on limestone, making it slick. Her feet couldn't find a grip. Her center of gravity was wrong to duck or dodge, and she knew she was about to take the force of the goat's attack in her face. Beneath and behind her, the two-meter drop would leave her sprawled over prickly pear and stone.

She straightened her back as much as she could, clucked her tongue, and then whistled a high, shrill whistle, like the wolf whistle men had so often aimed at her, but a single tone that echoed through the mountains.

Above, a soaring bird, a black kite, responded in kind. One note. High and shrill. The same note.

Beyond the goat, another whistle sounded. Again, the same note.

The goat lifted its head. Its eyes widened, and it peered for a moment at her. Then, it looked over its shoulder toward its own rear. It turned, and disappeared down the other side of the limestone shark fin.

She wasn't sure why she'd whistled like that; but wherever it came from, it had seemed to be the right thing to do.

She finished her climb, and when she had claimed the space the goat had surrendered, she sat panting and surveying her surroundings.

Out and downward, across the main valley and maybe three cigarettes away and two hundred meters beneath her on the right, the blocky fading colors of stucco walls, red tile roofs, and the brightly-painted wooden doors of the village glowed in the sun.

With her bleeding feet and shaking muscles, it might as well have been the other side of the world. Only the goat truly knew how long it might take on foot.

Cactus spines burned in the flesh of her feet. The rags she had used for shoes had helped, but the terrain shredded the rags. Now soaked in sweat and blood, her tattered rags stung like alcohol poured over her feet each time she moved. She couldn't continue ignoring her wounds.

Immediately below her, where the goat had gone, maybe fifty more fat-bellied, bony-shouldered goats of the mountains grazed.

She'd gone to find help for the Bull of the Mountain, and now she needed help.

It wasn't right. Not fair at all. She'd come to this place to build a new life and create freedom from people who tried to trap her, to manipulate her, to make her do things nobody should have to do. She'd come because she thought the work she did would be respected and admired. Instead, the manipulations, betrayals, and unwanted events were worse than ever.

The vultures circled overhead, five of them, black like Hades's shades spinning and descending toward her.

Even if she got to the village, she'd likely only end up with Andros again.

A bell rang—a bell on one of the goats.

A whistle just like hers sounded, and she thought it came from around the hillside and beyond her line of sight up the little valley. It might have been a bird. It might not. She decided she had no choice, so she tried to whistle again.

It took her two tries to get her mouth right. What she had done in desperation out of some weird instinct, she had trouble doing on purpose, but she managed a shrill response. Hers was not the same, matching, high note, but at least it was loud.

The distant whistle answered, and below her where the shoulder of the ridge came down to let the two valleys meet before both spilled into the main valley, a red scarf wrapped around a human head bobbed up into sight.

A few moments later, Nikkis sighed in relief.

Leeho.

The girl strode across the ground between them, scampered to the top of the stone, and embraced her.

"You look well, Sister." Leeho lied in a voice so casual that Nikkis almost believed the combat of the previous days had never happened, that the two of them were BFFs who had met for coffee the day before and chatted about their families, jobs, and men—the kinds of things simply not worthy of mention meeting today.

She went on. "And you've chosen a beautiful day to see the mountain."

Nikkis had to smile a little at the way the girl's clever eyes took in her situation while her voice showed no surprise at finding Nikkis once again.

"And you." Nikkis hoped her voice carried the same calm and nobility in adversity as Leeho's. She desperately needed the girl's help. "I hope your goats grow fat and happy."

"Lazy," Leeho said. "All lazy, and if they didn't give good milk, I think we would roast them all."

Nikkis surprised herself with a genuine laugh.

Leeho pulled a water skin from her shoulder and handed it to Nikkis. "Sti-yamas," she said.

"Para kalo." Nikkis drank. The water cooled her lips, throat, and mind.

When she'd drunk her fill, she returned the skin to Leeho, who capped it and shouldered it. "Would you like to come to dinner this evening?"

"I would, if you have room at your table and food enough," Nikkis said.

"Then we should start down."

"I suppose so." Taking a little pride in having settled into the mountain rhythm of the encounter, she added, "Though, it is nice here."

"Yes, but the goats are lazy." Leeho glanced at Nikkis's feet. "It will take them a very long time to get down."

"Of course," Nikkis said.

Leeho set about unwrapping Nikkis's feet, washing them, and making better sandals from bits of leather and rope she carried in her herder's bag. While Leeho worked, Nikkis told her of the Bull of the Mountain.

Secrets Revealed

Yiayia and Papu both looked relieved and excited to see Nikkis again. They tended her wounds and listened to her story. Leeho sat in a chair on the street by the front door watching for fascists while quietly, calmly sharpening her knives the way other women do needlepoint.

"We need a doctor for him," Nikkis said.

"The man in the cave?" Yiayia asked, spreading a salve of goat fat and mint-laced raki on Nikkis's feet.

The mixture burned. Nikkis winced. Then, the cool feeling that followed made her smile.

Yiayia's gnarled hands looked arthritic. They must have been broken by work many times, but her touch on Nikkis's feet was sure and strong.

"He is strong," Papu said.

Yiayia hissed.

"Let it go, Yiayia. She has met him twice. He sought her out. We have more here than we know. Perhaps this time–"

"Be quiet, old fool. Do not jinx the patterns placed by the gods so long ago."

"If the pattern is laid, we can't change it," Papu said. "She knows where he is, where he lives. Do you?"

"You believe me?" Nikkis was both surprised and relieved. The story she had told them sounded insane to her. She had expected to have to fight to convince them the man existed. And even if she convinced them of that, she expected to have to argue to convince them to help her.

Yiayia looked up from her work at Nikkis's feet. "Little one," she said. "Of course we believe you. You have been to the labyrinth and returned twice."

"Who is he?" Nikkis asked. "Why does he live there? Does his family carve the artifacts? His father? His grandfather?"

Yiayia tugged on the end of a bandage and finished her work. She slipped new sandals on Nikkis's feet—good sandals with automobile tire soles, sandals that fit perfectly. "Your mother's once," Yiayia said, "before she left us."

Papu spit on the floor.

"None of your disrespect, Old Man," Yiayia said. "Her daughter has come back to us. And there is the Bull of the Mountain. Now, finally, we see the workings of the minds of gods and goddesses, Papu."

He nodded. "I'm sorry," he said. "You are right." He slipped into the kitchen from which a feast had issued only two days before, days that felt like a lifetime.

"*He* was shot?" Yiayia asked. "The Bull?"

Nikkis nodded. "By Andros's men."

Yiayia nodded. "We will need your help, Nikkis. No ordinary man, this one."

"Who is he? What is he?"

"See if you can stand, Child. Stand, and we will help you help him."

Nikkis struggled to get up, to put weight on tender feet. The bandages and salve worked wonders, and she managed to stand without help, though Yiayia stood ready to catch and steady if needed. Nikkis believed the frail-looking woman was stronger than she looked and could, if needed, easily catch and hold her.

Papu came back from the kitchen. He carried a clay bowl in one hand, a lidded reed basket in the crook of his other arm, and he had a golden-handled, curve-bladed dagger tucked in the sash at his waist. "The Bull of the Mountain," Papu said. "He is our blessing from the gods."

Yiayia nodded. "He has always been there."

Nikkis stopped and sought answers in the dark mists of Yiayia's eyes. Finding none, she asked, "What do you mean he has always been there?"

Papu placed the bowl, the pot, and the knife on the table in the center of the room. "Not always. Sometimes, he is gone. During those times, I am keeper. The village must protect itself. Then, he comes back. Then, he goes again. He has been gone twice since I was a child."

"You're saying he's as old as you?" Nikkis asked.

Yiayia settled Nikkis back into her chair. "We will help him."

"He can't be that old," Nikkis said. "I've seen him. He isn't much older than me."

Papu laughed. "My grandfather knew him. His grandfather knew him. When the war came here, no German or Italian man ever went into that part of the mountains and returned. Not one."

"It's impossible," Nikkis said.

Papu shrugged. "Eh," he said. "So said the dead Nazis. In the mountains of Crete where Zeus himself was hidden from Kronos, who knows what is possible?"

Yiayia picked up the knife and the bowl. "Give me your hand, child," she said.

The blade flashed light from the windows. The edge had been sharpened many times, and where tang disappeared into the golden handle, the metal was twice as wide as the worn and sharpened blade. "Why?" Nikkis asked.

"Your blood, Nikkis," Yiayia said. "We will need it for your friend in the cave."

"He's not my friend," Nikkis protested. "I don't even know him."

"Perhaps," Papu said. "Perhaps not. Who can say about these things?"

Yiayia smiled.

"We've never met," Nikkis said.

Yiayia reached out her brown, callused hand.

"I think he's insane," Nikkis said.

Yiayia nodded.

Nikkis put her right hand in Yiayia's. "He's a brute, a madman."

Yiayia placed the cold steel against Nikkis's forearm. "Choose, child. Save him or let him die?"

Wide-eyed, she stared at the knife now pressed against her skin.

"Choose," Yiayia said again.

"He saved my life," Nikkis said. "He needs a doctor."

Yiayia frowned. "No. Not that man. That man needs the blood of a virgin and the venom of an asp."

Nikkis jerked her hand back.

More insanity. More superstition. Nikkis told herself she needed to get up and run from these people, from the Bull of the Mountain, from Andros. She told herself she would get up and run, and she would go home to her parents and the disgusting Dr. Karin Anderson, whom she could handle, who at least was rational on some level, even if she did abuse her power.

Instead, she returned her hand to Yiayia and said, "Do it."

The blade slipped painlessly into Nikkis's skin a quarter inch. The blood welled up around the gold sides of the blade, and Nikkis watched, amazed to see her own arm become a fountain of red fluid, amazed that she felt no pain where the blade entered her arm, and most amazed that she had given permission for this.

Yiayia placed the bowl under her hand, and Papu held Nikkis's arm so the blood dripped into the bowl—a lot of blood, more than Nikkis thought might be good.

Finally, Yiayia pressed a folded linen square against the wound. She pressed hard, and she gently folded Nikkis's arm as if Yiayia were a Red Cross nurse and Nikkis had just given blood. "Keep this tight for a while," Yiayia said.

"Papu?" Yiayia asked.

He lifted the lidded basket and held it out in front of Yiayia.

The old woman closed her eyes. She murmured something odd, something that sounded like the same dialect the Bull of the Mountain used. Before Nikkis could ask about the language, Yiayia pulled the lid off the basket and as casually as reaching into hay for a chicken's egg, she slipped her hand in up to the elbow. When her hand emerged, it held a brown-and-gold viper, a writhing snake with a triangular head and a very bad attitude.

Nikkis pushed back. Her chair scraped on the floor. "Oh my God!"

The serpent tried to strike Yiayia, but the old woman, even with her eyes closed, held the snake in a way that kept its thrusting head away from her flesh.

Yiayia opened her eyes and said, "A mainland adder. She is upset with me." To the snake, she spoke soothingly. She gathered the reptile in, and it seemed to listen to her, to calm down. Yiayia pressed the snake's nose to the lip of the bowl. Responding to her coaxing, it opened its mouth and bit the edge. Two milk-white fangs stretched out over the lip of the bowl. Viscous, honey-colored venom flowed from each fang, moved down the bowl's sides, and mingled with Nikkis's blood. Where the venom mixed, the blood turned darker until it looked like molten, red bronze mixed with the crimson given by the pumping of her heart.

"This can't help." Nikkis said. "This just can't help. He needs a doctor, not voodoo."

Yiayia put the snake back in the basket, and Papu took the basket back to the kitchen.

"Come," Yiayia said, "or stay. Now, we go to him." She took up the bowl and poured the blood and venom into a plastic water bottle, which she dropped into a bag that she slung over her shoulder. "Leeho! Pahmeh!" *we go*, she called. "Bring Virgil."

Virgil pushed his soft nose into her hand for a scratch as if they were old friends, and she realized they had met on the trail when she'd first come to the village. Apparently, he remembered her.

"Get on," Papu said.

Nikkis realized that Virgil was there to carry her and her damaged feet rather than Yiayia. Gratefully, she scratched Virgil's nose and agreed to ride on his back.

Papu and Leeho helped Nikkis mount, then Nikkis, Papu, Yiayia, Virgil, and Leeho set out from the village as the sun neared the western ridges.

By the time they passed the limestone outcropping where Nikkis had met up with Leeho, the sun had disappeared and a high, full moon cast silver light over the trail and hills. They covered the remaining ground, the same ground Nikkis thought it had taken hours to walk, in only a few minutes.

Nikkis showed them the bushes covering the mouth of the cavern.

"I have looked here," Yiayia said. "For sixty years, I have looked for him. I have stood in this exact spot many times and never seen–"

"What you were not meant to see," Papu finished for her.

"Until today." Yiayia raised her hands to the moonlight and intoned a prayer of gratitude.

Nikkis pushed the bushes aside and went in.

Papu took Virgil off onto the mountainside while Yiayia, Nikkis, and Leeho went into the cave.

Within, the Bull of the Mountain lay unconscious.

Yiayia pulled candles from her pouch, lit them, and set them on stones for light.

Nikkis and Leeho held the Bull's head and shoulders. They lifted him.

He roused a little, his muscles tensed, his mouth moved, and words Nikkis did not know came out. One word, she recognized—her name.

Yiayia's smile reminded Nikkis of her mother grinning because she thought she'd found some perfect man for Nikkis in some clerk at the mall or in the squint-eyed accountant son of a woman in her book group.

But Yiayia's smile held no judgment, no power to make Nikkis angry. Instead, Nikkis's face got hot and her heart jumped. Her hands warmed against the firm, muscled flesh of the man she held. His scent, the scent of his sweat and his work and the stone dust that clung to him became so sweet to her, so intoxicating, that she could not help herself. She inhaled deeply.

"Drink." Yiayia put the bottle of blood and venom to his lips. "Drink this, Old One."

His eyelids fluttered. His lips parted. The mixture poured into his mouth. Some spilled down his chin, through his beard, and onto the hollow of his neck where it met his broad chest. Some stayed in his mouth. He swallowed. Whether automatically or because he was conscious, he swallowed.

"Good," Yiayia said.

"He'll need stitches," Nikkis said. "Antibiotics. Clean bandages."

Yiayia clucked her tongue at Leeho, who nodded like she'd been given an order. The girl stood and left the cave.

Nikkis believed Yiayia might have given Leeho an order. The herders certainly had a language of clicks, clucks, and whistles.

Yiayia asked, "If you don't trust me, why did you come here, Nikkis?"

"This is a serious wound. It isn't a matter of trust."

Yiayia shook her head. "This *is* a matter of trust and family and love."

"Superstitions," Nikkis said. "We can use Virgil to get him down the mountain. We can get him to Iraklion—to a hospital."

"Or you, Nikkis, can hold him through the night and keep him warm and talk to him."

"He can't hear me."

"He knows. Talk to him. Give him a reason to stay in this world and not go in search of you yet again."

"You're crazy." Nikkis shook her head. "I don't know this man." She stared at the old woman in the candle-lit cavern. Yiayia became no more than a shadow, no more than a thin ghost that Nikkis couldn't be sure was there at all.

"By morning," Yiayia said. "We will know what choices have been made and what future will be written." Yiayia lifted the candle. She stood and moved to the white marble wall. "Have you looked at the wall, here, Nikkis?"

"He's a forger. He's been making the artifacts. Andros is hunting him."

"Have you looked with your heart?"

"Enough," Nikkis said. "I'm an expert in the language he's trying to trick people into believing he can write."

Yiayia walked farther into the cave where the marble became whiter. "Have you looked deeper?" Yiayia asked.

Nikkis remembered how excited she had been to find Andros, to tell him where this man was hiding, where the forgers made their fakes. She felt suddenly self-conscious and a little ashamed to say she had looked at the wall before.

Yiayia walked deeper into the shadows and held up her candle.

The marble there was slick with mineral deposits dripped from the roof of the cave, but it had once been as clean and as smooth as any museum-cleaned artifact. Even from where Nikkis cradled the Bull's head, she could see that the wall was covered in the script the Bull had carved—the script that was almost, but not quite, Linear-A.

Yiayia walked farther. More wall. More script. And farther, until Nikkis couldn't make out the script or the woman any longer. She could only see the light descending along the curved floor of the cave, deeper and nearer to the heart of the earth.

After a time, Yiayia returned, bringing the candle with her. She held it low so the light danced on the face of the Bull.

"Look at him, Nikkis. You want to know his secret? Look closely." Yiayia put the candle carefully on a stone so it lit the man's face and burned without being held. When the flame burned steady, she stood up and left the cave.

By candlelight, Nikkis cradled the Bull's head in her lap. She looked down into his face.

Nothing made sense anymore. Nothing.

She was a scholar—a damned scientist.

At least, she had been before she came here.

She'd spent too many years learning to be objective, learning to be smart, learning to defer and deflect the irrationality of men and women, learning to be a creature of intellect, a woman who could command respect on the merits of her studies and the logic of her arguments.

In English, she whispered to the unconscious, magnificent man she held, "I don't know you. I can't help you."

His chest rose and fell. Her blood still glistened on the ragged mustache below his rugged nose. The mustache shivered with his breath.

"Don't you understand?" she said. "This isn't possible. You're insane—you and my family. I see why my mother and father left this place. They had to get away from the superstitions. They had to raise me somewhere safe where people live by laws and rational standards."

A low moan escaped his lips.

Her heart jumped. In Greek she said, "I'm here." She pulled his head closer to her belly, cradled his face, closed her eyes and found herself rocking gently as if somehow her slight movement could make a difference in his dire circumstances, circumstances she should be doing something about.

Love Heals

Sometime in the night, the candle burned down and then out. Nikkis dozed in and out of the half-dream space between waking and sleeping. For a while, she held him and rocked him, and he was the Bull of the Mountain, a man troubled by some demon of torn psychology Nikkis wasn't qualified to understand or treat. Then, he was a real Bull, an animal, a thing so large and impossibly powerful that she couldn't imagine him as other than a force of nature, practically a god.

Some sound of the night or slight movement startled her drifting mind back to clarity, and he was a frail life lying in her lap, waiting for her to do some impossible, irrational miracle that would save him.

For a while, she walked in her dream place, and he was there, standing in the night, clean-shaven, wearing jeans and a t-shirt. He was younger, much thinner, but just as tall. He smiled and winked at her. Then, he turned, screamed at the sky and ran off into the night.

Again, she started to full consciousness. "Daed," she said.

"No." A light flared.

Nikkis shielded her eyes to look toward the cave entrance.

Andros stood inside the entrance to the cave unstrapping night-vision goggles from his face. Muscus stood beside him holding up a battery-powered floodlight. "Sweet Dr. Aristos," Andros said, "I've missed you."

His chilling gaze skipped quickly over Nikkis and went to the walls, to the script, to the thousands and thousands of lines of Linear-A. "By all the ancient gods." Avarice coated his words.

"What do you want?" Nikkis asked.

Andros grabbed the light from Muscus. He moved the light, playing the bright circle along the wall and deeper into the cave. He stepped past the Bull and Nikkis, and, like Yiayia during the night, he moved deeper into the cave.

"Yiayia?" Nikkis asked. "Papu and Leeho? Where are they?"

Muscus's whiny chuckle chilled Nikkis.

The Bull of the Mountain stirred.

Muscus jumped back and pulled a pistol.

The Bull's eyes opened. Brown and wide, he looked up at Nikkis. She peered down into his face. By the reflected light of Andros's lamp, she saw her own reflection in his eyes, imagined that she saw herself wearing a many-layered, multi-colored Minoan skirt, wearing her hair back save for the long ringlets beside her ears, draping swirls of darkness that swept downward and framed her pale face.

For a moment, she saw herself that way.

Then, she saw some deep rage—a redness far down inside his pupils, beyond his mind, beyond his thoughts.

The rising, crazed rage of the Bull made her shiver.

"Hush," she said. "I'm here."

His shoulders tensed.

Muscus pointed his pistol.

The Bull looked to Muscus and spoke one word. "Gask."

"I don't understand," Nikkis said.

"Put that away." Andros returned from the back of the cave. "Go get the old woman. Tell the old man if he makes trouble, he'll be lighting an oil lamp in a shrine for her."

Muscus grinned. His tangled fangs flashed and snapped. He slipped out of the cave.

For the first time, Nikkis saw that sunlight shone outside the entrance of the cave.

"What is it, then—this place?" Andros asked her. "I'm sure you know, and you also know that you and your boyfriend aren't going to leave here if you don't tell me."

"He's not my–" Nikkis cut herself off. She looked down at the Bull's face again. She didn't understand what was happening to her. This insane man was dying in her lap. For a moment, she'd believed he was Daed—older, but still Daed.

She couldn't—no, dammit—she *didn't* have feelings for him.

"What do you make of this, Dr. Aristos?" Andros asked.

The Bull moved in her lap. She cradled his head more tightly. "A family business, I think. Over generations."

"Maybe." Andros looked at the walls again. "If so, it is a very old family, and they have been doing this for a very long time."

"I'm sure I wouldn't know," Nikkis said.

The Bull moved again. He grunted.

"Ah, your meddling friend is awake. Good. I'll want him to watch the activities of the day. After what he has done to my work and my men, I think he will spend some time with me in the interest of cross-cultural understanding."

"What are you talking about? He's hurt. He's sick. He has no idea what's going on around him. He barely speaks Greek."

"Dr. Aristos, I'm surprised at you. Of course he speaks Greek. Listen closely. He speaks a very, very old dialect of Kritiki Greek."

"I work in ancient scripts."

"Oh, of course." Andros mocked her. "But we have a forensic advantage. We replayed the recording of his howling, crazed terrorist attack on a police operation." He flashed his predatory smile. "Did you know that he kidnapped a wounded American professor?"

"You were recording what you did to me?"

"Of course, my dear. I know men who would pay fortunes to watch me force a woman as beautiful and arrogant as you to respond to my love."

"Love had nothing to do with what–"

"Oh, but it did. I do love you, Dr. Nikkis Aristos. Surely, you know that. If I didn't have such inconvenient feelings for you, you would be dead."

She spat at him.

"I don't require that you love me back. Really, it simply isn't needed."

The Bull shook. He rolled a little to one side, and his hands moved to find the ground.

Andros smiled.

A steady stream of Greek cursing preceded Yiayia into the cave.

Muscus, assault rifle on his back, pistol in hand, and clearly angered by her invectives, followed.

"He's coming around," Andros said. "Now, we will learn a thing or two about this place."

"I won't tell you anything else, you pig," Nikkis said. She remembered the red rage deep in the eyes of the Bull, and suddenly she understood it, knew that she had once known it, too—a long time ago. In some impossible way, the Bull and she shared at least that one thing.

Andros held the light out to Muscus. The little man traded him the pistol. Andros aimed it at Yiayia. "What is this place?" he asked.

Yiayia laughed. "A cave, Fascist."

Andros lowered the muzzle and pulled the trigger. A bullet hit the dirt next to Yiayia's foot. The report, amplified in the cave, echoed in the deeps of the earth, and echoed, and echoed.

Nikkis covered her ears and stared in horror at Andros.

Recovering slightly, she turned her attention to Yiayia. The old woman hadn't so much as flinched, and the bullet had hit only a few centimeters from her foot. Pride in her grandmother's courage overwhelmed Nikkis's fear.

"Next one goes to flesh, witch woman," Andros said.

Yiayia spit.

Andros fired.

The Bull and Yiayia roared at the same time. The Bull jumped up like he had no wound. He was whole, angry, and ready to kill.

Without thought, Nikkis jumped up right behind him, screaming, "No! No! Please!"

Blood oozed like slick, red muck from Yiayia's boot, but her eyes focused on Andros. In spite of her wound, she leapt on the gunman. It was too late for Andros to lift his weapon and aim. "Run!" Yiayia yelled. "Save him!"

Nikkis grasped the Bull by the tied waist of his linen pants. With all her weight and strength, she dug in and pulled. "No!" she screamed. "Run!"

Yiayia clawed at Andros. They spun and fell to the ground. "Run!" the old woman screamed. "Don't die again. Not again."

In the chaos, Muscus dropped his light and scrambled to slip his rifle from his back to his hands.

The Bull glanced quickly from Andros to Muscus to Yiayia to Nikkis. He seemed to hear, to understand. He took Nikkis's hand and ran, pulling her with him deeper into the dark tunnels.

Two more shots echoed inside the cavern behind them.

The Bull pulled her along. Darkness enclosed them. The cave hid them, and the Bull ran on, blindly, deeper into the safety of the earth.

She was terrified, but his grip left her no choice but to follow.

He ran as if in full daylight. Somehow, impossibly, his touch conveyed certainty and power.

Trust was not a thing Nikkis had ever known well, but in this dark maze, she found that she trusted this stranger. As they ran, she thought of the walls that must be passing by, walls that represented generations of his family, walls near the cave entrance that he had carved, deeper walls that someone before him had carved, and someone before that, and someone and someone and finally who knows how long ago someone like him must have put hand to stone and begun the process.

Someone, perhaps, who had known Linear-A. Someone who, perhaps, had known it personally as a living language and passed it on to children.

Suddenly, she wished for a light, for some way of seeing the deepest cave walls, the walls that surely they must be running past now.

As if her desire had made it real, a flash illuminated the cavern walls—white light, brighter than the sun, brighter than Muscus's flood light had been.

She gasped.

The Bull stopped, pulled her to his chest and wrapped her in powerful arms.

Before she could protest, the ground bucked. A terrible, invisible force knocked the breath out of her like a blow from thick, wooden club. A moment later, a roaring hot wind whipped dust and debris through the cavern like a flash flood.

The Bull turned his back to the wind and pressed her against the wall. Cold, damp stone pressed through the tears in her tortured blouse, and the lime-encrusted edges of cut glyphs of Linear-A pressed into her flesh.

Her arms went around him, reached behind him, trying in vain to protect him for no reason she understood.

Darkness engulfed them once more.

Rumbling, roaring, and finally rattling reached them.

Behind the warm wind, like a swarm of gritty gnats pelting their skin, hot-smelling stone dust swept over them, and she knew in her soul that they were dead, that Yiayia, Papu, and Leeho were dead, that Virgil, if he was not dead, would die as surely as the rest of them.

Andros had buried them alive, sealed the cavern with them in it.

Small stones rained down on her head. She tried to cover his head, and he tried to cover hers. Something large hit his head and her hand.

Vertigo took her.

Wrapped in his arms, they fell in darkness so complete that the coming of floor or ceiling would have been the same. The falling was so like dreaming that in the falling she felt a sense of safety, of irrational warmth, grace, and joy that at least this time they were together—lost together in the maze of her fear and the darkness of the cavern.

~~~

Coming to consciousness in the darkness of the bowels of the earth confused her. Eyes opened or closed, the world was the same black place—black save for the hot red shapes that wandered through the darkness—artifacts of her mind, she knew, trying to create patterns where none could be found.

Thinking, "Oh, I'm awake," didn't help because she knew she could be dreaming; and dreaming, she might wake and find that she had been dreaming. The shapes were part of her dream, and they didn't care if she woke or slept.

In the end, after swimming in confusion, his warm, steady breath convinced her she was awake. More than that, his breathing told her they were alive.

His breath smelled of rich olives and silky, ancient red wines. It flowed over her in warm, strong waves. His arms still encircled her. His heart beat like the heart of the earth itself, pounding against her breast.

She pressed her head against his chest. His arms tightened around her.

He was awake, too.

Even so, they were dead. Rather, they would be dead. In time, the cave would cover them with soft, wet lime that might preserve their embrace forever.

Her mother and father flashed into her mind. What if someone did find her body? Did she want her parents to know she had been found like this—in the arms of a madman?

The thought made her laugh. It couldn't possibly matter to her or to them.

She inhaled the scent of him, the stone dust, the wine. There, in the dark, she looked up.

Silly, she thought, to look up for a sky that couldn't be seen through tons of rock. Then, she realized what she was looking for—the next shooting star.

The passing time of her whole life since the night Daed had run from her had been a dream—no time at all. She was sure a star would cut the darkness in half, that it would light his face, that her life of obsessive perfection, order, and intellectual
~~~

armor would disappear, a mere fantasy not yet lived, a vision lost in the sunlight of love and a new day.

Still, she searched the sky—knowing that searching was ridiculous.

The cavern was sealed.

No one knew they were there.

It was her fault. She'd come to Crete to prove herself, to prove her theories, to make a name in unassailable rational thought. Instead, she'd gotten her grandparents killed and helped evil men rob the village of this hero, this guardian they believed was some kind of demigod.

What had her education gotten her? Come-ons from socially inept professors, stalking lesbian predators, false successes in publication, fleeting joys among antiquities that had once had meaning to living people as gifts, as offerings of spirit and life that were now hidden away in dusty vaults to be seen only by passionless fools like her.

All wasted.

How, or even if, she was found didn't matter. Only how she lived each moment of life mattered—even her last moments—*especially these last moments.*

His nose grazed her cheek. His breath warmed her ear. His lips grazed the soft, short hair behind her ear. He whispered something in that odd dialect of his, and, for the first time, she heard the roots of ancient Greek buried in the odd words, the entire history of the language of an island people echoing in the warm whispers of a madman.

It had been there for her to hear all the time.

He kissed her ear, and her blood burned. It was the same shaking fire of need she'd felt so long ago in the arms of Daed inside his Helios.

And she wanted this man. Whether from fear, need of human contact, or something older and deeper, she wanted him.

So, she tried to push him away, but his embrace was too strong. Her will was too weak.

It didn't matter. What was a kiss now? He was already mad, so he could not go mad from her kiss. Sealed in a cavern, he could not open the car door and run away, screaming into the night.

Her lips found his.

His lips parted.

The tips of their tongues touched, unsure, gentle. Tip to tip, they met and slid slowly, tentatively, tenderly into a dance of love.

The pounding of his heart against hers hardened and deepened. Her own smaller pounding tried to match his hammering, sculptor's rhythms.

Perhaps he was mad. Perhaps she was mad. Madness was a label defined by blind books in the light. Madness in the dusty darkness of a cavern crypt meant nothing.

They kissed again.

Desire filled her, and though her eyes were closed and no crack in the rock offered sunlight, their hearts and minds found an ancient path to travel together.

They kissed; her darkness was gone.

He rolled onto his back.

She pushed her fingers through the silken hair on his chest, let them ride over the firm ridges of his belly, let her hands slide along the bandage.

She stopped her exploration, uncertain of his wound.

His hand found hers and helped her slip fingers under the bandage, along his side to the top of his hip where the bullet hole should have been.

Only skin—smooth and hot.

What was one more impossible thing in this moment?

She pressed her hungry mouth to his, and she knew from his moan and from the heat of his hip that he understood perfectly what she asked for, what she wanted from him. They were and had always been one mind and one heart. If they died that way, so much the better.

"Daed," she said.

"Nikkis," he whispered.

~~~

Nikkis woke in the deep cavern for the second time. She blinked, again confused, but this time her confusion was because of light instead of darkness.

Flickering yellow light danced on the slick, pale cavern walls above her.

A chill shook her, and she reached out for him.

Fingertips met cold stone. He was gone—*again.*

Panic gripped her heart. She sat up.

No. He was there, standing near the cavern wall, facing the smooth, damp stone, his right hand high, sliding slowly along a line of symbols. Beside him on
~~~

the dust-covered floor burned a very old oil lantern made of clay and wicked with knotted fiber.

Her panic subsided, and she stood and approached him.

His back to her, his giant's shoulders shook.

She hoped he wasn't hurt. She hoped his fever hadn't returned. She remembered that she'd been unable to find his wound, but it was impossible that it was gone.

She came up behind him. The shaking of his back coincided with small gasps. The Bull of the Mountain sobbed, slowly running his fingers over the glyphs.

She pressed her cheek to his back and caressed his shoulder.

"Nikkis," he said in perfect American English, "thirty-five hundred years."

Startled, she stood straight and backed away. "You speak English."

He turned to face her. His clear, dark eyes overflowed with love and tears.

She touched his cheek at the edge of his beard.

"I have always loved you, Nikkis," he said, "and no matter what, I always will."

"You *are* Daed," she gasped. "I thought my fear made that up."

He shook his head. "Daedalus," he said. "Daed, who rebuilt that old Ford, Helios, in this life."

Nausea and confusion shook her.

He steadied her and helped her to sit next to the lamp.

He held her while the wave washed through her, and like a wave changing the shape of a beach, it rearranged the sands of her mind. Each beat of his proud, faithful, courageous heart brought a lifetime of terrible memories to her and protected her from those terrors. Time passed, and in them the years unfolded. Had he not held her, she might have collapsed. Had he not held her, the memories of pain and loss might have torn away her mind.

When the memories had passed, becoming only haunts in the shadows of her mind, her heart slowed and her breath became once more her own to use as she willed, she said, "Thousands of years," she said. "Done. Broken. The curse is broken."

He nodded. "You found me. We are breaking it."

She grasped him. She dug her fingernails into his arm and held him, afraid she would lose him, afraid he wasn't real, afraid the ordeal wasn't over, that they weren't together. She feared thirty-five hundred years of pain and loss, and she feared that now their love would live only a short while.

He lifted her to her feet and wrapped her in his arms. For the first time in her life—for the first time in over 100 lives—Nikkis Aristos was fully alive and herself.

By feeble lamplight, they retraced their steps. It didn't take long before they came on the pile of rubble that blocked the cavern tunnel. Daedalus placed the little oil lamp high on the rockfall caused by Andros. The vertical flame did not waver.

"Sealed," she said. "No airflow."

"Andros must have followed us in. The entrance is at least 100 meters farther on."

"The others?" She asked.

"Maybe still alive."

"We have to get out," Nikkis said.

"Even if we get out," Daedalus said, "what?"

He was right. Once in the open air again, they'd face Andros and his armed mercenaries. Nobody except the villagers would believe that Andros, a respected detective, was a thief and worse.

Daedalus knelt, sat back on his heels, and placed his hands on the floor as if praying to the earth or searching for something. His head bent low. The muscles in his back and shoulders tensed, and she realized he battled his own frustration and despair. His hands twisted, twitched, and, she now understood, searched for answers to save them.

Even knowing that, something about the way he touched the floor of the cavern reminded her of a dream… or a memory… or…

"Daed!"

He looked up. Lamplight glistened in his ancient eyes.

"Your hands."

He lifted his hands and looked at his palms then up at her.

Once," she said, "long ago, you whispered to me through the stones of Knossos." She didn't need to say more.

The lamp glow in his eyes ignited. He nodded, smiled, and reached for her. "Here," he said. "Hold me. Make us whole, Nikkis."

She knelt behind him, wrapped her arms around his belly, and pressed her cheek to his warm, gritty back. She closed her eyes, and she let his heat, his stone scent, and their closeness fill her.

His hands.

She remembered the magic Queen Pasiphae had given Daedalus, Master Mason of Knossos. His hands had once reached out and touched the heart of Rhea herself.

Now, once again he reached, and she reached with him.

As one, their hearts and minds swam through the stone body of the goddess until they found the limestone shark fin, the slope, the cavern entrance.

There, the feet of their friends touched the earth. As with all things that touched the earth, each was known to Daedalus—and through him to her.

At gunpoint, Yiayia, Papu, and Leeho moved in and out of the cavern, forced to gather carved stones and pile them into packs on the back of Virgil.

"They're trying to dig us out," Nikkis said. "It was an accident."

"No." Daedalus said.

She knew it. She wanted to hope, but Andros also stood on the earth, and his heart held no love for her or for anyone. His heart held only anger and vengeful certainty that the people of Crete had stolen his family honor and fortune.

Daedalus said, "Even if we could go out the way we came in, he would see us leave the cave."

"Another path," she said. "I got out once. We can circle behind them."

He moved her hand to the place where he had been shot. The freshly healed flesh was hot to her touch where Yiayia's magic had healed the wound.

She remembered Yiayia's foot and the blood.

Guns.

She understood his thoughts and feelings—his fear for her and the others.

In spite of the dangers they faced, they could once more love and live. This new depth of connection, of understanding, gave her such pleasure that a little shiver of joy ran through her.

But what good would a life together be if their happiness caused death and suffering for the people who had helped them?

"We cannot let them die," he whispered.

He knew her thoughts and fears as well. It was as it had always been meant to be between them.

The curse seemed so frail a thing now. Minos had been a fool to think that a muddled mind could hold no love, that fragmented memories could keep her heart from Daedalus or his from hers.

Pasiphae, prisoner in her own kingdom, had known more of love than that ancient king could have imagined possible. Pasiphae had known that love transcends time, nations, and even the then uncharted continents. The queen had understood that magic is born in the heart and that the gods themselves revered the power of love.

"We have to help," she said. "Even if we return to our curse."

"The tablet isn't broken." He stated the fact with conviction. "If we die, we return to the cursed cycle."

With her own deep conviction, she added, "I found you once. If we let them die, we curse ourselves."

He turned, fully embraced her and kissed her. When they once more breathed their own breath, he said, "How, then, my lovely herdswoman? I can open the way, but Andros will turn guns on the others long before we can do anyone any good."

"I will not easily give up this life of love," she said. "You once told me that there is a path through every labyrinth. There is a path. There must be a path."

His breath warmed her ear as he whispered, "I know these caverns and hills better than any living man, but you know our enemies and this age in ways I cannot."

Think, Nikkis, she said to herself. To him, and to the ancient stone, she said, "Think."

Together, they sought a path. Their minds burned. Their hearts pounded.

His powerful arms held her and his breath was her hope. He trusted her as she trusted him.

She thought about the Linear A, about the warehouse full of enslaved women, about the restorations at Knossos, about the body of lifeless Yorgos. She found no answers in any of it.

His heart and mind saw Ikarus, winds, waves, their hands clasped in the chain of hands and hearts in the village. Against her back, he flexed his fingers, remembering the making of the mask he gave her father and the endless fevered years carving inscriptions into walls of the cavern labyrinth. Thirty-five hundred years ago, he began his work in the hidden halls of Knossos. This year, he carved the words Andros now forced others to steal for him.

Near tears, she shook her head. "I don't know."

Lovingly, he grasped her hands in his. "Once, many lives ago," he said, "you told me to feel your heart." He placed their hands between her breasts. "You put my hand on your chest—just here."

The warmth of his hand made her feel safe—loved. She wanted to touch his lips with hers. For this man's touch, she would do anything.

The flash came to her the way first light escapes the horizon and ignites the highest peaks of Crete. "Your hands!" She squeezed his hands. "You touched the goddess. Rhea bled for you. She shook the world for you. Thera exploded because of you."

By the lamplight, she saw deep sadness cloud his eyes. "No," he said. "Not that. Not again."

Their hearts and minds mingled, and they shared the dreamlike memory of his anger and will. In his dying rage, he had sunken a river and exploded a mountain. His despair and the gift of the priestess queen had let him level an empire.

Too many innocents had died.

"Thousands of years ago," she said.

"By my hand."

"In pain and rage." She held his face between her palms. "Not this time."

"If we are to have a new life, it cannot begin with horrors."

"Tied to a stake, burning alive, fighting to save me or avenge me, you unleashed your pain on those who caused it. The earth itself took up your cause."

"No," he whispered.

"We are not tied. We do not burn. We are free. This time, I am with you—part of you."

Daedalus looked at her for a long moment. His eyes cleared and warmed.

She remembered a thousand moments from a hundred lives. In each, she watched the thoughts behind his eyes, watched his clever hands twitch and turn while he thought, his fingers holding the invisible shapes of the things that lived in his mind.

She took his moving hands in hers and kissed them.

"Yes, my clever mason," she said. "Together. We are in a labyrinth."

He smiled. "Yes. The maze," he said. "Knossos. There was once a path to Knossos. I walked it once, but it caved in long ago."

"Your hands," she said. "We don't need to go there any more than you had to go to Thera."

"Help from Knossos?"

"Yes," she said. "There's a policeman there. Tylissus. A real policeman."

"You are brilliant, my love," he said.

She told him her idea, and they had their path, a simple answer born of mingled hearts and memories.

She said, "We only have to wait."

He nodded and kissed her again.

"Touch the stone, my clever Daedalus." She pressed his hands down to the earth. Her hands on his, they reached for the help of the goddess once more.

~~~

Tylissus had been a policeman of one type or another for twenty years, and a soldier before that, and he had seen things he could not explain. He had seen things he could explain but no one would believe, so he did not speak of them.

On one occasion, he was quite sure he had even met the ghost of a comrade who had been dead five years. The two of them had spent a pleasant hour together fishing and talking on the rocks of the north shore of Crete.

It was the kind of thing a policeman never spoke of if he wanted to keep his job.

So, standing beside the sealed case that presented the disk to the world amid the ruins of Knossos, he held his breath and tongue while he watched a hair-thin black fissure begin at one edge of the disk and cross its face like an undulating serpent until the disk split completely in two. Only the grip of the museum mounts held the halves together.

Before Tylissus marshalled coherent thoughts from his confusion and surprise, the old archaeologist screamed for him from inside the new tunnel.

Instantly, Tylissus became a cop. He turned from the display and ran toward the trouble.

Making his way past pale, frightened workmen who seemed to be running for their lives, he forgot the damaged disk and prepared for anything—tunnel collapse, a gruesome injury, or a new discovery that had set off the superstitious fears of the workmen. What he could not prepare for was the old man standing, pale and shaking and shining his light on the stone wall—just standing and staring.

Alone with the old man, Tylissus searched the ancient stone for whatever had frightened the workers and rendered the old man speechless.
~~~

All he found was an inscription. He couldn't read it, but he was pretty sure the old man could.

He followed the line of chiseled characters along the wall and down, and a vague bit of his mind noted that the words appeared to be newer, sharper than others he had seen on the site and in the museums.

When he came to the end, he finally understood what had frightened off the men.

It had to be a trick, he told himself.

He watched in silence as an invisible chisel struck by a spirit hammer held by a ghost cut into the stone. Chips and dust fell away. New characters appeared before his eyes.

Even he—a man who had watched other men die, a man who had once been trapped underwater in a sunken cave, a man who had pressed his hands over the bleeding artery of a friend to keep him alive—even he needed to blink, to breathe, to take a moment to compose himself.

Letters still slowly appearing, chiseled away dust falling from the wall to the ground at their feet, he said, "Can you read it?"

The bluster and self-importance of the old archaeologist abandoned him. The man didn't move, didn't breathe, didn't answer.

"Can you read it?" Tylissus repeated.

The old man slowly nodded.

"Well? What does it say?"

"It's impossible," the old man whispered. "English."

"Yes," Tylissus said. "I don't read it. What does it say?"

The old man looked at him and seemed to finally see him. "Of course," he said. "Yes." And he began to read:

I, Daedalus, The Bull of the Mountain, who has been cursed for thousands of years and is cursed no more, call you, Tylissus, to arms and to aid against those who steal from our people. Upon the White Mountain beyond the road's end past the guardians I carved from stone and above the rock blade with which Rhea would cut the sky, Andros, a liar and thief, hurts those I hold dear. Come to us now. Save your people from death as you are sworn to do.

The archeologist paused, but the letters continued to appear.

Tylissus said, "By the gods, what the–"

The old man interrupted:

Nikkis Aristos and I are trapped in a cave. Hurry.

The letters stopped forming. The dust stopped falling.

"The American Linguist," Tylissus turned to the old man to tell him to speak of this to no one, but it was too late. The old man had fainted.

Tylissus gathered him up, moved him out into the open air, and began barking orders.

~~~

Andros's life included so many large disappointments that he had long ago learned the value of savoring a moment, even a small moment. His project in the hills had been filled with disappointments, yet he had combined the precision in planning he had learned from his father and the angry passion and commitment that he had learned from his long-suffering mother to bring the project to this moment, and he savored it.

The women of the mountains of Crete had goaded the men into resistance against every invader in history, and the true power lay in their steel determination and willingness to sacrifice. The old woman hobbling back and forth, wounded by his bullet but still forced to work carrying broken rock from the cave entrance, gave him a sound feeling of triumph. As long as the old woman lived and hoped to uncover the corpses of the American and the madman, the young girl and the old man would continue to work beside her.

Two of his men watched the slaves. Three helped load the artifacts. The other three watched the hills. Muscus watched them all. For the moment, he enjoyed sunlight on his neck and shoulders. The night and most of a day had passed slowly. Watched by his mercenaries, his little slave group moved stone by hand and by donkey. Muscus sorted piles into loads for the helicopter. Only the best pieces were worth hauling out. If he were lucky, he would come back for more.

No one else knew this place, and all the witnesses currently worked to fill his coffers, to prepare his next effort at restoring his honor, and to give him this small moment of pleasure.

Overhead, a black kite turned on pin-feathers. He imagined for a moment that it was Daedalus of old saluting him from his wax and feather wings.
~~~

The thought made him laugh. No man could power wings like those Daedalus had supposedly made. Science had proven that, and he was about to use science to make himself wealthy.

No one believed these artifacts existed, so no one would suspect him of stealing them. He could find a new expert to authenticate them, and he would use them to restore his family lands, to buy influence, and to prove the influence of his people on Western Civilization.

Muscus sidled up to him.

The little weasel of a man grinned, his wicked teeth catching sunlight. "We're almost at carrying capacity for the copter."

Andros looked down on Muscus. "How many more loads?"

"Maybe two."

"Run four more to be sure," he said.

"Then?"

"We do what needs to be done. Set more charges in the cavern mouth. Don't let the slaves see you."

The little man smiled his nasty-toothed grin, and Andros wondered how much the little man weighed. If he left the little man buried under rubble with the bodies of the Kritikos, he might be able to carry another two or three blocks of Linear-A, and he certainly would be rid of another liability.

~~~

Nikkis and Daedalus, bodies, minds, and hearts entwined, held vigil. For a few moments after finishing their message, they enjoyed a sense of relief that Tylissus and other honest men would come and save Yiayia, Papu, Leeho, and Virgil.

For a few moments, they watched their friends through Daedalus's hands and the gift of Pasiphae. Yiayia, Papu, and Leeho, watched by Muscus and foreign soldiers, loaded the stoic Virgil and walked him to a helicopter where other men unloaded him and arranged the stone for flight.

With one mind, the lovers realized Andros would finish before Tylissus could arrive. Andros would kill the witnesses and claim they had been terrorists. Even if Nikkis and Daedalus escaped and testified against Andros, their friends would be dead.

Together, they once more searched several thousand years of memories.
~~~

Hadn't they survived the red dust storm only recently? Hadn't they burned as Daedalus's fury brought the blood of Rhea upward and outward from the heart of a mountain? Hadn't they married and seen the bliss in her father's face when Daedalus presented the bull's head mask to him?

In all of these memories, they relived pain and loss.

Her father, her first father, was dust and memory. Daedalus's son had long past become a part of the body and endless flow of Poseidon. Yorgos, who they now understood had been their friend in truth, heart, and soul for thirty-five hundred years, was once more dead in service to their love and honor.

All of this, and so much more, tore at them and taught them. From a moment's flash of remembered love, sacrifice, and pain, new hope emerged. Together, they found their answer—a new path—maybe.

The mask was here, deeper in the cave where The Bull slept and kept his tools. The clever hands of Daedalus had crafted it anew only one lifetime ago. A new bull's head—so much better than the one he had made so long ago.

The dust of the sorako still lay loose on the earth, still coated leaf and stone and grass. No cleansing rain had yet come to wash it away or mix it with the island's soil.

The hands and hearts of the lovers still touched earth, and Nikkis's soul soothed the rage of the Bull of the Mountain.

Together, they touched the land and shook free the loose dust.

The new dust cloud lived only on this mountain, only in this valley, and only around the liars and thieves who would hurt others for love of money and power. It surrounded their helicopter, the men, the guns, the donkey, and the trapped friends who labored to live a few minutes longer.

When the dust was full upon the thieves, Nikkis and Daedalus untangled their bodies, hearts, and minds. Standing once more as two people in the dim lamplight of an ancient labyrinth of cavern tunnels and chambers, they smiled.

The touch of her lover's mind lingered in her. Never, Nikkis knew, would they ever be truly apart again.

He moved with purpose back into the shadows of the cavern. She knew without his words what he sought, and she set to her own task of preparing help for Yiayia.

When he returned, she helped him don the mask of the bull.

Briefly, she let her fingers touch the warm, fresh scar on his side. It was all that needed to be done to show her concern, to know that he would be careful and to tell him that she, too, would take care in what they were about to do.

He placed his hands upon the stone.

She placed her hands upon his and slipped her fingers between his until her own fingertips also touched the living earth—Mother Rhea.

Justice

Daedalus reached through the stone that had been meant to kill them. Had Nikkis not been with him—touching him, feeling his ancient heart—he would have brought heated rage up from the earth as he had once done. He might have used his rage to heat and expand boulders and jagged stone, pressing each against others until all exploded outward to free them and to kill and terrify their enemies.

Nikkis, however, was with him—touching him, feeling his heart.

Her compassion and love tempered his rage. They found spaces, weak jumbles, and balance points that could be shifted to open a passage for them.

Gently, the stones that closed them in slipped downward or aside. The earth shook a little with each settling. Their joined hearts beat together, and only a few moments passed before a crooked path opened enough to let them move close to the cave entrance and the thick, rising cloud of red dust creating chaos beyond.

Near the entrance, Nikkis gathered the bottle of Yiayia's medicine, the bandages, and the gauze into the old woman's bag. When she was as ready as she could be, she faced him and nodded.

Daedalus, who wore the bull's head and could see, went first.

Nikkis, her hand in his, followed, doing her best to guard her eyes and cover her mouth and nose.

They both knew the dust cloud they had created would not last and that they faced guns and men trained to use them.

What were short-sighted men with guns to reunited lovers who had lived lives of torture and terror for thousands of years? Both joined hearts knew that neither could abandon the caring people who had befriended them and helped them to break the cycle of pain so long ago created by the King of Bulls.

~~~

With his pistol, Andros struck Leeho across the cheek.

The ignorant hill-child fell to her knees. Her cheek bled, but she didn't cry out.

He looked down into her face for signs of submission, but her eyes still burned with defiance. He wondered if shooting her there and then would speed up or slow down the loading.

Around her folded legs, loose red dust that had settled out from the storm days before shifted as if it were somehow suddenly going out of focus.

He blinked to clear his eyes, but the movement of the dust was real and not a trick of light or perception.

For perhaps three seconds, the layer of dust shifted like smoke, swirling and twisting against itself, as if many conflicting breezes blew along the ground.

The girl began to laugh.

"What's so funny, little mountain bitch?" Andros decided he didn't really want an answer. He wanted faster loading. Shooting her would, after all, let him focus on the others, and she wasn't helping that much.

But the disturbed dust began to rise. It crawled up and over the kneeling girl's calves, up her thighs, and up his own boots.

He stepped back.

The dust around him rose. As it stirred, the heated desert death smell replaced fresh mountain air.

In seconds, the dust swallowed half the girl.

She laughed harder. Tears rolled down her cheeks, and he thought she looked up at him with pity.

"What in hell?" he managed.

The girl couldn't answer. She laughed too hard.

From a few paces away, Papu answered. "The Bull of the Mountain comes for you."

"Superstitious crap," Andros said. But the dust rose faster in spite of an eerie stillness in the air.

The red Saharan fog rose like the Greek earth itself had rejected the touch of foreign dust. It covered the kneeling, laughing girl. She became a shadow in red haze.

Abruptly, her laughing stopped.

He aimed for the silhouette of her head, but her shadow melted away.
~~~

He fired into the rising dust. The round hit earth with a dry thump.

"Muscus!" he yelled.

As always, the little man suddenly appeared close by his side.

Andros said, "Trouble."

"Afraid of the dust?"

Andros turned his pistol on the little man.

Muscus flinched. "Orders?"

"Helicopter. We're leaving."

"Villagers? Men?"

Andros shook his head. "You have three minutes."

Muscus slipped away into the red fog.

Andros waved uselessly at the dust in front of him. He couldn't see his own boots on his feet. If that dust got into the copter's intakes, he would have to wait it out and clean the engines before he could leave. That would not be good.

By feel and memory, he made his way to the helicopter.

~~~

Nikkis hid in the brush between boulders near the entrance to the cave. There, she waited in the red blindness for Daedalus to bring her the wounded Yiayia.

He moved away through the dust as if he had been born to live in a world of burned stone stench and endless red emptiness. Three steps away he became the shadowy minotaur of legend.

Seeing his monster's silhouette in the red fog almost made Nikkis laugh aloud because it came to her that he was, indeed, the legendary minotaur. Daedalus, her love, her life, her clever mason, and her endlessly loyal man, was certainly the very source of the tales that had become the myth of the man-beast.

Poor Pasiphae, Nikkis thought. The queen didn't deserve to be remembered for worse than what she had actually done. Pasiphae had nurtured her dark arts in order to protect her people, but she had never truly lost the light in her heart. The men who wrote her history had feared her and sought power over her by spinning a tale that made the monster her child.

If they survived, perhaps, Nikkis thought, she and Daedalus could use what the ages had taught them to rewrite some of that history.
~~~

~~~

With cunning skill, the mason who had hidden himself in these mountains for thousands of years stalked those who had come to steal and kill.

The first mercenary Daedalus found did not have time to scream before he lay unconscious on the ground. The second, however, managed to fire one wild round and scream.

That lone shot called out for a response. Gunfire erupted from several places.

The men on the mountain fired at shadows, crickets, and rustling grass.

The helicopter's turbines began to whine. Daedalus understood machines—even the machines of this new age. If the engine reached compression and fired up, Andros would be gone.

He couldn't let that happen.

Yiayia could wait. Her wound was not mortal. He hoped she had Papu and Leeho with her.

Daedalus stepped silently from a shadow behind one of his enemies. He wrapped his great hands around a big soldier's neck.

Breath and blood ceased to flow.

Silently, the unconscious man collapsed.

The next man Daedalus came upon turned. Blinded by red murk, he fired wide. He was not as lucky as the previous man. He left Daedalus no time for mercy. The gunman died.

Daedalus, mythic monster and determined man, moved toward the rising whine of the helicopter's engines.

Away to his right, a man screamed. It was not Papu, and the scream ended in a low, liquid grunt.

Daedalus's grim smile stretched and cracked his dry lips. He was not the only death moving in the fog.

Perhaps Leeho?

He hoped so, and he wished her well.

~~~

Her Daedalus was gone into the dust, but his thoughts touched her just as they had so long ago when his heart had reached out from his cell, through earth and stone, and into her room to save her from the king and to soothe her heart and mind.

She understood what he now did—what he wanted her to do.

Nikkis lifted her tattered shirt, bit through the stitching, ripped a wide strip from the bottom, and tied it over her mouth and nose. Her eyes closed tight, she listened to the slow hissing of dust moving over stone.

A man screamed.

Gunshots made eerie, dust-damped echoes.

A very unhappy donkey brayed.

Nikkis smiled and whispered, "Thank you, Virgil."

Blind, she stepped into the dust and moved along the wall of stone. She hoped she would find Yiayia, Papu, and Leeho near the long-suffering Virgil.

~~~

Tylissus looked down from the Super Puma helicopter carrying him and his security squad. At 7000 feet, they had traveled above a deep drainage that sent finger valleys out like a fan in all directions. He had no idea what he was looking for until he saw an impossible, almost perfectly circular Saharan dust cloud covering an area near the mouth of one of the finger valleys below. The cloud's unnatural curved edge butted up against a stone escarpment on one edge of the broad valley. The other edge defined a curve across open ground. Below the cloud and maybe 100 meters above the point where two valleys met and spilled into the main drainage, a sharp ridge of pale stone cut upward from the earth and across the bottom of the valley. That stone, he was sure, was the blade of Rhea mentioned in the miraculous message at Knossos.

Shadows moved within the dust, but he couldn't make out who or what they were. From above the low, flat circle of dust, he could, however, make out the slowly moving rotors and top quarter of a troop helicopter almost identical to his own.

He wanted to land as close to that copter as possible.

He tapped his cousin's helmet to get his attention then pointed to a flat, clear area just upslope of the cloud.

With luck, the prop wash of their landing would clear away some of the strange dust cloud.

His cousin shot him a wary look. Over helmet com, he said, "If the intakes suck in dust, we fall."

He nodded and offered a hard smile. "Today is a day of miracles."
~~~

His cousin nodded and turned to his task.

Tylissus told himself that the choice to land was based on a good cop's instinct, but he knew he lied to himself. He had seen the words appear on the wall. Now, he descended toward an impossible, circular dust cloud.

The events of the day forced him to admit that someone else's hands shaped his destiny today.

~~~

In thirty-five hundred years, Daedalus had not encountered a machine that he could not understand by merely placing his hands upon it.

The helicopter was a machine.

He placed his hand on the heat-laminated glass of the nose.

He would have laughed at the simultaneous strength and fragility of this modern war machine, but the rotors above him moved. He had no time to indulge in the pleasure of irony.

This flying machine is, he thought, *much like a war chariot pulled by strong horses.* To defeat a chariot, break the axle. If the driver survives the crash, he becomes merely a man without cover. Kill him, and only splinters and livestock in want of food and water remain.

Movement beyond the glass caught his attention.

Two figures. One was the pilot.

The other was not a man. It was the monster himself, Andros.

The monster's wide eyes glared at Daedalus. The monster yelled something Daedalus couldn't hear at the pilot. Spit sprayed from his tight mouth.

Like a horse whipped to a sudden gallop, the pilot worked his machine with hands, feet, and head.

Daedalus reached heart and mind through hands and became, for just a moment, the oils and sands that had been cleaned, purified, mixed, melted, and shaped into the laminate glass and polycarbonate he touched.

Just as he had once sought and found the weak points that let him separate layers of mica one from the other to create the skylights of a great palace, he now found a tiny, invisible bubble of air between layers in the windscreen.

Like a grandfather flicking a child's forehead to chastise, he snapped a hard finger against that spot.
~~~

The windshield shattered into a thousand, thousand fragments that fell away, leaving the two shocked men facing flowing dust and the unrestrained wrath of the Bull of the Mountain.

~~~

Nikkis groped her way along the wall.

Very near, Virgil complained loudly.

She opened her eyes and regretted it immediately. Eyes watering, blinking fast to keep out the burning dust, she searched the red fog for dark, ghostly figures that might be friend or foe.

She found neither before she tripped over something soft.

The yelp and curse that came from the ground at her feet turned the pounding fear in her heart to joy. She whispered, "Yiayia?" She let herself fall to the ground. Into the hissing dust, she said it again, "Yiayia?"

"Clumsy child."

"I thought.... I was afraid you–"

"I'm too old to die today."

Very close by, Virgil brayed his agreement that the old woman was too tough to ever die.

"Hush," Yiayia hissed. "Shut that animal up, Old Man. He'll be the death of us."

Even though Nikkis couldn't make out the old man or the donkey, Papu's hushing and shooshing came to her as a soft addition to the hissing of dust against rock and earth.

"Leeho?" Nikkis pulled the medicine bottle, bandages, and gauze from her satchel.

"Gone in the dust," Yiayia said. "You should go, too, child. Take this loud old man with you."

"No." Papu's low voice carried stubbornness that should have belonged to Virgil.

"Stupid old shit," Yiayia said.

Nikkis tore at her shirt again. She poured venom and blood onto the gauze and said, "He can't leave you any more than I could leave the Bull."

Yiayia pushed her hands back. "Help the Bull, Child. Go. Be his heart. He needs you."
~~~

"I am helping him," she said. "He sent me to you. Without you, who will tell the police what happened here? Me? The American hired by the thieves?" She swabbed over the wound opening.

Yiayia gasped. "You will kill me with that."

"You made it," Nikkis said.

"Give it to me. Since I made it. Let me do it."

"No." Nikkis kept working.

Yiayia said, "The police won't believe us. The police think we are insurgents—terrorists."

Virgil brayed in protest.

"He is a very patriotic donkey," Papu said. "He doesn't like being called a terrorist."

"Shut up, Old Man. Don't make me laugh."

"It's good to laugh while dying," Papu said.

"I'm not dying, you old shit."

"Good," he said. "I would miss your insults."

In spite of the dust stinging her eyes and penetrating her makeshift mask, Nikkis found herself smiling and wondering if someday the love she and Daedalus shared would become like the love shared by Yiayia and Papu. She hoped so. Theirs was a good love.

A flurry of muted shots reminded her of their danger. She pushed away all thoughts except those she needed to care for Yiayia's wounds.

Somewhere in the dust, the Bull and Leeho each fought while she tended Yiayia. At best, it was two against many. She hoped that if they all died today they would meet again in a new life in which the curse would be truly and completely broken.

The thwapping echo of an arriving helicopter battling air filled the valley.

The rising whine of Andros's helicopter became a scream in the dust.

"The gods have brought someone new to the mountain," Yiayia said.

Nikkis hoped that she knew who, but even after having seen so many wonders and miracles, her memory of countless lives of disappointment combined with her academic training to make her doubt any gods would nod in their direction today.

She tied off the temporary bandage over Yiayia's wound. "We need to move," she said. "Can you tie Virgil? Leave him here?"

"He is very brave donkey," Papu said. "He deserves better."

"They won't kill him," Nikkis said. "He can't speak their names."

"Do it, Old Man," Yiayia said.

Papu grunted his assent. After a moment and a final protest from Virgil, Papu appeared from the dust.

Grasping Yiayia's arms between them, Papu and Nikkis supported the woman and made their way downslope along the cliff wall.

~~~

The monster in front of Andros was a thing of myth. Its bull's eyes glowed red, and hot breath from its snout fogged the windshield.

It was that man thing. He had killed it twice. He had shot it. He had buried it under a mountain with Nikkis. Still, it was here.

Panic made Andros scream into the pilot's ear to take off.

The man worked his controls frantically.

The thing tapped the windshield. It was just a finger tap, but the entire front of the helicopter exploded inward.

Andros covered his face. Broken glass pelted his arms.

When he brought his arms down, the pilot and his entire seat were gone.

Just gone.

Somewhere in the dust behind the monster the missing man groaned.

Long arms and giant, hard hands reached for Andros.

Andros fought his seat harness with one hand while trying to raise his pistol with the other.

The thing caught his wrist in a huge hand and squeezed.

Andros's hand lived in a night terror. He willed his finger to pull the trigger, but tendons and muscles failed to move. His trigger finger could not squeeze, but his other hand managed to hit the harness quick release and free him from his seat.

The strength of the thing was terrifying. It hauled him outward, upward, over its head. For what seemed minutes, he flew through the infinite confusion of the red fog.

This, he thought, is my death.

From hidden places in the fog, his mother, his father, and his grandfather laughed at him.
~~~

The ground slapped him hard, knocking all the air from his lungs. For a moment, he couldn't inhale. When he did, he choked on dust. Instinctively, he brought his hand up to cover his mouth.

Still locked in his desperate grip, the pistol hit his forehead.

He tested his fingers. White hot pain filled his arm, but his fingers obeyed him.

Good. That thing would be on him in moments.

He spun toward the whine of the helicopter and fired three times before he realized he was shooting at a thing that wouldn't die.

He scrambled on hands and knees to one side, hoping to hide his position.

It was a man. It had to be a man. There was no such thing as an immortal Bull of the Mountain. No such thing.

Coughing and shaking, he managed to get his feet under him.

His only hope was to find a place to hide, to get away from the dust, to find a place to think. He had to think.

With his first running step, he tripped on his own feet, and the ground pulled him down again.

He called out for Muscus. For the first time since they had met, the little man did not appear next to him.

He spat.

He cursed his father.

He cursed Nikkis and the ignorance of the hill people of Crete.

Renewed rage drove him to control his cough, his breath. He rose once more, and he managed a quick shuffle downslope, away from the sound of the helicopter and, he hoped, toward cover.

~~~

The whining of the two helicopters died off.

Gunshots and screams ceased to echo in the valley.

Nikkis, Yiayia, and Papu broke free of the dust near the shark fin rock where the valley broke into open, rubble-strewn slope. Together, they took shelter behind the edge of stone and rested.

From their hiding place, Nikkis watched the police moving quickly toward the edge of the dust. She considered calling to them, but she couldn't be sure they would help.
~~~

She just couldn't.

The only people she trusted in the world stood beside her or fought within the dust.

One of the policemen, a big man, barked orders she couldn't make out. He gestured. She thought he might be the policeman they had called from Knossos.

She hoped he was. Yorgos had trusted that man, and Andros hadn't liked the man at all.

The first two policemen reached the wall of dust.

Their touch seemed to end the magic of Daedalus. The dust fell. The air cleared.

As if a strobe had fired in theater darkness, the valley became a frozen stage. Deathly silence she had hoped only lived in sealed caverns filled the valley.

Surprise had frozen the policemen.

Leeho lay face down in the dust.

Muscus, suddenly in the open, his pistol casually aimed at Leeho's head, looked around, his rat's eyes wide with surprise.

Close to the rock face, Andros faced across the valley, watching the arriving police.

No mercenaries still stood. Half a dozen bodies lay in the dust.

The Minotaur, her Daedalus, was the only moving thing in sight. Very nearly at the entrance to the cave, he tore away his mask and dropped it.

Beyond him, a few dozen yards from the cave that had been the tomb from which she and her love had been reborn, Virgil shook dust from his coat, threw back his head, and shattered the stillness with a scream of protest to the gods.

The semicircle of police moved toward Daedalus.

Andros turned his weapon toward her love.

Nikkis jumped up from her hiding place and screamed. "Bastard!"

"Nikkis." Daedalus's calm, rich voice stopped her. She couldn't be sure if he spoke in her heart or across the meters of death and dust that separated them.

It didn't matter. She heard him. She understood him.

She wondered at this man she had loved over so many centuries. Part of her was still Dr. Nikkis Aristos, and that part of her wondered how she could have changed so much so quickly. The other part of her, the part that was Nikkis, ageless beauty cursed by a Minoan king, didn't need to wonder. That part of her loved Daedalus, and that part of her trusted his mind, his heart, and his hands.

Daedalus's eyes had become more sure and dark, but they still held in them some of the red rage of the bull, though it was focused, more like a laser she had once seen in the labs at the university than the pointless, diffuse anger of the red dust storms.

This was the man of her past.

And, she realized, the man of her future.

Nikkis smiled, held up her arms, and waved them about to be sure she would be seen by all. She called out, "Andros is a murderer!"

It was all the distraction Leeho needed. She was around and driving her fist into the solar plexus of the man who had been about to kill her.

The big policeman's voice boomed over the landscape. "Hold! Hold!"

The voice made Nikkis sure. The policeman was Tylissus from the ruins of Knossos.

His men fanned out.

Daedalus stood very still. He nodded approval to Nikkis.

Tylissus called out, "You will all stand very still, please."

Andros straightened and trained his pistol on Daedalus. "Tylissus." He smiled for the policemen. "Good to have backup."

Confusion radiated from Tylissus.

"Please, old friend." Andros's voice was olive oil smooth but labyrinth dark. He said, "Arrest–"

"Help us," Nikkis called. "He's a murderer."

The darkness in Andros's eyes deepened, and he poured on the oil. "Arrest these people. They are the forgers and thieves of antiquities we've been hunting." His gun still pointed at Daedalus. "I've caught them in the act."

Leeho cried out, "Lies! Fascist!"

Tylissus leveled a short, automatic rifle on Andros. "We'll sort it out, Andros," he said. "Put the weapon down."

The men with Tylissus, all stone-faced and professional, moved cautiously to make a closing semicircle around Andros, Daedalus, Leeho, and Muscus.

Nikkis had never truly appreciated the look her old friend Yorgos had worn so often, but she was grateful to have known him long enough to now know that these men would soon be her friends.

Muscus rolled over, stood, fired a shot, and darted away from Leeho. He was gone and into the cover of a scattering of rocks and boulders before anyone could respond.

Two men returned fire in short bursts.

As fast as a viper, Andros shifted his aim and fired once.

The bullet hit Tylissus's shoulder. The big policeman grunted and went down on one knee.

Daedalus made quick use of the distraction. He closed the distance to Andros in a single heartbeat and drove one fist forward, a stone mallet driven by an arm that had spent a lifetime cutting stone and by a spirit that had spent many lifetimes fighting madness. He caught Andros on the side of the head.

Andros flew. The gun flew.

Daedalus advanced. Fires of rage burned in his eyes.

Nikkis left Yiayia and Papu. She ran to him.

A policeman called to her to halt, but she reached Daedalus, grasped his great arm, and pulled him. It was like grabbing the leg of a bull. All her strength was nothing compared to his. He took another step, pulling her along like she was nothing more than his shirt sleeve tugged by the wind.

For a fleeting moment, she imagined what Daedalus would do to the monster lying on the earth before them. For a moment, the anger, fear, and pain of many lives burned bright, and she almost let the vengeful rage of Daedalus rule his blood and their future.

"Enough." Her word surprised her. Seeing Andros down, disarmed, and beaten, her desire to see him dead suddenly drained away. "Better that they take him," she said. "Better to let him live in dishonor and shame and prison."

Daedalus froze. His heavy breath slowed. The knots of muscle under her hands relaxed. He nodded.

Andros rolled, jumped up, and bolted, running for his life down slope.

Tylissus called after him, "Stop! There is no place to run!"

One of the policemen tended Tylissus, who now sat on the stony hillside. The wounded man spoke to Nikkis. "He has no place to go. My men will pick him up."

"There is a place." Daedalus said. "The labyrinth. If he finds a way in, he will be gone." He pulled his arm free from Nikkis's grasp and ran after Andros.

"No!" Nikkis glanced to Tylissus and his men. Some had followed Muscus. Some helped Yiayia and Papu. None gave chase to Andros and Daedalus.

She sprinted after her love.

Tylissus called after her, but she ignored him. Down the hill at breakneck speed, she ran, legs loose and quick with the memory of lifetimes spent in these hills or hills like them. Her eyes stayed focused on the back of the man she needed, the man she wanted to live, to be with her for the rest of their natural lives and perhaps, if ancient gods could be kind, many lives to come.

Eyes on him, her so recently wounded feet felt strong and sure. The sandals Yiayia had fashioned for her gripped like tailor-fit running shoes. Without looking, her herder's feet found the stones, the ridges of packed ground, the right places to tread, to spring, to jump. It was like she had never been hurt. She imagined that she had been raised like Leeho and had run the paths and stones of these hills her whole life.

In the back of her mind, Dr. Nikkis Aristos marveled at herself. She thrilled at the feeling of running like this. *Finally*, she thought, she could run like a goat over the hills. The running made her feel free. At last, she lived out her dreams—the dreams in which she could fly across the land.

Daedalus, ahead of her, turned into a cleft.

She recognized the cut in the stones, the curve of the drainage. It was the box canyon where the village kept their bull.

"No!" Nikkis called.

She ran faster. She leapt and danced and spun. She came to the rock cut, and she stopped. Within, Daedalus walked cautiously forward. The gate to the stone fence that cut the little canyon in half stood open.

"Wait," Nikkis said

Daedalus moved to the gate, through it, and into the corral.

She followed, scanning the sheer rock walls for signs of Muscus, signs of Andros—for signs of more treachery.

Titan, the bull, stood off to one side of the canyon near the rock wall. It watched them, head low, thick neck flat as if the massive animal's spine were a metal beam that extended into the creature's skull. The long, double-curved horns stretched out, forward, and then upward into sharp tips.

Nikkis trotted to the gate. She smelled the scent of the bull, Daedalus's stone dust, and the sweat of his passing.

And she smelled fear. Andros.

"Daedalus!" The old language rolled off her tongue. "He's here. He plays us."

Before she could find the words in English or the new Greek, the bull lifted its head and trotted forward toward her like a giant dog coming to greet its owner.

Daedalus turned.

The bull caught sight of his motion. It paused. It lowered its giant head and faced Daedalus.

"Nikkis." Andros's olive oil breath was hot and slick on her neck. She stiffened. His cruel hand slipped around her waist. His other hand gripped her throat. He kissed her behind her ear, a hard, cruel kiss.

Daedalus screamed, "No!" The word echoed in the box canyon.

The bull's eyes showed their whites. It rolled its head back and forth, horns tearing at the air.

"Yes." Andros's grip around the base of her ribs sent shooting pain into Nikkis's skull. He pushed her forward.

"Watch, Nikkis," Andros said. "Watch him die."

The bull lowered its head. Deadly horns aimed for Daedalus.

Nikkis couldn't watch. She closed her eyes.

Behind her lids, her memories showed her a very young and beautiful Yiayia, breasts bare, a serpent in each hand, blessing her. Daedalus leapt a living bull as if it were a toy. She remembered running like her feet knew every centimeter of the hills here—running and laughing like Leeho.

She opened her eyes.

The bull's flanks quivered as if shaking off flies.

Daedalus backed away from the beast until his back was against the opposite stone wall. He had no place to run.

Nikkis strained against Andros's grip. She lifted her head.

She had an idea. It was an insane idea. Probably a fantasy, but so many things had worked that shouldn't. So many impossible things had happened. Perhaps her thoughts now were memories and not wishes.

She whistled loud, sharp, and clear.

The bull turned.

She whistled again, calling the animal to dinner like Leeho calling a goat.

Head up again, the bull trotted toward her.

Andros squeezed her neck.

Nikkis kicked up dust and screamed as best she could.

"No, Nikkis!" Daedalus yelled. "No!"

Against Andros's punishing grip, Nikkis managed to say, "I called it to feed."

The bull began to trot. It picked up speed.

Andros stepped back. "Call it off." He shook her.

The bull gained speed. "We're between it and the stalls," she said.

His hard hand gripped her windpipe and cut off her air. She was suffocating, getting dizzy.

The ground shook and thundered. The bull dropped its head and horns to gore and smash any obstacle between it and its feasting. It came on.

Andros shook. His grip broke. The coward ran.

Free, Nikkis sucked in a huge breath. Her vision cleared.

The earth shook, and the bull came at her in full charge, horns low, eyes enraged and confused.

Nikkis embraced her past lives and chose her next moment.

She sprinted toward the bull. She dipped her head low, as low as she could.

The bull matched her dip.

When she imagined that the heat of the bull's breath was on her, she lifted her head, leapt, grasped the horns, and vaulted.

The bull lifted its head to follow, and she used the boost to send her flying into a flip. She tucked, she spun, she put out her hands.

No thought.

No memory.

Her body did what it needed to do.

She opened from her flip. Ever so briefly, her hands touched the rump of the bull, and her feet came over, and she was once more spinning in the air.

Her feet reached for and found the earth. She carried her momentum perfectly into a run to Daedalus and a leap into the power and warmth of his arms.

He held her, pulled her into his chest, and cradled one great hand around her head.

After a few long, relieved breaths, she pulled back and searched the canyon for the monster and the bull she had set upon him.

Where Andros had been, only a mangled mass of meat, bone, and clothing remained.

Where the bull had been, only billows of rust-colored dust settled onto the trail back to the village, his cows, and his grain.

She buried her head again in his chest. "I couldn't lose you," she said.

"You leapt the bull."

"You did it once for me," she said.

"And it got us both killed."

"We're getting better at this sort of thing."

He laughed and kissed her.

Leeho interrupted their kiss. "Gross."

Startled, they pulled apart and turned.

The girl stood near Andros's remains. A long, bloody knife in one hand, she held Muscus's flack vest in the other. She used it to wipe the blood from her blade before tossing the vest onto Andros's twisted corpse.

"Muscus?" Nikkis asked.

"He thought he knew how to stalk me in our land." Leeho's quick smile was perhaps the most terrifying smile Nikkis had ever seen, and it made Nikkis grateful for the girl's friendship.

Reunion

Nikkis thought she heard Titan's bell. She looked up from her notes. The sun still illuminated the triptych of Daedalus fighting the dragon. She had tried to buy it from the Inn, but the woman would not take her money. Now, it hung on the wall of her study, a newly remodeled room in the back of Papu's shop.

The slanted sunlight through her sheet-mica skylight told her that her parents should be arriving soon, but she wasn't sure she'd heard the bell at all. Still, she stood and made her way to the doors onto the village street.

The movements of shadows in the street had become a part of her life the way the rising and setting of the sun had changed her sense of days and the milking of the goats had given her time to think about and feel the world around her.

The shade of the shop kept her cool enough, and she watched downslope along the bright cobbles of the village for the first sign of her parents.

Across the street and down a few doors, the steady, sure *clang* and *chink* of Daedalus's hammer on chisel and chisel on marble issued from the shadowed interior of a storeroom Papu had given him for a workshop.

The hammer stopped.

The door of the warehouse opened, and Daedalus appeared there, marble dust on his naked chest, a pale patina that made him look like a partially painted statue sculpted from living rock by the patient, ancient efforts of nature. Two lines of sweat traced through the marble dust to the leather belt holding the apron at his waist. As usual, he wore nothing else.

She smelled his scent on the breeze and smiled.

He saw her, and where he had been a statue, he became a man, smiling, proud, and filled with the life of love.

In the distance, the bell rang again and Titan bellowed.

"They are here," he said. He strode across the street and took her in his arms. They kissed, and his apron moved between them.

"I think," Nikkis said, "you should put on pants before my mother arrives. This is not the Crete of our first lives."

He looked down. They laughed.

Titan's bell sounded again, closer.

"I have always wanted to see my mother ride a donkey," Nikkis said.

Daedalus moved away toward their home and modern clothes. Nikkis walked along the cobbles toward the path to the guardian statues Daedalus had carved a thousand years ago to honor men who had once honored them.

At the low end of the village, Titan, Papu, and three donkeys appeared.

Nikkis's mother, grinning, or perhaps grimacing, rode Virgil.

Her father, certainly smiling, rode one of Virgil's friends.

Dr. Karin Anderson, whose job now depended on her ability to keep the very famous Dr. Nikkis Aristos on the faculty no matter where Nikkis chose to live, rode the third. Karin was the unhappiest woman Nikkis had ever seen, and Nikkis felt no guilt in taking pleasure in that fact.

Daedalus returned, now wearing jeans and a t-shirt, but still barefoot. "Shall we meet them, then?" he asked. "I think it is time I requested the honor of your hand."

She laughed. "Again?"

"One simple, honorable life is worthy of a second request after thousands of years of separation and suffering."

For the first time in over three millennia, death and loss had no place in her heart when she pressed her lips to his. Their embrace warmed and tightened. The kiss deepened. Their breath mingled, and the sweet peace of love, trust, and tomorrows together joined their souls.

THE END

Thank you for your time and participation.

Author's Note

When this project began, Linear-A and the unique inscription language on the Phaistos Disk were still an unsolved mystery. Recent developments in archeolinguistics have led to speculation, controversy, and debated translations. Several scholars now posit that the disk contains a prayer to a mother goddess. Personally, with just the right squint, I still see the battle between ancient male and female energies. I can also, with some liberal interpretation, see the curse of Nikkis and Daedalus along with a promise of salvation.

About the Author

Eric M. Witchey lives in Oregon where the fly fishing is good and deer like to sleep in his yard. He has made a living as a freelance writer, communication consultant, teacher, and speaker for over 25 years. In addition to many contracted and ghost-written non-fiction titles, he has sold more than 100 stories. His stories have appeared in multiple genres and on six continents. He's still working on Antarctica. He has received awards or recognition from New Century Writers, Writers of the Future, Writer's Digest, The Eric Hoffer Prose Award Program, Short Story America, the Irish Aeon Awards, and a number of other organizations. His how-to articles have appeared in The Writer Magazine, Writer's Digest Magazine, and other print and online magazines.

If you enjoyed this story, **please let the author know by rating the book or leaving a review at the purchase site and on Goodreads.com** (or the review site of your choice). Other stories written by this author and published by IFD Publishing are listed in the next section, and you can find even more by searching on "Eric Witchey" in your favorite search engine.

You can contact the author through the publisher at www.IFDPublishing.com or through any of the following:

Email: eric@ericwitchey.com

Web Site: www.ericwitchey.com

Shared Blog: http://shadowspinners.wordpress.com/

Twitter: @EWitchey

Other Books from IFD Publishing

You can find the following titles at most distribution points for ereading platforms.

Ebook Novels:

Bull's Labyrinth, by Eric Witchey
Beyond the Serpent's Heart, by Eric Witchey
Lizzie Borden, by Elizabeth Engstrom
Lizard Wine, by Elizabeth Engstrom
Northwoods Chronicles: A Novel in Short Stories, by Elizabeth Engstrom
Siren Promised, by Alan M. Clark and Jeremy Robert Johnson
To Kill a Common Loon, by Mitch Luckett
The Blood of Father Time: Book 1, The New Cut, by Alan M. Clark, Stephen C. Merritt & Lorelei Shannon
The Blood of Father Time: Book 2, The Mystic Clan's Grand Plot, by Alan M. Clark, Stephen C. Merritt & Lorelei Shannon
Candyland, by Elizabeth Engstrom
How I Met My Alien Bitch Lover: Book 1 from the Sunny World Inquisition Daily Letter Archives, by Eric Witchey
Baggage Check, by Elizabeth Engstrom
Death is a Star, by Christina Lay
D. D. Murphry, Secret Policeman, by Alan M. Clark and Elizabeth Massie
Black Leather, by Elizabeth Engstrom
York's Moon, by Elizabeth Engstrom
Jack the Ripper Victims Series: The Double Event, by Alan M. Clark
A Parliament of Crows, by Alan M. Clark

Ebook Collections:

Suspicions, by Elizabeth Engstrom
Professor Witchey's Miracle Mood Cure, by Eric Witchey

Ebook Novelettes:

The Tao of Flynn, by Eric Witchey
To Build a Boat, Listen to Trees, by Eric Witchey
Beware the Boojum, by Eric Witchey

Ebook Children's Illustrated:

The Christmas Thingy, by F. Paul Wilson. Illustrated by Alan M. Clark

Ebook Short Fiction:

"Brittle Bones and Old Rope," by Alan M. Clark
"Crosley," by Elizabeth Engstrom
"The Apple Sniper," by Eric Witchey

Ebook Non-Fiction:

How to Write a Sizzling Sex Scene, by Elizabeth Engstrom

Trade Paper:

Bull's Labyrinth—Eric Witchey
Professor Witchey's Miracle Mood Cure—Eric Witchey
Baggage Check—Elizabeth Engstrom
How to Write a Sizzling Sex Scene—Elizabeth Engstrom
The Surgeon's Mate: A Dismemoir—Alan M. Clark
Death is a Star—Christina Lay

Over-sized paperback:

Pain and Other Petty Plots to Keep You in Stitches—Alan M. Clark and Friends

Over-sized paperback and hardcover full-color art book:

The Paint in My Blood: Illustration and Fine Art—Alan M. Clark

Hardcover limited editions anthology:

Imagination Fully Dilated, Volume II—Edited by Elizabeth Engstrom

Hardcover limited editions collection:

Escaping Purgatory, Fables in Words and Pictures—Alan M. Clark and Gary A. Braunbeck

Audio books:

The Surgeon's Mate: A Dismemoir—Alan M. Clark
The Door That Faced West—Alan M. Clark
A Parliament of Crows—Alan M. Clark
Jack the Ripper Victims Series: A Brutal Chill in August—Alan M. Clark
Jack the Ripper Victims Series: The Double Event—Alan M. Clark
Jack the Ripper Victims Series: Of Thimble and Threat—Alan M. Clark
Jack the Ripper Victims Series: Say Anything but Your Prayers—Alan M. Clark